ROADSIDE CROSSES

Jeffery DEAVER

HODDER

First published in the United States of America in 2009 by Simon & Schuster, Inc.
First published in Great Britain in 2009 by Hodder & Stoughton
An Hachette UK company

This Hodder paperback edition 2010

1

A CIP catalogue record for this title is available from the British Library

A format paperback ISBN 978 0 340 93727 3
B format paperback ISBN 978 0 340 99404 7

Typeset in Fairfield Light by
Palimpsest Book Production Limited, Grangemouth, Stirlingshire

Printed and bound by Clays Ltd, St Ives plc

Hodder & Stoughton policy is to use papers that are natural, renewable and
recyclable products and made from wood grown in sustainable forests.
The logging and manufacturing processes are expected to conform to the
environmental regulations of the country of origin.

Hodder & Stoughton Ltd
338 Euston Road
London NW1 3BH

www.hodder.co.uk

Author's Note

One theme of this novel is the blurring of the line between the 'synthetic world' – the online life – and the real world. Accordingly, if you happen to come across a website address in the pages that follow, you might wish to type it into your browser and go where it takes you. You won't need what's in those websites to enjoy the novel, but you may just find a few extra clues that will help you unravel the mystery. You might also simply be interested – or disturbed – by what you find there.

[W]hat the Internet and its cult of anonymity do is to provide a blanket sort of immunity for anybody who wants to say anything about anybody else, and it would be difficult in this sense to think of a more morally deformed exploitation of the concept of free speech.

— RICHARD BERNSTEIN IN *THE NEW YORK TIMES*

MONDAY

1

Out of place.

The California Highway Patrol trooper, young with bristly yellow hair beneath his crisp hat, squinted through the windshield of his Crown Victoria Police Interceptor as he cruised south along Highway 1 in Monterey. Dunes to the right, modest commercial sprawl to the left.

Something was out of place. What?

Heading home at 5:00 p.m. after his tour had ended, he surveyed the road. The trooper didn't write a lot of tickets here, leaving that to the county deputies – professional courtesy – but he occasionally lit up somebody in a German or Italian car if he was in a mood, and this was the route he often took home at this time of day, so he knew the highway pretty well.

There . . . that was it. Something colorful, a quarter mile ahead, sat by the side of the road at the base of one of the hills of sand that cut off the view of Monterey Bay.

What could it be?

He hit his light bar – protocol – and pulled over onto the right shoulder. He parked with the hood of the Ford pointed leftward toward traffic, so a rear-ender would shove the car away from, not over, him, and climbed out. Stuck in the sand just beyond the shoulder was a cross – a roadside memorial. It was about eighteen inches high and homemade, cobbled together out of dark, broken-off branches, bound with wire like florists use. Dark red roses lay in a splashy bouquet at the base. A cardboard disk was in the center, the date of the accident written on it in blue ink. There were no names on the front or back.

Officially these memorials to traffic accident victims were discouraged, since people were occasionally injured, even killed, planting a cross or leaving flowers or stuffed animals.

Usually the memorials were tasteful and poignant. This one was spooky.

What was odd, though, was that he couldn't remember any accidents along here. In fact this was one of the safest stretches of Highway 1 in California. The roadway becomes an obstacle course south of Carmel, like that spot of a really sad accident several weeks ago: two girls killed coming back from a graduation party. But here, the highway was three lanes and mostly straight, with occasional lazy bends through the old Fort Ord grounds, now a college, and the shopping districts.

The trooper thought about removing the cross, but the mourners might return to leave another one and endanger themselves again. Best just to leave it. Out of curiosity he'd check with his sergeant in the morning and find out what had happened. He walked back to his car, tossed his hat on the seat and rubbed his crew cut. He pulled back into traffic, his mind no longer on roadside accidents. He was thinking about what his wife would be making for supper, about taking the kids to the pool afterward.

And when was his brother coming to town? He looked at the date window on his watch. He frowned. Was that right? A glance at his cell phone confirmed that, yes, today was June 25.

That was curious. Whoever had left the roadside cross had made a mistake. He remembered that the date crudely written on the cardboard disk was June 26, Tuesday, tomorrow.

Maybe the poor mourners who'd left the memorial had been so upset they'd jotted the date down wrong.

Then the images of the eerie cross faded, though they didn't vanish completely and, as the officer headed down the highway home, he drove a bit more carefully.

TUESDAY

2

The faint light – the light of a ghost, pale green – danced just out of her reach.

If she could only get to it.

If she could only reach the ghost she'd be safe.

The glow, floating in the dark of the car's trunk, dangled tauntingly above her feet, which were duct-taped together, as were her hands.

A ghost . . .

Another piece of tape was pasted over her mouth and she was inhaling stale air through her nose, rationing it, as if the trunk of her Camry held only so much.

A painful bang as the car hit a pothole. She gave a brief, muted scream.

Other hints of light intruded occasionally: the dull red glow when he hit the brake, the turn signal. No other illumination from outside; the hour was close to 1:00 a.m.

The luminescent ghost rocked back and forth. It was the emergency trunk release: a glow-in-the-dark hand pull emblazoned with a comical image of a man escaping from the car.

But it remained just out of reach of her feet.

Tammy Foster had forced the crying to stop. The sobs had begun just after her attacker came up behind her in the shadowy parking lot of the club, slapped tape on her mouth, taped her hands behind her back and shoved her into the trunk. He'd bound her feet as well.

Frozen in panic, the seventeen-year-old had thought: He doesn't want me to see him. That's good. He doesn't want to kill me.

He just wants to scare me.

She'd surveyed the trunk, spotting the dangling ghost. She'd tried to grip it with her feet but it slipped out from between her shoes. Tammy was in good shape, soccer and cheerleading. But, because of the awkward angle, she could keep her feet raised for only a few seconds.

The ghost eluded her.

The car pressed on. With every passing yard, she felt more and more despair. Tammy Foster began to cry again.

Don't, don't! Your nose'll clog up, you'll choke.

She forced herself to stop.

She was supposed to be home at midnight. She'd be missed by her mother – if she wasn't drunk on the couch, pissed about some problem with her latest boyfriend.

Missed by her sister, if the girl wasn't online or on the phone. Which of course she was.

Clank.

The same sound as earlier: the bang of metal as he loaded something into the backseat.

She thought of some scary movies she'd seen. Gross, disgusting ones. Torture, murder. Involving tools.

Don't think about that. Tammy focused on the dangling green ghost of the trunk release.

And heard a new sound. The sea.

Finally they stopped and he shut off the engine.

The lights went out.

The car rocked as he shifted in the driver's seat. What was he doing? Now she heard the throaty croak of seals nearby. They were at a beach, which at this time of night, around here, would be completely deserted.

One of the car doors opened and closed. And a second opened. The clank of metal from the backseat again.

Torture . . . tools.

The door slammed shut, hard.

And Tammy Foster broke. She dissolved into sobs, struggling to suck in more lousy air. 'No, please, please!' she cried, though the words were filtered through the tape and came out as a sort of moan.

Tammy began running through every prayer she could remember as she waited for the click of the trunk.

The sea crashed. The seals hooted.

She was going to die.

'Mommy.'

But then . . . nothing.

The trunk didn't pop, the car door didn't open again, she heard no footsteps approaching. After three minutes she controlled the crying. The panic diminished.

Five minutes passed, and he hadn't opened the trunk.

Ten.

Tammy gave a faint, mad laugh.

It was just a scare. He wasn't going to kill her or rape her. It was a practical joke.

She was actually smiling beneath the tape, when the car rocked, ever so slightly. Her smile faded. The Camry rocked again, a gentle push-pull, though stronger than the first time. She heard a splash and felt a shudder. Tammy knew an ocean wave had struck the front end of the car.

Oh, my God, no! He'd left the car on the beach, with high tide coming in!

The car settled into the sand, as the ocean undermined the tires.

No! One of her worst fears was drowning. And being stuck in a confined space like this . . . it was unthinkable. Tammy began to kick at the trunk lid.

But there was, of course, no one to hear, except the seals.

The water was now sloshing hard against the sides of the Toyota.

The ghost . . .

Somehow she *had* to pull the trunk release lever. She worked off her shoes and tried again, her head pressing hard against the carpet, agonizingly lifting her feet toward the glowing pull. She got them on either side of it, pressed hard, her stomach muscles quivering.

Now!

Her legs cramping, she eased the ghost downward.

A tink.

Yes! It worked!

But then she moaned in horror. The pull had come away in her feet, without opening the trunk. She stared at the green ghost lying near her. He must've cut the wire! After he'd dumped her into the trunk, he'd cut it. The release pull had been dangling in the eyelet, no longer connected to the latch cable.

She was trapped.

Please, somebody, Tammy prayed again. To God, to a passerby, even to her kidnapper, who might show her some mercy.

But the only response was the indifferent gurgle of saltwater as it began seeping into the trunk.

The Peninsula Garden Hotel is tucked away near Highway 68 – the venerable route that's a twenty-mile-long diorama, 'The Many Faces of Monterey County.' The road meanders west from the Nation's Salad Bowl – Salinas – and skirts the verdant Pastures of Heaven, punchy Laguna Seca racetrack, settlements of corporate offices, then dusty Monterey and pine-and-hemlock-filled Pacific Grove. Finally the highway deposits those drivers, at least those bent on following the complex via from start to finish, at legendary Seventeen Mile Drive – home of a common species around here: People With Money.

'Not bad,' Michael O'Neil said to Kathryn Dance as they climbed out of his car.

Through narrow glasses with gray frames, the woman surveyed the Spanish and deco main lodge and half-dozen adjacent buildings. The inn was classy though a bit worn and dusty at the cuffs. 'Nice. I like.'

As they stood surveying the hotel, with its distant glimpse of the Pacific Ocean, Dance, an expert at kinesics, body language, tried to read O'Neil. The chief deputy in the Monterey County Sheriff's Office Investigations Division was hard to analyze. The solidly built man, in his forties, with salt-and-pepper hair, was easygoing, but quiet unless he knew you. Even then he was economical of gesture and expression. He didn't give a lot away kinesically.

At the moment, though, she was reading that he wasn't at all nervous, despite the nature of their trip here.

She, on the other hand, was.

Kathryn Dance, a trim woman in her thirties, today wore her dark blond hair as she often did, in a French braid, the feathery tail end bound with a bright blue ribbon her daughter had selected that morning and tied into a careful bow. Dance was in a long, pleated black skirt and matching jacket over a white blouse. Black ankle boots with two-inch heels – footwear she'd admired for months but been able to resist buying only until they had gone on sale.

O'Neil was in one of his three or four civilian configurations: chinos and powder blue shirt, no tie. His jacket was dark blue, in a faint plaid pattern.

The doorman, a cheerful Latino, looked them over with an expression that said, You seem like a nice couple. 'Welcome. I hope you enjoy your stay.' He opened the door for them.

Dance smiled uncertainly at O'Neil and they walked through a breezy hallway to the front desk.

From the main building, they wound through the hotel complex, looking for the room.

'Never thought this would happen,' O'Neil said to her.

Dance gave a faint laugh. She was amused to realize that her eyes occasionally slipped to doors and windows. This was a kinesic response that meant the subject was subconsciously thinking about ways to escape – that is, was feeling stress.

'Look,' she said, pointing to yet another pool. The place seemed to have four.

'Like Disneyland for adults. I hear a lot of rock musicians stay here.'

'Really?' She frowned.

'What's wrong?'

'It's only one story. Not much fun getting stoned and throwing TVs and furniture out the window.'

'This is Carmel,' O'Neil pointed out. 'The wildest they'd get here is pitching recyclables into the trash.'

Dance thought of a comeback line but kept quiet. The bantering was making her more nervous.

She paused beside a palm tree with leaves like sharp weapons. 'Where are we?'

The deputy looked at a slip of paper, oriented himself and pointed to one of the buildings in the back. 'There.'

O'Neil and Dance paused outside the door. He exhaled and lifted an eyebrow. 'Guess this is it.'

Dance laughed. 'I feel like a teenager.'

The deputy knocked.

After a short pause the door opened, revealing a narrow man, hovering near fifty, wearing dark slacks and a white shirt and striped tie.

'Michael, Kathryn. Right on time. Come on in.'

Ernest Seybold, a career district attorney for Los Angeles County, nodded them into the room. Inside, a court reporter sat beside her three-legged dictation machine. Another young woman rose and greeted the new arrivals. She was, Seybold said, his assistant from L.A.

Earlier this month, Dance and O'Neil had run a case in Monterey – the convicted cult leader and killer Daniel Pell had escaped from prison and remained on the Peninsula, targeting more victims. One of the people involved in the case had turned out to be somebody very different from the person Dance and her fellow officers had believed. The consequences of that involved yet another murder.

Dance adamantly wanted to pursue the perp. But there was

much pressure not to follow up – from some very powerful organizations. Dance wouldn't take no for an answer, though, and while the Monterey prosecutor had declined to handle the case, she and O'Neil learned that the perp had killed earlier – in Los Angeles. District Attorney Seybold, who worked regularly with Dance's organization, the California Bureau of Investigation, and was a friend of Dance's, agreed to bring charges in L.A.

Several witnesses, though, were in the Monterey area, including Dance and O'Neil, and so Seybold had come here for the day to take statements. The clandestine nature of the get-together was due to the perp's connections and reputation. In fact, for the time being they weren't even using the killer's real name. The case was known internally as *The People v. J. Doe.*

As they sat, Seybold said, 'We might have a problem, I have to tell you.'

The butterflies Dance had felt earlier – that something would go wrong and the case would derail – returned.

The prosecutor continued, 'The defense's made a motion to dismiss based on immunity. I honestly can't tell you what the odds are it'll succeed. The hearing's scheduled for day after tomorrow.'

Dance closed her eyes. 'No.' Beside her O'Neil exhaled in anger.

All this work . . .

If he gets away, Dance thought . . . but then realized she had nothing to add to that, except: If he gets away, I lose.

She felt her jaw trembling.

But Seybold said, 'I've got a team putting together the response. They're good. The best in the office.'

'Whatever it takes, Ernie,' Dance said. 'I want him. I want him real bad.'

'A lot of people do, Kathryn. We'll do everything we can.'

If he gets away . . .

'But I want to proceed as if we're going to win.' He said this confidently, which reassured Dance somewhat. They got started,

Seybold asking dozens of questions about the crime – what Dance and O'Neil had witnessed and the evidence in the case.

Seybold was a seasoned prosecutor and knew what he was doing. After an hour of interviewing them both, the wiry man sat back and said he had enough for the time being. He was momentarily expecting another witness – a local state trooper – who had also agreed to testify.

They thanked the prosecutor, who agreed to call them the instant the judge ruled in the immunity hearing.

As Dance and O'Neil walked back to the lobby, he slowed, a frown on his face.

'What?' she asked.

'Let's play hooky.'

'What do you mean?'

He nodded at the beautiful garden restaurant, overlooking a canyon with the sea beyond. 'It's early. When was the last time anybody in a white uniform brought you eggs Benedict?'

Dance considered. 'What year is it again?'

He smiled. 'Come on. We won't be that late.'

A glance at her watch. 'I don't know.' Kathryn Dance hadn't played hooky in school, much less as a senior agent with the CBI.

Then she said to herself: Why're you hesitating? You love Michael's company, you get to spend hardly any downtime with him.

'You bet.' Feeling like a teenager again, though now in a good way.

They were seated beside each other at a banquette near the edge of the deck, overlooking the hills. The early sun was out and it was a clear, crisp June morning.

The waiter – not fully uniformed, but with a suitably starched white shirt – brought them menus and poured coffee. Dance's eyes strayed to the page on which the restaurant bragged of their famous mimosas. No way, she thought, and glanced up to see O'Neil looking at exactly the same item.

They laughed.

'When we get down to L.A. for the grand jury, or the trial,' he said, 'champagne then.'

'Fair enough.'

It was then that O'Neil's phone trilled. He glanced at Caller ID. Dance was immediately aware of his body language changing – shoulders slightly higher, arms closer to his body, eyes focused just past the screen.

She knew whom the call was from, even before he said a cheerful, 'Hi, dear.'

Dance deduced from his conversation with his wife, Anne, a professional photographer, that a business trip had come up unexpectedly soon and she was checking with her husband about his schedule.

Finally O'Neil disconnected and they sat in silence for a moment while the atmosphere righted itself and they consulted their menus.

'Yep,' he announced, 'eggs Benedict.'

She was going to have the same and glanced up for the waiter. But then *her* phone vibrated. She glanced at the text message, frowned, then read it again, aware that her own body orientation was changing quickly. Heart rate revving, shoulders lifted, foot tapping on the floor.

Dance sighed, and her gesture to the waiter changed from a polite beckon to one of mimicking signing the check.

3

The California Bureau of Investigation's west-central regional headquarters is in a nondescript modern building identical to those of the adjacent insurance companies and software consulting firms, all tucked neatly away behind hills and decorated with the elaborate vegetation of Central Coast California.

The facility was near the Peninsula Garden, and Dance and O'Neil arrived from the hotel in less than ten minutes, minding traffic but not red lights or stop signs.

Climbing out of his car, Dance slung her purse over her shoulder, and hefted her bulging computer bag – which her daughter had dubbed 'Mom's purse annex', after the girl had learned what *annex* meant – and she and O'Neil walked into the building.

Inside they headed immediately to where she knew her team would be assembled: her office, in the portion of the CBI known as the Gals' Wing, or 'GW' – owing to the fact that it was populated exclusively by Dance, fellow agent Connie Ramirez, as well as their assistant, Maryellen Kresbach, and Grace Yuan, the CBI administrator, who kept the entire building humming like a timepiece. The name of the wing derived from an unfortunate comment by an equally unfortunate, and now former, CBI agent, who coined the designation while trying to press his cleverness on a date he was touring around the headquarters.

Everyone on the GW still debated if he – or one of his dates

– had ever found all the feminine hygiene products Dance and Ramirez had seeded into his office, briefcase and car.

Dance and O'Neil now greeted Maryellen. The cheerful and indispensable woman could easily run both a family and the professional lives of her charges without a bat of one of her darkly mascaraed eyelashes. She also was the best baker Dance had ever met. 'Morning, Maryellen. Where are we?'

'Hi, Kathryn. Help yourself.'

Dance eyed, but didn't give in to, the chocolate chip cookies in the jar on the woman's desk. They had to be a biblical sin. O'Neil, on the other hand, didn't resist. 'Best breakfast I've had in weeks.'

Eggs Benedict . . .

Maryellen gave a pleased laugh. 'Okay, I called Charles *again* and left *another* message. Honestly.' She sighed. 'He wasn't picking up. TJ and Rey are inside. Oh, Deputy O'Neil, one of your people is here from MCSO.'

'Thanks. You're a dear.'

In Dance's office wiry young TJ Scanlon was perched in her chair. The redheaded agent leapt up. 'Hi, boss. How'd the audition go?'

He meant the deposition.

'I was a star.' Then she delivered the bad news about the immunity hearing.

The agent scowled. He too had known the perp and was nearly as adamant as Dance about winning a conviction.

TJ was good at his job, though he was the most unconventional agent in a law enforcement organization noted for its conventional approach and demeanor. Today he was wearing jeans, a polo shirt and plaid sports coat – madras, a pattern on some faded shirts in her father's storage closet. TJ owned one tie, as far as Dance had been able to tell, and it was an outlandish Jerry Garcia model. TJ suffered from acute nostalgia for the 1960s. In his office two lava lamps bubbled merrily away.

Dance and he were only a few years apart, but there was a generational gap between them. Still, they clicked professionally, with a bit of mentor-mentee thrown in. Though TJ tended to run solo, which was against the grain in the CBI, he'd been filling in for Dance's regular partner – still down in Mexico on a complicated extradition case.

Quiet Rey Carraneo, a newcomer to the CBI, was about as opposite to TJ Scanlon as one could be. In his late twenties, with dark, thoughtful features, he today wore a gray suit and white shirt on his lean frame. He was older in heart than in years, since he'd been a beat cop in the cowboy town of Reno, Nevada, before moving here with his wife for the sake of his ill mother. Carraneo held a coffee cup in a hand that bore a tiny scar in the Y between thumb and forefinger; it was where a gang tat had resided not too many years ago. Dance considered him to be the calmest and most focused of all the younger agents in the office and she sometimes wondered, to herself only, if his days in the gang contributed to that.

The deputy from the Monterey County Sheriff's Office – typically crew cut and with a military bearing – introduced himself and explained what had happened. A local teenager had been kidnapped from a parking lot in downtown Monterey, off Alvarado, early that morning. Tammy Foster had been bound and tossed into her own car trunk. The attacker drove her to a beach outside of town and left her to drown in high tide.

Dance shivered at the thought of what it must've been like to lie cramped and cold as the water rose in the confined space.

'It was her car?' O'Neil asked, sitting in one of Dance's chairs and rocking on the back legs – doing exactly what Dance told her son not to do (she suspected Wes had learned the practice from O'Neil). The legs creaked under his weight.

'That's right, sir.'

'What beach?'

'Down the coast, south of the Highlands.'

'Deserted?'

'Yeah, nobody around. No wits.'

'Witnesses at the club where she got snatched?' Dance asked.

'Negative. And no security cameras in the parking lot.'

Dance and O'Neil took this in. She said, 'So he needed other wheels near where he left her. Or had an accomplice.'

'Crime scene found some footprints in the sand, headed for the highway. Above the tide level. But the sand was loose. No idea of tread or size. But definitely only one person.'

O'Neil asked, 'And no signs of a car pulling off the road to pick him up? Or one hidden in the bushes nearby?'

'No, sir. Our people did find some bicycle tread marks but they were on the shoulder. Could've been made that night, could've been a week old. No tread match. We don't have a bicycle database,' he added to Dance.

Hundreds of people biked along the beach in that area daily.

'Motive?'

'No robbery, no sexual assault. Looks like he just wanted to kill her. Slowly.'

Dance exhaled a puffy breath.

'Any suspects?'

'Nope.'

Dance then looked at TJ. 'And what you told me earlier, when I called? The weird part. Anything more on that?'

'Oh,' the fidgety young agent said, 'you mean the roadside cross.'

The California Bureau of Investigation has broad jurisdiction but usually is involved only in major crimes, like gang activity, terrorism threats and significant corruption or economic offenses. A single murder in an area where gangland killings occur at least once a week wouldn't attract any special attention.

But the attack on Tammy Foster was different.

The day before the girl had been kidnapped, a Highway Patrol trooper had found a cross, like a roadside memorial, with the next day's date written on it, stuck in the sand along Highway 1.

When the trooper heard of the attack on the girl, not far off the same highway, he wondered if the cross was an announcement of the perp's intentions. He'd returned and collected it. The Monterey County Sheriff's Office's Crime Scene Unit found a tiny bit of rose petal in the trunk where Tammy had been left to die – a fleck that matched the roses from the bouquet left with the cross.

Since on the surface the attack seemed random and there was no obvious motive, Dance had to consider the possibility that the perp had more victims in mind.

O'Neil now asked, 'Evidence from the cross?'

His junior officer grimaced. 'Truth be told, Deputy O'Neil, the Highway Patrol trooper just tossed it and the flowers in his trunk.'

'Contaminated?'

'Afraid so. Deputy Bennington said he did the best he could to process it.' Peter Bennington – the skilled, diligent head of the Monterey County Crime Scene Lab. 'But didn't find anything. Not according to the preliminary. No prints, except the trooper's. No trace other than sand and dirt. The cross was made out of tree branches and florist wire. The disk with the date on it was cut out of cardboard, looked like. The pen, he said, was generic. And the writing was block printing. Only helpful if we get a sample from a suspect. Now, here's a picture of the cross. It's pretty creepy. Kind of like *Blair Witch Project,* you know.'

'Good movie,' TJ said, and Dance didn't know if he was being facetious or not.

They looked at the photo. It *was* creepy, the branches like twisted, black bones.

Forensics couldn't tell them anything? Dance had a friend she'd worked with not long ago, Lincoln Rhyme, a private forensic consultant in New York City. Despite the fact he was a quadriplegic, he was one of the best crime scene specialists in the country. She wondered, if he'd been running the scene, would he have found something helpful? She suspected he would have. But perhaps the most universal rule in police work was this: You go with what you've got.

She noticed something in the picture. 'The roses.'

O'Neil got her meaning. 'The stems are cut the same length.'

'Right. So they probably came from a store, not clipped from somebody's yard.'

TJ said, 'But, boss, you can buy roses about a thousand places on the Peninsula.'

'I'm not saying it's leading us to his doorstep,' Dance said. 'I'm saying it's a fact we might be able to use. And don't jump to conclusions. They might've been *stolen*.' She felt grumpy, hoped it didn't come off that way.

'Gotcha, boss.'

'Where exactly was the cross?'

'Highway One. Just south of Marina.' He touched a location on Dance's wall map.

'Any witnesses to leaving the cross?' Dance now asked the deputy.

'No, ma'am, not according to the CHP. And there are no cameras along that stretch of highway. We're still looking.'

'Any stores?' O'Neil asked, just as Dance took a breath to ask the identical question.

'Stores?'

O'Neil was looking at the map. 'On the east side of the highway. In those strip malls. Some of them have to have security cameras. Maybe one was pointed toward the spot. At least we could get a make and model of the car – if he was in one.'

'TJ,' Dance said, 'check that out.'

'You got it, boss. There's a good Java House there. One of my favorites.'

'I'm so pleased.'

A shadow appeared in her doorway. 'Ah. Didn't know we were convening here.'

Charles Overby, the recently appointed agent in charge of this CBI branch, walked into her office. In his midfifties, tanned; the pear-shaped man was athletic enough to get out on the golf or tennis courts several times a week but not so spry to keep up a long volley without losing his breath.

'I've been in my office for . . . well, quite some time.'

Dance ignored TJ's subtle glance at his wristwatch. She suspected that Overby had rolled in a few minutes ago.

'Charles,' she said. 'Morning. Maybe I forgot to mention where we'd be meeting. Sorry.'

'Hello, Michael.' A nod toward TJ too, whom Overby sometimes gazed at curiously as if he'd never met the junior agent – though that might have just been disapproval of TJ's fashion choices.

Dance had in fact informed Overby of the meeting. On the drive here from the Peninsula Garden Hotel, she'd left a message on his voice mail, giving him the troubling news of the immunity hearing in L.A. and telling him of the plan to get together here, in her office. Maryellen had told him about the meeting too. But the CBI chief hadn't responded. Dance hadn't bothered to call back, since Overby usually didn't care much for the tactical side of running cases. She wouldn't have been surprised if he'd declined attending this meeting altogether. He wanted the 'big picture,' a recent favorite phrase. (TJ had once referred to him as Charles Overview; Dance had hurt her belly laughing.)

'Well. This girl-in-the-trunk thing . . . the reporters are calling already. I've been stalling. They hate that. Brief me.'

Ah, reporters. That explained the man's interest.

Dance told him what they knew at this point, and what their plans were.

'Think he's going to try it again? That's what the anchors are saying.'

'That's what they're *speculating*,' Dance corrected delicately.

'Since we don't know why he attacked her in the first place, Tammy Foster, we can't say,' O'Neil said.

'And the cross is connected? It was left as a message?'

'The flowers match forensically, yes.'

'Ouch. I just hope it doesn't turn into a Summer of Sam thing.'

'A . . . what's that, Charles?' Dance asked.

'That guy in New York. Leaving notes, shooting people.'

'Oh, that was a movie.' TJ was their reference librarian of popular culture. 'Spike Lee. The killer was *Son* of Sam.'

'I know,' Overby said quickly. 'Just making a pun. Son and Summer.'

'We don't have any evidence one way or the other. We don't know *anything* yet, really.'

Overby was nodding. He never liked not having answers. For the press, for his bosses in Sacramento. That made him edgy, which in turn made everybody else edgy too. When his predecessor, Stan Fishburne, had had to retire unexpectedly on a medical and Overby had assumed the job, dismay was the general mood. Fishburne was the agents' advocate; he'd take on anybody he needed to in supporting them. Overby had a different style. Very different.

'I got a call from the AG already.' Their ultimate boss. 'Made the news in Sacramento. CNN too. I'll have to call him back. I wish we had *something* specific.'

'We should know more soon.'

'What're the odds that it was just a prank gone bad? Like hazing the pledges. Fraternity or sorority thing. We all did that in college, didn't we?'

Dance and O'Neil hadn't been Greek. She doubted TJ had been, and Rey Carraneo had gotten his bachelor's in criminal justice at night while working two jobs.

'Pretty grim for a practical joke,' O'Neil said.

'Well, let's keep it as an option. I just want to make sure that we stay away from panic. That won't help anything. Downplay any serial-actor angle. And don't mention the cross. We're still reeling from that case earlier in the month, the Pell thing.' He blinked. 'How did the deposition go, by the way?'

'A delay.' Had he not listened to her message at all?

'That's good.'

'Good?' Dance was still furious about the motion to dismiss.

Overby blinked. 'I mean it frees you up to run this Roadside Cross Case.'

Thinking about her old boss. Nostalgia can be such sweet pain.

'What are the next steps?' Overby asked.

'TJ's checking out the security cameras at the stores and car dealerships near where the cross was left.' She turned to Carraneo.

'And, Rey, could you canvass around the parking lot where Tammy was abducted?'

'Yes, ma'am.'

'What're you working on now, Michael, at MCSO?' Overby asked.

'Running a gang killing, then the Container Case.'

'Oh, that.'

The Peninsula had been largely immune to terrorist threats. There were no major seaports here, only fishing docks, and the airport was small and had good security. But a month or so ago a shipping container had been smuggled off a cargo ship from Indonesia docked in Oakland and loaded on a truck headed south toward L.A. A report suggested that it had gotten as far as Salinas, where, possibly, the contents had been removed, hidden and then transferred to other trucks for forward routing.

Those contents might've been contraband – drugs, weapons . . . or, as another credible intelligence report went, human beings sneaking into the country. Indonesia had the largest Islamic population in the world and a number of dangerous extremist cells. Homeland Security was understandably concerned.

'But,' O'Neil added, 'I can put that on hold for a day or two.'

'Good,' Overby said, relieved that the Roadside Cross Case would be task-forced. He was forever looking for ways to spread the risk if an investigation went bad, even if it meant sharing the glory.

Dance was simply pleased she and O'Neil would be working together.

O'Neil said, 'I'll get the final crime scene report from Peter Bennington.'

O'Neil's background wasn't specific to forensic science, but the solid, dogged cop relied on traditional techniques for solving crimes: research, canvassing and crime scene analysis. Occasionally head-butting. Whatever his concoction of techniques, though, the senior detective was good at his job. He had one of the highest arrest – and more important – *conviction* records in the history of the office.

Dance glanced at her watch. 'And I'll go interview the witness.'

Overby was silent for a moment. 'Witness? I didn't know there was one.'

Dance didn't tell him that that very information too was in the message she'd left her boss. 'Yep, there is,' she said, and slung her purse over her shoulder, heading out of the door.

4

'Oh, that's sad,' the woman said.

Her husband, behind the wheel of their Ford SUV, which he'd just paid $70 to fill, glanced at her. He was in a bad mood. Because of the gas prices and because he'd just had a tantalizing view of Pebble Beach golf course, which he couldn't afford to play even if the wife would let him.

One thing he definitely didn't want to hear was something sad.

Still, he'd been married for twenty years, and so he asked her, 'What?' Maybe a little more pointedly than he intended.

She didn't notice, or pay attention to, his tone. 'There.'

He looked ahead, but she was just gazing out of the windshield at this stretch of deserted highway, winding through the woods. She wasn't pointing at anything in particular. That made him even more irritated.

'Wonder what happened.'

He was about to snap, 'To what?' when he saw what she was talking about.

And he felt instantly guilty.

Stuck in the sand ahead of them, about thirty yards away, was one of those memorials at the site of a car accident. It was a cross, kind of a crude thing, sitting atop some flowers. Dark red roses.

'Is sad,' he echoed, thinking of their children – two teenagers who still scared the hell out of him every time they got behind the wheel. Knowing how he'd feel if anything happened to them in an accident. He regretted his initial snippiness.

He shook his head, glancing at his wife's troubled face. They drove past the homemade cross. She whispered. 'My God. It *just* happened.'

'It did?'

'Yep. It's got today's date on it.'

He shivered and they drove on toward a nearby beach that somebody had recommended for its walking trails. He mused, 'Something odd.'

'What's that, dear?'

'The speed limit's thirty-five along here. You wouldn't think somebody'd wipe out so bad that they'd die.'

His wife shrugged. 'Kids, probably. Drinking and driving.'

The cross sure put everything in perspective. Come on, buddy, you could be sitting back in Portland crunching numbers and wondering what kind of insanity Leo will come up with at the next team rally meeting. Here you are in the most beautiful part of the state of California, with five days of vacation left.

And you couldn't come close to par at Pebble Beach in a million years. Quit your moaning, he told himself.

He put his hand on his wife's knee and drove on toward the beach, not even minding that fog had suddenly turned the morning gray.

Driving along 68, Holman Highway, Kathryn Dance called her children, whom her father, Stuart, was driving to their respective day camps. With the early-morning meeting at the hotel, Dance had arranged for Wes and Maggie – twelve and ten – to spend the night with their grandparents.

'Hey, Mom!' Maggie said. 'Can we go to Rosie's for dinner tonight?'

'We'll have to see. I've got a big case.'

'We made noodles for the spaghetti for dinner last night,

Grandma and me. And we used flour and eggs and water. Grandpa said we were making them from scratch. What does "from scratch" mean?'

'From all the ingredients. You don't buy them in a box.'

'Like, I know *that*. I mean, what does "scratch" mean?'

'Don't say "like." And I don't know. We'll look it up.'

'Okay.'

'I'll see you soon, sweetie. Love you. Put your brother on.'

'Hey, Mom.' Wes launched into a monologue about the tennis match planned for today.

Wes was, Dance suspected, just starting the downhill coast into adolescence. Sometimes he was her little boy, sometimes a distant teenager. His father had died two years ago, and only now was the boy sliding out from under the weight of that sorrow. Maggie, though younger, was more resilient.

'Is Michael still going out on his boat this weekend?'

'I'm sure he is.'

'That rocks!' O'Neil had invited the boy to go fishing this Saturday, along with Michael's young son, Tyler. His wife, Anne, rarely went out on the boat and, though Dance did from time to time, seasickness made her a reluctant sailor.

She then spoke briefly to her father, thanking him for baby-sitting the children, and mentioned that the new case would be taking up a fair amount of time. Stuart Dance was the perfect grandfather – the semiretired marine biologist could make his own hours and truly loved spending time with the children. Nor did he mind playing chauffeur. He did, however, have a meeting today at the Monterey Bay aquarium but assured his daughter that he'd drop the children off with their grandmother after camp. Dance would pick them up from her later.

Every day Dance thanked fate or the gods that she had loving family nearby. Her heart went out to single mothers with little support.

She slowed, turned at the light and pulled into the parking lot of Monterey Bay Hospital, studying a crowd of people behind a row of blue sawhorse barriers.

More protesters than yesterday.

And yesterday had seen more than the day before.

MBH was a famed institution, one of the best medical centers in the region, and one of the most idyllic, set in a pine forest. Dance knew the place well. She'd given birth to her children here, sat with her father as he recovered from major surgery. She'd identified her husband's body in the hospital's morgue.

And she herself had recently been attacked here – an incident related to the protest Dance was now watching.

As part of the Daniel Pell case, Dance had sent a young Monterey County deputy to guard the prisoner in the county courthouse in Salinas. The convict had escaped and, in the process, had attacked and severely burned the deputy, Juan Millar, who'd been brought here to intensive care. That had been such a hard time – for his confused, sorrowful family, for Michael O'Neil, and for his fellow officers at the MCSO. For Dance too.

It was while she was visiting Juan that his distraught brother, Julio, had assaulted her, enraged that she was trying to take a statement from his semiconscious sibling. Dance had been more startled than hurt by the attack and had chosen not to pursue a case against the hysterical brother.

A few days after Juan was admitted, he'd died. At first, it seemed that the death was a result of the extensive burns. But then it was discovered that somebody had taken his life – a mercy killing.

Dance was saddened by the death, but Juan's injuries were so severe that his future would have been nothing but pain and medical procedures. Juan's condition had also troubled Dance's mother, Edie, a nurse at the hospital. Dance recalled standing in her kitchen, her mother nearby, gazing into the distance. Something was troubling her deeply, and she soon told Dance what: she'd been checking on Juan when the man had swum to consciousness and looked at her with imploring eyes.

He'd whispered, 'Kill me.'

Presumably he'd delivered this plea to anybody who'd come to visit or tend to him.

Soon after that, someone had fulfilled his wish.

No one knew the identity of the person who had combined the drugs in the IV drip to end Juan's life. The death was now officially a criminal investigation – being handled by the Monterey County Sheriff's Office. But it wasn't being investigated very hard; doctors reported that it would have been highly unlikely for the deputy to live for more than a month or two. The death was clearly a humane act, even if criminal.

But the case had become a cause célèbre for pro-lifers. The protesters that Dance was now watching in the parking lot held posters emblazoned with crosses and pictures of Jesus and of Terry Schiavo, the comatose woman in Florida, whose right-to-die case the U.S. Congress itself became entwined in.

The placards being waved about in front of Monterey Bay Hospital decried the horrors of euthanasia and, apparently because everyone was already assembled and in a protesting mood, abortion. They were mostly members of Life First, based in Phoenix. They'd arrived within days of the young officer's death.

Dance wondered if any of them caught on to the irony of protesting death outside a hospital. Probably not. They didn't seem like folks with a sense of humor.

Dance greeted the head of security, a tall African-American, standing outside the main entrance. 'Morning, Henry. They keep coming, it looks like.'

'Morning, Agent Dance.' A former cop, Henry Bascomb liked using departmental titles. He gave a smirk, nodding their way. 'Like rabbits.'

'Who's the ringleader?' In the center of the crowd was a scrawny balding man with wattles beneath his pointy chin. He was in clerical garb.

'That's the head, the minister,' Bascomb told her. 'Reverend R. Samuel Fisk. He's pretty famous. Came all the way from Arizona.'

'R. Samuel Fisk. Very ministerial-sounding name,' she commented.

Beside the reverend stood a burly man with curly red hair and a buttoned dark suit. A bodyguard, Dance guessed.

'Life is sacred!' somebody called, aiming the comment to one of the news trucks nearby.

'Sacred!' the crowd took up.

'Killers,' Fisk shouted, his voice surprisingly resonant for such a scarecrow.

Though it wasn't directed at her, Dance felt a chill and flashed back to the incident in the ICU, when enraged Julio Millar had grabbed her from behind as Michael O'Neil and another companion intervened.

'Killers!'

The protesters took up the chant. 'Kill-ers. Kill-ers!' Dance guessed they'd be hoarse later in the day.

'Good luck,' she told the security chief, who rolled his eyes uncertainly.

Inside, Dance glanced around, half expecting to see her mother. Then she got directions from reception and hurried down a corridor to the room where she'd find the witness in the Roadside Cross Case.

When she stepped into the open doorway, the blond teenage girl inside, lying in the elaborate hospital bed, looked up.

'Hi, Tammy. I'm Kathryn Dance.' Smiling at the girl. 'You mind if I come in?'

5

Although Tammy Foster had been left to drown in the trunk, the attacker had made a miscalculation.

Had he parked farther from shore the tide would have been high enough to engulf the entire car, dooming the poor girl to a terrible death. But, as it happened, the car had gotten bogged down in loose sand not far out, and the flowing tide had filled the Camry's trunk with only six inches of water.

At about 4:00 a.m. an airline employee on his way to work saw the glint from the car. Rescue workers got to the girl, half conscious from exposure, bordering on hypothermia, and raced her to the hospital.

'So,' Dance now asked, 'how you feeling?'

'Okay, I guess.'

She was athletic and pretty but pale. Tammy had an equine face, straight, perfectly tinted blond hair and a pert nose that Dance guessed had started life with a somewhat different slope. Her quick glance at a small cosmetic bag suggested to Dance that she rarely went out in public without makeup.

Dance's badge appeared.

Tammy glanced at it.

'You're looking pretty good, all things considered.'

'It was so cold,' Tammy said. 'I've never been so cold in my life. I'm still pretty freaked.'

'I'm sure you are.'

The girl's attention swerved to the TV screen. A soap opera was on. Dance and Maggie watched them from time to time, usually when the girl was home sick from school. You could miss months and still come back and figure out the story perfectly.

Dance sat down and looked at the balloons and flowers on a nearby table, instinctively searching for red roses or religious gifts or cards emblazoned with crosses. There were none.

'How long are you going to be in the hospital?'

'I'm getting out today, probably. Maybe tomorrow, they said.'

'How're the doctors? Cute?'

A laugh.

'Where do you go to school?'

'Robert Louis Stevenson.'

'Senior?'

'Yeah, in the fall.'

To put the girl at ease, Dance made small talk: asking about whether she was in summer school, if she'd thought about what college she wanted to attend, her family, sports. 'You have any vacations plans?'

'We do *now*,' she said. 'After this. My mom and sister and me are going to visit my grandmother in Florida next week.' There was exasperation in her voice and Dance could tell that the last thing the girl wanted to do was go to Florida with the family.

'Tammy, you can imagine, we really want to find whoever did this to you.'

'Asshole.'

Dance lifted an agreeing eyebrow. 'Tell me what happened.'

Tammy explained about being at a club and leaving just after midnight. She was in the parking lot when somebody came up from behind, taped her mouth, hands and feet, threw her in the trunk and then drove to the beach.

'He just left me there to, like, drown.' The girl's eyes were hollow. Dance, empathetic by nature – a gift from her mother – could feel the horror herself, a hurting tickle down her spine.

'Did you know the attacker?'

The girl shook her head. 'But I know what happened.'

'What's that?'

'Gangs.'

'He was in a gang?'

'Yeah, everybody knows about it. To get into a gang, you have to kill somebody. And if you're in a Latino gang you have to kill a white girl. Those're the rules.'

'You think the perp was Latino?'

'Yeah, I'm sure he was. I didn't see his face but got a look at his hand. It was darker, you know. Not black. But he definitely wasn't a white guy.'

'How big was he?'

'Not tall. About five-six. But really, really strong. Oh, something else. I think last night I said it was just one guy. But I remembered this morning. There were two of them.'

'You saw two of them?'

'More, I could *feel* somebody else nearby, you know how that happens?'

'Could it have been a woman?'

'Oh, yeah, maybe. I don't know. Like I was saying, I was pretty freaked out.'

'Did anybody touch you?'

'No, not that way. Just to put tape on me and throw me in the trunk.' Her eyes flashed with anger.

'Do you remember anything about the drive?'

'No, I was too scared. I think I heard some clanks or something, some noise from inside the car.'

'Not the trunk?'

'No. Like metal or something, I thought. He put it in the car after he got me in the trunk. I saw this movie, one of the *Saw* movies. And I thought maybe he was going to use whatever it was to torture me.'

The bike, Dance was thinking, recalling the tread marks at the beach. He'd brought a bicycle with him for his escape. She suggested this, but Tammy said that wasn't it; there was no way to get a bike in the backseat. She added gravely. 'And it didn't sound like a bike.'

'Okay, Tammy.' Dance adjusted her glasses and kept looking at the girl, who glanced at the flowers and cards and stuffed animals. The girl added, 'Look at everything people gave me. That bear there, isn't he the best?'

'He's cute, yep . . . So you're thinking it was some Latino kids in a gang.'

'Yeah. But . . . well, you know, like now, it's kind of over with.'

'Over with?'

'I mean, I didn't get killed. Just a little wet.' A laugh as she avoided Dance's eyes. 'They're definitely freaking. It's all over the news. I'll bet they're gone. I mean, maybe even left town.'

It was certainly true that gangs had initiation rites. And some involved murder. But killings were rarely outside the race or ethnicity of the gang and were most often directed at rival gang members or informants. Besides, what had happened to Tammy was too elaborate. Dance knew from running gang crimes that they were business first; time is money and the less spent on extracurricular activities the better.

Dance had already decided that Tammy didn't think her attacker was a Latino gangbanger at all. Nor did she believe there were two of them.

In fact, Tammy knew more about the perp than she was letting on.

It was time to get to the truth.

The process of kinesic analysis in interviewing and inter-rogation is first to establish a baseline — a catalog of behaviors that subjects exhibit when telling the truth: where do they put their hands, where do they look and how often, do they swallow or clear their throats often, do they lace their speech with 'Uhm,' do they tap their feet, do they slouch or sit forward, do they hesitate before answering?

Once the truthful baseline is determined, the kinesic expert will note any deviations from it when the subject is asked questions to which he or she might have reason to answer falsely.

When most people lie, they feel stress and anxiety and try to relieve those unpleasant sensations with gestures or speech patterns that differ from the baseline. One of Dance's favorite quotes came from a man who predated the coining of the term 'kinesics' by a hundred years: Charles Darwin, who said, 'Repressed emotion almost always comes to the surface in some form of body motion.'

When the subject of the attacker's identity had arisen, Dance observed that the girl's body language changed from her baseline: she shifted her hips uneasily and a foot bobbed. Arms and hands are fairly easy for liars to control but we're much less aware of the rest of our body, especially toes and feet.

Dance also noted other changes: in the pitch of the girl's voice, fingers flipping her hair and 'blocking gestures,' touching her mouth and nose. Tammy also offered unnecessary digressions, she rambled and she made overgeneralized statements ('Everybody knows about it'), typical of someone who's lying.

Convinced that the girl was withholding information, Kathryn Dance now slipped into her analytic mode. Her approach to getting a subject to be honest consisted of four parts. First, she asked: what's the subject's role in the incident? Here, Tammy was a victim and a witness only, Dance concluded. She wasn't a participant – either involved in another crime or staging her own abduction.

Second, what's the motive to lie? The answer, it was pretty clear, was that the poor girl was terrified of reprisal. This was common, and made Dance's job easier than if Tammy's motive were to cover up her own criminal behavior.

The third question: what's the subject's general personality type? This determination would suggest what approach Dance should adopt in pursuing the interrogation – should she, for instance, be aggressive or gentle; work toward problem solving or offer emotional support; behave in a friendly manner or detached? Dance categorized her subjects according to attributes in the Myers-Briggs personality type indicator, which assesses whether someone is an extravert or introvert, thinking or feeling, sensing or intuitive.

The distinction between extravert and introvert is about attitude. Does the subject act first and then assess the results (an extravert), or reflect before acting (introvert)? Information gathering is carried out either by trusting the five senses and verifying data (sensing) or relying on hunches (intuitive). Decision making occurs by either objective, logical analysis (thinking) or by making choices based on empathy (feeling).

Although Tammy was pretty, athletic and apparently a popular girl, her insecurities – and, Dance had learned, an unstable home life – had made her an introvert, and one who was intuitive and feeling. This meant Dance couldn't use a blunt approach with the girl. Tammy would simply stonewall – and be traumatized by harsh questioning.

Finally, the fourth question an interrogator must ask is: what kind of *liar's* personality does the subject have?

There are several types. Manipulators, or 'High Machiavellians' (after the Italian political philosopher who, literally, wrote the book on ruthlessness), see absolutely nothing wrong with lying; they use deceit as a tool to achieve their goals in love, business, politics or crime and are very, very good at deception. Other types include social liars, who lie to entertain; adaptors, insecure people who lie to make positive impressions; and actors, who lie for control.

Dance decided Tammy was a combination of adaptor and actor. Her insecurities would make her lie to boost her fragile ego, and she would lie to get her way.

Once a kinesic analyst answers these four questions, the rest of the process is straightforward. She continues questioning the subject, noting carefully those queries that elicit stress reactions – indicators of deception. Then she keeps returning to those questions, and related ones, probing further, closing in on the lie, and noting how the subject is handling the increasing levels of stress. Is she angry, in denial, depressed or trying to bargain her way out of the situation? Each of these states requires different tools to force or trick or encourage the subject to finally tell the truth.

This is what Dance did now, sitting forward a bit to put herself in a close but not invasive 'proxemic zone' – about three feet away from Tammy. This would make her uneasy, but not overly threatened. Dance kept a faint smile on her face and decided not to exchange her gray-rimmed glasses for her black frames – her 'predator specs' – which she wore to intimidate High Mach subjects.

'That's very helpful, Tammy, everything you've said. I really appreciate your cooperation.'

The girl smiled. But she also glanced at the door. Dance read: guilt.

'But one thing,' the agent added, 'we have some reports from the crime scene. Like on *CSI*, you know?'

'Sure. I watch it.'

'Which one do you like?'

'The original. You know, Las Vegas.'

'That's the best, I hear.' Dance had never seen the show. 'But from the evidence it doesn't seem like there were two people. Either in the parking lot or at the beach.'

'Oh. Well, like I said, it was just a, like, feeling.'

'And one question I had. That clanking you heard? See, we didn't find any other car wheel tread marks either. So we're real curious how he got away. Let's go back to the bicycle. I know you didn't think that was the sound in the car, the clanking, but any way it could have been, you think?'

'A bicycle?'

Repeating a question is often a sign of deception. The subject is trying to buy time to consider the implications of an answer and to make up something credible.

'No, it couldn't. How could he get it inside?' Tammy's denial was too fast and too adamant. She'd considered a bicycle too but didn't want to admit the possibility, for some reason.

Dance lifted an eyebrow. 'Oh, I don't know. One of my neighbors has a Camry. It's a pretty big car.'

The girl blinked; she was surprised, it seemed, that Dance knew the make of her car. That the agent had done her homework was making Tammy uneasy. She looked at the window. Subconsciously, she was seeking a route of escape from the unpleasant anxiety. Dance was on to something. She felt her own pulse tap harder.

'Maybe. I don't know,' Tammy said.

'So, he could've had a bike. That might mean he was somebody your age, a little younger. Adults ride bikes, sure, but you see teenagers with them more. Hey, what do you think about it being somebody in school with you?'

'School? No way. Nobody I know would do something like that.'

'Anybody ever threaten you? Have any fights with anybody at Stevenson?'

'I mean, Brianna Crenshaw was pissed when I beat her for cheerleader. But she started going out with Davey Wilcox. Who I had a crush on. So it kind of evened out.' A choked laugh.

Dance smiled too.

'No, it was this gang guy. I'm sure of it.' Her eyes grew wide. 'Wait, I remember now. He made a call. Probably to the gang leader. I could hear him open his phone and he said, "*Ella esta en el coche.*"'

She's in the car, Dance translated to herself. She asked Tammy, 'You know what that means?'

'Something like "I've got her in the car."'

'You're studying Spanish?'

'Yeah.' This was all very breathless and told in a voice with a higher pitch than normal. Her eyes locked onto Dance's but her hand flicked her hair away and paused to scratch her lip.

The Spanish quotation was a complete lie.

'What I'm thinking,' Dance began reasonably, 'is that he was just *pretending* to be a gangbanger. To cover up his identity. That means there was another reason to attack you.'

'Like, why?'

'That's what I'm hoping you can help me with. You get any look at him at all?'

'Not really. He was behind me the whole time. And it was

really, really dark in the parking lot. They ought to put lights in. I think I'm going to sue the club. My father's a lawyer in San Mateo.'

The angry posturing was meant to deflect Dance's questioning; Tammy had seen something.

'Maybe as he came up toward you, you saw a reflection in the windows.'

The girl was shaking her head no. But Dance persisted. 'Just a glimpse. Think back. It's always cold at night here. He wouldn't've been in shirtsleeves. Was he wearing a jacket? A leather one, cloth? A sweater? Maybe a sweatshirt. A hoodie?'

Tammy said no to all of them, but some no's were different from others.

Dance then noticed the girl's eyes zip to a bouquet of flowers on the table. Beside it the get-well card read: *Yo, girl, get your a** out of there soon! Love J, P, and the Beasty Girl.*

Kathryn Dance looked at herself as a journeyman law enforcer who succeeded largely because of doing her homework and not taking no for an answer. Occasionally, though, her mind did a curious jump. She'd pack in the facts and impressions and suddenly there'd be an unexpected leap – a deduction or conclusion that seemed to arise as if by magic.

A to B to X . . .

This happened now, seeing Tammy look at the flowers, eyes troubled.

The agent took a chance.

'See, Tammy, we know that whoever attacked you also left a roadside cross – as a message of some sort.'

The girl's eyes grew wide.

Gotcha, Dance thought. She *does* know about the cross.

She continued her improvised script, 'And messages like that are always sent by people who know the victims.'

'I . . . I *heard* him speaking Spanish.'

Dance knew this was a lie, but she'd learned that with subjects who had a personality type like Tammy's, she needed to leave them an escape route, or they'd shut down completely. She said agreeably, 'Oh, I'm sure you did. But I think he was trying to cover up his identity. He wanted to fool you.'

Tammy was miserable, the poor thing.

Who terrified her so much?

'First of all, Tammy, let me reassure you that we'll protect you. Whoever did this won't get near you again. I'm going to have a policeman stay outside your door here. And we'll have one at your house too until we catch the person who did this.'

Relief in her eyes.

'Here's a thought: what about a stalker? You're very beautiful. I'll bet you have to be pretty careful.'

A smile – very cautious, but pleased nonetheless at the compliment.

'Anybody been hassling you?'

The young patient hesitated.

We're close. We're really close.

But Tammy backed away. 'No.'

Dance did too. 'Have you had any problems with people in your family?' This was a possibility. She'd checked. Her parents were divorced – after a tough courtroom battle – and her older brother lived away from home. An uncle had a domestic abuse charge.

But Tammy's eyes made it clear that relatives probably weren't behind the attack.

Dance continued to fish. 'You have any trouble with anybody you've been e-mailing? Maybe somebody you know online, through Facebook or MySpace? That happens a lot nowadays.'

'No, really. I'm not online that much.' She was flicking fingernail against fingernail, the equivalent of wringing hands.

'I'm sorry to push, Tammy. It's just so important to make sure this doesn't happen again.'

Then Dance saw something that struck her like a slap. In the girl's eyes was a recognition response – a faint lifting of the brows and lids. It meant that Tammy *was* afraid that this would happen again – but, since she'd have her police guard, the implication was that the attacker was a threat to others too.

The girl swallowed. She was clearly in the denial phase of stress reaction, which meant she was hunkered down, defenses raised high.

'It was somebody I didn't know. I swear to God.'

A deception flag: 'I swear.' The deity reference too. It was as if she were shouting, I'm lying! I want to tell the truth but I'm afraid.

Dance said, 'Okay, Tammy. I believe you.'

'Look, I'm really, really tired. I think maybe I don't want to say anything else until my mom gets here.'

Dance smiled. 'Of course, Tammy.' She rose and handed the girl one of her business cards. 'If you could think about it a bit more and let us know anything that occurs to you.'

'I'm sorry I'm, like, not all that helpful.' Eyes down. Contrite. Dance could see that the girl had used pouting and insincere self-deprecation in the past. The technique, mixed with a bit of flirt, would work with boys and her father; women wouldn't let her get away with it.

Still, Dance played to her. 'No, no, you've been very helpful. Gosh, honey, look at all you've been through. Get some rest. And put on some sitcoms.' A nod at the TV. 'They're good for the soul.'

Walking out the door, Dance reflected: another few hours and she might have gotten the girl to tell the truth, though she wasn't sure; Tammy was clearly terrified. Besides, however talented the interrogator, sometimes subjects simply would not tell what they knew.

Not that it mattered. Kathryn Dance believed she'd learned all the information she needed.

A to B to X . . .

6

In the lobby of the hospital Dance used a pay phone – no mobiles allowed – and called in a deputy to guard Tammy Foster's room. She then went to reception and had her mother paged.

Three minutes later Edie Dance surprised her daughter by approaching not from her station at Cardiac Care but from the intensive care wing.

'Hi, Mom.'

'Katie,' said the stocky woman with short gray hair and round glasses. Around her neck was an abalone and jade pendant that she'd made herself. 'I heard about the attack – that girl in the car. She's upstairs.'

'I know. I just interviewed her.'

'She'll be okay, I think. That's the word. How did your meeting go this morning?'

Dance grimaced. 'A setback, it looks like. The defense is trying to get the case dismissed on immunity.'

'Doesn't surprise me' was the cold response. Edie Dance was never hesitant to state her opinions. She had met the suspect, and when she learned what he'd done, she'd grown furious – an emotion evident to Dance in the woman's calm visage and faint smile. Never raising her voice. But eyes of steel.

If looks could kill, Dance remembered thinking about her mother when she was young.

'But Ernie Seybold's a bulldog.'

'How's Michael?' Edie Dance had always liked O'Neil.

'Fine. We're running this case together.' She explained about the roadside cross.

'No, Katie! Leaving a cross *before* somebody dies? As a message?'

Dance nodded. But she noted that her mother's attention continued to be drawn outside. Her face was troubled.

'You'd think they'd have more important things to do. That reverend gave a speech the other day. Fire and brimstone. And the hatred in their faces. It's vile.'

'Have you seen Juan's parents?'

Edie Dance had spent some time comforting the burned officer's family, his mother in particular. She had known that Juan Millar probably wouldn't survive, but she'd done everything she could to make the shocked and bewildered couple understand that he was getting the best care possible. Edie had told her daughter that the woman's emotional pain was as great as her son's physical agony.

'No, they haven't been back. Julio has. He was here this morning.'

'He was? Why?'

'Maybe collecting his brother's personal effects. I don't know . . .' Her voice faded. 'He was just staring at the room where Juan died.'

'Has there been an inquiry?'

'Our board of ethics was looking into it. And a few policemen have been here. Some county deputies. But when they look at the report – and see the pictures of his injuries – nobody's actually that upset that he died. It really *was* merciful.'

'Did Julio say anything to you when he was here today?'

'No, he didn't talk to anybody. You ask me, he's a bit scary. And I couldn't help but remember what he did to you.'

'He was temporarily insane,' Dance said.

'Well, that's no excuse for attacking my daughter,' Edie said with a staunch smile. Then her eyes slipped out the glass doors and examined the protesters once more. A dark look. She said, 'I better get back to my station.'

'If it's okay, could Dad bring Wes and Maggie over here later? He's got a meeting at the aquarium. I'll pick them up.'

'Of course, honey. I'll park 'em in the kids' play area.'

Edie Dance headed off once more, glancing outside. Her visage was angry and troubled. It seemed to say: you've got no business being here, disrupting our work.

Dance left the hospital with a glance toward Reverend R. Samuel Fisk and his bodyguard or whoever the big man was. They'd joined several other protesters, clasped hands and lowered their heads in prayer.

'Tammy's computer,' Dance said to Michael O'Neil.

He lifted an eyebrow.

'It's got the answer. Well, maybe not *the* answer. But *an* answer. To who attacked her.'

They were sipping coffee as they sat outside at Whole Foods in Del Monte Center, an outdoor plaza anchored by Macy's. She once calculated that she'd bought at least fifty pairs of shoes here – footwear, her tranquilizer. In fairness, though, that otherwise embarrassing number of purchases had taken place over a few years. Often, but not always, on sale.

'Online stalker?' O'Neil asked. The food they ate wasn't poached eggs with delicate hollandaise sauce and parsley garnish, but a shared raisin bagel with low-fat cream cheese in a little foil envelope.

'Maybe. Or a former boyfriend who threatened her, or somebody she met on a social networking site. But I'm sure she knows his identity, if not him personally. I'm leaning toward somebody from her school. Stevenson.'

'She wouldn't say, though?'

'Nope, claimed it was a Latino gangbanger.'

O'Neil laughed. A lot of fake insurance claims started with, 'A Hispanic in a mask broke into my jewelry store.' Or 'Two

African-Americans wearing masks pulled guns and stole my Rolex.'

'No description, but I think he was wearing a sweatshirt, a hoodie. She gave a different negation response when I mentioned that.'

'Her computer,' O'Neil mused, hefting his heavy briefcase onto the table and opening it. He consulted a printout. 'The good news: we've got it in evidence. A laptop. It was in the backseat of her car.'

'And the bad news is it went for a swim in the Pacific Ocean?'

'"Significant seawater damage,"' he quoted.

Dance was discouraged. 'We'll have to send it to Sacramento or the FBI up in San Jose. It'll take weeks to get back.'

They watched a hummingbird brave the crowds to hover for breakfast at a red hanging plant. O'Neil said, 'Here's a thought. I was talking to a friend of mine in the Bureau up there. He'd just been to a presentation on computer crime. One of the speakers was local – a professor in Santa Cruz.'

'UC?'

'Right.'

One of Dance's alma maters.

'He said the guy was pretty sharp. And he volunteered to help if they ever needed him.'

'What's his background?'

'All I know is he got out of Silicon Valley and started to teach.'

'At least there're no bursting bubbles in education.'

'You want me to see if I can get his name?'

'Sure.'

O'Neil lifted a stack of business cards from his attaché case, which was as neatly organized as his boat. He found one and made a call. In three minutes he'd tracked down his friend and had a brief conversation. The attack had already attracted the FBI's attention, Dance deduced. O'Neil jotted down a name and thanked the agent. Hanging up, he handed the slip to Dance. *Dr Jonathan Boling*. Below it was a number.

'What can it hurt? . . . Who's got the laptop itself?'

'In our evidence locker. I'll call and tell them to release it.'

Dance unholstered her cell phone and called Boling, got his voice mail and left a message.

She continued to tell O'Neil about Tammy, mentioning that much of the girl's emotional response was from her fear that the attacker would strike again – and maybe target others.

'Just what we were worried about,' O'Neil said, running a thick hand through his salt-and-pepper hair.

'She also was giving off signals of guilt,' Dance said.

'Because she might've been partly responsible for what happened?'

'That's what I'm thinking. In any case, I really want to get inside that computer.' A glance at her watch. Unreasonably, she was irritated that this Jonathan Boling hadn't returned her call of three minutes before.

She asked O'Neil, 'Any more leads on the evidence?'

'Nope.' He told her what Peter Bennington had reported about the crime scene: that the wood in the cross was from oak trees, of which there were about a million or two on the Peninsula. The green florist wire binding the two branches was common and untraceable. The cardboard was cut from the back of a pad of cheap notebook paper sold in thousands of stores. The ink couldn't be sourced either. The roses couldn't be traced to a particular store or other location.

Dance told him the theory of the bicycle. O'Neil was one step ahead, though. He added that they'd reexamined the lot where the girl had been kidnapped and the beach where the car was left, and found more bicycle tread marks, none identifiable, but they were fresh, suggesting that this was the perp's likely means of transport. But the tread marks weren't distinctive enough to trace.

Dance's phone rang – the Warner Brothers' Looney Tunes theme, which her children had programmed in as a practical joke. O'Neil smiled.

Dance glanced at the Caller ID screen. It read *J. Boling*. She lifted an eyebrow, thinking – again unreasonably – it was about time.

7

The noise outside, a snap from behind the house, brought back an old fear.

That she was being watched.

Not like at the mall or the beach. She wasn't afraid of leering kids or perverts. (That was irritating or flattering – depending, naturally, on the kid or the perv.) No, what terrified Kelley Morgan was some *thing* staring at her from outside the window of her bedroom.

Snap . . .

A second sound. Sitting at the desk in her room, Kelley felt a shivering so sudden and intense that her skin stung. Her fingers were frozen, pausing above the computer keyboard. Look, she told herself. Then: no, don't.

Finally: Jesus, you're seventeen. Get over it!

Kelley forced herself to turn around and risk a peek out the window. She saw gray sky above green and brown plants and rocks and sand. Nobody.

And no-*thing*.

Forget about it.

The girl, physique slim and brunette hair dense, would be a senior in high school next fall. She had a driver's license. She'd surfed Maverick Beach. She was going skydiving on her eighteenth birthday with her boyfriend.

No, Kelley Morgan didn't spook easily.

But she had one intense fear.

Windows.

The terror was from when she was a little girl, maybe nine or ten and living in this same house. Her mother read all these overpriced home design magazines and thought curtains were totally out and would mess up the clean lines of their modern house. Not a big deal, really, except that Kelley had seen some stupid TV show about the Abominable Snowman or some monster like that. It showed this CG animation of the creature as it walked up to a cabin and peered through the window, scaring the hell out of the people in bed.

Didn't matter that it was cheesy computer graphics, or that she knew there wasn't any such thing in real life. That was all it took, one TV show. For years afterward, Kelley would lie in bed, sweating, head covered by her blanket, afraid to look for fear of what she'd see. Afraid not to, for fear she'd have no warning of it – whatever *it* was – climbing through the window.

Ghosts, zombies, vampires and werewolves didn't exist, she told herself. But all she'd need to do was read a Stephenie Meyer *Twilight* book and, bang, the fear would come back.

And Stephen King? Forget about it.

Now, older and not putting up with as much of her parents' weirdness as she used to, she'd gone to Home Depot and bought curtains for her room and installed them herself. Screw her mother's taste in décor. Kelley kept the curtains drawn at night. But they were open at the moment, it being daytime, with pale light and a cool summer breeze wafting in.

Then another snap outside. Was it closer?

That image of the effing creature from the TV show just never went away, and neither did the fear it injected into her veins. The yeti, the Abominable Snowman, at her window, staring, staring. A churning now gripped her in the belly, like the time she'd tried that liquid fast then gone back to solid foods.

Snap . . .

She risked another peek.

The blank window yawned at her.

Enough!

She returned to her computer, reading some comments on the OurWorld social networking site about that poor girl from Stevenson High, Tammy, who'd been attacked last night – Jesus, thrown into a trunk and left to drown. Raped or at least molested, everybody was saying.

Most of the postings were sympathetic. But some were cruel and *those* totally pissed Kelley off. She was staring at one now.

Okay Tammy's going to be all right and thank God. But I have to say one thing. IMHO, she brought it on herself. she has GOT to learn not to walk around like a slutcat from the eighties with the eyeliner and where does she get those dresses? she KNOWS what the guys are thinking, what did she expect????

—AnonGurl

Kelley banged out a response.

OMG, how can you say that? She was almost killed. And anybody who says a woman ASKS to be raped is a mindless lOOser. u should be ashamed!!!

—BellaKelley

She wondered if the original poster would reply, hitting back.

Leaning toward the computer, Kelley heard yet another noise outside.

'That's it,' she said aloud. She rose, but didn't go to the window. Instead she walked out of her room and into the kitchen, peeking outside. Didn't see anything . . . or did she? Was there a shadow in the canyon behind the shrubs at the back of the property?

None of her family was home, her parents working, her brother at practice.

Laughing uneasily to herself: it was less scary for her to go outside and meet a hulking pervert face-to-face than to see him looking into her window. Kelley glanced at the magnetic knife rack. The blades were totally sharp. Debated. But she left the weapons where they were. Instead she held her iPhone up to her ear and walked outside. 'Hi, Ginny, yeah, I heard something outside. I'm just going to go see.'

The conversation was pretend, but he – or it – wouldn't know that.

'No, I'll keep talking. Just in case there's some asshole out there.' Talking loud.

The door opened onto the side yard. She headed toward the back, then, approaching the corner, she slowed. Finally she stepped tentatively into the backyard. Empty. At the end of the property, beyond a thick barrier of plants, the ground dropped away steeply into county land – a shallow canyon filled with brush and some jogging trails.

'So, how's it going? Yeah . . . yeah? Sweet. Way sweet.'

Okay. Don't overdo it, she thought. Your acting sucks.

Kelley eased to the row of foliage and peered through it into the canyon. She thought she saw someone moving away from the house.

Then, not too far away, she saw some kid in sweats on a bike, taking one of the trails that was a shortcut between Pacific Grove and Monterey. He turned left and vanished behind a hill.

Kelley put the phone away. She started to return to the house when she noticed something out of place in the back planting beds. A little dot of color. Red. She walked over to it and picked up the flower petal. A rose. Kelley let the crescent flutter back to the ground.

She returned to the house.

A pause, looking back. No one, no animals. Not a single Abominable Snowman or werewolf.

She stepped inside. And froze, gasping.

In front of her, ten feet away, a human silhouette was approaching, features indistinct because of the backlighting from the living room.

'Who—?'

The figure stopped. A laugh. 'Jesus, Kel. You are *so* freaked. You look . . . gimme your phone. I want a picture.'

Her brother, Ricky, reached for her iPhone.

'Get *out*!' Kelley said, grimacing and twisting away from his outstretched hand. 'Thought you had practice.'

'Needed my sweats. Hey, you hear about that girl in the trunk? She goes to Stevenson.'

'Yeah, I've seen her. Tammy Foster.'

'She hot?' The lanky sixteen-year-old, with a mop of brown hair that matched her own, headed for the refrigerator and grabbed a power drink.

'Ricky, you're so gross.'

'Uh-huh. So? Is she?'

Oh, she hated brothers. 'When you leave, lock the door.'

Ricky screwed his face into a huge frown. 'Why? Who'd wanna molest you?'

'Lock it!'

'Like, okay.'

She shot him a dark look, which he missed completely.

Kelley continued to her room and sat down at the computer again. Yep, AnonGurl had posted an attack on Kelley for defending Tammy Foster.

Okay, bitch, you're going down. I am gonna own you so bad.

Kelley Morgan began to type.

Professor Jonathan Boling was in his forties, Dance estimated. Not tall, a few inches over her height, with a frame that suggested either a tolerance for exercise or a disdain for junk food. Straight brownish hair similar to Dance's, though she suspected that *he* didn't sneak a box of Clairol into his shopping cart at Safeway every couple of weeks.

'Well,' he said, looking around the halls as she escorted him from the lobby to her office at the California Bureau of Investigation. 'This isn't quite what I pictured. Not like *CSI*.'

Did everybody in the universe watch that show?

Boling wore a digital Timex on one wrist and a braided bracelet on the other – perhaps symbolizing support for something or another. (Dance thought about her children, who would cover their wrists with so many colored bands she was never sure what the latest causes were.) In jeans and a black polo shirt, he was handsome in a subdued, National Public Radio kind of way. His brown eyes were steady, and he seemed fast with a smile.

Dance decided he could have any grad student he set his sights on.

She asked, 'You ever been in a law enforcement office before?'

'Well, sure,' he said, clearing his throat and giving off odd kinesic signals. Then a smile. 'But they dropped the charges. I mean, what else could they do when Jimmy Hoffa's body never turned up?'

She couldn't help but laugh. Oh, you poor grad students. Beware.

'I thought you consulted with police.'

'I've *offered* to, at the end of my lectures to law enforcement agencies and security companies. But nobody's taken me up on it. Until now. You're my maiden voyage. I'll try not to disappoint.'

They arrived in her office and sat across from each other at her battered coffee table.

Boling said, 'I'm happy to help however I can but I'm not sure exactly what I can do.' A bolt of sunlight fell across his loafers and he glanced down, noticed that one sock was black and one navy blue. He laughed without embarrassment. In another era Dance would have deduced that he was single; nowadays, with two busy working partners, fashion glitches like this were inadmissible evidence. He didn't, however, wear a wedding ring.

'I have a hardware and software background but for serious technical advice, I'm afraid I'm over the legal age limit and I don't speak Hindi.'

He told her that he'd gotten joint degrees in literature and engineering at Stanford, admittedly an odd combination, and after a bit of 'bumming around the world' had ended up in Silicon Valley, doing systems design for some of the big computer companies.

'Exciting time,' he said. But, he added, eventually he'd been turned off by the greed. 'It was like an oil rush. Everybody was asking how could they get rich by convincing people they had these needs that computers could fill. I thought maybe we should look at it the other way: find out what needs people *actually* had and then ask how computers could help them.' A cocked head. 'As between their position and mine. I lost big-time. So I took some stock money, quit, bummed around again. I ended up in Santa Cruz, met somebody, decided to stay and tried teaching. Loved it. That was almost ten years ago. I'm still there.'

Dance told him that after a stint as a reporter she'd gone back to college – the same school where he taught. She studied communications and psychology. Their time had coincided, briefly, but they didn't know anyone in common.

He taught several courses, including the Literature of Science Fiction, as well as a class called Computers and Society. And in the grad school Boling taught what he described as some boring technical courses. 'Sort of math, sort of engineering.' He also consulted for corporations.

Dance interviewed people in many different professions. The majority radioed clear signals of stress when speaking of their jobs, which indicated either anxiety because of the demands of the work, or, more often, depression about it – as Boling had earlier when speaking about Silicon Valley. But his kinesic behavior now, when discussing his present career, was stress free.

He continued to downplay his technical skill, though, and Dance was disappointed. He seemed smart and more than willing to help – he'd driven down here on a moment's notice – and she would have liked to use his services, but to get into Tammy Foster's computer it sounded like they'd need more of a hands-on tech person. At least, she hoped, he could recommend someone.

Maryellen Kresbach came in with a tray of coffee and cookies. Attractive, she resembled a country-western singer, with her coiffed brown hair and red Kevlar fingernails. 'The guard desk called. Somebody's got a computer from Michael's office.'

'Good. You can bring it up.'

Maryellen paused for a moment and Dance had an amusing idea that the woman was checking out Boling as romantic fodder. Her assistant had been waging a none-too-subtle campaign to find Dance a husband. When the woman eyed Boling's naked left ring finger and lifted her brow at Dance, the agent flashed her an exasperated glance, which was duly noted and summarily ignored.

Boling called his thanks and, after pouring three sugars into his coffee, dug into the cookies and ate two. 'Good. No, better than good.'

'She bakes them herself.'

'Really? People do that? They don't all come out of a Keebler bag?'

Dance went for half a cookie and enjoyed a sip of coffee, though she was caffeinated enough from her earlier meeting with Michael O'Neil.

'Let me tell you what's going on.' She explained to Boling about the attack on Tammy Foster. Then said, 'And we have to get into her laptop.'

Boling nodded understandingly. 'Ah, the one that went for a swim in the Pacific Ocean.'

'It's toast . . .'

He corrected, 'With the water, more likely it's oatmeal – if we're keeping to breakfast food metaphors.'

Just then a young MCSO deputy stepped into Dance's office, carrying a large paper bag. Good-looking and eager, though more cute than handsome, he had bright blue eyes, and for a moment he seemed about to salute. 'Agent Dance?'

'That's right.'

'I'm David Reinhold. Crime Scene at the Sheriff's Office.'

She nodded a greeting. 'Nice to meet you. Thanks for bringing that over.'

'You bet. Anything I can do.'

He and Boling shook hands. Then the trim officer, in a perfectly pressed uniform, handed Dance the paper bag. 'I didn't put it in plastic. Wanted it to breathe. Get as much moisture out as we could.'

'Thanks,' Boling said.

'And I took the liberty of taking the battery out,' the young deputy said. He held up a sealed metal tube. 'It's a lithium-ion. I thought if water got inside there could be a fire risk.'

Boling nodded, clearly impressed. 'Good thinking.'

Dance had no clue what he was talking about. Boling noticed her frown and explained that some lithium batteries, under certain circumstances, could burst into flames when exposed to water.

'You a geek?' Boling asked him.

The deputy replied, 'Not really. Just stuff you pick up, you know.' He held out a receipt for Dance to sign and then pointed out the chain-of-custody card, attached to the bag itself. 'If there's anything else I can do, let me know.' He handed her a business card.

She thanked him, and the young man retreated.

Dance reached inside the bag and extracted Tammy's laptop. It was pink.

'What a color,' Boling said, shaking his head. He turned it over and examined the back.

Dance asked him, 'So, do you know somebody who could get it running and take a look at her files?'

'Sure. Me.'

'Oh, I thought you said you weren't that much of a tech anymore.'

'That's not tech, not by today's standards.' He smiled again. 'It's like rotating your tires on a car. Only I need a couple of tools.'

'We don't have a lab here. Nothing as sophisticated as you probably need.'

'Well, that depends. I see you collect shoes.' Her closet door was open and Boling must've glanced inside, where a dozen pairs sat, more or less ordered, on the floor – for those nights when she went out after work, without stopping at home. She gave a laugh.

Busted.

He continued, 'How 'bout personal care appliances?'

'Personal care?'

'I need a hair dryer.'

She chuckled. 'Sadly, all my beauty aids are at home.'

'Then we better go shopping.'

8

Jon Boling needed a bit more than a hair dryer, as it turned out. Though not much.

Their shopping spree had yielded a Conair, a set of miniature tools and a metal box called an enclosure – a three-by-five-inch rectangle from which sprouted a wire that ended in a USB plug.

These items now sat on Dance's coffee table in her office at the CBI.

Boling surveyed Tammy Foster's designer laptop. 'I can take it apart? I'm not going to screw up any evidence, am I?'

'It's been dusted for prints. All we found were Tammy's. Go ahead and do what you want – she's not a suspect. Besides, she lied to me, so she's in no position to complain.'

'Pink,' he said again, as if this was a shocking breach of propriety.

He turned the machine over and, with a tiny Phillips-head screwdriver, had the panel off the back in a few minutes. He then extracted a small metal-and-plastic rectangle.

'The hard drive,' he explained. 'By next year this'll be considered huge. We're going to flash memory in central processing units. No hard drives – no moving parts at all.' The subject seemed to excite him but he sensed a lecture was a digression inappropriate at the moment. Boling fell silent and examined the drive closely. He didn't seem to wear contacts; Dance, who'd worn glasses since girlhood, had a mild attack of eye envy.

The professor then gently rattled the drive beside his ear. 'Okay.' He set it on the table.

'Okay?'

He grinned, unpacked the hair dryer, plugged it in and wafted a stream of balmy heat over the drive. 'Shouldn't be long. I don't think it's wet but we can't take the chance. Electricity and water equal uh-oh.'

With his free hand he sipped the coffee. He mused, 'We professors're very envious of the private sector, you know. "Private sector" – that's Latin for "actually making money".' He nodded at the cup. 'Take Starbucks . . . Coffee was a pretty good idea for a franchise. I keep looking for the next big one. But all I could think of were things like House O' Pickles and Jerky World. Beverages're the best, but all the good ones're taken.'

'Maybe a milk bar,' Dance suggested. 'You could call it Elsie's.'

His eyes brightened. 'Or how 'bout "Just An-Udder Place".'

'That was really bad,' she said as they shared a brief laugh.

When he finished drying the hard drive he slipped it into the enclosure. He then plugged the USB connection into his own laptop, which was a somber gray, apparently the shade computers should be.

'I'm curious what you're doing.' She was watching his sure fingers pound the keys. Many of the letters were worn off. He didn't need to see them to type.

'The water would've shorted out the computer itself, but the hard drive should be okay inside. I'm going to turn it into a readable drive.' After a few minutes he looked up and smiled. 'Nope, it's good as new.'

Dance scooted her chair closer to his.

She glanced at the screen and saw that Windows Explorer was reading Tammy's hard drive as 'Local Disk (G)'.

'It'll have everything on it – her emails, the websites she's browsed, her favorite places, records of her instant messages. Even deleted data. It's not encrypted or password-protected – which, by the way, tells me that her parents are very uninvolved in her life. Kids whose folks keep a close eye on them learn to use all kinds of tricks for privacy. Which I, by the way, am pretty good at cracking.' He unplugged the disk from his computer and handed it and the cable to her. 'It's all yours. Just plug it in and read to your heart's content.' He shrugged. 'My first assignment for the police . . . short but sweet.'

With a good friend, Kathryn Dance owned and operated a website devoted to homemade and traditional music. The site was pretty sophisticated technically but Dance knew little of the hardware and software; her friend's husband handled that side of the business. She now said to Boling, 'You know, if you're not too busy, any chance you could stay around for a little? Help me search it?'

Boling hesitated.

'Well, if you have plans . . .'

'How much time are we talking? I've got to be in Napa on Friday night. Family reunion sort of thing.'

Dance said, 'Oh, nothing that long. A few hours. A day at the most.'

Eyes brightening again. 'I'd love to. Puzzles are an important food group to me . . . Now, what would I be looking for?'

'Any clues as to the identity of Tammy's attacker.'

'Oh, *Da Vinci Code*.'

'Let's hope it's not as tricky and that whatever we find won't get us excommunicated . . . I'm interested in any communications that seem threatening. Disputes, fights, comments about stalkers. Would instant messages be there?'

'Fragments. We can probably reconstruct a lot of them.' Boling plugged the drive back into his computer and leaned forward.

'Then social networking sites,' Dance said. 'Anything to do with roadside memorials or crosses.'

'Memorials?'

She explained, 'We think he left a roadside cross to announce the attack.'

'That's pretty sick.' The professor's fingers snapped over the keys. As he typed, he asked, 'Why do you think her computer's the answer?'

Dance explained about the interview with Tammy Foster.

'You picked up all that just from her body language?'

'That's right.'

She told him about the three ways humans communicate. First, through verbal content – *what* we say. 'That's the meaning of the words themselves. But content is not only the least reliable and most easily faked, it's actually only a small portion of the way we send messages to each other. The second and third are much more important: verbal quality – *how* we say the words. That would be things like pitch of voice, how fast we talk, whether we pause and use "uhm" frequently. And then, third, kinesics – our body's behavior. Gestures, glances, breathing, posture, mannerisms. The last two are what interviewers are most interested in, since they're much more revealing than speech content.'

He was smiling. Dance lifted an eyebrow.

Boling explained, 'You sound as excited about your work as—'

'You and your flash memory.'

A nod. 'Yep. They're amazing little guys . . . even the pink ones.'

Boling continued to type and scroll through page after page of the guts of Tammy's computer, speaking softly. 'Typical rambling of a teenage girl. Boys, clothes, makeup, parties, a little bit about school, movies and music . . . no threats.'

He scrolled quickly through various screens. 'So far, negative on the emails, at least the ones for the past two weeks. I can go back and check the earlier ones if I need to. Now, Tammy's in all the big social networking sites – Facebook, MySpace, OurWorld, Second Life.' Though Boling was offline, he could pull up and view recent pages Tammy had read. 'Wait. Wait . . . Okay.' He was sitting forward, tense.

'What is it?'

'She was almost drowned?'

'That's right.'

'A few weeks ago she and some of her friends started a discussion in OurWorld about what scared them the most. One of Tammy's big fears was drowning.'

Dance's mouth tightened. 'Maybe he picked the means of death specifically for her.'

In a surprisingly vehement tone, Boling said, 'We give away too much information about ourselves online. Way too much. You know the term "escribitionist"?'

'Nope.'

'A term for blogging about yourself.' A grimacing smile. 'Tells it pretty well, doesn't it? And then there's "dooce".'

'That's new too.'

'A verb. As in "I've been dooced". It means getting fired because of what you posted on your blog – whether facts about yourself or your boss or job. A woman in Utah coined it. She posted some things about her employer and got laid off. "Dooce" comes from a misspelling of "dude", by the way. Oh, and then there's pre-doocing.'

'Which is?'

'You apply for a job and the interviewer asks you, "You ever write anything about your former boss in a blog?" Of course, they already know the answer. They're waiting to see if you're honest. And if you have posted anything bad? You were knocked out of contention before you brushed your teeth the morning of the interview.'

Too much information. Way too much . . .

Boling continued to type, lightning fast. Finally he said, 'Ah, think I've got something.'

'What?'

'Tammy posted a comment on a blog a few days ago. Her screen name is TamF1399.' Boling spun the computer around for Dance to look at.

Reply to Chilton, posted by TamF1399.

[The driver] is effing weird, i mean dangerous. 1 time after cheerleader practice he was hanging out outside our locker room, like he was trying to look inside and get pictures on his phone. I go up to him and I'm like, what're you doing here, and he looks at me like he was going to kill me. He's a total fr33k. i know a girl who goes to [deleted] with us and she told me [the driver] grabbed her boobs, only she's afraid to say anything because she thinks he'll come get her or start shooting people, like in Virginia Tech.

Boling added, 'What's interesting is that she posted that in a part of the blog called "Roadside Crosses".'

Dance's heart rate pumped up a bit. She asked, 'Who's "the driver"?'

'Don't know. The name's deleted in all the posts.'

'A blog, hmm?'

'Right.' Boling gave a brief laugh and said, 'Mushrooms.'

'What?'

'Blogs are the mushrooms of the Internet. They're sprouting up everywhere. A few years ago everybody in Silicon Valley was wondering what would be the next big thing in the dot-com world. Well, it turned out to be not a revolutionary new type of hardware or software, but online content: games, social networking sites . . . and blogs. You can't write about computers now without studying them. The one Tammy posted to was *The Chilton Report*.'

Dance shrugged. 'Never heard of it.'

'I have. It's local but it's well known in blogging circles. It's like a California-based Matt Drudge, only more fringe. Jim Chilton's a bit of a character.' He continued to read. 'Let's go online and check it out.'

Dance got her own laptop from her desk. 'What's the URL?' she asked.

Boling gave it to her.

http://www.thechiltonreport.com

The professor tugged his chair closer and together they read the homepage.

THE CHILTON REPORT™

THE MORAL VOICE OF AMERICA. A COLLECTION OF MUSINGS ABOUT WHERE THIS COUNTRY'S GOING WRONG . . . AND WHERE IT'S GOING RIGHT.

Dance chuckled. '"Where it's going *right*." Clever. He's Moral Majority, conservative, I take it.'

Boling shook his head. 'From what I know he's more cut-and-paste.'

She lifted an eyebrow.

'I mean that he picks and chooses his causes. He's more right than left but he'll take on anybody who falls short of his standards of morality or judgment or intelligence. That's one of the points of blogs, of course: to stir things up. Controversy sells.'

Below was a greeting to the readers.

Dear Reader

Whether you've ended up here because you're a subscriber or a fan or simply because you happened to be browsing the Web and stumbled across the *Report*, welcome.

Whatever your positions on political and social issues, I hope you'll find something in my reflections here that, at the very least, makes you question, makes you doubt, makes you want to know more.

For that is what journalism is all about.
James Chilton

Below that was: 'Mission Statement.'

OUR MISSION STATEMENT

We can't make judgments in a vacuum. Will business, will government, will corrupt politicians and criminal and debauched individuals be honest about what they're up to? Of course not. It's our job in the *Report* to shine the light of truth into the shadows of deceit and greed – to give you the facts you need to make informed decisions about the pressing issues of the day.

Dance also found a brief biography of Chilton, then a section about personal news. She glanced over the listings.

ON THE HOME FRONT

GO TEAM!

I'm happy to say that after this weekend's game the Older Boy's team is 4–0! Go, Jayhawks! Now, parents: listen to me. Your youngsters should give up baseball and football for soccer, which is the safest and healthiest team sport there is. (See *The Chilton Report* of April 12 for my comments about sports injuries among children.) And by the way, make sure you call it 'soccer,' not 'football,' the way the foreigners do. When in America, do as Americans!

A PATRIOT

Yesterday the Younger Boy knocked the socks off the audience in his day camp recital by singing 'America the Beautiful'. All by himself! Makes a dad swell up with pride.

SUGGESTIONS, ANYONE?

We're coming up on our nineteenth anniversary, Pat and I. And I need ideas for presents! (Out of self-interest I've decided against getting her a high-speed fiber optic upgrade for the computer!) You ladies out there, send me your ideas. And, no, Tiffany's is not out of the question.

WE'RE GOING GLOBAL!

Am pleased to report that the *Report* has been getting raves from around the world. It's been selected as one of the lead blogs in a new RSS feed (we'll call it 'Really Simple Syndication') that will link thousands of other blogs, websites and bulletin boards throughout the world. Kudos to you, my readers, for making The Report as popular as it is.

WELCOME HOME

Heard some news that made me smile. Those of you who've followed the *Report* may remember glowing comments over the years about this

humble reporter's dear friend Donald Hawken – we were pioneers in this
crazy computer world so many years ago I don't like to think about it.
Donald escaped the Peninsula for greener pastures in San Diego. But I'm
delighted to say that he's come to his senses and is returning, along
with his bride, Lily, and his two wonderful children. Welcome home,
Donald!

HEROES

Hats off to the brave firefighters of Monterey County . . . Pat and I
happened to be downtown on Alvarado last Tuesday when calls for help
rang out and smoke sprouted from a construction site. Flames blocked the
exit . . . with two construction workers trapped on the upper floors. Within
minutes two dozen firemen and women were on the scene and a fire
truck had stretched its ladder to the roof. The men were plucked from
harm's way, and the flames were extinguished. No injuries, minimal
damage.

In most of our lives bravery involves little more than arguing politics or, at
the most physical, snorkeling at fancy resorts or mountain biking.

How rarely are we called on to exhibit true courage – the way the men and
women of Monterey County Fire and Rescue do every single day, without a
moment's hesitation or complaint.

Bravo to you all!

Accompanying this posting was a dramatic photo of a fire
truck in downtown Monterey.

'Typical of blogs,' Boling said. 'Personal information, gossip.
People like to read that.'

Dance also clicked on a link called 'Monterey'.

She was taken to a page that extolled 'Our Home: the Beautiful
and Historic Monterey Peninsula', featuring artistic photos of
the shoreline and boats near Cannery Row and Fisherman's
Wharf. There were a number of links to local sights.

Another link led them to maps of the area, including one that
depicted her town: Pacific Grove.

Boling said, 'This is all gingerbread. Let's look at the content of the blog . . . that's where we'll find the clues.' He frowned. 'Do you call them "clues"? Or "evidence"?'

'You can call 'em broccoli if it helps us find the perp.'

'Let's see what the veggies reveal.' He gave her another URL.

http://www.thechiltonreport.com/html/june26.html

This was the crux of the blog: Chilton's mini-essays.

Boling explained, 'Chilton's the "OP", the original poster. Which, if you're interested, is derived from "OG", Original Gangsta", for the leaders of gangs, like Bloods and Crips. Anyway, he uploads his commentary and then leaves it there for people to respond to. They agree or disagree. Sometimes they go off on tangents.'

The original comment by Chilton, Dance noticed, remained at the top, and below were the replies. Mostly people replied directly to the blogger's comment, but sometimes they responded to other posters.

'Each separate article and all the related posts are called a "thread",' Boling explained. 'Sometimes the threads can go on for months or years.'

Dance began skimming. Under the clever heading 'HypoCHRISTcy', Chilton attacked the very man Dance had just seen at the hospital, the Reverend Fisk, and the Life First movement. Fisk, it seemed, had once said that murdering abortion doctors was justified. Chilton wrote that he was adamantly against abortion, but condemned Fisk for the statement. Two of Fisk's defenders, CrimsoninChrist and LukeB1734, viciously attacked Chilton. The former said the blogger himself should be crucified. With the reference to the color in his name, Dance wondered if CrimsoninChrist was the minister's large, redheaded bodyguard she'd seen earlier at the hospital protest.

The 'Power to the People' thread was an exposé about a California state representative – Brandon Klevinger, who was head of the Nuclear Facilities Planning Committee. Chilton had found out that Klevinger had gone on a golfing junket with a developer who was proposing a new nuclear plant near Mendocino, when it would have been cheaper and more efficient to build it closer to Sacramento.

In 'Desalinate . . . and Devastate' the blogger took on a plan to build a desalination plant near the Carmel River. The comment included a personal attack on the man behind the project, Arnold Brubaker, painted by Chilton as an interloper from Scottsdale, Arizona, a man with a sketchy past and possible underworld connections.

Two of the postings represented the citizens' two positions on the desalination issue.

Reply to Chilton, posted by Lyndon Strickland.

I have to say you've opened my eyes on this issue. Had no idea that somebody's ramrodding this through. I reviewed the filed proposal at the County Planning Office and must say that, though I am an attorney familiar with environmental issues, it was one of the most obfuscatory documents I've ever tried to wade through. I think we need considerably more transparency in order to have meaningful debate on this matter.

Reply to Chilton, posted by Howard Skelton.

Do you know that America will run out of freshwater by 2023? And 97 percent of the earth's water is salt water. Only an idiot would not take advantage of that. We need desalination for our survival, if we're to continue to maintain our position as the most productive and efficient country in the world.

In the 'Yellow Brick Road' thread Chilton talked about a project by the state Department of Transportation – Caltrans. A new highway was being built from Highway 1 through Salinas and on to Hollister, through farm country. Chilton was questioning the lightning speed with which the project had been approved, as well as the meandering route, which would benefit some farmers far more than others. He hinted at payoffs.

Chilton's social conservative side shone through in 'Just Say

No', a thread condemning a proposal for increased sex education in middle schools. (Chilton called for abstinence.) A similar message could be found in 'Caught in the Act . . . NOT', about a married state court judge caught leaving a motel with a young clerk, half his age. Chilton was incensed at the recent development that the judge had received a wrist slap from the judicial ethics committee. He felt the man should have been removed from the bench and disbarred.

Kathryn Dance then came to the crucial thread, beneath a sad picture of crosses, flowers and a stuffed animal.

ROADSIDE CROSSES

Posted by Chilton.

I recently drove past the spot on Highway 1 where two roadside crosses, and some bright bouquets, sit. They marked the site of that terrible accident on June 9, where two girls died following a graduation party. Lives ended . . . and lives of loved ones and friends changed forever.

I realized that I hadn't heard much about any police investigation into the crash. I made some calls and found there'd been no arrests. No citations were even issued.

That struck me as odd. Now, no ticket means a determination that the driver – a high school student, so no names – was not to blame. So then what was the cause of the accident? As I drove along the road I noticed it was windswept and sandy and had no lights or guardrails near the spot where the car veered off the road. A caution sign was weathered and would have been hard to see in the dark (the accident occurred around midnight). There was no drainage; I could see pools of standing water on the shoulder and on the highway itself.

Why didn't the police do a thorough accident reconstruction (they have people on staff who do that, I've learned)? Why didn't Caltrans immediately send a team to examine the surface of the road, the grading, the markings? I could find no record of any such examination.

Maybe the road is as safe as can be expected.

But is it fair to us – whose children regularly drive that stretch of highway – for the authorities to dismiss the tragedy so quickly? It seems to me that their attention has faded quicker than the flowers sitting sorrowfully beneath those roadside crosses.

Reply to Chilton, posted by Ronald Kestler.

If you look at the budget situation in Monterey County and in the state in general, you will find that one area taking the brunt of our economic woes is adequate warning measures along high-risk highways. My son was killed in an accident along Highway 1 because the Curve sign had become covered with mud. It would have been an easy thing for state workers to find and clean it, but did they do this? No. Their neglect was inexcusable. Thank you, Mr Chilton, for calling attention to this problem.

Reply to Chilton, posted by A Concerned Citizen.

Highway workers make obscene amounts of money and sit on their fat [deleted] all day long. you've seen them, everybody has, standing by the road not doing anything when they could be fixing dangerous highways and making sure we're safe. another example of our tax dollars NOT at work.

Reply to Chilton, posted by Robert Garfield, California Department of Transportation.

I wish to assure you and your readers that the safety of our citizens is Caltrans's number one priority. We make every effort to maintain the highways of our state in good repair. The portion of road where the accident you're referring to occurred is, like all highways under state control, regularly inspected. No violations or unsafe conditions were found. We urge all drivers to remember that highway safety in California is everyone's responsibility.

Reply to Chilton, posted by Tim Concord.

Your comment is EPIC WIN, Chilton! The police will get away with murder if we let them! I was pulled over on Sixty-eight because I'm African-American. The police made me sit on the ground for half an hour before they let me go and they wouldn't tell me what I'd done wrong, except for a light that was out. The government should be protecting lives not dissing innocent citizens. Thank you.

Reply to Chilton, posted by Ariel.

On Friday me and my friend went to see the place where it happened and we were crying when we saw the crosses and flowers there. We were sitting there and we looked all over the highway and there were no police there, I mean, none! Just after it happened! Where were the police? And maybe it was there were no warning signs or the road was slippery, but it looked pretty safe to me, even tho it was sandy, that's true.

Reply to Chilton, posted by SimStud.

I drive that stretch of highway all the time and it's not the most dangerous place in the world, so what I'm wondering is, did the police really look at who was behind the wheel, I know [the driver] from school and I don't think he's the best driver in the world.

Reply to SimStud, posted by Footballrulz.

Dude, not the BEST driver in the world???? H8 to break it to you but [the driver] is a total fr33k and a luser, he CANT drive. I don't even think he has a license. Why didn't the cops find THAT out? Too busy going for dounuts and coffee. LOL.

Reply to Chilton, posted by MitchT.

Chilton, You're always trashing the government which is total win but in this case forget the road. It's fine. That guy from Caltrans said so. I've drove down there a hundred times and if you missed that curve because your drunk or stoned. If the police [deleted] up its because they didn't look at [the driver] close enough. He's a n00b and scary too. SimStud OWNS this thread.

Reply to Chilton, posted by Amydancer44.

This is weird cause my parents read the *Report* but I don't usually so it's weird that I'm here. But I heard around school what you'd posted about the accident and so I logged on. I read everything and I think you're one hundred percent right, and what that other poster said too. Everybody is innocent until proven guilty but I don't understand why the police just dropped the investigation.

Somebody who knows [the driver] was telling me that he was up all night before the party, I mean 24 hours, playing computer games. IMHO, he fell asleep driving, And another thing – those gamers think they're hot [deleted] behind the wheel b/c they play those driving games in the arcades but it's not the same thing.

Reply to Chilton, posted by Arthur Standish.

Federal funds for road maintenance have decreased consistently over the years, while the budget for U.S. military operations and foreign aid has quadrupled. Perhaps we should be more concerned about the lives of our citizens than those of people in other countries.

Reply to Chilton, posted by TamF1399.

[The driver] is effing weird, i mean dangerous. 1 time after cheerleader practice he was hanging out outside our locker room, like he was trying to look inside and get pictures on his phone. I go up to him and I'm like, what're you doing here and he looks at me like he was going to kill me. He's a total fr33k. i know a girl who goes to [deleted] with us and she told me [the driver] grabbed her boobs, only she's afraid to say anything because she thinks he'll come get her or start shooting people, like in Virginia Tech.

Reply to Chilton, posted by BoardtoDeath.

i heard somebody who knows a dude was at the party that night and he saw [the driver] before he got in the car and he was walking around all [deleted] up. And that's why they crashed. It was the POLICE lost the breathaliser results and it was embarrassing, so they had to let him go. And that's WORD.

Reply to Chilton, posted by SarafromCarmel.

I don't think it's fair what everybody in this thread is saying. We don't know the facts. The crash was a terrible tragedy and the police didn't press charges, so we have to go with that. Think what [the driver]'s going through. He was in my chemistry class and he never bothered anybody. He was pretty smart and helped our Table Team a lot. I'll bet he feels real bad about those girls. He's got to live with that for the rest of his life. I feel sorry for him.

Reply to SarafromCarmel, posted by Anonymous.

Sara U R a lame [deleted]. if he was driving the car then he DID something that made those girls die. How can you say he didn't? Jesus its people like you who let hitler gas the jews and bush go into Iraq. why dont you call [the driver] up and have him take you for a nice ride? i'll come put a cross at your [deleted]ing grave, you [deleted].

Reply to Chilton, posted by Legend666.

[The driver]'s brother is retarded and it might look bad for the police to arrest [the driver], cause of all this political correct stuff which makes me sick. Also they should check out the girls purses, I mean the girls in the crash, because I heard he ripped them off before the ambulances got there. His families so poor that they can't even afford a washer and drier. I've seen him and his mom and his [deleted]-up little brother at the laundromat on Billings all the time. Who goes to laundromats? Lusers that's who.

Reply to Chilton, posted by SexyGurl362.

My best friend is a junior at [deleted] with [the driver] and she was talking to somebody who was at the party where the girls who died were. [The driver] was sitting in a corner with his sweats hood up staring at everybody and talking to himself and somebody found him in the kitchen just looking at the knives. Everybody was like, what the hells he doing here? Why did he come?

Reply to Chilton, posted by Jake42.

U totally OWN it, Chilton!! Yeah [the driver] [deleted]ed up. Look at the luser, his life is epic FAIL!!! He's always faking he's sick in PE class to get out of working out. He only goes to the gym to hang around in the locker room and stare at everybody's [deleted]. He is totally gay, somebody told me that.

Reply to Chilton, posted by CurlyJen.

Me and my friends were talking and last week somebody saw [the driver] on Lighthouse doing donuts in a car he stole from his grandmother without permission. He was trying to get [deleted] to show her thong. (like she'd care, LOL!!!). And when she ignored him he started wacking off right in front of her, right there on Lighthouse at the same time he was driving. he definitely was doing the same thing that night he crashed.

Reply to Chilton, posted by Anonymous.

I go to [deleted], I'm a sophomore, and I know him and everybody knows about him. IMHO, I mean, he's all right. He games a lot, but so what? I play soccer a lot, that doesn't make me a killer.

Reply to Anonymous, posted by BillVan.

[Deleted] you, [deleted]. if you know so much whats your sauce oh genius? You don't even have the balls to post under your real name. Afraid he'd come and [deleted] you up the [deleted]?

Reply to Chilton, posted by BellaKelley.

u r so right!!! Me and my friend were at that party on the 9th where it happened and [the driver] was coming on to [deleted] and they were like, just go away. But he didn't, he followed them out the door when they were leaving. But we have ourselves to blame too for not doing anything, all of us who were there. We all knew [the driver] is a luser and perv and we should have called the police or somebody when they left. I had this bad feeling like in Ghost Whisperer. And look what happened.

Reply to Chilton, posted by Anonymous.

Somebody goes into Columbine or Virginia Tech with a gun and they're criminals but when [the driver] kills somebody with a car nobody does anything about it. Something is very messed up here.

Reply to Chilton, posted by WizardOne.

I think we need a time out. Some poster dissed [the driver] because he didn't like sports and he played games. What's the BFD? There are millions of people who don't play sports but like games. I don't know [the driver] real good but we're in the same class at [deleted]. He isn't a bad dude at all. Everybody's dissing him but does anybody here actually KNOW him? Whatever happened, he didn't hurt anybody on purpose and we all know people who do, everyday. IMHO, he feels bad about what happened. The police didn't arrest him because, duh, he didn't do anything illegal.

Reply to WizardOne, posted by Halfpipe22.

Another gamer-lamer. Look at the name. LOOZR!!! FOAD wizard!

Reply to Chilton, posted by Archenemy.

[The driver] is a total phr33k. In his locker at school, he has pictures of the d00ds from Columbine and Virginia Tech, and those dead bodies from the concentration camps. He walks around in some ch33p ass hoodie trying to look kewl but hes a luser on roids, thats all he'll ever be.

[The driver] if your reading this, d00d, and not hanging with the elves and fairies, remember: we OWN U. Why don't you U just do us all a favor and blow you're [deleted]ing brains out. Your death = EPIC WIN!

9

Kathryn Dance sat back, shaking her head. 'A lot of hormones there,' she said to Jon Boling.

She was troubled by the viciousness of the blog posts – and most of them written by young people.

Boling scrolled back to the original post. 'Look what happened. Chilton makes a simple observation about a fatal accident. All he does is question whether the road was safely maintained. But look at how the responding posts arc. They go from discussing what Chilton brought up – highway safety – then move on to government finances and then to the kid who was driving, even though he apparently didn't do anything wrong. The posters get more and more agitated as they attack him and finally the blog turns into a barroom brawl among the posters themselves.'

'Like the game of Telephone. By the time the message moves along, it's distorted. "I heard . . ." "Somebody knows somebody who . . ." "A friend of mine told me . . ."' She scanned the pages again. 'One thing I noticed, Chilton doesn't fight back. Look at the post about Reverend Fisk and the right-to-life group.'

Reply to Chilton, posted by CrimsoninChrist.
You are a sinner who cannot comprehend the goodness within the heart of
Rev. R. Samuel Fisk. He has devoted his life to Christ and all of His works,

while you do nothing but pander to the masses for your own pleasure and profit. Your misreading of the great Reverend's views is pathetic and libelous. You should be nailed up on a cross yourself.

Boling told her, 'No, the serious bloggers don't argue back. Chilton will give a reasoned response, but flame wars – attacks among posters – get out of control and become personal. The postings become about the *attack,* not the substance of the topic. That's one of the problems with blogs. In person, people would never feud like this. The anonymity of the blogs mean the fights go on for days or weeks.'

Dance looked through the text. 'So the boy *is* a student.' She recalled her deduction from the interview with Tammy Foster. 'Chilton deleted his name and the name of the school but it's got to be Robert Louis Stevenson. Where Tammy goes.'

Boling tapped the screen. 'And there's her post. She was one of the first to say something about the boy. And everyone else jumped on board after that.'

Maybe the post was the source of the guilt Dance had picked up on during the interview. If this boy *was* behind the attack, then Tammy, as Dance and O'Neil had speculated, would feel partly responsible for the assault on her; she'd brought it on herself. And perhaps guilty too if he went on to hurt someone else. This explained why Tammy wouldn't like the suggestion that her abductor had a bike in the car: that would lead Dance to consider a younger suspect – a student whose identity the girl didn't want to reveal because she still considered him a threat.

'It's all so vicious,' Dance said, nodding at the screen.

'Did you hear about the Litter Boy?'

'Who?'

'Happened in Kyoto a few years ago. Japan. A teenage boy tossed a fast food wrapper and soda cup on the ground in a park. Somebody shot a picture of the kid doing it on their cell phone and uploaded it to his friends. Next thing, it started appearing on blogs and social networking sites all over the country.

Cybervigilantes tracked him down. They got his name and address and posted the info online. It spread to thousands of blogs. The whole thing became a witch hunt. People began showing up at his house – throwing trash in the yard. He nearly killed himself – that kind of dishonor is significant in Japan.' Boling's tonal quality and body language revealed anger. 'Critics say, oh, it's just words or pictures. But they can be weapons too. They can cause just as much damage as fists. And, frankly, I think the scars last longer.'

Dance said, 'I don't get some of the vocabulary in the posts.'

He laughed. 'Oh, in blogs and bulletin boards and social networking sites, it's in to misspell, abbreviate and make up words. "Sauce" for "source". "Moar" for "more". "IMHO" is "in my humble opinion".'

'Do I dare ask? "FOAD".'

'Oh,' he said, 'a polite valediction to your note. It means "Fuck off and die". All caps, of course, is the same as shouting.'

'And what is "p-h-r-3–3-k"?'

'That's leetspeak for "freak".'

'Leetspeak?'

'It's a sort of language that's been created by teens over the past few years. You only see it with keyboarded text. Numbers and symbols take the place of letters. And spellings are altered. Leetspeak comes from "elite", as in the best and the chicest. It can be incomprehensible to us old folks. But anybody who's mastered it can write and read it as fast as we do English.'

'Why do kids use it?'

'Because it's creative and unconventional . . . and cool. Which, by the way, you should spell "K-E-W-L".'

'The spelling and grammar are awful.'

'True, but it doesn't mean the posters are necessarily stupid or uneducated. It's just the convention nowadays. And speed is important. As long as the reader can understand what you're saying, you can be as careless as you want.'

Dance said, 'I wonder who the boy is. I guess I could call CHP about the accident Chilton refers to.'

'Oh, I'll find it. The online world is huge but it's also small. I've got Tammy's social networking site here. She spends most of her time in one called OurWorld. It's bigger than Facebook and MySpace. It's got a hundred thirty million members.'

'A hundred thirty *million?*'

'Yep. Bigger than most countries.' Boling was squinting as he typed. 'Okay, I'm in her account, just do a little cross-referencing . . . There. Got him.'

'That fast?'

'Yep. His name's Travis Brigham. You're right. He's a junior at Robert Louis Stevenson High in Monterey. Going to be a senior this fall. Lives in Pacific Grove.'

Where Dance and her children lived.

'I'm looking over some of the postings in OurWorld about the accident. Looks like he was driving a car back from a party and lost control. Two girls were killed, another one ended up in the hospital. He wasn't badly injured. No charges were filed – there *was* some question about the condition of the road. It'd been raining.'

'That! Sure. I remember it.' Parents always recall fatal car crashes involving youngsters. And, of course, she felt a sting of memory from several years ago: the highway patrol officer calling her at home, asking if she was FBI Agent Bill Swenson's wife. Why was he asking? she'd wondered.

I'm sorry to tell you, Agent Dance . . . I'm afraid there's been an accident.

She now pushed the thought away and said, 'Innocent but he's still getting vilified.'

'But innocence is boring,' Boling said wryly. 'It's no fun to post about that.' He indicated the blog. 'What you've got here are Vengeful Angels.'

'What's that?'

'A category of cyberbullies. Vengeful Angels are vigilantes. They're attacking Travis because they think he got away with something – since he wasn't arrested after the accident. They don't believe, or trust, the police. Another category is the Power

Hungry – they're closest to typical school-yard bullies. They need to control others by pushing them around. Then there are the Mean Girls. They bully because, well, they're little shits. Girls, mostly, who're bored and post cruel things for the fun of it. It borders on sadism.' A tinge of anger again in Boling's voice. 'Bullying . . . it's a real problem. And it's getting worse. The latest statistics are that thirty-five percent of kids have been bullied or threatened online, most of them multiple times.' He fell silent and his eyes narrowed.

'What, Jon?'

'Interesting that there's one thing we *don't* see.'

'What's that?'

'*Travis* fighting back in the blog, flaming the people who attacked him.'

'Maybe he doesn't know about it.'

Boling gave a thin laugh. 'Oh, believe me, he would've known about the attacks five minutes after the first post in the Chilton thread.'

'Why's it significant he's not posting?'

'One of the most persistent categories of cyberbullying is called Revenge of the Nerds, or the Victims of Retaliators. Those are people who've been bullied and are fighting back. The social stigma of being outed or bullied or humiliated at that age is over-whelming. I guarantee he's furious and he's hurt and he wants to get even. Those feelings have to come out somehow. You get the implication?'

Dance understood. 'It suggests that he *is* the one who attacked Tammy.'

'If he's not going after them online, it's all the more likely he'd be inclined to get them in real life.' A troubled glance at the screen. 'Ariel, BellaKelley, SexyGurl362, Legend666, Archenemy – they all posted attacks on him. Which means they're all at risk – if he's the one.'

'Would it be hard for him to get their names and addresses?'

'Some, sure, short of hacking into routers and servers. The "Anonymous" postings, of course. But a lot of them would be as easy to find as my getting his name. All he'd need would be a few high school yearbooks or class directories, access to OurWorld, Facebook or MySpace. Oh, and everybody's favorite – Google.'

Dance noted a shadow had fallen over them and Jonathan Boling was looking past her.

Michael O'Neil stepped into the office. Dance was relieved to see him. They shared smiles. The professor stood. Dance introduced them. The two men shook hands.

Boling said, 'So, I have you to thank for my first outing as a cop.'

'If "thank" is the right word,' O'Neil said with a wry smile.

They all sat at the coffee table, and Dance told the deputy what they'd found . . . and what they suspected: that Tammy might have been attacked because she'd posted a comment on a blog about a high school student who'd been responsible for a car crash.

'Was that the accident on One a couple of weeks ago? About five miles south of Carmel?'

'Right.'

Boling said, 'The boy's name is Travis Brigham and he's a student at Robert Louis Stevenson, where the victims went.'

'So he's a person of interest, at least. And it's possible – what we were afraid of?' O'Neil asked Dance. 'He wants to keep going?'

'Very likely. Cyberbullying pushes people over the edge. I've seen it happen dozens of times.'

O'Neil put his feet on the coffee table and rocked back in the chair. Two years ago she'd bet him ten dollars that someday he'd fall over backward. So far she had yet to collect. He asked Dance, 'Anything more on witnesses?'

Dance explained that TJ hadn't reported back yet about the security camera near the highway where the first cross had been left, nor had Rey responded about witnesses near the club where Tammy had been abducted.

O'Neil said that there hadn't been any breakthroughs with the physical evidence. 'Only one thing – Crime Scene found a gray fiber, cotton, on the cross.' He added that the lab in Salinas couldn't match it to a specific database, other than to report that it was probably from clothing, not from carpet or furniture.

'That's all, nothing else? No prints, tread marks?'

O'Neil shrugged. 'The perp's either very smart or very lucky.'

Dance walked to her desk and went into the state databases of warrants and records. She squinted over the screen and read, 'Travis Alan Brigham, age seventeen. Driver's license puts him at four oh eight Henderson Road.' She pushed her glasses up on her nose as she read. 'Interesting. He's got a record.' Then she shook her head. 'No, sorry. My mistake. It's not him. It's *Samuel* Brigham, at the same address. He's fifteen. Juvie record. Arrested twice on peeping, once on misdemeanor assault. Both dismissed, subject to psych treatment. Looks like he's a brother. But Travis? No, he's clean.'

She called Travis's DMV picture up on the screen. A dark-haired boy with eyes closely set together, beneath thick brows, stared at the camera. He wasn't smiling.

'I'd like to find out more about the accident,' O'Neil said.

Dance placed a call to the local office of the Highway Patrol, the official name for California's state police. After a few minutes of being transferred around she ended up with a Sergeant Brodsky, put the call on speaker and asked about the accident.

Brodsky slipped immediately into the tone you hear when police take the stand at trial. Emotionally flat, precise. 'It was just before midnight on Saturday, June nine. Four juveniles, three female, one male, were heading north on Highway One about three miles south of Carmel Highlands, near Garrapata State Beach Reserve. The male was driving. The vehicle was a late-model Nissan Altima. It appears that the car was traveling at about forty-five. He missed a curve, skidded and went over a cliff. The girls in the back weren't wearing their seat belts. They died instantly. The girl in the passenger seat had a concussion. She was in the hospital for a few days. The driver was admitted, examined and released.'

'What'd Travis say happened?' Dance asked.

'Just lost control. It'd rained earlier. There was water on the highway. He changed lanes and went into a skid. It was one of the girls' cars and the tires weren't the best. He wasn't speeding, and he tested negative for alcohol and controlled substances. The girl who survived corroborated his story.' A defensive echo sounded in his voice. 'There *was* a reason we didn't charge him, you know. Whatever anybody said about the investigation.'

So he'd read the blog too, Dance deduced.

'You going to reopen the investigation?' Brodsky asked warily.

'No, this is about that attack Monday night. The girl in the trunk.'

'Oh, that. The boy did it, you think?'

'Possibly.'

'Wouldn't surprise me. Not one bit.'

'Why do you say that?'

'Sometimes you get a feeling. Travis was dangerous. Had eyes just like the kids at Columbine.'

How could he possibly know the visage of the killers in that horrific 1999 murder spree?

Then Brodsky added, 'He was a fan of theirs, you know, the shooters. Had pictures up in his locker.'

Did he know that independently, or from the blog? Dance recalled that someone had mentioned it in the 'Roadside Crosses' thread.

'Did you think he was a threat?' O'Neil asked Brodsky. 'When you interviewed him?'

'Yes, sir. Kept my cuffs handy the whole time. He's a big kid. And wore this hooded sweatshirt. Just stared at me. Freaky.'

At this reference to the garment, Dance recalled what Tammy had given away about the attacker wearing a hoodie.

She thanked the officer and they hung up. After a moment she looked over at Boling. 'Jon, any insights you can give us about Travis? From the postings?'

Boling reflected for a moment. 'I do have a thought. If he's a gamer, like they're saying, that fact could be significant.'

O'Neil asked, 'You mean by playing those games he's

programmed to be violent? We saw something on Discovery Channel about that the other night.'

But Jon Boling shook his head. 'That's a popular theme in the media. But if he's gone through relatively normal childhood developmental stages, then I wouldn't worry too much about that. Yes, some children can become numb to the consequences of violence if they're continually exposed in certain ways – generally visual – too early. But at the worst that just desensitizes you; it doesn't *make* you dangerous. The tendency to violence in young people almost always comes from rage, not watching movies or TV.

'No, I'm speaking of something else when I say that gaming probably affects Travis fundamentally. It's a change we're seeing throughout society now among young people. He could be losing the distinction between the synthetic world and the real world.'

'Synthetic world?'

'It's a term I got from Edward Castronova's book on the subject. The synthetic world is the life of online games and alternative reality websites, like *Second Life*. They're fantasy worlds you enter through your computer – or PDA or some other digital device. People in our generation usually draw a clear distinction between the synthetic world and the real one. The real world is where you have dinner with your family or play softball or go out on a date after you log out of the synthetic world and turn off the computer. But younger people – and nowadays I mean people in their twenties and even early thirties – don't see that distinction. More and more, the synth worlds are becoming real to them. In fact, there was a study recently that showed nearly a fifth of the players in one online game felt that the real world was only a place to eat and sleep, that the synthetic world was their true residence.'

This surprised Dance.

Boling smiled at her apparently naive expression. 'Oh, an average gamer can easily spend thirty hours a week in the synth world, and it's not unusual for people to spend twice that. There are hundreds of millions of people who have *some* involvement in the synth world, and tens of millions who spend much of their day there. And we're not talking *Pac-Man* or *Pong*. The level of realism in the synthetic world is astonishing. You — through an avatar, a character that represents you — inhabit a world that's as complex as what we're living in right now. Child psychologists have studied how people create avatars; players actually use parenting skills subconsciously to form their characters. Economists have studied games too. You have to learn skills to support yourself or you'll starve to death. In most of the games you earn money, payable in game currency. But that currency actually trades against the dollar or pound or euro on eBay — in their gaming category. You can buy and sell virtual items — like magic wands, weapons, or clothing or houses or even avatars themselves — in real-world money. In Japan, not too long ago, some gamers sued hackers who stole virtual items from their synth world homes. They won the case.'

Boling leaned forward, and Dance again noticed the sparkle in his eyes, the enthusiasm in his voice. 'One of the best examples of the synth and real worlds coinciding is in a famous online game, *World of Warcraft*. The designers created a disease as a debuffer — that's a condition that reduces the health or power of characters. It was called Corrupted Blood. It would weaken powerful characters and kill the ones who weren't so strong. But something odd happened. Nobody's quite sure how, but the disease got out of control and spread on its own. It became a virtual black plague. The designers never intended that to happen. It could be stopped only when the infected characters died out or adapted to it. The Centers for Disease Control in Atlanta heard about it and had a team study the spread of the virus. They used it as a model for real-world epidemiology.'

Boling sat back. 'I could go on and on about the synth world. It's a fascinating subject, but my point is that whether or not Travis is desensitized to violence, the real question is which world does he inhabit most, the synth or the real? If it's synth, then he runs his life according to a whole different set of rules. And we don't know what those are. Revenge against cyberbullies — or anyone who humiliates him – could be perfectly accepted. It could be encouraged. Maybe even *required*.

'The comparison is to a paranoid schizophrenic who kills someone because he genuinely believes that the victim is a threat to the world. He isn't doing anything wrong. In fact, to him, killing you is heroic. Travis? Who knows what he's thinking? Just remember it's possible that attacking a cyberbully like Tammy Foster meant no more to him than swatting a fly.'

Dance considered this and said to O'Neil, 'Do we go talk to him or not?'

Deciding when to initially interview a suspect was always tricky. Travis would probably not yet think he was a suspect. Speaking to him now would catch him off guard and might make him blurt out statements that could be used against him; he might even confess. On the other hand, he could destroy evidence or flee.

Debating.

What finally decided it for her was a simple memory. The look in Tammy Foster's eyes – the fear of reprisal. And the fear that the perp would attack someone else.

She knew they had to move fast.

'Yep. Let's go see him.'

10

The Brigham family lived in a scabby bungalow whose yard was strewn with car parts and old appliances, half dismantled. Green garbage bags, out of which flowed trash and rotting leaves, sat amid broken toys and tools. A scruffy cat stared cautiously out from a nest of vines beneath an overgrown hedgerow. It was too lazy or full to care about a pudgy gray rat that skittered past. O'Neil parked in the gravel drive, forty feet or so away from the house, and he and Dance climbed out of his unmarked MCSO car.

They studied the area.

It was like a scene from the rural South, vegetation thick, no other houses in sight, dereliction. The dilapidated state of the house and the pungent aroma suggesting a nearby, and inefficient, sewer or a swamp explained how the family could afford such secluded property in this high-priced part of the state.

As they started toward the house she found her hand dangling near her pistol butt, her jacket unbuttoned.

She was spooked, alert.

Still, it was a shock when the boy attacked them.

They had just passed a patch of anemic, reedy grass beside the lopsided detached garage when she turned to O'Neil and found the deputy stiffen as he looked past her. His arm rose and gripped her jacket, pulling her forward to the ground.

'Michael!' she cried.

The rock sailed over her head, missing her by inches, and crashed through a garage window. Another followed a moment later. O'Neil had to duck fast to avoid getting hit. He crashed into a narrow tree.

'You all right?' he asked quickly.

A nod. 'You see where it was from?'

'No.'

They were scanning the thicket of woods bordering the property.

'There!' she called, pointing at the boy, in sweats and a stocking cap, who was staring at them. He turned and fled.

Dance debated only a moment. Neither of them had radios; this hadn't been planned as a tactical mission. And to return to O'Neil's car to call in a pursuit to Dispatch would have taken too long. They had a chance to catch Travis now and instinctively they went after him, sprinting forward.

CBI agents learn basic hand-to-hand combat skills – though most, Dance included, had never been in a fistfight. They also are required to have physical fitness checkups every so often. Dance was in fair shape, though not thanks to the CBI's regimen but to her treks into the wilderness to track down music for her website. Despite the impractical outfit – black skirt suit and blouse – she now eased ahead of Michael O'Neil as they pushed fast into the woods in pursuit of the boy.

Who was moving just a little faster.

O'Neil had his cell phone out and was breathlessly calling in a request for backup.

They were both gasping hard and Dance wondered how Dispatch could understand him.

The boy vanished for a moment and the officers slowed. Then Dance cried, 'Look,' spotting him emerge from bushes about fifty feet away. 'Weapon?' she gasped. He held something dark in his hand.

'Can't tell.'

Could have been a gun, though maybe a pipe or a knife.

Either way . . .

He vanished into a dense part of the woods, beyond which Dance could just see a glimmer of a green pond. Probably the source of the stench.

O'Neil glanced at her.

She sighed and nodded. Simultaneously they drew their Glocks.

They pushed forward again.

Dance and O'Neil had worked a number of cases together and fell instinctively into a symbiotic mode on an investigation. But they were at their best when solving intellectual puzzles, not playing soldier.

She had to remind herself: finger off the trigger, never cross in front of your partner's weapon and lift your muzzle if he crosses in front of you, fire only if threatened, check your backdrop, shoot in bursts of three, count your rounds.

Dance hated this.

Yet it was a chance to stop the Roadside Cross attacker. Picturing Tammy Foster's terrified eyes, Dance rushed through the woods.

The boy vanished again, and she and O'Neil pulled up, where two paths diverged. Travis had probably taken one – the vegetation was very thick here, impassible in parts. O'Neil silently pointed left, then right, raising an eyebrow.

Flip a coin, she thought, angry and unsettled that she'd have to separate from O'Neil. She nodded toward the left.

They began easing carefully down their respective routes.

Dance was moving through the thickets, thinking how unsuited she was to this role. Her world was one of words and expressions and nuances of gesture. Not tactical work, like this.

She knew how people got hurt, how they died, stepping out of the zones they were in harmony with. A sense of foreboding filled her.

Stop, she told herself. Find Michael, go back to the car and wait for backup.

Too late.

Just then Dance heard a rustling at her feet, and glanced down to see that the boy, hiding in the bushes next to her, had flung a large branch in her way. It caught her foot as she tried to jump over it and she went down hard. Struggling to keep from falling, Dance rolled onto her side.

Which had the effect of saving her wrist.

And another consequence: the boxy, black Glock flew from her hand and vanished into the bushes.

Only seconds later, Dance heard the rustle of bushes once more as the boy, apparently waiting to make certain she was alone, charged out of the bushes.

Careless, Michael O'Neil thought angrily.

He was running in the direction of Dance's cry, but realized now he had no idea where she was.

They should have stayed together. Careless to split up. Yes, it made sense – to cover as much ground as they could – but while he'd been in several firefights and a couple of street pursuits, Kathryn Dance had not.

If anything happened to her . . .

In the distance sirens sounded, growing louder. The backup was getting closer. O'Neil slowed to a walk, listening carefully. Maybe the rustle of bushes nearby. Maybe not.

Careless too because Travis would know this area perfectly. It was, literally, his backyard. He'd know where to hide, what paths to escape down.

The gun, weighing nothing in his large hand, swung ahead of O'Neil, as he looked for the attacker.

Frantic.

Pushing ahead another twenty feet. Finally he had to risk some noise. 'Kathryn?' he called in a whisper.

Nothing.

Louder: 'Kathryn?'

The wind rustled brush and trees.

Then: 'Michael, here!' A choked sound. From nearby. He raced toward her words. Then he found her ahead of him on a path, on her hands and knees. Her head down. He heard gasping. Was she wounded? Had Travis struck her with a pipe? Stabbed her?

O'Neil had to suppress his overwhelming urge to tend to her, see how badly hurt she was. He knew procedures. He ran closer, stood over her, his eyes scanning, swiveling around, looking for a target.

At last, some distance away, he saw Travis's back vanish.

'He's gone,' Dance said, pulling her weapon from a thicket of bushes and rising to her feet. 'Headed that way.'

'You hurt?'

'Sore, that's all.'

She did seem to be unharmed, but she was dusting at her suit in a way that was troubling to him. She was uncharacteristically shaken, disoriented. He could hardly blame her. But Kathryn Dance had always been a bulwark he could count on, a standard he measured his own behavior against. Her gestures reminded him that they were out of their element here, that this case wasn't a typical gangbanger hit or a weapons smuggling ring cruising up and down the 101.

'What happened?' he asked.

'Tripped me, then took off. Michael, it wasn't Travis.'

'What?'

'I got a fast look at him. He was blond.' Dance grimaced at a tear in her skirt, then gave up on the clothing. She started scanning the ground. 'He dropped something . . . Okay, there.' She picked it up. A can of spray paint.

'What's this all about?' he wondered aloud.

She tucked the gun away in her hip holster and turned back toward the house. 'Let's go find out.'

They arrived back at the Brigham house simultaneously with the backup – two Pacific Grove town police cars. A longtime resident, Dance knew the officers and waved hello.

They joined her and O'Neil.

'You all right, Kathryn?' one cop asked, noting her disheveled hair and dusty skirt.

'Fine.' She filled them in on the attack and pursuit. One officer used his shoulder-mounted Motorola to report the incident.

Dance and O'Neil had no sooner gotten to the house when a woman's voice called out from behind the screen, 'Did you get him?' The door opened and the speaker stepped out on the porch. In her forties, Dance guessed, she had a round figure and her face was moonish. She wore painfully taut jeans and a billowy gray blouse with a triangle of stain on the belly. Kathryn Dance noted that the woman's cream pumps were hopelessly limp and scuffed from bearing her weight. From inattention too.

Dance and O'Neil identified themselves. The woman was Sonia Brigham and she was Travis's mother.

'Did you get him?' she persisted.

'Do you know who he was, why he attacked us?'

'He wasn't attacking *you*,' Sonia said. 'He probably didn't even see you. He was going for the windows. They've already got three of 'em.'

One of the Pacific Grove officers explained, 'The Brighams've been the target of vandalism lately.'

'You said "he",' Dance said. 'Do you know who he was?'

'Not that particular one. There's a bunch of them.'

'Bunch?' O'Neil asked.

'They're coming by all the time. Throwing rocks, bricks, painting stuff on the house and garage. That's what we've been living with.' A contemptuous wave of the hand, presumably toward where the vandal had disappeared. 'After everybody started saying those bad things about Travis. The other day, somebody threw a brick through the living room window, nearly hit my younger son. And look.' She pointed to green spray paint graffiti on the side of a large lopsided shed in the side yard, about fifty feet away

KILL3R!!

Leetspeak, Dance noted.

Dance handed the spray paint to one of the Pacific Grove officers, who said they'd follow up on it. She described the boy – who looked like one of five hundred high school students in the area. They took a brief statement from both Dance and O'Neil, as well as Travis's mother, then climbed back into their cars and left.

'They're after my boy. And he didn't do anything! It's like the goddamn Ku Klux Klan! That brick nearly hit Sammy. He's a little troubled. He went crazy. Had an episode.'

Vengeful Angels, Dance reflected. Though the bullying was no longer cyber; it had moved from the synth world into the real.

A round-faced teenager appeared on the porch. His wary smile made him look slow, but his eyes seemed fully comprehending as he took them in. 'What is it, what is it?' His voice was urgent.

'It's okay, Sammy. Go back inside. You go to your room.'

'Who're they?'

'You go on back to your room. You stay inside. Don't go to the pond.'

'I want to go to the pond.'

'Not now. Somebody was out there.'

He ambled off into the house.

Michael O'Neil said, 'Mrs Brigham, there was a crime last night, an attempted murder. The victim was someone who'd posted a comment against Travis on a blog.'

'Oh, that Chilton crap!' Sonia spat out between yellow teeth that had aged even faster than the woman's face. 'That's what started it all. Somebody should throw a brick through *his* window. Now everybody's ganging up on our boy. And he didn't *do* anything. Why does everybody think he did? They said he stole my mother's car and was driving it on Lighthouse, you know, exposing himself. Well, my mother sold her car four years ago. That's how much they know.' Then Sonia had a thought and the seesaw returned to the side of wariness. 'Oh, wait, that girl in the trunk, going to be drowned?'

'That's right.'

'Well, I'll tell you right now, my boy wouldn'ta done anything like that. I swear to God! You're not going to arrest him, are you?' She looked panicked.

Dance wondered: too panicked? *Did* she in fact suspect her son?

'We'd just like to talk to him.'

The woman was suddenly uneasy. 'My husband isn't home.'

'You alone is fine. Both parents aren't necessary.' But Dance could see that the problem was that she didn't want the responsibility.

'Well, Trav isn't here either.'

'Will he be back soon?'

'He works part-time, at Bagel Express, for pocket money. His shift's in a little while. He'll have to come back here to pick up his uniform.'

'Where is he now?'

A shrug. 'Sometimes he goes to this video game place.' She fell silent, probably thinking she shouldn't be saying anything. 'My husband will be back soon.'

Dance noted again the tone with which Sonia delivered those words. *My husband.*

'Was Travis out last night? Around midnight?'

'No.' Offered fast.

'Are you sure?' Dance asked with a crisp tone. Sonia had just exhibited aversion – looking away – and blocking, touching her nose, a gesture Dance had not observed earlier.

Sonia swallowed. 'Probably he was here. I'm not exactly sure. I went to bed early. Travis stays up till all hours. He might've gone out. But I didn't hear anything.'

'And your husband?' She'd noted the singular pronoun regarding her bedtime. 'Was he here around that time?'

'He plays poker some. I think he was at a game.'

O'Neil was saying, 'We really need to—'

His words braked to a halt as a tall, lanky teenager, shoulders and stance wide, appeared from the side yard. His black jeans were faded, patches of gray showing, and an olive-drab combat jacket covered a black sweatshirt. It didn't have a hood, Dance noted. He stopped suddenly, blinking in surprise at the visitors. A glance at the unmarked CBI car, which any viewer of a cop show on TV in the last ten years would instantly recognize for what it was.

Dance noted in the boy's posture and expression the typical reaction of someone spotting law enforcers, whether they were guilty or innocent: caution . . . and thinking quickly.

'Travis, honey, come over here.'

He remained where he was, and Dance sensed O'Neil tensing.

But a second foot pursuit wasn't needed. Expressionless, the boy slouched forward to join them.

'These're police officers,' his mother said. 'They want to talk to you.'

'I guess. What about?' His voice was casual, agreeable. He stood with his long arms dangling at his side. His hands were dirty and there was grit under his nails. His hair seemed washed, though; she supposed he did this regularly to combat the sprinkling of acne on his face.

She and O'Neil said hello to the boy and offered their IDs. He studied them for a long moment.

Buying time? Dance wondered.

'Somebody else was here,' Sonia said to her son. She nodded at the graffiti. 'Broke a couple more windows.'

Travis took this news from his mother without emotion. He asked, 'Sammy?'

'He didn't see.'

O'Neil asked, 'You mind if we go inside?'

He shrugged and they walked into the house, which smelled of mold and cigarette smoke. The place was ordered but grimy. The mismatched furniture seemed secondhand, slipcovers worn and pine legs sloughing off varnish. Dim pictures covered the walls, mostly decorative. Dance could see part of a *National Geographic* magazine logo just below the frame of a picture of Venice. A few were of the family. The two boys, and one or two of Sonia when she was younger.

Sammy appeared, as before, big, moving quickly, grinning again.

'Travis!' He charged toward his sibling. 'Did you bring me M's?'

'Here you go.' Travis dug into his pocket and handed the boy a packet of M&M's.

'Yeah!' Sammy opened the package carefully, looked inside. Then gazed at his brother. 'The pond was nice today.'

'Was it?'

'Yeah.' Sammy returned to his room, clutching the candy in his hand.

Travis said, 'He doesn't look good. Did he take his pills?'

His mother looked away. 'They . . .'

'Dad wouldn't get the prescription refilled because the price went up. Right?'

'He doesn't think they do that much good.'

'They do a lot of good, Mom. You know how he gets when he doesn't take them.'

Dance glanced into Sammy's room and saw that the boy's desk was covered with complicated electronic components, parts of computers and tools – along with toys for children much younger. He was reading a Japanese graphic novel as he slouched in a chair. The boy glanced up and stared at Dance intently, studying her. He gave a faint smile and nodded toward the book. Dance smiled back at the cryptic gesture. He returned to reading. His lips moved.

She noticed on a hall table a laundry basket filled with clothes. She tapped O'Neil's arm and glanced at a gray sweatshirt sitting on the top. It was a hoodie.

O'Neil nodded.

'How are you feeling?' Dance asked Travis. 'After the accident?'

'Okay, I guess.'

'It must've been terrible.'

'Yeah.'

'But you weren't hurt bad?'

'Not really. The airbag, you know. And I wasn't going that fast . . . Trish and Van.' A grimace. 'If they'd had their seat belts on they would've been fine.'

Sonia repeated, 'His father should be home anytime now.'

O'Neil continued evenly, 'Just have a few questions.' Then he stepped back to the corner of the living room, leaving the questioning to Dance.

She asked, 'What grade are you in?'

'Just finished junior year.'

'Robert Louis Stevenson, right?'

'Yeah.'

'What're you studying?'

'I don't know, stuff. I like computer science and math. Spanish. Just, you know, what everybody's taking.'

'How's Stevenson?'

'It's okay. Better than Monterey Public or Junipero.' He was answering agreeably, looking directly into her eyes.

At Junipero Serra School, uniforms were required. Dance supposed that more than stern Jesuits and long homework assignments, the dress code was the most hated aspect of the place.

'How're the gangs?'

'He's not in a gang,' his mother said. Almost as if she wished he were.

They all ignored her.

'Not bad,' Travis responded. 'They leave us alone. Not like Salinas.'

The point of these questions wasn't social. Dance was asking them to determine the boy's baseline behavior. After a few minutes of these harmless inquiries, Dance had a good feel for the boy's nondeceptive mode. Now she was ready to ask about the assault.

'Travis, you know Tammy Foster, don't you?'

'The girl in the trunk. It was on the news. She goes to Stevenson. She and me don't talk or anything. Maybe we had a class together freshman year.' He then looked Dance straight in the eye. His hand occasionally strayed across his face but she wasn't sure whether it was a blocking gesture, signifying deception, or because he was ashamed of the acne. 'She posted some stuff about me in *The Chilton Report*. It wasn't true.'

'What did she say?' Dance asked, though she recalled the post, about his trying to take pictures of the girls' locker room after cheerleading practice.

The boy hesitated, as if wondering if she was trying to trap him. 'She said I was taking pictures. You know, of the girls.'

His face grew dark. 'But I was just on the phone, you know, talking.'

'Really,' his mother interjected. 'Bob'll be home any minute now. I might rather wait.'

But Dance felt a certain urgency to keep going. She knew without doubt that if Sonia wanted to wait for her husband, the man would put a fast end to the interview.

Travis asked, 'Is she going to be okay? Tammy?'

'Looks like it.'

He glanced at the scarred coffee table, where an empty but smudged ashtray rested. Dance didn't think she'd seen an ashtray in a living room for years. 'You think I did it? Tried to hurt her?' How easily his dark eyes, set deep beneath those brows, held hers.

'No. We're just talking to everybody who might have information about the situation.'

'Situation?' he asked.

'Where were you last night? Between eleven and one?'

Another sweep of the hair. 'I went to the Game Shed about ten-thirty.'

'What's that?'

'This place where you can play video games. Like an arcade. I kind of hang there some. You know where it is? It's by Kinko's. It used to be that old movie theater but that got torn down and they put it in. It's not the best, the connections aren't so good, but it's the only one that's open late.'

Dance noted the rambling. She asked, 'You were alone?'

'There were, like, other kids there. But I was playing alone.'

'I thought you were here,' Sonia said.

A shrug. 'I *was* here. I went out. I couldn't sleep.'

'At the Game Shed were you online?' Dance asked.

'Like, no. I was playing pinball, not RPG.'

'Not what?'

'Role-playing games. For shooter and pinball and driving games you don't go online.'

He said this patiently, though he seemed surprised she didn't know the distinction.

'So you weren't logged on?'

'That's what I'm saying.'

'How long were you there?' His mother had taken on the interrogation.

'I don't know, an hour, two.'

'What do those games cost? Fifty cents, a dollar every few minutes?'

So that was Sonia's agenda. Money.

'If you play good, it lets you keep on going. Cost me three dollars for the whole night. I used money I made. And I got some food too and a couple of Red Bulls.'

'Travis, can you think of anybody who saw you there?'

'I don't know. Maybe. I'll have to think about it.' Eyes studying the floor.

'Good. And what time did you come home?'

'One-thirty. Maybe two. I don't know.'

She asked more questions about Monday night and then about school and his classmates. She wasn't able to decide whether or not he was telling the truth since he wasn't deviating much from his baseline. She thought again about what Jon Boling had told her about the synth world. If Travis was mentally there, not in the real world, baseline analysis might be useless. Maybe a whole different set of rules applied to people like Travis Brigham.

Then the mother's eyes flickered toward the doorway. The boy's too.

Dance and O'Neil turned to see a large man enter, tall and broad. He was wearing workmen's overalls streaked in dirt, *Central Coast Landscaping* embroidered on his chest. He looked at everybody in the room, slowly. Dark eyes still and unfriendly beneath a fringe of thick, brown hair.

'Bob, these are police—'

'They're not here with the report for the insurance, are they?'

'No. They—'

'You have a warrant?'

'They're here to—'

'I'm talking to her.' A nod at Dance.

'I'm Agent Dance with the California Bureau of Investigation.' She offered an ID he didn't look at. 'And this is Senior Deputy O'Neil, Monterey County Sheriff's Office. We're asking your son a few questions about a crime.'

'There was no crime. It was an accident. Those girls died in an accident. That's all that happened.'

'We're here about something else. Someone who'd posted a message about Travis was attacked.'

'Oh, that blog bullshit.' He growled. 'That Chilton is a danger to society. He's like a fucking poisonous snake.' He turned to his wife. 'Joey, down at the dock, nearly got hisself popped in the mouth, the stuff he was saying about me. Egging on the other boys. Just 'cause I'm his father. They don't read the newspaper, they don't read *Newsweek*. But they read that Chilton crap. Somebody should . . .' His voice faded. He turned toward his son. 'I told you not to say anything to anybody without we have a lawyer. Did I tell you that? You say the wrong fucking thing to the wrong person, and we get sued. And they take the house away and half my paycheck for the rest of my life.' He lowered his voice. 'And your brother goes into a home.'

'Mr Brigham, we're not here about the accident,' O'Neil reminded him. 'We're investigating the assault last night.'

'Doesn't matter, does it? Things get written down and go into the record.'

He seemed more concerned about responsibility for the accident than that his son might get arrested for attempted murder.

Ignoring them completely, he said to his wife, 'Why'd you let 'em in? This ain't Nazi Germany, not yet. You can tell 'em to shove it.'

'I thought—'

'No, you didn't. You didn't think at all.' To O'Neil: 'Now, I'll ask you to leave. And if you come back it better be with a warrant.'

'Dad!' Sammy cried, racing from his bedroom, startling Dance. 'It's working! I wanta show you!' He was holding up a circuit board, from which wires sprouted.

Brigham's gruffness vanished instantly. He hugged the younger son and said kindly, 'We'll look at it later, after supper.'

Dance was watching Travis's eyes, which grew still at the display of affection toward his younger brother.

'Okay.' Sammy hesitated, then went out the back door and clomped down the porch and headed toward the shed.

'Stay close,' Sonia called.

Dance noted that she hadn't told her husband about the vandalism that had just occurred. She'd be afraid of delivering bad news. She did, however, say of Sammy, 'Maybe he *should* be on his pills.' Eyes everywhere but at her husband.

'They're a rip-off, what they cost. Weren't you listening to me? And what's the point, if he stays home all day?'

'But he doesn't stay home all day. That's—'

'Because Travis don't watch him like he should.'

The boy listened passively, apparently unmoved by the criticism.

O'Neil said to Bob Brigham, 'A serious crime was committed. We need to talk to everyone who might be involved. And your son *is* involved. Can you confirm he was at the Game Shed last night?'

'I was out. But that's none of your business. And listen up, my boy didn't have nothing to do with any attacks. You staying's trespassing, isn't it?' He lifted a bushy eyebrow as he lit a cigarette, waved the match out and dropped it accurately into the ashtray. 'And you,' he snapped to Travis. 'You're going to be late for work.'

The boy went into his bedroom.

Dance was frustrated. He was their prime suspect, but she simply couldn't tell what was going on in Travis's mind.

The boy returned, carrying a brown-and-beige-striped uniform jacket on a hanger. He rolled it up and stuffed it into his backpack.

'No,' Brigham barked. 'Your mother ironed it. Put it on. Don't crumple it up like that.'

'I don't want to wear it now.'

'Show some respect to your mother, after all her work.'

'It's a bagel shop. Who cares?'

'That's not the point. Put it on. Do what I'm telling you.'

The boy stiffened. Dance gave an audible gasp seeing Travis's face. Eyes widening, shoulders rising. His lips drew back like those of a snarling animal. Travis raged to his father, 'It's a stupid fucking uniform. I wear it on the street and they laugh at me!'

The father leaned forward. 'You do not ever talk to me that way, and *never* in front of other people!'

'I get laughed at *enough*. I'm not going to wear it! You don't have any fucking idea!' Dance saw the boy's frantic eyes flicker around the room and settle on the ashtray, a possible weapon. O'Neil noticed this too and tensed, in case a fight was about to break out.

Travis had become somebody else entirely, possessed with anger.

The tendency to violence in young people almost always comes from rage, not watching movies or TV . . .

'I didn't do anything wrong!' Travis growled, wheeled around and pushed through the screen door, letting it snap back loudly. He hurried into the side yard, grabbed his bike, which was leaning against a broken fence, and walked it down a path through the woods bordering the backyard.

'You two, thanks for fucking up our day. Now get out.'

With neutral-toned good-byes, Dance and O'Neil headed for the door, Sonia offering a timid glance of apology. Travis's father strode into the kitchen. Dance heard the refrigerator door open; a bottle fizzed open.

Outside, she asked, 'How'd you do?'

'Not bad, I think,' O'Neil offered and held up a tiny tuft of gray. He'd tugged it off the sweatshirt in the laundry basket when he'd stepped away to let Dance take over the questioning.

They sat in the front seat of O'Neil's cruiser. The doors slammed simultaneously. 'I'll drop the fiber off with Peter Bennington.'

It wouldn't be admissible – they had no warrant – but it would at least tell them that Travis was the likely suspect.

'If it matches, put him under surveillance?' she asked.

A nod. 'I'll stop by the bagel shop. If his bike's outside, I can get a soil sample from the treads. I think a magistrate'd go with a warrant if the dirt matches the beach scene.' He looked Dance's way. 'Gut feeling? You think he did it?'

Dance debated. 'All I can say is that I only got clear deception signals twice.'

'When?'

'First when he said he was at the Game Shed last night.'

'And the second time?'

'When he said he didn't do anything wrong.'

11

Dance returned to her office at the CBI. She smiled at Jon Boling. He reciprocated, but then his face grew grim. He nodded at his computer. 'More postings about Travis on *The Chilton Report*. Attacking him. And then other posts, attacking the attackers. It's an all-out flame war. And I know you wanted to keep the connection between the Roadside Cross Case and the attack secret, but somebody caught on.'

'How on earth?' Dance asked angrily.

Boling shrugged. He nodded to a recent posting.

Reply to Chilton, posted by BrittanyM.

Is anybody watching the news???? Somebody left a cross and then went out and attacked that girl. What's that all about? OMG, I'll bet it's [the driver]!

Subsequent postings suggested Tammy was attacked by Travis because she'd posted a critical comment in *The Chilton Report*. And he had become the 'Roadside Cross Killer', even though Tammy had survived.

'Great. We try to keep it secret and we get outed by a teenage girl named Brittany.'

'Did you see him?' Boling asked.

'Yes.'

'You think he's the one?'

'I wish I could say. I'm leaning toward it.' She explained her theory that it was hard to read Travis because he was living more in the synth world than the real, and he was masking his kinesic responses. 'I will say there's a huge amount of anger there. How 'bout we take a walk, Jon? There's somebody I want you to meet.'

A few minutes later they arrived at Charles Overby's office. On the phone, as he often was, her boss gestured Dance and Boling in, with a glance of curiosity at the professor.

The agent-in-charge hung up. 'They made the connection, the press did. He's now the "Roadside Cross Killer".'

BrittanyM . . .

Dance said, 'Charles, this is Professor Jonathan Boling. He's been helping us.'

A hearty handshake. 'Have you now? What area?'

'Computers.'

'That's your profession? Consultant?' Overby let this hang like a balsa-wood glider over the trio for a moment. Dance spotted her cue and was about to say that Boling was volunteering his time when the professor said, 'I teach mostly, but, yes, I do some consulting, Agent Overby. It's really how I make most of my money. You know, academia pays next to nothing. But as a consultant I can charge up to three hundred an hour.'

'Ah.' Overby looked stricken. 'Per hour. Really?'

Boling held a straight face for exactly the right length of time before adding, 'But I get a real kick out of volunteering for free to help organizations like yours. So I'm tearing up my bill in your case.'

Dance nearly had to bite the inside of her cheek to keep from laughing. Boling, she decided, could have been a good psychologist; he'd deduced Overby's prissy frugality in ten seconds flat, defused it – and slipped in a joke. For her benefit, Dance noted – since she was the only member of the audience.

'It's getting hysterical, Kathryn. We've had a dozen reports of killers wandering around in backyards. A couple of people've already taken some shots at intruders, thinking it's him. Oh, and there've been a couple more reports of crosses.'

Dance was alarmed. *'More?'*

Overby held up a hand. 'They were all real memorials, apparently. Accidents that had happened in the past few weeks. None with *prospective* dates on them. But the press is all over it. Even Sacramento's heard.' He nodded at the phone, presumably indicating a call from their boss – the director of the CBI. Possibly even *his* boss, the attorney general.

'So where are we?'

Dance brought him up to date on Travis, the incidents at his parents' house, her take on the boy. 'Definitely a person of interest.'

'But you didn't bring him in?' Overby asked.

'No probable cause. Michael's checking out some physical evidence right now to link him to the scene.'

'And no other suspects?'

'No.'

'How the hell is a *kid* doing this, a kid riding around on a bicycle?'

Dance pointed out that local gangs, centered primarily in and around Salinas, had terrorized people for years, and many of them had members much younger than Travis.

Boling added, 'And one thing we've found out about him. He's very active in computer games. Young people who are good at them learn very sophisticated combat and evasion techniques. One of the things military recruiters always ask is how much the applicants game; everything else being equal they'd take a gamer over another kid any day.'

Overby asked, 'Motive?'

Dance then explained to her boss that if Travis was the killer, his motive was probably revenge based on cyberbullying.

'Cyberbullying,' Overby said, gravely. 'I was just reading up on that.'

'You were?' Dance asked.

'Yep. There was a good article in *USA Today* last weekend.'

'It's become a popular topic,' Boling said. Did Dance detect slight dismay about the sources that informed the head of a regional office of the CBI?

'That's enough to turn him to violence?' Overby asked.

Boling continued, nodding, 'He's being pushed over the edge. The postings and the rumors have spread. And it's become physical bullying too. Somebody's put up a YouTube video about him. They got him in a happy slap vid.'

'A what?'

'It's a cyberbullying technique. Somebody came up to Travis at Burger King and pushed him. He stumbled – it was embarrassing – and one of the other kids was waiting to record it on a cell phone. Then they uploaded it. It's been viewed two hundred thousand times so far.'

It was then that a slightly built, unsmiling man stepped out of the conference room across the hall and into the doorway of Overby's office. He noted the visitors and ignored them.

'Charles,' he said in a baritone.

'Oh . . . Kathryn, this is Robert Harper,' Overby said. 'From the AG's office in San Francisco. Special Agent Dance.'

The man walked into the room and shook her hand firmly, but kept a distance, as if she'd think he was coming on to her.

'And Jon . . .' Overby tried to recall.

'Boling.'

Harper gave the professor a distracted glance. Said nothing to him.

The man from San Francisco had an unrevealing face and perfectly trimmed black hair. He wore a conservative navy blue suit and white shirt, a red-and-blue striped tie. On his lapel was an American flag pin. His cuffs were perfectly starched, though she noticed a few stray gray threads at the ends. A professional state's attorney, long after his colleagues had gone into private practice and were making buckets of money. She put him in his early fifties.

'What brings you to Monterey?' she asked.

'Caseload evaluations.' Offering nothing more.

Robert Harper seemed to be one of those people who, if he had nothing to say, was comfortable with silence. Dance believed too she recognized in his face an intensity, a sense of devotion to his mission, akin to what she'd seen in the Reverend Fisk's face at the hospital protest. Though how much of a mission caseload analysis would entail was a mystery to her.

He turned his attention to her briefly. She was used to being looked over, but usually by suspects; Harper's perusal was unsettling. It was as if she held the key to an important mystery for him.

Then he said to Overby, 'I'm going to be outside for a few minutes, Charles. If you could keep the door to the conference room locked, I'd appreciate it.'

'Sure. Anything else you need, just let me know.'

A chilly nod. Then Harper was gone, fishing a phone from his pocket.

'What's the story with *him*?' Dance asked.

'Special prosecutor from Sacramento. Had a call from upstairs—'

The attorney general.

'—to cooperate. He wants to know about our caseload. Maybe something big's going down and he needs to see how busy we are. He spent some time at the sheriff's office too. Wish he'd go back and bug them. Fellow's a cold fish. Don't know what to say to him. Tried some jokes. They fell flat.'

But Dance was thinking about the Tammy Foster case; Robert Harper was gone from her mind.

She and Boling returned to her office and she'd just sat down at her desk when O'Neil called. She was pleased. She guessed he'd have the results of the analysis of the bike tread dirt and the gray fiber from the sweatshirt.

'Kathryn, we have a problem.' His voice was troubled.

'Go on.'

'Well, first, Peter says the gray fiber they found in the cross? It matches what we found at Travis's.'

'So he *is* the one. What'd the magistrate say about the warrant?'

'Didn't get that far. Travis's on the run.'

'What?'

'He didn't show up for work. Or, he did show up – there were fresh bike tread marks behind the place. He snuck into the back room, stole some bagels and some cash from the purse of one of the workers . . . and a butcher's knife. Then he disappeared. I called his parents, but they haven't heard from him and claim they don't have any idea where he might go.'

'Where are you?'

'In my office. I'm going to put out a detain alert on him. Us, Salinas, San Benito, surrounding counties.'

Dance rocked back, furious with herself. Why hadn't she planned better and had somebody follow the boy when he left his house? She'd managed to establish his guilt – and simultaneously let him slip through her fingers.

And, hell, now she'd have to tell Overby what had happened. *But you didn't bring him in?*

'There's something else. When I was at the bagel place, I looked up the alley. There's that deli near Safeway.'

'Sure, I know it.'

'They have a flower stand on the side of the building.'

'Roses!' she said.

'Exactly. I talked to the owner.' O'Neil's voice went flat. 'Yesterday, somebody snuck up to the place and stole all the bouquets of red roses.'

She understood now why he was sounding so grave. 'All? . . . How many did he take?'

A slight pause. 'A dozen. It looks like he's just getting started.'

12

Dance's phone rang. A glance at Caller ID.

'TJ. Was just about to call you.'

'Didn't have any luck with security cameras but there's a sale on Blue Mountain Jamaican coffee at Java House. Three pounds for the price of two. Still sets you back close to fifty bucks. But that coffee is the best.'

She made no response to his banter. He noticed it. 'What's up, boss?'

'Change of plans, TJ.' She told him about Travis Brigham, the forensics match and the dozen stolen bouquets.

'He's on the run, boss? He's planning *more*?'

'Yep. I want you to get to Bagel Express, talk to his friends, anybody who knows him, find out where he might go. People he might be staying with. Favorite places.'

'Sure, I'll get right on it.'

Dance then called Rey Carraneo, who was having no luck in his search for witnesses near the parking lot where Tammy Foster had been abducted. She briefed him as well and told him to head over to the Game Shed to find any leads to where the boy might've gone.

After hanging up, Dance sat back. A frustrating sense of helplessness came over her. She needed witnesses, people to interview. This was a skill she was born to, one she enjoyed and was good at. But now the case slogged along in the world of evidence and speculation.

She glanced at the printouts of *The Chilton Report*.

'I think we better start contacting the potential victims and warning them. Are people attacking him in the social sites too, MySpace, Facebook, OurWorld?' she asked Boling.

'It's not as big a story in those; they're international sites. *The Chilton Report* is local, so that's where ninety percent of the attacks on Travis are. I'll tell you one thing that would help: getting the Internet addresses of the posters. If we could get those, we can contact their service providers and find their physical addresses. It would save a lot of time.'

'How?'

'Have to be from Chilton himself or his webmaster.'

'Jon, can you tell me anything about him that'll help me persuade him to cooperate, if he balks?'

'I know about his blog,' Boling responded, 'but not much about him personally. Other than the bio in the *Report* itself. But I'd be happy to do some detective work.' His eyes had taken on the sparkle she'd seen earlier. He turned back to his computer.

Puzzles . . .

While the professor was lost in his homework assignment Dance took a call from O'Neil. A Crime Scene team had searched the alley behind Bagel Express and found traces of sand and dirt where the tread marks showed Travis had left his bike; they matched the sandy soil where Tammy's car had been left on the beach. He added that an MCSO team had canvassed the area but nobody had seen him.

O'Neil told her too that he'd gotten a half dozen other officers from Highway Patrol to join in the manhunt. They were coming in from Watsonville.

They disconnected and Dance slumped back in her chair.

After a few minutes, Boling said that he'd gotten some background on Chilton from the blog itself and from other research. He called up the homepage again, which had the bio Chilton himself had written.

http://www.thechiltonreport.com

Scrolling down, Dance began to skim the blog while Boling offered, 'James David Chilton, forty-three years old. Married to Patrizia Brisbane, two boys, ten and twelve. Lives in Carmel. But he also has property in Hollister, vacation house, it looks like, and some income property around San Jose. They inherited it when the wife's father died a few years ago. Now, the most interesting thing I found out about Chilton is that he's always had a quirky habit. He'd write letters.'

'Letters?'

'Letters to the editor, letters to his congressmen, op ed pieces. He started with snail mail – before the Internet really took off – then emails. He's written thousands of them. Rants, criticism, praise, compliments, political commentary. You name it. He was quoted as saying one of his favorite books was *Herzog,* the Saul Bellow novel about a man obsessed with writing letters. Basically Chilton's message was about upholding moral values, exposing corruption, extolling politicians who do good, trashing the ones who don't – exactly what his blog does now. I found a lot of them online. Then, it seems, he found out about the blogosphere. He started *The Chilton Report* about five years ago. Now before I go on, it might be helpful to know a little history of blogs.'

'Sure.'

'The term comes from "weblog", which was coined by a computer guru in nineteen ninety-seven, Jorn Barger. He wrote an online diary about his travels and what he'd been looking at on the Web. Now, people'd been recording their thoughts online for years but what made blogs distinctive was the concept of *links*. That's the key to a blog. You're reading something and you come to that underlined or boldface reference in the text and click on it and that takes you someplace else.

'Linking is called "hypertext". The *H-T-T-P* in a website address? It stands for "hypertext transfer protocol". That's the software that lets you create links. In my opinion it was one of the most significant aspects of the Internet. Maybe the most significant.

'Well, once hypertext became common, blogs started to take off. People who could write code in HTML – hypertext markup language, the computer language of links – could create their own blogs pretty easily. But more and more people wanted in and not everybody was tech savvy. So companies came up with programs that anybody, well, almost anybody, could use to create linked blogs with – Pitas, Blogger and Groksoup were the early ones. Dozens of others followed. And now all you have to do is have an account with Google or Yahoo and, poof, you can make a blog. Combine that with the bargain price of data storage nowadays – and getting cheaper every minute – and you've got the blogosphere.'

Boling's narrative was animated and ordered. He'd be a great professor, she reflected.

'Now, before Nine-eleven,' Boling explained, 'blogs were mostly computer-oriented. They were written by tech people for tech people. After September Eleventh, though, a new type of blog appeared. They were called war blogs, after the attacks and the Afghanistan and Iraq wars. Those bloggers weren't interested in technology. They were interested in politics, economics, society, the world. I describe the distinction this way: while pre-Nine-eleven blogs were inner-directed – toward the Internet itself – the war blogs are outer-directed. Those bloggers look at themselves as journalists, part of what's known as the New Media. They want press credentials, just like CNN and *Washington Post* reporters, and they want to be taken seriously.

'Jim Chilton is the quintessential war blogger. He doesn't care about the Internet per se or the tech world, except to the extent it lets him get his message out. He writes about the real world. Now the two sides – the original bloggers and the war bloggers – constantly battle for the number-one spot in the blogosphere.'

'It's a contest?' she asked, amused.

'To them it is.'

'They can't coexist?'

'Sure, but it's an ego-driven world and they'll do anything they can to be top of the heap. And that means two things. One, having as many subscribers as possible. And two, more import-ant – having as many other blogs as possible include links to yours.'

'Incestuous.'

'Very. Now, you asked what could I tell you to get Chilton's cooperation. Well, you have to remember that *The Chilton Report* is the real thing. It's important and influential. You notice that one of the early posts in the "Roadside Crosses" thread was from an executive at Caltrans? He wanted to defend their inspection of the highway. That tells me that government officials and CEOs read the blog regularly. And get pretty damn upset if Chilton says anything bad about them.

'The *Report* leans toward local issues but local in this case is California, which isn't really local at all. Everybody in the world keeps an eye on us. They either love or hate the state, but they *all* read about it. Also, Chilton himself's emerged as a serious journalist. He works his sources, he writes well. He's reasonable and he picks real issues – he's not sensationalist. I searched for Britney Spears and Paris Hilton in his blog, going back four years, and neither name came up.'

Dance had to be impressed with that.

'He's not a part-timer, either. Three years ago he began to work on the report full-time. And he campaigns it hard.'

'What does that mean, "campaign"?'

Boling scrolled down to the 'On the Home Front' thread on the homepage.

http://www.thechiltonreport.com.

WE'RE GOING GLOBAL!

Am pleased to report that the *Report* has been getting raves from around the world. It's been selected as one of the lead blogs in a new RSS feed (we'll call it 'Really Simple Syndication') that will link thousands of other blogs, websites and bulletin boards throughout the world. Kudos to you, my readers, for making the *Report* as popular as it is.

'RSS is another next big thing. It actually stands for RDF Site Syndication — "RDF" is Resource Description Framework, if you're interested, and there's no reason for you to be. RSS is a way of customizing and consolidating updated material from blogs and websites and podcasts. Look at your browser. At the top is a little orange square with a dot in the corner and two curved lines.'

'I've seen it.'

'That's your RSS feeds. Chilton is trying hard to get picked up by other bloggers and websites. That's important to him. And it's important to you too. Because it tells us something about him.'

'He's got an ego I can stroke?'

'Yep. That's one thing to remember. I'm also thinking of something else you can try with him, something more nefarious.'

'I like nefarious.'

'You'll want to somehow hint that his helping you will be good publicity for the blog. It'll get the name of the *Report* around in the mainstream media. Also, you could hint that you or somebody at CBI could be a source for information in the future.' Boling nodded at the screen, where the blog glowed. 'I mean, first and foremost, he's an investigative reporter. He appreciates sources.'

'Okay. Good idea. I'll try it.'

A smile. 'Of course, the other thing he might do is consider your request an invasion of journalistic ethics. In which case he'll slam the door in your face.'

Dance looked at the screen. 'These blogs — they're a whole different world.'

'Oh, that they are. And we're just beginning to comprehend the power they have — how they're changing the way we get information and form opinions. There are probably sixty million of them now.'

'That many?'

'Yep. And they do great things – they prefilter information so you don't have to Google your way through millions of sites, they're a community of like-minded people, they can be funny, creative. And, like *The Chilton Report,* they police society and keep us honest. But there's a dark side too.'

'Propagating rumors,' Dance said.

'That's one thing, yes. And another problem is what I said earlier about Tammy: they encourage people to be careless. People feel protected online and in the synth world. Life seems anonymous, posting under a nym or nic – a screen name – so you give away all sorts of information about yourself. But remember: every single fact about you – or lie – that you post, or somebody posts about you, is there forever. It will never, ever go away.'

Boling continued, 'But I feel the biggest problem is that people tend not to question the accuracy of the reporting. Blogs give an impression of authenticity – the information's more democratic and honest because it comes from the people, not from big media. But my point – and it's earned me plenty of black eyes in academia and in the blogosphere – is that that's bullshit. The *New York Times* is a for-profit corporation but is a thousand times more objective than most blogs. There's very little accountability online. Holocaust denials, Nine-eleven conspiracies, racism, they all thrive, thanks to blogs. They take on an authenticity some weirdo at a cocktail party doesn't have when he spouts off that Israel and the CIA were behind the Trade Towers attack.'

Dance returned to her desk and lifted her phone. 'I think I'll put all your research to use, Jon. Let's see what happens.'

James Chilton's house was in an upscale area of Carmel, the yard close to an acre, and filled with trimmed but hodgepodge gardens, which suggested that husband, wife or both spent plenty of weekend hours extracting weeds and inserting plants, rather than paying pros to do it.

Dance gazed at the outside décor enviously. Gardening, though much appreciated, wasn't one of her skills. Maggie said that if plants didn't have roots they'd run when her mother stepped into the garden.

The house was an expansive ranch, about forty years old, and squatted at the back of the property. Dance estimated six bedrooms. Their cars were a Lexus sedan and a Nissan Quest, sitting in a large garage filled with plenty of sports equipment, which unlike similar articles in Dance's garage, actually appeared well used.

She had to laugh at the bumper stickers on Chilton's vehicles. They echoed headlines from his blog: one against the desalination plant and one against the sex education proposal. Left and right, Democrat and Republican.

He's more cut-and-paste . . .

There was another car here too, in the drive; a visitor, probably, since the Taurus bore the subtle decal of a rental car company. Dance parked and walked to the front door, rang the bell.

Footsteps grew louder, and she was greeted by a brunette woman in her early forties, slender, wearing designer jeans and a white blouse, the collar turned up. A thick Daniel Yurman knotted necklace, in silver, was at her throat.

The shoes, Dance couldn't help but identify, came from Italy and were knockouts.

The agent identified herself, proffering her ID. 'I called earlier. To see Mr Chilton.'

The woman's face eased into the hint of a frown that typically forms when one meets law enforcers. Her name was Patrizia – she pronounced it Pa-*treet*-sia.

'Jim's just finishing up a meeting. I'll go tell him you're here.'

'Thank you.'

'Come on in.'

She led Dance to a homey den, the walls covered with pictures of family, then disappeared into the house for a moment. Patrizia returned. 'He'll be just a moment.'

'Thank you. These are your boys?' Dance was pointing at a picture of Patrizia, a lanky balding man she took to be Chilton and two dark-haired boys, who reminded her of Wes. They were all smiling at the camera. The woman proudly said, 'Jim and Chet.'

Chilton's wife continued through the photos. From the pictures of the woman in her youth – at Carmel Beach, Point Lobos, the Mission – Dance guessed she was a native. Patrizia explained that, yes, she was; in fact, she'd grown up in this very house. 'My father had been living here alone for years. When he passed, about three years ago, Jim and I moved in.'

Dance liked the idea of a family home, passed down from generation to generation. She reflected that Michael O'Neil's parents still lived in the oceanview house where he and his siblings had grown up. With his father suffering from senility, his mother was thinking of selling the place and moving into a retirement community. But O'Neil was determined to keep the property in the family.

As Patrizia was pointing out photos that displayed the family's exhausting athletic accomplishments – golf, soccer, tennis, triathlons – Dance heard voices in the front hall.

She turned to see two men. Chilton – she recognized him from the pictures – wore a baseball cap, green polo shirt and chinos. Blondish hair eased in tufts from under the hat. He was tall and apparently in good shape, with only a bit of belly swelling above his belt. He was speaking to another man, sandy-haired, wearing jeans, a white shirt and a brown sports coat. Dance started toward them but Chilton quickly ushered the man out of the door. Her kinesic reading was that he didn't want the visitor, whoever he was, to know that a law enforcement agent had come to see him.

Patrizia repeated, 'He'll just be a minute.'

But Dance sidestepped her and continued into the hall, sensing the wife stiffen, protective of her husband. Still, an interviewer has to take immediate charge of the situation; subjects can't set the rules. But by the time Dance got to the front door Chilton was back and the rental car heading off, gravel crunching under tires.

His green eyes – similar to her shade – turned their attention her way. They shook hands and she read in the blogger's face, tanned and freckled, curiosity and a certain defiance, more than wariness.

Another flash of the ID. 'Could we talk somewhere for a few minutes, Mr Chilton?'

'My office, sure.'

He led her up the hall. The room they entered was modest and a mess, filled with towers of magazines and clippings and computer printouts. Underscoring what she'd learned from Jon Boling, the officer revealed that indeed the reporter's game was changing: small rooms in houses and apartments just like this were replacing city-desk rooms of newspapers. Dance was amused to see a cup of tea beside his computer – the scent of chamomile filled the room. No cigarettes, coffee or whisky for today's hard-edged journalists, apparently.

They sat and he lifted his eyebrow. 'So he's been complaining, has he? But I'm curious. Why the police, why not a civil suit?'

'How's that?' Dance was confused.

Chilton rocked back in his chair, removed his cap, rubbed his balding head and slipped the hat back on. He was irritated. 'Oh, he bitches about libel. But it's not defamation if it's true. Besides, even if what I wrote was false, which it isn't, libel's not a crime in this country. Would be in Stalinist Russia, but it's not here yet. So why're you involved?' His eyes were keen and probing, his mannerisms intense; Dance could imagine how it might soon get tiring to spend much time in his presence.

'I'm not sure what you mean.'

'Aren't you here because of Arnie Brubaker?'

'No. Who's that?'

'He's the man who wants to destroy our shoreline by putting in that desalination plant.'

She recalled the blog postings in *The Chilton Report* critical of the plant. And the bumper sticker.

'No, this has nothing to do with that.'

Chilton's forehead crinkled. 'He'd love to stop me. I thought maybe he'd trumped up some criminal complaint. But sorry. I was making assumptions.' The defensiveness in his face relaxed. 'It's just, well, Brubaker's really a . . . pain.'

Dance wondered what the intended descriptive of the developer was going to have been.

'Excuse me.' Patrizia appeared in the doorway and brought her husband a fresh cup of tea. She asked Dance if she'd like anything. She was smiling now but still eyed the agent suspiciously.

'Thanks, no.'

Chilton nodded at the tea and charmingly winked his thanks to his wife. She left and closed the door behind her.

'So, what can I do for you?'

'Your blog about the roadside crosses.'

'Oh, the car accident?' He regarded Dance closely. Some of the defensiveness was back; she could read the stress in his posture. 'I've been following the news. That girl was attacked, the press is saying, because she posted something on the blog. The posters are starting to say the same thing. You want the boy's name.'

'No. We have it.'

'Is he the one who tried to drown her?'

'It seems so.'

Chilton said quickly, 'I didn't attack *him*. My point was, did the police drop the ball on the investigation and did Caltrans adequately maintain the road? I said up front that he wasn't to blame. And I censored his name.'

'It didn't take long for a mob to form and find out who he is.'

Chilton's mouth twisted. He'd taken the comment as criticism of him or the blog, which it wasn't. But he conceded. 'That does happen. Well, what *can* I do for you?'

'We have reason to believe that Travis Brigham may be considering attacking other people who posted comments against him.'

'Are you sure?'

'No, but we have to consider it's a possibility.'

Chilton grimaced. 'I mean, can't you arrest him?'

'We're looking for him now. We aren't sure where he is.'

'I see.' Chilton said this slowly and Dance could see from his lifted shoulders and the tension in his neck he was wondering what exactly she wanted. The agent considered Jon Boling's advice and said, 'Now, your blog is known all over the world. It's very respected. That's one of the reasons so many people are posting on it.'

The flash of pleasure in his eyes was faint but obvious to Dance; it told her that even obvious flattery went down very well with James Chilton.

'But the problem is that all the posters attacking Travis are potential targets. And the number's increasing every hour.'

'The *Report* has one of the highest hit ratings in the country. It's the most-read blog in California.'

'I'm not surprised. I really enjoy it.' Keeping an eye on her own mannerisms, so as not to telegraph the deception.

'Thank you.' A full smile joined the eye crinkle.

'But see what we're facing: every time somebody posts to the "Roadside Crosses" thread they become a possible target. Some of those people are completely anonymous, some are out of the area. But some are nearby and we're afraid Travis will find out their identities. And then he'll go after them too.'

'Oh,' Chilton said, his smile vanishing. His quick mind made the leap. 'And you're here for their Internet addresses.'

'For their protection.'

'I can't give those out.'

'But these people are at risk.'

'This country operates on the principle of separation of media and state.' As if this flippant recitation skewered her argument.

'That girl was thrown into a trunk and left to drown. Travis could be planning another attack right now.'

Chilton held up a finger, shushing her like a schoolteacher. 'It's a slippery slope. Agent Dance, who do you work for? Your ultimate boss?'

'The attorney general.'

'Okay, well, say I give you the addresses of posters on the "Roadside Crosses" thread. Then next month you come back and ask for the address of a whistleblower who was fired by the attorney general for, oh, let's pick harassment. Or maybe you want the address of somebody who posted a comment critical of the governor. Or the president. Or – how 'bout this – someone who says something favorable about al-Qaeda? You say to me: "You gave me the information last time. Why not again?"'

'There won't be an again.'

'You say that but . . .' As if government employees lied with every breath. 'Does this boy know you're after him?'

'Yes.'

'Then he's run off somewhere, wouldn't you think? He's not going to show himself by attacking somebody else. Not if the police are looking for him.' His voice was stern.

Hers was reasonable as she continued slowly, 'Still. You know, Mr Chilton, sometimes life is about compromises.'

She let this comment linger.

He cocked an eyebrow, waiting.

'If you gave us the addresses – just of the locals who wrote the most vicious posts about Travis – we'd really appreciate it. Maybe . . . well, maybe we could do something to help you, if you ever needed a hand.'

'Like what?'

Thinking again about Boling's suggestions, she said, 'We'd be happy to issue a statement about your cooperation. Good publicity.'

Chilton considered this. But then frowned. 'No. if I were to help you it'd probably be best not to mention it.'

She was pleased; he was negotiating. 'Okay, I can understand that. But maybe there's something else we could do.'

'Really? What?'

Thinking about another suggestion the professor had made, she said, 'Maybe, well, if you need any contacts in the California law enforcement agencies . . . Sources. High-up ones.'

He leaned forward, eyes flaring. 'So you *are* trying to bribe me. I thought so. Just had to draw you out a little. Got you, Agent Dance.'

She sat back as if she'd been slapped.

Chilton continued, 'Appealing to my public spirit is one thing. This . . .' he waved his hand at her, '. . . is distasteful. And corrupt, if you ask me. It's the kind of maneuvering I expose in my blog every day.'

Of course, the other thing he might do is consider your request an invasion of journalistic ethics. In which case he'll slam the door in your face.

'Tammy Foster was almost killed. There could be others.'

'I'm very sorry for that. But the *Report* is too important to jeopardize. And if people think they can't post anonymously it'll change the integrity of the entire blog.'

'I'd like you to reconsider.'

The blogger's strident facade faded. 'That man I was meeting with when you got here?'

She nodded.

'Gregory Ashton.' He said this with some intensity, the way people will when speaking about someone significant to them, but who have no meaning to you. Chilton noted the blank expression. He continued, 'He's starting a new network of blogs and websites, one of the biggest in the world. I'll be at the flagship level. He's spending millions to promote it.'

This was the issue that Boling had explained to her. Ashton must have been the one behind the RSS feed Chilton was referring to in the 'We're Going Global' posting.

'That expands the scope of the *Report* exponentially. I can take on problems around the world. AIDS in Africa, human rights violations in Indonesia, atrocities in Kashmir, environmental disasters in Brazil. But if word were to get out that I gave away the Internet address of my posters, that could put the sanctity of the *Report* at risk.'

Dance was frustrated, though part of her, as a former journalist, grudgingly understood. Chilton wasn't resisting out of greed or ego, but from a genuine passion for his readers.

Though that hardly helped her out.

'People could die,' she persisted.

'This question has come up before, Agent Dance. The responsibility of bloggers.' He stiffened slightly. 'A few years ago I did an exclusive post about a well-known writer who I found out had plagiarized some passages from another novelist. He claimed it was an accident, and begged me not to run the story. But I ran it anyway. He started drinking again and his life fell apart. Was that my goal? God, no. But either the rules exist or they don't. Why should he get away with cheating when you and I don't?

'I did a blog about a deacon from San Francisco who was head of an antigay movement – and, it turned out, a closet homosexual. I had to expose the hypocrisy.' He looked right into Dance's eyes. 'And the man killed himself. Because of what I wrote. Killed himself. I live with that every day. But did I do the right thing? Yes. If Travis attacks somebody else, then I'll feel terrible about that too. But we're dealing with bigger issues here, Agent Dance.'

'I was a reporter too,' she said.

'You were?'

'Crime reporter. I'm against censorship completely. We're not talking about the same thing. I'm not telling you to change your postings. I just want to know the names of people who've posted so we can protect them.'

'Can't do it.' The flint was back in his voice. He looked at his watch. She knew the interview was over. He rose.

Still, one last shot. 'No one will ever know. We'll say we found out through other means.'

Escorting her to the door, Chilton gave a genuine laugh. 'Secrets in the blogosphere, Agent Dance? Do you know how fast word spreads in today's world? . . . At the speed of light.'

13

As she drove along the highway, Kathryn Dance called Jon Boling.

'How did it go?' he asked brightly.

'What was that phrase that was in the blog about Travis? One of the kids posted it. "Epic" something . . .'

'Oh.' Less cheer now. 'Epic fail.'

'Yeah, that describes it pretty well. I tried for the good-publicity approach but he went for door number two: the fascists trammeling free press. With a touch of "the world needs me".'

'Ouch. Sorry about that. Bad call.'

'It was worth a shot. But I think you'd better start trying to get as many names as you can on your own.'

'I already have. Just in case Chilton gave you the boot. I should have some names soon. Oh, did he say he'd get even in a blog posting about you for suggesting it?'

She chuckled. 'Came close. The headline would've been "CBI agent in attempted bribe".'

'I doubt he will – you're small potatoes. Nothing personal. But with hundreds of thousands of people reading what he writes, he sure does have the power to make you worry.' Then Boling's voice grew somber. 'I should tell you the postings are getting worse. Some of the posters are saying they've seen Travis doing devil worship, sacrificing animals. And there are stories about him groping other students, girls and boys. All sounds bogus to me, though. It's like they're trying to one-up each other. The stories are getting more outlandish.'

Rumors . . .

'The one thing that's a recurring reference, which makes me think there's some truth in it, is the online role-playing games. They're talking about the kid being obsessed with fighting and death. Especially with swords and knives and slashing his victims.'

'He's slipped into the synthetic world.'

'Seems that way.'

After they disconnected, Dance turned up the volume on her iPod Touch – she was listening to Badi Assad, the beautiful Brazilian guitarist and singer. It was illegal to listen through the ear buds while driving, but running the music through the speakers in a cop car didn't produce the most faithful sound quality.

And she needed a serious dose of soul-comforting music.

Dance felt the urgency to pursue the case, but she was a mother too and she'd always balanced her two worlds. She'd now pick up her children from her mother's care at the hospital, spend a little time with them and drop them off at her parents' house, where Stuart Dance would resume baby-sitting, after he returned from his meeting at the aquarium. And she would head back to the CBI to continue the hunt for Travis Brigham.

She continued the drive in the big, unmarked CVPI – her Police Interceptor Ford. It handled like a combination race car and tank. Not that Dance had ever pushed the vehicle to its limits. She wasn't a natural driver and, though she'd taken the required high-speed-pursuit course in Sacramento, couldn't picture herself actually chasing another driver along the winding roads of central California. With this thought, an image from the blog came to mind – the photo of the roadside crosses at the site of the terrible accident on Highway 1 on June 9, the tragedy that had set all of this subsequent horror in motion.

She now pulled up in the hospital lot and noticed several California Highway Patrol cars, and two unmarkeds, parked in front of the hospital. She couldn't remember a report about any police action involving injuries. Climbing from the car, she observed a change in the protesters. For one thing, there were more of them. Three dozen or so. And they'd been joined by two more news crews.

Also, she noticed, they were boisterous, waving their placards and crosses like sports fans. Smiling, chanting. Dance noticed that the Reverend Fisk was being approached by several men, shaking his hands in sequence. His red-haired minder was carefully scanning the parking lot.

And then Dance froze, gasping.

Walking out the front door of the hospital were Wes and Maggie – faces grim – accompanied by an African-American woman in a navy blue suit. She was directing them to one of the unmarked sedans.

Robert Harper, the special prosecutor she'd met outside Charles Overby's office, emerged.

And behind him walked Dance's mother. Edie Dance was flanked by two large uniformed CHP troopers, and she was in handcuffs.

Dance jogged forward.

'Mom!' twelve-year-old Wes shouted and ran across the parking lot, pulling his sister after him.

'Wait, you can't do that!' shouted the woman who'd been accompanying them. She started forward, fast.

Dance knelt, embracing her son and daughter.

The woman's stern voice resounded across the parking lot. 'We're taking the children—'

'You're not taking anybody,' Dance growled, then turned again to her children: 'Are you all right?'

'They arrested Grandma!' Maggie said, tears welling. Her chestnut braid hung limply over her shoulder, where it had jumped in the run.

'I'll talk to them in a minute.' Dance rose. 'You're not hurt, are you?'

'No.' Lean Wes, nearly as tall as his mother, said in a shaky voice, 'They just, that woman and the police, they just came and got us and said they're taking us someplace, I don't know where.'

'I don't want to leave you, Mommy!' Maggie clung to her tightly.

Dance reassured her daughter, 'Nobody's taking you anywhere. Okay, go get in the car.'

The woman in the blue suit approached and said in a low tone, 'Ma'am, I'm afraid—' And found herself talking to Dance's CBI identification card and shield, thrust close to her face. 'The children are going with me,' Dance said.

The woman read the ID, unimpressed. 'It's procedure. You understand. It's for their own good. We'll get it all sorted out and if everything checks out—'

'The children are going with me.'

'I'm a social worker with Monterey County Child Services.' Her own ID appeared.

Dance was thinking that there were probably negotiations that should be going on at the moment but still she pulled her hand-cuffs out of her back holster in a smooth motion and swung them open like a large crab claw. 'Listen to me. I'm their mother. You know my identity. You know theirs. Now back off, or I'm arresting you under California Penal Code section two-oh-seven.'

Observing this, the TV reporters seemed to stiffen as one, like a lizard sensing the approach of an oblivious beetle. Cameras swung their way.

The woman turned toward Robert Harper, who seemed to debate. He glanced at the reporters and apparently decided that, in this situation, bad publicity was worse than no publicity. He nodded.

Dance smiled to her children, hitching the cuffs away, and walked them to her car. 'It's going to be okay. Don't worry. This is just a big mix-up.' She closed the door, locking it with the remote. She stormed past the social worker, who was glaring back with sleek, defiant eyes, and approached her mother, who was being eased into the back of a squad car.

'Honey!' Edie Dance exclaimed.

'Mom, what's—'

'You can't talk to the prisoner,' Harper said.

She whirled and faced Harper, who was exactly her height. 'Don't play games with me. What's this all about?'

He regarded her calmly. 'She's being taken to the county lockup for processing and a bail hearing. She's been arrested and informed of her rights. I have no obligation to say anything to you.'

The cameras continued to pick up every second of the drama.

Edie Dance called, 'They said I killed Juan Millar!'

'Please be quiet, Mrs Dance.'

The agent raged at Harper, 'That "caseload evaluation"? It was just bullshit, right?'

Harper easily ignored her.

Dance's cell phone rang and she stepped aside to answer it. 'Dad.'

'Katie, I just got home and found the police here. State police. They're searching everything. Mrs Kensington next door said they took away a couple of boxes of things.'

'Dad, Mom's been arrested . . .'

'What?'

'That mercy killing. Juan Millar.'

'Oh, Katie.'

'I'm taking the kids to Martine's, then meet me at the court-house in Salinas. She's going to be booked and there'll be a bond hearing.'

'Sure. I . . . I don't know what to do, honey.' His voice broke.

It cut her deeply to hear her own father – normally unflappable and in control – sounding so helpless.

'We'll get it worked out,' she said, trying to sound confident but feeling just as uncertain and confused as he would be. 'I'll call later, Dad.' They disconnected.

'Mom,' she called through the car window, looking down at her mother's grim face. 'It'll be all right. I'll see you at the court-house.'

The prosecutor said sternly, 'Agent Dance, I don't want to remind you again. No talking to the prisoner.'

She ignored Harper. 'And don't say a word to anyone,' she warned her mother.

'I hope we're not going to have a security problem here,' the prosecutor said stiffly.

Dance glared back, silently defying him to make good on his threat, whatever it might be. Then she glanced at the CHP troopers nearby, one of whom she'd worked with. His eyes avoided hers. Everybody was in Harper's pocket on this one.

She turned and strode back toward her car, but diverted to the woman social worker.

Dance stood close. 'Those children have cell phones. I'm number two on speed dial, right after nine-one-one. And I *guarantee* they told you I'm a law enforcement officer. Why the fuck didn't you call me?'

The woman blinked and reared back. 'You can't talk to me that way.'

'Why the fuck didn't you call?'

'I was following procedures.'

'Procedures are the welfare of the child comes first. You contact the parent or guardian in circumstances like this.'

'Well, I was doing what I was told.'

'How long've you had this job?'

'That's none of your business.'

'Well, I'll tell you, miss. There're two answers: either not long enough, or way *too* long.'

'You can't—'

But Dance was gone by then and climbing back into her car, grinding the starter; she'd never shut the engine off when she'd arrived.

'Mom,' Maggie asked, weeping with heartbreaking whimpers. 'What's going to happen to Grandma?'

Dance wasn't going to put on a false facade for the children; she'd learned as a parent that in the end it was better to confront pain and fear, rather than to deny or defer them. But she had to struggle to keep panic from her voice. 'Your grandmother's going to see a judge and I hope she'll be home soon. Then we're going to find out what's happened. We just don't know yet.'

She'd take the children to the home of her best friend, Martine Christensen, with whom she operated her music website.

'I don't like that man,' Wes said.

'Who?'

'Mr Harper.'

'I don't like him either,' Dance said.

'I want to go to the courthouse with you,' Maggie said.

'No, Mags. I don't know how long I'm going to be there.'

Dance glanced back and gave a reassuring smile to the children.

Seeing their wan, forlorn faces, she grew all the angrier at Robert Harper.

Dance plugged in her phone's hands-free mike, thought for a moment and called the best defense lawyer she could think of. George Sheedy had once spent four hours trying to discredit Dance on the witness stand. He'd come close to winning a verdict of not guilty for a Salinas gang leader who clearly was. But the good guys had won and the punk got life. After the trial, Sheedy had come up to Dance and shaken her hand, complimenting her on the solid job she'd done testifying. She'd told him too that she'd been impressed by his skill.

As her call was being transferred to Sheedy, she noticed that the cameramen continued to record the excitement, every one of them focused on the car in which her mother sat, handcuffed. They looked like insurgents firing rocket launchers at shell-shocked troops.

Calm now, after the intruder in the backyard turned out not to be the Abominable Snowman, Kelley Morgan was concentrating on her hair.

The teenager was never far from her curlers.

Her hair was the most frustrating thing in the world. A little humidity and it went all frizzy. Pissed her off *sooo* much.

She had to meet Juanita and Trey and Toni on Alvarado in forty minutes, and they were *such* great friends that if she was more than ten minutes late they'd ditch her. She lost track of time writing a post on Bri's Town Hall board on OurWorld, about Tammy Foster.

Then Kelley'd looked up, into the mirror, and realized that the damp air had turned the strands into this total *creature*. So she logged off and attacked the brunette tangles.

Somebody had once posted on a local blog – anonymously, of course:

Kelley Morgan . . . whats with her hair?????? its like shes a mushroom. I dont like girls with shaved heads but she should go for THAT look. LOL. yikes why dosnt she get a clue.

Kelley had sobbed, paralyzed at the terrible words, which cut her like a razor.

That post was the reason she'd defended Tammy on OurWorld and flamed AnonGurl (who she *did* end up owning, big-time).

Even now, thinking of the cruel post about her hair, she shivered with shame. And anger. Never mind that Jamie said he loved everything about her. The posting had devastated her and made her hypersensitive about the subject. And had cost her countless hours. Since that April 4 post, she hadn't once gone outside without battling the do into shape.

Okay, get to work, girl.

She rose from her desk and went to her dressing table and plugged in the heated rollers. They gave her split ends but at least the heat tamed the worst of the renegade tresses.

She flicked the dressing table light on and sat down, stripped off her blouse and tossed it onto the floor, then pulled two tank tops over her bra, liking the look of the three straps: red, pink and black. Tested the curlers. A few more minutes. Almost right. She started to brush. It was *soooo* unfair. Pretty face, nice boobs, great ass. And this effing hair.

She happened to glance at her computer and saw an instant message from a friend.

Check out TCR, I mean NOW!!!!!!!!

Kelley laughed. Trish was *so* exclamation point.

Usually she didn't read *The Chilton Report* – it was more politics than she cared about – but she'd put it on her RSS feed after Chilton had begun posting about the accident on June 9 under the 'Roadside Crosses' thread. Kelley had been at the party that night and, just before Caitlin and the other girls left, had seen Travis Brigham arguing with Caitlin.

She swung to the keyboard and typed, Don't Xplode. Y?

Trish responded, Chilton took out names but people are saying Travis attacked Tammy!!

Kelley typed, Is this win or r u guessing?

The response: WIN, WIN!!!! Travis is pissed b/c she flamed him in the blog, READ IT!!!! THE DRIVER = TRAVIS and THE VICTIM = TAMMY.

Sick to her stomach, Kelley began pounding the keys, calling up *The Chilton Report* and plowing through the 'Roadside Crosses' thread. Toward the end, she read:

Reply to Chilton, posted by BrittanyM.

Is anybody watching the news???? Somebody left a cross and then went out and attacked that girl. What's that all about? OMG, I'll bet it's [the driver]!

Reply to Chilton, posted by CTO93.

Where the [deleted] are the police? I heard that that girl in the trunk was raped and had crosses carved on her, then he LEFT her in the trunk to drown. Just because she dissed him – [the driver], I mean I just looked at the news and he hasn't been arrested yet. WHY NOT?????

Reply to Chilton, posted by Anonymous.

Me and my friends were near the beach where [the victim] was found and they heard the police talking about this cross. They were like he left it as a warning for people to shut up. [The victim] was attacked and raped because she dissed [the driver] HERE, i mean what she wrote in the blog!!! Listen if you flamed him here and you're not using proxies or posting anon, you're totally [deleted], he's going to get you!!

Reply to Chilton, posted by Anonymous.

I know a d00d where [the driver] goes to game and he was saying that [the driver] was saying he was going to get everybody who was posting stuff about him, he planned to cut their throats like terrorists do on arab TV, hey, cops, [the driver] is the Roadside Cross killer!!! And that's WORD!!!

No . . . God, no! Kelley thought back to what she'd posted about Travis. What'd she said? Would the boy be mad at *her*? She frantically scrolled up and found her post.

Reply to Chilton, posted by BellaKelley.

u r so right!!! Me and my friend were at that party on the 9th where it happened and [the driver] was coming on to [deleted] and they were like, just go away. But he didn't, he followed them out the door when they were leaving. But we have ourselves to blame too for not doing anything, all of us who were there. We all knew [the driver] is a luser and perv and we should have called the police or somebody when they left. I had this bad feeling like in Ghost Whisperer. And look what happened.

Why? Why did I say that?

I was all, Leave Tammy alone. Don't flame people online. And then I went and said something about Travis.

Shit. Now he's going to get me too! Is *that* what I'd heard outside earlier? Maybe he really was outside and, when my brother showed up, that scared him off.

Kelley thought of the bicyclist she'd seen. Hell, Travis rode a bike all the time; a lot of kids at school made fun of him because he couldn't afford a car.

Dismayed, angry, scared . . .

Kelley was staring at the posts on the screen of the computer, when she heard a noise behind her.

A snap, like earlier.

Another.

She turned.

A wrenching scream poured from Kelley Morgan's lips.

A face – the most frightening face she'd ever seen – was staring at her from the window. Kelley's rational thinking stopped cold. She dropped to her knees, feeling the warm liquid gush between her legs as she lost control of her bladder. A pain spurted in her chest, spread to her jaw, her nose, eyes. She nearly stopped breathing.

The face, motionless, staring with its huge black eyes, scarred skin, slits for the nose, the mouth sewn shut and bloody.

The pure horror from her childhood fears flooded through her.

'No, no, no!' Sobbing like a baby, Kelley was scrabbling away as fast as she could and as far as she could. She slammed into the wall and sprawled, stunned, on the carpet.

Eyes staring, black eyes.

Staring right at her.

'No . . .'

Jeans drenched with pee, stomach churning, Kelley crawled desperately toward the door.

The eyes, the mouth with the bloody stitching in it. The yeti, the Abominable Snowman. Somewhere in that portion of her mind that still worked she knew it was only a mask, tied to the crape myrtle tree outside the window.

But that didn't lessen the fear it ignited within her – the rawest of her childhood fears.

And she knew too what it meant.

Travis Brigham was here. He'd come to kill her, just like he'd tried to kill Tammy Foster.

Kelley finally managed to climb to her feet and stumbled to her door. Run. Get the fuck out.

In the hall she turned toward the front door.

Shit! It was open! Her brother hadn't locked it at all.

Travis was here, in the house!

Should she just sprint through the living room?

As she stood frozen in fear, he got her from behind, his arm snaking around her throat.

She struggled – until he jammed a gun against her temple.

Sobbing. 'Please, no, Travis.'

'Perv?' he whispered. 'Luser?'

'I'm sorry, I'm *sorry*, I didn't mean it!'

As he dragged her backward, toward the basement door, she felt his arm flex harder until her pleas and the choking grew softer and softer and the glare from the spotless living room window turned gray and then went black.

Kathryn Dance was no stranger to the American justice system. She had been in magistrates' offices and courtrooms as a crime journalist, a jury consultant, a law enforcement officer.

But she'd never been the relative of the accused.

After leaving the hospital, she'd dropped the children off at Martine's and called her sister, Betsey, who lived with her husband down in Santa Barbara.

'Bet, there's a problem with Mom.'

'What? Tell me what happened.' There'd been a rare edge in the voice of the otherwise flighty woman, younger than Dance by several years. Betsey had curly angelic hair and flitted from career to career like a butterfly testing out flowers.

Dance had run through the details she knew.

'I'll call her now,' Betsey had announced.

'She's in detention. They've got her phone. There'll be a bail hearing soon. We'll know more then.'

'I'm coming up.'

'It might be better later.'

'Sure, of course. Oh, Katie, how serious is this?'

Dance had hesitated. She recalled Harper's still, determined eyes, missionary's eyes. Finally she'd said, 'It could be bad.'

After they'd disconnected, Dance had continued here, to the magistrate's office at the courthouse, where she now sat with her father. The lean, white-haired man was even paler than usual (he'd learned the hard way of the dangers a marine biologist faces in the ocean sun and was now a sunscreen and hat addict). His arm was around her shoulders.

Edie had spent an hour in the holding cell – the intake area in which many of Dance's collars had been booked. Dance knew the procedures well: all personal effects were confiscated. You went through the warrant check and the inputting of information, and you sat in a cell, surrounded by other arrestees. And then you waited and waited.

Finally you were brought here, into the magistrate's chilly impersonal room for a bail hearing. Dance and her father were surrounded by dozens of family members of arrestees. Most of the accused here, some in street clothes, some in red Monterey County jumpsuits, were young Latino men. Dance recognized plenty of gang tats. Some were sullen whites, scruffier than the Latinos, with worse teeth and hair. In the back sat the public defenders. The bail bondsmen, too, waiting to pick up their 10 percent from the carcasses.

Dance lifted her eyes to her mother as she was brought in. It broke her heart to see the woman in handcuffs. She wasn't in a jumpsuit. But her hair, normally perfectly done, was in a shambles. Her homemade necklace had been taken from her upon processing. Her wedding and engagement rings too. Her eyes were red.

Lawyers milled about, some not much spiffier than their clients; only Edie Dance's attorney was in a suit that had been shaped by a tailor after purchase. George Sheedy had been practicing criminal law on the Central Coast for two decades. He had abundant gray hair, a trapezoidal figure with broad shoulders and a bass voice that would have done a stunning version of 'Old Man River'.

After the brief phone conversation with Sheedy from the car, Dance had immediately called Michael O'Neil, who'd been shocked at the news. She then called the Monterey County prosecutor, Alonzo 'Sandy' Sandoval.

'I just heard about it, Kathryn,' Sandoval muttered angrily. 'I'm being straight with you: we've had MCSO looking into the Millar death, sure, but I had no idea that's what Harper was in town for. And a public arrest.' He was bitter. 'That was inexcusable. If the AG insisted on a prosecution, I would've had her surrender with you bringing her in.'

Dance believed him. She and Sandy had worked together for years and had put a lot of bad people in jail, thanks in part to mutual trust.

'But I'm sorry, Kathryn. Monterey has nothing to do with the case. It's in Harper's and Sacramento's hands now.'

She'd thanked him and hung up. But at least she had been able to get her mother's bail hearing handled quickly. Under California law the time of the hearing is at the magistrate's discretion. In some places, like Riverside and Los Angeles, prisoners are often in a cell for twelve hours before they appear in front of the magistrate. Since the case was murder it was possible the magistrate might not set bail at all, leaving that to the discretion of the judge at the arraignment, which in California would have to occur within a few days.

The door to the outer hallway kept opening and Dance noticed that many of the recent arrivals were wearing media identification cards around their necks. No cameras were allowed, but there were plenty of pads of paper.

A circus . . .

The clerk called out, 'Edith Barbara Dance', and, somber and red-eyed and still cuffed, her mother rose. Sheedy joined her. A jailor was beside them. This session was devoted exclusively to the bail; pleas were entered later, at the arraignment. Harper asked that Edie be held without bail, which didn't surprise Dance. Her father stiffened at the prosecutor's harsh words, which made Edie out to be a dangerous Jack Kevorkian, who, if released on bail, would target other patients for death and then flee to Canada.

Stuart gasped, hearing his wife spoken about in this way.

'It's okay, Dad,' his daughter whispered. 'That's just the way they talk.' Though the words broke her heart too.

George Sheedy argued articulately for an OR release – on Edie's own recognizance, pointing to her lack of a criminal record and to her roots in the community.

The magistrate, a quick-eyed Latino who had met Kathryn Dance, exuded considerable stress, which she could easily read in his posture and facial expressions. He wouldn't want this case at all; he'd have loyalty to Dance, who was a reasonable law officer, cooperative. But he would also be aware that Harper was a big name from the big city. And the magistrate would be very aware of the media too.

The arguments continued.

Dance the law enforcer found herself looking back to earlier that month, reliving the circumstances of the officer's death. Trying to match facts with facts. Whom had she seen in the hospital around the time Juan Millar died? What exactly were the means of death? Where had her mother been?

She now glanced up and found Edie staring at her. Dance gave a pale smile. Edie's face was expressionless. The woman turned back to Sheedy.

In the end the magistrate compromised. He set the bail at a half million dollars, which wasn't atypical for a murder, but also wasn't overly burdensome. Edie and Stuart weren't wealthy but they owned their house outright; since it was in Carmel, not far from the beach, it had to be worth two million. They could put it up as security.

Harper took the news stoically – his face unsmiling, his posture upright but relaxed. Dance's reading was that he was completely stress free, despite the setback. He reminded her of the killer in Los Angeles, J. Doe. One of the reasons she'd had such a hard time spotting that perp's deception was that a highly driven, focused person reveals, and feels, little distress when lying in the name of his cause. This certainly defined Robert Harper.

Edie was hustled back to the cell and Stuart rose and went to see the clerk to arrange for the bail.

As Harper buttoned his jacket and walked toward the door,

his face a mask, Dance intercepted him. 'Why are you doing this?'

He regarded her coolly, said nothing.

She continued, 'You could've let Monterey County handle the case. Why'd you come down from San Francisco? What's your agenda?' She was speaking loudly enough for the reporters nearby to hear.

Harper said evenly, 'I can't discuss this with you.'

'Why my mother?'

'I have nothing to say.' And he pushed through the door and onto the steps of the courthouse, where he paused to address the press – to whom he apparently had *plenty* to say.

Dance returned to a hard bench to await her father and mother.

Ten minutes later, George Sheedy and Stuart Dance joined her.

She asked her father, 'It went okay?'

'Yes,' he answered in a hollow voice.

'How soon will she be out?'

Stuart looked at Sheedy, who said, 'Ten minutes, maybe less.'

'Thank you.' He shook the lawyer's hand. Dance nodded her gratitude to Sheedy, who told them he was returning to the office and would get started on the defense immediately.

After he'd gone, Dance asked her father, 'What did they take from the house, Dad?'

'I don't know. The neighbor said they seemed most interested in the garage. Let's get out of here. I hate this place.'

They walked out into the hallway. Several reporters saw Dance and approached. 'Agent Dance,' one woman asked, 'is it troubling to know your mother's been arrested for murder?'

Well, *there's* some cutting-edge interviewing. She wanted to fire back with something sarcastic, but she remembered the number-one rule in media relations: assume everything you say in a reporter's presence will appear on the six o'clock news or on tomorrow's front page. She smiled. 'There's no doubt in my mind that this is a terrible misunderstanding. My mother has been a nurse for years. She's devoted herself to saving lives, not taking them.'

'Did you know that she signed a petition supporting Jack Kevorkian and assisted suicide?'

No, Dance didn't know that. And, she wondered, how had the press come by the information so fast? Her reply: 'You'll have to ask her about that. But petitioning to change the law isn't the same as breaking it.'

It was then that her phone sounded. It was O'Neil. She stepped away to take the call. 'Michael, she's getting out on bail,' she told him.

There was a moment's pause. 'Good. Thank God.'

Dance realized he was calling about something else, and something that was serious. 'What is it, Michael?'

'They've found another cross.'

'A real memorial, or with a future date?'

'Today. And it's identical to the first one. Branches and florist wire.'

Her eyes closed in despair. Not again.

Then O'Neil said, 'But, listen. We've got a witness. A guy who saw Travis leave it. He might've seen where he went or saw something about him that'll tell us where he's hiding. Can you interview him?'

Another pause. Then: 'I'll be there in ten minutes.'

O'Neil gave her the address. They disconnected.

Dance turned to her father. 'Dad, I can't stay. I'm so sorry.'

He turned his handsome, distraught face toward his daughter. 'What?'

'They found another cross. The boy's going after somebody else, it looks like. Today. But there's a witness. I have to interview them.'

'Of course you do.' Yet he sounded uncertain. He was going through a nightmare at the moment – nearly as bad as her mother's – and he'd want his daughter, with her expertise and her connections, nearby.

But she couldn't get images of Tammy Foster out of her mind, lying in the trunk, the water rising higher.

Images of Travis Brigham's eyes too, cold and dark beneath their abundant brows, as he gazed at his father, as if his character in a game, armed with knife or sword, was debating stepping out of the synth world and into the real, to slaughter the man.

She had to go. And now. 'I'm sorry.' She hugged her father. 'Your mother will understand.'

Dance ran to her car and started the engine. As she was pulling out of the parking lot she glanced in the rearview mirror and saw her mother emerge from the door to the lockup. Edie stared at her daughter's departure. The woman's eyes were still, her face revealing no emotion.

Dance's foot slipped to the brake. But then she pressed down once more on the accelerator and hit the grille flashers.

Your mother will understand . . .

No, she won't, Dance thought. She absolutely won't.

14

After all these years in the area Kathryn Dance had never quite grown used to the Peninsula fog. It was like a shape-shifter – a character out of the fantasy books that Wes liked. Sometimes it was wisps that hugged the ground and swept past you like ghosts. Other times it was smoke squatting in depressions of land and highway, obscuring everything.

Most often it was a thick cotton bedspread floating several hundred feet in the air, mimicking cloud and ominously darkening everything below it.

This was the breed of fog today.

The gloom thickened as Dance, listening to Raquy and the Cavemen, a North African group known for their percussion, drove along a quiet road running through state land between Carmel and Pacific Grove. The landscape was mostly woods, untended, filled with pine, scrub oak, eucalyptus and maple, joined by tangles of brush. She drove through the police line, ignoring the reporters and camera crews. Were they here for the crime, or because of her mother? Dance wondered cynically.

She parked, greeted the deputies nearby and joined Michael O'Neil. They began walking toward the cordoned-off shoulder, where the second cross had been found.

'How's your mother doing?' O'Neil asked.

'Not good.'

Dance was so glad he was here. Emotion swelled like a balloon within her, and she couldn't speak for a moment, as the image of her mother in handcuffs, and the run-in with the social worker about her children, surfaced.

The senior deputy couldn't help but give a faint smile. 'Saw you on TV.'

'TV?'

'Who was the woman, the one who looked like Oprah? You were about to arrest her.'

Dance sighed. 'They got that on camera?'

'You looked' – he searched for a word – 'imposing.'

'She was taking the kids to Social Services.'

O'Neil looked shocked. 'It was Harper. Tactics. He nearly got his flunky collared, though. Oh, I would've pushed the button on that one.' She added, 'I've got Sheedy on the case.'

'George? Good. Tough. You need tough.'

'Oh, and then Overby let Harper into CBI. To go through my files.'

'No!'

'I think he was looking to see if I suppressed evidence or tinkered with the files about the Juan Millar case. Overby said he went through your office's files too.'

'MCSO?' he asked. Dance could read his anger like a red highway flare. 'Did Overby know Harper was making a case against Edie?'

'I don't know. At the least he should've thought: what the hell is this guy from San Francisco prowling around in our files for? "Caseload evaluations". Ridiculous.' Her own fury swelled again and, with effort, she finally managed to bank it.

They approached the spot where the cross was planted, on the shoulder of the road. The memorial was like the earlier one: broken-off branches bound with wire, and a cardboard disk with today's date on it.

At the base was another bouquet of red roses.

She couldn't help but think: whose murder would this one represent?

And ten more waiting.

This cross had been left on a deserted stretch of barely paved road about a mile from the water. Not highly traveled, this route was a little-known shortcut to Highway 68. Ironically, this was one of the roads that would lead to that new highway that Chilton had written about in his blog.

Standing on a side road near the cross was the witness, a businessman in his forties, to look at him, into real estate or insurance, Dance guessed. He was round, his belly carrying his blue dress shirt well over a tired belt. His hair had receded and she saw sun freckles on his round forehead and balding crown. He stood beside a Honda Accord that had seen better days.

They approached and O'Neil said to her, 'This is Ken Pfister.'

She shook his hand. The deputy said he was going to supervise the crime scene search and headed across the street.

'Tell me what you saw, Mr Pfister.'

'Travis. Travis Brigham.'

'Did you know it was him?'

A nod. 'I saw his picture online when I was at lunch about a half hour ago. That's how I recognized him.'

'Could you tell me exactly what you saw?' she asked. 'And when?'

'Okay, it was around eleven this morning. I had a meeting in Carmel. I run an Allstate agency.' He said this proudly.

Got that one right, she thought.

'I left about ten-forty and was driving back to Monterey. Took this shortcut. It'll be nice when that new highway's open, won't it?'

She smiled noncommittally, not a smile really.

'And I pulled off onto that side road' – he gestured – 'to make some phone calls.' He gave a broad smile. 'Never drive and talk. That's my rule.'

Dance's lifted eyebrow prodded him to continue.

'I looked out my windshield and I saw him walking along the shoulder. From that direction. He didn't see me. He was kind of shuffling his feet. It seemed like he was talking to himself.'

'What was he wearing?'

'One of those hooded sweatshirts like the kids have.'

Ah, the hoodie.

'What color was it?'

'I don't remember.'

'Jacket, slacks?'

'Sorry. I wasn't paying much attention. I didn't know who he was at that point – I hadn't heard about the Roadside Cross stuff. All I knew was that he was weird and scary. He was carrying that cross, and he had a dead animal.'

'An animal?'

A nod. 'Yeah, a squirrel or groundhog or something. It had its throat cut.' He gestured with his finger at his own neck.

Dance hated any atrocities committed against animals. Still, she kept her voice even as she asked, 'Had he just killed it?'

'I don't think so. There wasn't much blood.'

'Okay, then what happened?'

'Then he looks up and down the road and when he doesn't see anybody he opens his backpack and—'

'Oh, he had a backpack?'

'That's right.'

'What color was it?'

'Uhm, black, I'm pretty sure. And he takes a shovel out, a little one. The sort that you'd use on a camping trip. And he opens it up and digs a hole and then puts the cross in the ground. Then . . . this is really weird. He goes through this ritual. He walks around the cross three times, and it looks like he's chanting.'

'Chanting?'

'That's right. Muttering things. I can't hear what.'

'And then?'

'He picks up the squirrel and walks around the cross again *five* times – I was counting. Three and five . . . Maybe it was a message, a clue, if somebody could figure it out.'

After *The Da Vinci Code*, Dance had observed, a lot of witnesses tended to decrypt their observations rather than just say what they'd seen.

'Anyway, he opened his backpack again and pulled out this stone and a knife. He used the stone to sharpen the blade. Then he held the knife over the squirrel. I thought he was going to cut it up, but he didn't. I saw his lips moving again, then he wrapped the body up in some kind of weird yellow paper, like parchment, and put it in the backpack. Then it looked like he said one last thing and went up the road the way he came. Loping, you know. Like an animal.'

'And what did you do then?'

'I left and went on to a few more meetings. I went back to the office. That's when I went online and saw the news about the boy. I saw his picture. I freaked out. I called nine-one-one right away.'

Dance gestured Michael O'Neil over.

'Michael, this is interesting. Mr Pfister's been real helpful.'

O'Neil nodded his thanks.

'Now could you tell Deputy O'Neil here what you saw?'

'Sure.' Pfister explained again about pulling over to make calls. 'The boy had a dead animal of some sort. A squirrel, I think. He walked around in a circle three times without the body. Then he plants the cross and walks around it five times. He was talking to himself. It was weird. Like a different language.'

'And then?'

'He wrapped the squirrel up in this parchment paper and held the knife over it. He said something else in that weird language again. Then he left.'

'Interesting,' O'Neil said. 'You're right, Kathryn.'

It was then that Dance pulled off her pale-pink-framed glasses and polished them. And subtly swapped them for a pair with severe black frames.

O'Neil caught on immediately that she was putting on her predator specs and stepped back. Dance moved closer to Pfister, well into his personal proxemic zone. Immediately, she could see, he felt a sense of threat.

Good.

'Now, Ken, I know you're lying. And I need you to tell me the truth.'

'Lying?' He blinked in shock.

'That's right.'

Pfister'd been pretty good at his deception, but certain comments and behaviors had tipped her off. Her suspicions arose initially because of content-based analysis: considering *what* he said rather than *how* he said it. Some of his explanations sounded too incredible to be true. Claiming he didn't know who the boy was and that he'd never heard about the Roadside Cross attack – when he seemed to go online regularly to get news. Claiming Travis was wearing a hoodie, which several of the posters to *The Chilton Report* had said, but not remembering the color – people tend to remember the hues of clothing far better than the garments themselves.

Pfister had also paused frequently – liars often do this as they try to craft credible deceptive lines. And he'd used at least one 'illustrator' gesture – the finger at the throat; people use these subconsciously to reinforce spurious statements.

So, suspicious, Dance had then used a shorthand technique to test for deception: in determining if somebody's lying, an interviewer will ask to hear his story several times. One who's telling the truth may edit the narrative some and remember things forgotten the first time through, but the chronology of events will always be the same. A liar, though, often forgets the sequence of occurrences within his fictional narrative. This happened with Pfister in retelling the story to O'Neil; he'd mixed up when the boy had planted the cross.

Also, while honest witnesses may recall new facts during the second telling, they'll rarely contradict the first version. Initially Pfister had said that Travis was whispering and that he couldn't hear the words. The second version included the detail that he couldn't *understand* the words, which were 'weird,' implying that he *had* heard them.

Dance concluded without a doubt that Pfister was fabricating.

In other circumstances Dance would have handled the interrogation more subtly, tricked the witness into revealing the truth. But this was a man whose liar's personality – she assessed him as a social deceiver – and slippery personal attitude would mean a long bout of tough interviewing to get to the truth. She didn't have time. The second cross, containing today's date, meant that Travis might be planning the next attack right now.

'So, Ken, you're real close to going to jail.'

'What? No!'

Dance didn't mind a bit of double teaming. She glanced at O'Neil, who said, 'You sure are. And we need the truth.'

'Oh, please. Look . . .' But he offered nothing for their examination. 'I didn't lie! Really. Everything I told you is true.'

This was different from assuring her that he'd actually seen what he said he had. Why did the guilty always think they were so clever? She asked, 'Did you *witness* what you told me?'

Under her laser gaze, Pfister looked away. His shoulders slumped. 'No. But it's all true. I *know* it!'

'How can you?' she asked.

'Because I read that somebody saw him doing what I told you. On this blog. *The Chilton Report*.'

Her eyes slipped to O'Neil's. His expression matched hers. She asked, 'Why did you lie?'

He lifted his hands. 'I wanted to make people aware of the danger. I thought people should be more careful with this psycho out there. They should take more precautions, especially with their children. We have to be careful with our children, you know.'

Dance noted the hand gesture, heard the slight hitch in his throat. She knew his liar's mannerisms by now. 'Ken? We have no time for this.'

O'Neil unleashed his handcuffs.

'No, no. I . . .' The head dropped in complete surrender. 'I made some bad business deals. My loans got called and I can't pay them. So I . . .' He sighed.

'So you lied to be a hero? Get some publicity?' O'Neil's face registered disgust as he glanced at the news crews, cordoned off, fifty yards away.

Pfister began to protest. Then his hand drooped. 'Yes. I'm sorry.'

O'Neil jotted something in his notebook. 'I'll have to speak to the prosecutor about this.'

'Oh, please . . . I'm sorry.'

'So you didn't see him at all, but you knew somebody had just left the cross and you knew who it was.'

'Okay, I had an idea. I mean, yes, I knew.'

'Why did you wait hours before telling us?' she snapped.

'I . . . I was afraid. Maybe he was still waiting around here.'

O'Neil asked in a low, ominous voice, 'It didn't occur to you that telling all that crap about ritual sacrifices might've sent us in the wrong direction?'

'I thought you knew all those things anyway. The stories were in that blog. They *have* to be true, don't they?'

Dance said patiently, 'Okay, Ken. Let's start over.'

'Sure. Anything.'

'Were you really in that meeting?'

'Yes, ma'am.'

He was so deeply into the last stage of emotional response in interrogation – acceptance and confession – that she nearly laughed. He was now the epitome of cooperation.

'And what happened then?'

'Okay, I was driving along and I pulled off on the side road here.' He pointed emphatically at his feet. 'When I made the turn there wasn't any cross. I made a couple of phone calls, then turned around and drove back to the intersection. I waited for traffic and looked up the road. There it was.' He pointed again. This time at the cross. 'I didn't see him at all. The hoodie and everything? I got that from the blog. All I can say is that I didn't pass anybody on the shoulder, so he must've come out of the woods. And, yeah, I knew what it meant. The cross. And it scared the shit out of me. The killer had just been there, right in front of me!' A sour laugh. 'I locked the doors so fast . . . I've never done anything brave in my life. Not like my father. He was a fireman, volunteer.'

This happened often with Kathryn Dance. The most important aspect of interrogation and interviewing is to be a good listener, nonjudgmental and aware. Because she honed this skill daily, witnesses — and suspects too — tended to look at her as a therapist. Poor Ken Pfister was confessing.

But he'd have to lie down on somebody else's couch. It wasn't her job to explore his demons.

O'Neil was looking into the trees. Based on what Pfister had originally told them the officers were searching the shoulder. 'We better check out the woods.' An ominous glance at Pfister. 'At least *that* might be helpful.' He called several deputies after him and they headed across the road to search in the forest.

'The traffic you waited for?' she asked Pfister. 'Could the driver have seen anything?'

'I don't know. Maybe, if Travis was still there. They'd have a better view than me.'

'You get a license number, make?'

'No, it was dark, a van or truck. But I remember it was official.'

'Official?'

'Yeah, it said "state" on the back.'

'Which organization?'

'I didn't see. Honest.'

That could be helpful. They'd contact all the California agencies that might've had vehicles in the area. 'Good.'

He seemed ecstatic at the faint praise.

'All right. You're free to go now, Ken. But remember there's still an open complaint against you.'

'Yes, sure, absolutely. Look, I'm really sorry. I didn't mean anything bad.' He scurried off.

As she crossed the road to join O'Neil and the team searching the woods, she watched the pathetic businessman climb into his dinged car.

The stories were in that blog. They have to be true, don't they?

She wanted to die.

Kelley Morgan was silently asking that her prayers be answered. The fumes were choking her. Her vision was going. Her lungs stung, eyes and nose were inflamed.

The pain . . .

But more horrifying than that was the thought of what was happening to her, the terrible changes to her skin and face from the chemicals.

Her thoughts were fuzzy. She had no memory of Travis dragging her down the stairs. She'd come back to consciousness here, in her father's darkened wine cellar in the basement, chained to a pipe. Her mouth taped, her neck aching from where he'd half strangled her.

And choking fiercely from whatever he'd poured onto the floor, the chemical now burning her eyes, her nose, her throat.

Choking, choking . . .

Kelley tried to scream. It was pointless, with the tape covering her face. Besides, there was nobody to hear. Her family was out, wouldn't be back till much later.

The pain . . .

Raging, she'd tried to kick the copper pipe away from the wall. But the metal wouldn't give.

Kill me!

Kelley understood what Travis Brigham was doing. He could've strangled her to death – just kept going another few minutes. Or shot her. But that wasn't good enough for him. No, the luser and perv was getting even by destroying her looks.

The fumes would eat away her eyelashes and brows, destroy her smooth skin, probably even make her hair fall out. He didn't want her to die; no, he wanted to turn her into a monster.

The geeky kid, face all broken out, the luser, the perv . . . He wanted to turn her into what he was.

Kill me, Travis. Why didn't you just kill me?

She thought of the mask. That's why he'd left it. It was a message about what she'd look like when the chemicals were done.

Her head drooped, her arms. She slumped against the wall.

I want to die.

She began to inhale deeply, through her stinging nose.

Everything began to fade. The pain was going, her thoughts, the choking, the stinging in her eyes, the tears.

Drifting away. Light going dark.

Deeper, breathe deeper.

Breathe the poison in.

And, yeah, it was working!

Thank you.

The pain was growing less, the worry less.

Warm relief replaced vanishing consciousness, and her last thought before the darkness grew complete was that at last she was going to be safe from her fears forever.

As she stood beside the roadside cross, staring down at the flowers, Dance was startled by her trilling phone – no cartoon music now; she'd put the ringer back on default. A glance at Caller ID.

'TJ.'

'Boss. Another cross? I just heard.'

'Yeah, today's date too.'

'Oh, man. *Today?*'

'Yep. What'd you find?'

'I'm at Bagel Express. Weird, but nobody here really knows anything about Travis. They said he showed up for work, but kept to himself. Didn't socialize, didn't say much, just left. He talked to one kid here about online games some. But that's it. And nobody's got any idea where he might go. Oh, and his boss said that he was going to fire Travis anyway. Ever since the blog postings he's been getting threats himself. Business is down. Customers're afraid to come in.'

'All right, get back to the office. I need you to call all the state agencies who might've had vehicles in the area this morning. No make or tag. Probably dark, but search for anything.' She told him what Pfister had seen. 'Check with Parks, Caltrans, Fisheries, Environment, everybody you can think of. And find out if Travis has a cell phone and who the provider is. See if they can trace it. I meant to do that earlier.'

They disconnected. Dance called her mother. No answer. She tried her father and the man picked up on the second ring.

'Katie.'

'She's okay?'

'Yes. We're at the house, but we're packing up.'

'What?'

Stuart said, 'The protesters from the hospital? They found out where we live. They're picketing outside.'

'No!' Dance was furious.

He said grimly, 'Interesting to watch your neighbors leave for work and find a dozen people with signs calling you a murderer. One of the posters was quite clever. It said, "Dance of Death". You have to give them credit.'

'Oh, Dad.'

'And somebody taped a poster of Jesus on the front door. He was being crucified. I think they're blaming Edie for that too.'

'I can get you a room anonymously at the inn we use for witnesses.'

'George Sheedy's already gotten us a room under a fake name,' Stuart said. 'I don't know how you feel about it, honey, but I think your mom'd love to see the kids. She's worried about how scared they got when the police came into the hospital.'

'That's a great idea. I'll pick them up from Martine's and bring them to you. When're you checking in?'

'Twenty minutes.' He gave her the address.

'Can I talk to her?'

'She's on the phone, honey, with Betsey. You can see her when you drop the kids off. Sheedy's coming over about the case.'

They disconnected. O'Neil returned from the woods. She asked, 'You find anything?'

'Some footprints that aren't helpful, a little bit of trace – a gray fiber, like the one we found earlier, and a shred of brown paper. An oat flake or grain of some kind. Could be from a bagel, I was thinking. Peter's waiting for it now. He'll get us the analysis as soon as he can.'

'That's great for the case against him. But what we need now is something to tell us where he's hiding.'

And the other question: who's he about to attack next?

As Dance lifted her phone to call Jon Boling, the ring tone sounded. She gave a faint smile at the coincidence. His name showed in Caller ID.

'Jon,' she answered.

As she listened to his words, her smile quickly faded.

15

Kathryn Dance climbed out of her Crown Vic in front of Kelley Morgan's house.

The Monterey County Crime Scene people were here, along with a dozen other state and town law enforcement officers.

Reporters too, plenty of them, most asking about the whereabouts of Travis Brigham. Why exactly hadn't the CBI or the MCSO or the Monterey city police or *anybody* arrested him yet? How hard could it be to find a seventeen-year-old who paraded around dressed like the Columbine and Virginia Tech killers? Who carried knives and machetes, sacrificed animals in bizarre rituals and left roadside crosses on public highways.

He's very active in computer games. Young people who are good at them learn very sophisticated combat and evasion techniques . . .

Dance ignored them all and pushed on, under the police cordon. She arrived at one of the ambulances, the one nearest the house. A young, intense medic with slicked-back dark hair climbed out of the back door. He closed it and then pounded on the side.

The boxy vehicle, containing Kelley, her mother and brother, raced off to the emergency room.

Dance joined Michael O'Neil and the tech. 'How is she?'

'Still unconscious. We've got her on a portable ventilator.' A shrug. 'She's unresponsive. We'll just have to wait and see.'

It was a near miracle that they'd saved Kelley at all.

And Jonathan Boling was to thank. At the news that a second cross had been located, the professor had gone into a frenzy of work to identify the posters critical of Travis in *The Chilton Report,* by correlating posting nics – nicknames – and information from social networking sites and other sources. He'd even compared grammar, word choice and spelling styles in the *Report* posts to those in networking sites and comments in high school yearbooks to identify anonymous posters. He'd enlisted his students too. They'd finally managed to find a dozen names of people in the area who'd posted the blog replies most critical of Travis.

His call a half hour ago was to give Dance their names. She'd immediately ordered TJ, Rey Carraneo and big Al Stemple to start calling and warning them they might be at risk. One of the posters, BellaKelley, the screen name for Kelley Morgan, was unaccounted for. Her mother said she was supposed to be meeting with friends, but hadn't shown up.

Stemple had led a tactical team to her house.

Dance glanced at him now, sitting on the front steps. The huge, shaved-headed man, hovering around forty, was the closest thing that the CBI had to a cowboy. He knew his weaponry, he loved tactical situations and he was pathologically quiet, except when it came to talking about fishing and hunting (accordingly he and Dance had had very few social conversations). Stemple's bulky frame was leaning against the banister of the front porch, as he breathed into an oxygen mask attached to a green tank.

The tech nodded Stemple's way. 'He's okay. Did his good deed for the year. Travis had her chained to a water pipe. Al ripped the pipe out with his bare hands. Problem was, it took him ten minutes. He sucked in a lot of fumes.'

'You okay, Al?' Dance called.

Stemple said something through the mask. Mostly he looked bored. Dance also read irritation in his eyes – probably that he hadn't gotten to shoot the perp.

The tech then said to O'Neil and Dance, 'There's something

you oughta know. Kelley was conscious for a minute or two when we got her out. She told me that Travis has a gun.'

'Gun? He's armed?' Dance and O'Neil shared a troubled gaze.

'That's what she said. I lost her after that. Didn't say anything else.'

Oh, no. An unstable adolescent with a firearm. Nothing was worse, in Dance's opinion.

O'Neil called in the information about the weapon to MCSO, who in turn would relay it to all the officers involved in the search for Travis.

'What was the gas?' Dance asked the tech as they walked to another ambulance.

'We aren't sure. It was definitely toxic.'

The Crime Scene Unit was searching carefully for evidence while a team canvassed the neighborhood for witnesses. Everyone on the block was concerned, everyone was sympathetic. But they were also terrified; no accounts were forthcoming.

But perhaps there simply *were* no witnesses. Bike tread marks in the canyon behind the house suggested how the boy might have snuck up unnoticed to attack Kelley Morgan.

One Crime Scene officer arrived, carrying what turned out to be an eerie mask in a clear evidence bag.

'What the hell's that?' O'Neil asked.

'It was tied to a tree outside her bedroom window, pointing in.'

It was hand-made from papier-mâché, painted white and gray. Bony spikes, like horns, extended from the skull. The eyes were huge and black. The narrow lips were sewn shut, bloody.

'To freak her out, the poor thing. Imagine looking out your window and seeing that.' Dance actually shivered.

As O'Neil took a call, Dance phoned Boling. 'Jon.'

'How is she?' the professor asked eagerly.

'In a coma. We don't know how she'll be. But at least we saved her life . . . *you* saved her life. Thank you.'

'It was Rey too. And my students.'

'Still, I mean it. We can't thank you enough.'

'Any leads to Travis?'

'Some.' She declined to tell him about the eerie mask. Her phone buzzed, call waiting. 'I've got to go. Keep looking for names, Jon.'

'I'm on the case,' he said.

Smiling, she rang off the line with Boling and answered, 'TJ.'

'How's the girl doing?'

'We don't know. Not good. What'd you find?'

'No luck, boss. About eighteen vans, trucks, SUVS or cars registered to the state were in the area this morning. But the ones I've been able to track down, they weren't near where the cross was left. And Travis's phone? The cell provider says he's taken out the battery. Or destroyed it. They can't trace it.'

'Thanks. I've got a couple more jobs. There's a mask the perp left here.'

'Mask? Ski mask?'

'No. It's ritual, looks like. I'm going to have Crime Scene upload a picture of it before they take it to Salinas. See if you can source it. And get the word out to everybody: he's armed.'

'Oh, man, boss. Keeps gettin' better and better.'

'I want to know if there've been any reports of stolen weapons in the county. And find out if the father or any relatives have registered firearms. Check the database. Maybe we can ID the weapon.'

'Sure . . . Oh, wanta say: heard about your mother.' The young man's voice had grown even more sober. 'Anything I can do?'

'Thanks, TJ. Just find out about the mask and the gun.'

After they hung up she examined the mask, thinking: could the rumors have been true? Was Travis into some type of ritualistic practice? Here she'd been skeptical of the posters on the blog, but maybe *she'd* been making a mistake by not paying attention to them.

TJ called back within minutes. There'd been no stolen guns reported in the past two weeks. He'd also looked through the state's firearms database. California liberally allows the purchase of pistols, but all sales must be through a licensed dealer and recorded. Robert Brigham, Travis's father, owned a Colt revolver, .38 caliber.

After she disconnected, Dance noticed O'Neil, his face still, looking into the distance.

She walked up to him. 'Michael, what is it?'

'Got to get back to the office. Something urgent on another case.'

'The Homeland Security thing?' she asked, referring to the Indonesian container case.

He nodded. 'I've got to get in right away. I'll call you as soon as I know more.' His face was grave.

'Okay. Good luck.'

He grimaced, then turned quickly and walked to his car.

Dance felt concern – and emptiness – watching him go. What was so urgent? And why, she thought bitterly, had it struck now, just when she needed him with her?

She called Rey Carraneo. 'Thanks for the work with Jon Boling. What did you find at the Game Shed?'

'Well, he *wasn't* there last night. He lied about that, like you were saying. But as for friends . . . he doesn't really hang out with people there. He'd just go, play games and then leave.'

'Anybody covering for him?'

'That's not my impression.'

Dance then told the young agent to meet her at Kelley Morgan's house.

'Sure.'

'Oh, and Rey, one thing?'

'Yes, ma'am?'

'I need you to pick up something from the supply room at HQ.'

'Sure. What?'

'Body armor. For both of us.'

Approaching the Brigham house, Carraneo beside her, Kathryn Dance wiped her palm on her dark slacks. Touched the grip of her Glock.

I don't want to use it, she thought. Not on a boy.

It wasn't likely that Travis was here; MCSO had been running surveillance on the place since the boy had vanished from the bagel shop. Still, he could have snuck back in. And, Dance was reflecting, if it came to a firefight, she'd shoot if she had to. The rationale was simple. She'd kill another human being for the sake of her own children. She wouldn't let them grow up without any parent at all.

The body armor chafed but gave her some confidence. She forced herself to stop patting the Velcro tabs.

With two county deputies behind them, they stepped onto the spongy front porch, keeping as far from the windows as possible. The family car was in the driveway. The landscape service truck too, a pickup with hollies and rose bushes in the bed.

In a whisper, she briefed Carraneo and the other officers about the younger brother, Sammy. 'He's big and he'll seem unstable, but he probably isn't dangerous. Use nonlethal if it comes down to it.'

'Yes, ma'am.'

Carraneo was wary but calm.

She sent the deputies to the back of the property, and the CBI agents flanked the front door. 'Let's do it.' She banged on the rotting wood. 'Bureau of Investigation. We have a warrant. Open the door, please.'

Another pounding. 'Bureau of Investigation. Open up!'

Hands near their weapons.

An interminable moment later, as she was about to knock again, the door opened and Sonia Brigham stood there staring with eyes wide. She'd been crying.

'Mrs Brigham, is Travis here?'

'I . . .'

'Please. Is Travis home? It's important that you tell us.'

'No. Really.'

'We have a warrant to collect his belongings.' Handing her the blue-backed document, Dance entered, Carraneo behind her. The living room was empty. She noticed both boys' doors were open. She saw no sign of Sammy and glanced into his room, noting elaborate charts, filled with hand-drawn pictures.

She wondered if he was trying to write his own comic or Japanese manga.

'Is your other son here? Sammy?'

'He's out playing. Down by the pond. Please, do you know anything about Travis? Has anybody seen him?'

A creak from the kitchen. Her hand dropped to her gun.

Bob Brigham appeared in the kitchen doorway. He was holding a can of beer. 'Back again,' he muttered. 'With . . .' His voice faded as he snatched the warrant away from his wife and made a pretense of reading it.

He looked at Rey Carraneo as if he were a busboy.

Dance asked, 'Have you heard from Travis?' Eyes swiveling around the house.

'Nope. But you can't be blaming us for what he's up to.'

Sonia snapped, 'He didn't do anything!'

Dance said, 'I'm afraid that the girl today who was attacked identified him.'

Sonia began to protest but fell silent and futilely fought tears.

Dance and Carraneo searched the house carefully. It didn't take long. No sign the boy had been here recently.

'We know you own a pistol, Mr Brigham. Could you check to see if it's missing?'

His eyes narrowed as if he were considering the implications of this. 'It's in my glove compartment. In a lockbox.'

Which California law required in a household where children under eighteen lived.

'Loaded?'

'Uh-huh.' He looked defensive. 'We do a lot of landscaping in Salinas. The gangs, you know.'

'Could you see if it's still there?'

'He's not going to take my gun. He wouldn't dare. He'd get a whipping like he wouldn't believe.'

'Could you check, please?'

The man gave her a look of disbelief. Then he stepped outside. Dance motioned Carraneo to follow him.

Dance looked at the wall and noticed a few pictures of the

family. She was struck by a much happier-looking, and much younger, Sonia Brigham, standing behind the counter at a booth at the Monterey County Fairgrounds. She was thin and pretty. Maybe she'd run the concession before she'd gotten married. Maybe that's where she and Brigham had met.

The woman asked, 'Is the girl all right? The one who got attacked?'

'We don't know.'

Tears dotted her eyes. 'He's got problems. He gets mad some. But . . . this has to be a terrible mistake. I know it!'

Denial was the most intractable of emotional responses to hardship. Tough as a walnut shell.

Travis's father, accompanied by the young agent, returned to the living room. Bob Brigham's ruddy face was troubled. 'It's gone.'

Dance sighed. 'And you wouldn't have it anyplace else?'

He shook his head, avoided Sonia's face.

Timidly she said, 'What good comes of a gun?'

He ignored her.

Dance asked, 'When Travis was younger, were there places he'd go?'

'No,' the father said. 'He was always disappearing. But who knows where he went?'

'How about his friends?'

Brigham snapped, 'Doesn't have any. He's always online. With that computer of his . . .'

'All the time,' echoed his wife softly. 'All the time.'

'Call us if he contacts you. Don't try to get him to surrender, don't take the gun away. Just call us. It's for his own good.'

'Sure,' she said. 'We will.'

'He'll do what I say. Exactly what I say.'

'Bob . . .'

'Shhhh.'

'We're going through his room now,' Dance said.

'Is that all right?' Sonia was nodding at the warrant.

'They can take whatever the fuck they want. Anything that'll help find him before he gets us into more trouble.' Brigham lit a cigarette and dropped the match into the ashtray, a smoking arc. Sonia's face sank as she realized she'd become her son's sole advocate.

Dance pulled her radio off her hip, called the deputies outside. One of them radioed back that he'd found something. The young officer arrived. He held up a lockbox in a latex-gloved hand. It had been smashed open. 'Was in some bushes behind the house. And this too.' An empty box of Remington .38 Special rounds.

'That's it,' the father muttered. 'Mine.'

The house was eerily quiet.

The agents walked into Travis's room. Pulling on her gloves, Dance said to Carraneo, 'I want to see if we can find anything about friends, addresses, places he might like to hang out.'

They searched through the effluence of a teenager's room – clothes, comics, DVDs, manga, anime, games, computer parts, notebooks, sketchpads. She noticed there was little music and nothing at all about sports.

Dance blinked as she looked through a notebook. The boy had done a drawing of a mask identical to the one outside Kelley Morgan's window.

Even the small sketch chilled her.

Hidden away in a drawer were tubes of Clearasil and books about remedies for acne, diet and medication and even dermabrasion to remove scarring. Though Travis's problem was less serious than with many teens, it was probably what he saw as a major reason he was an outcast.

Dance continued to search. Under the bed she found a strongbox. It was locked but she had seen a key in the top desk drawer. It worked in the box. Expecting drugs or porn, she was surprised at the contents: stacks of cash.

Carraneo was looking over her shoulder. 'Hmm.'

About four thousand dollars. The bills were crisp and ordered, as if he'd gotten them from a bank or an ATM, not from buyers in drug deals. Dance added the box to the evidence they'd take back. Not only did she not want to fund Travis's escape, if he came back for it, but she didn't doubt that his father would pilfer the money in an instant, if he found the stash.

'There's this,' Carraneo said. He was holding up printouts of pictures, mostly candids, of pretty girls about high school age, taken around Robert Louis Stevenson High School. None obscene or taken up the girls' skirts, though, or of locker rooms or bathrooms.

Stepping outside the room, Dance asked Sonia, 'Do you know who they are?'

Neither parent did.

She turned back to the pictures. She realized that she'd seen one of the girls before – in a news story about the June 9 crash. Caitlin Gardner, the girl who'd survived. The photo was more formal than the others – the pretty girl looking off to the side, smiling blandly. Dance turned the thin, glossy rectangle of paper over and noted a portion of a picture of a sports team on the other side. Travis had cut the picture out of a yearbook.

Had he asked Caitlin for a picture and been refused? Or had he been too shy even to ask?

The agents searched for a half hour but found no clues as to where Travis might be, no phone numbers, email addresses or friends' names. He kept no address book or calendar.

Dance wanted to see what was on his laptop. She opened the lid. It was in hibernate mode and booted up immediately. She wasn't surprised when it asked for a password. Dance asked the boy's father, 'Do you have any idea what the code is?'

'Like he'd tell us.' He gestured at the computer. 'Now, that's the problem right there, you know. That's what went wrong, playing all those games. All the violence. They shoot people and cut them up, do all kinds of shit.'

Sonia seemed to reach a breaking point. 'Well, you played soldier when you were growing up, I know you did. All boys play games like that. It doesn't mean they turn into killers!'

'That was a different time,' he muttered. 'It was better, healthier. We only played killing Indians and Viet Cong. Not normal people.'

Carrying the laptop, notebooks, strongbox and hundreds of

pages of printouts and notes and pictures, Dance and Carraneo walked to the door.

'Did you ever think about one thing?' Sonia asked.

Dance paused, turned.

'That even if he did it, went after those girls, that maybe it wasn't his fault. All those terrible things that they said about him just pushed him over the edge. They attacked *him,* with those words, those hateful words. And my Travis never said a single word against any one of them.' She controlled her tears. '*He's* the victim here.'

16

On the highway to Salinas, not far from beautiful Laguna Seca racecourse, Kathryn Dance braked her unmarked Ford to a halt in front of a construction worker holding a portable stop sign. Two large bulldozers slowly traversed the highway in front of her, shooting ruddy dust into the air.

She was on the phone with Deputy David Reinhold, the young officer who'd delivered Tammy Foster's computer to her and Boling. Rey Carraneo had sped to the MCSO Crime Scene Unit in Salinas and dropped Travis's Dell off for processing into evidence.

'I've logged it in,' Reinhold told her. 'And run it for prints and other trace. Oh, and it probably wasn't necessary, Agent Dance, but I ran a nitrate swab for explosives too.'

Computers were occasionally booby-trapped – not as IED weapons, but to destroy compromising data contained in the files.

'Good, Deputy.'

The officer certainly had initiative. She recalled his quick blue eyes and his smart decision to pull out the battery of Tammy's computer.

'Some of the prints are Travis's,' the young deputy said. 'But there are others too. I ran them. A half dozen were from Samuel Brigham.'

'The boy's brother.'

'Right. And a few others. No match in AIFIS. But I can tell you they're larger, probably male.'

Dance wondered if the boy's father had tried to get inside.

Reinhold said, 'I'm happy to try to crack into the system, if you want. I've taken some courses.'

'Appreciate it, but I'm having Jonathan Boling – you met him in my office – handle that.'

'Sure, Agent Dance. Whatever you'd like. Where are you?'

'I'm out now, but you can have it delivered to the CBI. Have Agent Scanlon take custody. He'll sign the card and receipt.'

'I'll do it right now, Kathryn.'

They disconnected and she looked around impatiently, waiting for the construction flagman to allow her through. She was surprised to see the area dug up so completely – dozens of trucks and road-grading equipment were tearing apart the ground. She'd driven here just last week and the work hadn't yet begun.

This was the big highway project that Chilton had written about in the blog, the shortcut to Highway 101, in the thread titled 'Yellow Brick Road', suggesting gold – and wondering if somebody was profiting illegally on the project.

She noted that the equipment belonged to Clint Avery Construction, one of the largest companies on the Peninsula. The workers here were large men, working hard, sweaty. They were mostly white, which was unusual. Much of the labor on the Peninsula was performed by Latino workers.

One of them looked at her solemnly – recognizing her car for an unmarked law enforcement vehicle – but he made no special effort to speed her through.

Finally, at his leisure, he waved the traffic on, his eyes looking over Dance closely, it seemed to her.

She left the extensive roadwork behind and cruised down the highway and onto side streets until she came to Central Coast College, where summer session was under way. A student pointed out Caitlin Gardner sitting at a picnic bench with several other girls, who hovered around her protectively. Caitlin was pretty and blond and sported a ponytail. Tasteful studs and hoops decorated both ears. She resembled any one of the hundreds of coeds here.

After leaving the Brighams, Dance had called the Gardner house and learned from Caitlin's mother that the girl was taking some college courses here for credit at Robert Louis Stevenson High, where she'd start her senior year in a few months.

Caitlin's eyes, Dance noticed, were focused away and then her gaze shifted to Dance. Not knowing who she was – probably thinking she was another reporter – she began to gather her books. Two of the other girls followed their friend's troubled eyes and rose in a phalanx to give cover so Caitlin could escape.

But they then noticed Dance's body armor and weapon. And grew cautious, pausing.

'Caitlin,' Dance called.

The girl stopped.

Dance approached and showed her ID, introduced herself. 'I'd like to talk to you.'

'She's pretty tired,' a friend said.

'And upset.'

Dance smiled. To Caitlin she said, 'I'm sure you are. But it's important that I talk to you. If you don't mind.'

'She shouldn't even be in school,' another girl said. 'But she's taking classes out of respect to Trish and Vanessa.'

'That's good of you.' Dance wondered how attending summer school honored the dead.

The curious icons of adolescents . . .

The first friend said firmly, 'Caitlin's, like, really, really—'

Dance turned to the frizzy-haired brunette, her personality brittle, lost the smile and said bluntly, 'I'm speaking to Caitlin.'

The girl fell silent.

Caitlin mumbled, 'I guess.'

'Come on over here,' Dance said pleasantly. Caitlin followed her across the lawn and they sat at another picnic table. She clutched her book bag to her chest and was looking around the campus nervously. Her foot bobbed and she tugged at an earlobe.

She appeared terrified, even more so than Tammy.

Dance tried to put her at ease. 'So, summer school.'

'Yeah. My friends and me. Better than working, or sitting home.'

The last word has been delivered in a tone that suggested a fair amount of parental hassle.

'What're you studying?'

'Chemistry and biology.'

'That's a good way to ruin your summer.'

She laughed. 'It's not so bad. I'm kinda good at science.'

'Headed for med school?'

'I'm hoping.'

'Where?'

'Oh, I don't know yet. Probably Berkeley undergrad. Then I'll see.'

'I spent time up there. Great town.'

'Yeah? What'd you study?'

Dance smiled and said, 'Music.'

In fact she hadn't taken a single class on that campus of the University of California. She'd been a busker – a musician playing guitar and singing for money on the streets of Berkeley – very little money, in her case.

'So, how you doing with all of this?'

Caitlin's eyes went flat. She muttered, 'Not so great. I mean, it's so terrible. The accident, that was one thing. But then, what happened to Tammy and Kelley . . . that was awful. How is she?'

'Kelley? We don't know yet. Still in a coma.'

One of the friends had overheard and called, 'Travis bought this poison gas online. Like from neo-Nazis.'

True? Or rumor?

Dance said, 'Caitlin, he's disappeared. He's hiding somewhere and we have to find him before he causes more harm. How well did you know him?'

'Not too good. We had a class or two together. I'd see him in the halls sometimes. That's all.'

Suddenly she started in panic and her eyes jumped to a nearby stand of bushes. A boy was pushing his way through them. He looked around, retrieved a football and then returned into the foliage for the field on the other side.

'Travis had a crush on you, right?' Dance pressed on.

'No!' she said. And Dance deduced that the girl did in fact think this; she could tell from the rise in the pitch of her voice, one of the few indicators of deception that can be read without the benefit of doing a prior baseline.

'Not just a little?'

'Maybe he did. But a lot of boys . . . You know what it's like.' Her eyes did a sweep of Dance – meaning: boys might've had a crush on you too. Even if it was a long, long time ago.

'Did you two talk?'

'Sometimes about assignments. That's all.'

'Did he ever mention anyplace he liked to hang out at?'

'Not really. Nothing, like, specific. He said there were some neat places he liked to go. Near the water, mostly. The shore reminded him of some places in this game he played.'

This was something, that he liked the ocean. He could be hiding out in one of the shorefront parks. Maybe Point Lobos. In this land of temperate climate he could easily survive with a waterproof sleeping bag.

'Does he have any friends he might be staying with?'

'Really, I don't know him real well. But he didn't have any friends I ever saw, not like my girlfriends and me. He was, like, online all the time. He was smart and everything. But he wasn't into school. Even at lunch or study period, he'd just sit outside with his computer and if he could hack into a signal he'd go online.'

'Are you scared of him, Caitlin?'

'Well, yeah.' As if it was obvious.

'But you haven't said anything bad about him on *The Chilton Report* or social networking sites, have you?'

'No.'

What was the girl so upset about? Dance couldn't read her emotions, which were extreme. More than just fear. 'Why haven't you posted anything about him?'

'Like, I don't go there. It's bullshit.'

'Because you feel sorry for him.'

'Yeah.' Caitlin frantically played with one of the four studs in her left ear. 'Because . . .'

'What?'

The girl was very upset now. Tension bursting. Tears dotted her eyes. She whispered, 'Because it's my fault what happened.'

'What do you mean?'

'The accident. It's my fault.'

'Go on, Caitlin.'

'See, there was this guy at the party? A guy I kind of like. Mike D'Angelo.'

'At the party?'

'Right. And he was totally ignoring me. Hanging out with this other girl, Brianna, rubbing her back, you know. Right in front of me. I wanted to make him jealous, so I walked up to Travis and was hanging out with him. I gave him my car keys right in front of Mike and asked him to take me home. I was, like, oh, let's drop Trish and Vanessa off and then you and me can hang out.'

'And you thought it would make Mike feel bad?'

She nodded tearfully. 'It was so stupid! But he was acting like such a shit, flirting with Brianna.' Her shoulders were arched in tension. 'I shouldn't've. But I was so hurt. If I hadn't done that, nothing would've happened.'

This explained why Travis had been driving that night.

All to make another boy jealous.

The girl's explanation also suggested a whole new scenario. Maybe on the drive back Travis had realized that he was being used by Caitlin, or maybe he was angry at her for having a crush on Mike. Had he intentionally crashed the car? Murder/suicide – an impulsive gesture, not unheard of when it came to young love.

'So he's got to be mad at me.'

'What I'm going to do is put an officer outside your house.'

'Really?'

'Sure. It's still early at summer school, right? You don't have any tests coming up, do you?'

'No. We just started.'

'Well, why don't you head home now?'

'You think?'

'Yeah. And stay there until we find him.' Dance took down the girl's address. 'If you can think of anything more – about where he might be – please let me know.'

'Sure.' The girl took Dance's card. Together they walked back to her crew.

Floating through her ears was the haunting quena flute of Jorge Cumbo, with the South American group Urubamba. The music calmed her, and it was with some regret that Dance pulled into the Monterey Bay Hospital parking lot, parked and paused the music.

Of the protesters, only about half remained. The Reverend Fisk and his redheaded bodyguard were absent.

Probably trying to track down her mother.

Dance walked inside.

Several nurses and doctors came up to express their sympathy – two nurses wept openly when they saw their coworker's daughter.

She walked downstairs to the office of the head of security. The room was empty. She glanced up the hall toward the intensive care unit. She headed in that direction and pushed through the door.

Dance blinked as she turned to the room where Juan Millar had died. It was cordoned off with yellow police tape. Signs read *Do Not Enter. Crime Scene*. It was Harper's doing, she reflected angrily. This was idiocy. There were only five intensive care rooms down here – three were occupied – and the prosecutor had sealed one of them? What if two more patients were admitted? And what's more, she thought, the crime had taken place nearly a month ago, the room occupied by presumably a dozen patients since then, not to mention cleaned by fastidious crews. There couldn't possibly be more evidence to collect.

Grandstanding and public relations.

She started away.

And nearly ran right into Juan Millar's brother, Julio, the man who had attacked her earlier in the month.

The dark, compact man, in a dark suit, pulled up short, eyes fixed on her. He was carrying a folder of papers, which sagged in his hand, as he stared at Dance, only four or five feet away.

Dance tensed and stepped back slightly, to give her time to get to her pepper spray or cuffs. If he came at her again she was prepared to defend herself, though she could imagine what the media would do with the story of the daughter of a suspected mercy killer Macing the brother of the euthanized victim.

But Julio simply stared at her with a curious look – not of anger or hate, but almost amusement at the coincidence of running into her. He whispered, 'Your mother . . . how could she?'

The words sounded rehearsed, as if he'd been waiting for the chance to recite them.

Dance began to speak, but Julio clearly expected no response. He walked slowly out of the door that led to the back exit.

And that was it.

No harsh words, no threats, no violence.

How could she?

Her heart pounding furiously from the bewildering confrontation, she recalled that her mother had said Julio had been here earlier. Dance wondered why he was back now.

With a last glance at the police tape, Dance left the ICU and walked to the office of the head of security.

'Oh, Agent Dance,' Henry Bascomb said, blinking.

She smiled a greeting. 'They've got the room taped off?'

'You were back there?' he asked.

Dance immediately noted the stress in the man's posture and voice. He was thinking quickly and he was uneasy. What was that about? Dance wondered.

'Sealed off?' she repeated.

'Yeah, that's right, ma'am.'

Ma'am? Dance nearly laughed at the formal word. She, O'Neil, Bascomb and some of his former deputy buddies had shared beer and quesadillas down on Fisherman's Wharf a few months ago. She decided to get to the nut of it: 'I've only got a minute or two, Henry. It's about my mother's case.'

'How's she doing?'

Dance was thinking: I don't know any better than you do, Henry. She said, 'Not great.'

'Give her my best.'

'I'll do that. Now, I'd like to see the employee and front desk logs of who was at the hospital when Juan died.'

'Sure.' Only he didn't mean sure at all. He meant what he said next: 'But the thing is, I can't.'

'Why's that, Henry?'

'I've been told I can't let you see anything. No paperwork. We're not even supposed to be talking to you.'

'Whose orders?'

'The board,' Bascomb said tentatively.

'And?' Dance continued, prodding.

'Well, it was Mr Harper, that prosecutor. He talked to the board. And the chief of staff.'

'But that's discoverable information. The defense attorney has a right to it.'

'Oh, I know that. But he said that's how you'll have to get it.'

'I don't want to take it. Just look through it, Henry.'

There was absolutely nothing illegal about her looking through the material, and it wouldn't ultimately affect the case because what was contained in the logs and sign-in sheets would come out eventually.

Bascomb's face revealed how torn he was. 'I understand. But I can't. Not unless there's a subpoena.'

Harper had spoken to the security chief for one purpose only: to bully Dance and her family.

'I'm sorry,' he said sheepishly.

'No, that's okay, Henry. Did he give you a reason?'

'No.' He said this too quickly, and Dance could easily see eye aversion that differed from what she knew of the man's baseline behavior.

'What did he say, Henry?'

A pause.

She leaned toward him.

The guard looked down. 'He said . . . he said he didn't trust you. And he didn't like you.'

Dance stoked her smile as best she could. 'Well, that's the good news, I suppose. He's the last person in the world I'd want a thumbs-up from.'

The time was now 5:00 p.m.

From the hospital lot, Dance called the office and learned there'd been no significant developments in the hunt for Travis Brigham. The Highway Patrol and sheriff's office were running a manhunt, focusing on the traditional locales and sources for information about runaways and juvenile fugitives: his school and classmates and the shopping malls. That his transportation was limited to a bike was helpful, in theory, but hadn't led to any sightings.

Rey Carraneo had learned little from Travis's rambling notes and drawings, but was still sifting through them for leads to the boy's whereabouts. TJ was trying to track down the source of the mask, and calling the potential victims from the blog. Since Dance had learned from Caitlin that Travis liked the shore, she gave him the added task of contacting the parks department and alerting them that the boy might be hiding out somewhere in the thousands of square acres of state land in the area.

'Okay, boss,' he said wearily, revealing not fatigue but the same hopelessness that she felt.

She then spoke to Jon Boling.

'I got the boy's computer. That deputy dropped it off, Reinhold. He sure knows his stuff when it comes to computers.'

'He shows initiative. He'll go places. You having any luck?'

'No. Travis is smart. He's not relying on your basic password protection alone. He's got some proprietary encryption programs that have locked his drive. We may not be able to crack it, but I've called an associate at school. If anybody can get inside, they can.'

Hmm, Dance thought, how gender-neutral: 'associate' and 'they'. Dance translated the words as 'young, gorgeous female grad student, probably blond and voluptuous'.

Boling added in techspeak that a brute force attack was under way via an uplink to a supercomputer at UC-Santa Cruz. 'The system might crack the code within the next hour—'

'Really?' she asked brightly.

'Or, I was going to say, within the next two or three hundred years. It depends.'

Dance thanked him and told him to head home for the evening. He sounded disappointed and, after explaining that he had no plans for that night, said he'd continue to search for the names of posters who might be at risk.

She then collected the children from Martine's and they all drove to the inn where her parents were hiding out.

As she drove, she was recalling the incidents surrounding young Juan Millar's death, but in truth she hadn't focused on them much at the time. The manhunt had demanded all her attention: Daniel Pell – the cult leader, killer and vicious manipulator – and his partner, a woman equally dangerous, had remained on the Peninsula after his escape, to stalk and murder new victims. Dance and O'Neil had worked nonstop pursuing them, and Juan Millar's death had not occupied her thoughts, other than to engender a piercing remorse for the part, though small, she'd played in it.

If she'd guessed that her mother might have become entwined in the case, she would have been much more attentive.

Ten minutes later Dance parked the car in the gravel lot of the inn. Maggie offered, 'Wow', bouncing on the seat as she examined the place.

'Yeah, neat.' Though Wes was more subdued.

The quaint cottage – part of the luxurious Carmel Inn – was

one of a dozen stand-alone cabins separate from the main building.

'There's a pool!' Maggie cried. 'I want to go swimming.'

'Sorry, I forgot your suits.' Dance nearly suggested Edie and Stuart could take them shopping for swimwear, but then recalled that her mother shouldn't be out in public – not with Reverend Fisk and his birds of prey on the loose. 'I'll bring them by tomorrow. And, hey, Wes, there's a tennis court. You can practice with Grandpa.'

'Okay.'

They climbed out, Dance collecting their suitcases, which she'd packed earlier. The children would be staying here tonight with their grandparents.

They walked along the path bordered with vines and low, green chick-and-hen succulents.

'Which one's theirs?' Maggie asked, bouncing along the trail.

Dance pointed it out and the girl launched herself forward fast. She hit the buzzer and a moment later, just as Dance and Wes arrived, the door opened and Edie smiled at her grand-children and let them inside.

'Grandma,' Maggie called. 'This is cool!'

'It's very nice. Come on in.'

Edie gave a smile to Dance, who tried to read it. But the expression was as informative as a blank page.

Stuart hugged the children.

Wes asked, 'You okay, Grandma?'

'I'm absolutely fine. How're Martine and Steve?'

'Okay,' the boy said.

'The twins and I built a mountain out of pillows,' Maggie said. 'With caves.'

'You'll have to tell me all about it.'

Dance saw they had a visitor. Distinguished defense attorney George Sheedy rose and stepped forward, shaking Dance's hand and saying hello in his basso profundo voice. A briefcase was open on the coffee table in the sitting area of the suite, and yellow pads and printouts sat in cluttered stacks. The lawyer said hello to the children. He was courteous, but from his posture and expression Dance could tell immediately that the conversation she'd interrupted was a hard one. Wes regarded Sheedy suspiciously.

After Edie dispensed treats to the children, they headed outside to a playground.

'Stay with your sister,' Dance commanded.

'Okay. Come on,' the boy said to Maggie and, juggling juice boxes and cookies, they left. Dance glanced out the window and noted that she could see the playground from here. The pool was behind a locked gate. With children, you could never be too vigilant.

Edie and Stuart returned to the couch. Three cups of coffee rested, largely untouched, on a low driftwood table. Her mother would have instinctively prepared them the moment Sheedy arrived.

The lawyer asked about the case and the hunt for Travis Brigham.

Dance gave sketchy answers – which, in fact, were the best she could offer.

'And that girl, Kelley Morgan?'

'Still unconscious, it seems.'

Stuart shook his head.

The subject of the Roadside Cross attacks was tucked away and Sheedy glanced at Edie and Stuart, eyebrow raised. Dance's father said, 'You can tell her. Go ahead. Everything.'

Sheedy explained, 'We're tipping to what Harper's game plan seems to be. He's very conservative, he's very religious and he's on record as opposing the Death with Dignity Act.'

The proposal cropped up every so often in California; it was a statute, like Oregon's, that would allow physicians to assist people who wished to end their lives. Like abortion, it was a controversial topic and the pros and cons were highly polarized. Presently in California if somebody helped a person commit suicide, that assistance was considered a felony.

'So he wants to make an example of Edie. The case isn't about assisted suicide – your mother tells me that Juan was too badly injured to administer the drugs to himself. But Harper wants to send a message that the state will seek tough penalties against anybody who helps with a suicide. His meaning: don't support the law because DAs will be looking real closely at each case. One step out of line and doctors or anybody helping someone die will get prosecuted. Hard.'

The distinguished voice continued grimly, speaking to Dance, 'That means he's not interested in plea bargains. He wants to go to trial and run a big, splashy, public relations–driven contest. Now, in this instance, because somebody killed Juan, that makes it murder.'

'First degree,' Dance said. She knew the penal code the way some people knew the *Joy of Cooking*.

Sheedy nodded. 'Because it's premeditated and Millar was a law enforcement officer.'

'But not special circumstances,' Dance said, looking at her mother's pale face. Special circumstances would allow for the death penalty. But for that punishment to apply, Millar would have had to've been on duty at the time he was killed.

But Sheedy said, scoffing, 'Believe it or not, he's considering that.'

'How? How can he possibly be?' Dance asked heatedly.

'Because Millar was never officially signed out of his tour.'

'He's playing a technicality like that?' Dance snapped in disgust.

'Is Harper mad?' Stuart muttered.

'No, he's driven and he's self-righteous. Which is scarier than being mad. He'll get better publicity with a capital case. And that's what he wants. Don't worry, there is no way you'd be convicted of special circumstance murder,' he said, turning toward Edie. 'But I think he's going to start there.'

Still, Murder One was harrowing enough. That could mean twenty-five years in prison for Edie.

The lawyer continued, 'Now, for our defense, justification doesn't apply, or mistake or self-defense. Ending the man's pain and suffering would be relevant at sentencing. But if the jury believed you intended to end his life, however merciful your motive, they would have to find you guilty of first-degree murder.'

'The defense, then,' Dance said, 'is on the facts.'

'Exactly. First, we attack the autopsy and the cause of death. The coroner's conclusion was that Millar died because the morphine drip was open too far and that an antihistamine had been added to the solution. That led to respiratory, and then cardiac, failure. We'll get experts to say that this was wrong. He died of natural causes as a result of the fire. The drugs were irrelevant.

'Second, we assert that Edie didn't do it at all. Somebody else administered the drugs either intentionally to kill him, or by mistake. We want to try to find people who might've been around – somebody who might've seen the killer. Or somebody who might *be* the killer. What about it, Edie? Was anybody near ICU around the time Juan died?'

The woman replied, 'There were some nurses down on that wing. But that was all. His family was gone. And there were no visitors.'

'Well, I'll keep looking into it.' Sheedy's face was growing grave. 'Now, we come to the big problem. The medication that was added to the IV was diphenhydramine.'

'The antihistamine,' Edie said.

'In the police raid on your house, they recovered a bottle of a brand-name version of diphenhydramine. The bottle was empty.'

'What?' Stuart gasped.

'It was found in the garage, hidden under some rags.'

'Impossible.'

'And a syringe with a small bit of dried morphine on it. The same brand of morphine that was in Juan Millar's IV drip.'

Edie muttered, 'I didn't put it there. Of course I didn't.'

'We know that, Mom.'

The lawyer added, 'Apparently no fingerprints or significant trace.'

Dance said, 'The perp planted it.'

'Which is what we'll try to prove. Either he or she intended to kill Millar, or did it by mistake. In either case, they hid the bottle and syringe in your garage to shift the blame.'

Edie was frowning. She looked at her daughter. 'Remember earlier in the month, just after Juan died, I told you I heard a noise outside. It was coming from the garage. I'll bet somebody was there.'

'That's right,' Dance agreed, though she couldn't actually recall it – the manhunt for Daniel Pell had occupied all her thoughts then.

'Of course . . .' Dance fell silent.

'What?'

'Well, one thing we'll have to work around. I'd stationed a deputy outside their house – for security. Harper will want to know why he didn't see anything.'

'Or,' Edie said, 'we should find out if he *did* see the intruder.'

'Right,' Dance said quickly. She gave Sheedy the name of the deputy.

'I'll check that out too.' He added, 'The only other thing we have is a report that the patient told you, "Kill me." And you told several people that. There are witnesses.'

'Right,' Edie said, sounding defensive, her eyes slipping to Dance.

The agent suddenly had a terrible thought: would she be called to testify against her mother? She felt physically ill at this idea. She said, 'But she wouldn't tell anybody that if she were really intent on killing somebody.'

'True. But remember, Harper is going for splash. Not for logic. A quote like that . . . well, let's hope Harper doesn't find out about it.' He rose. 'When I hear from the experts and get details of the autopsy report, I'll let you know. Are there any questions?'

Edie's face revealed that, yes, she had about a thousand. But she merely shook her head.

'It's not hopeless, Edie. The evidence in the garage is troublesome but we'll do the best we can with that.' Sheedy gathered up his papers, organized them and put them into his briefcase. He shook everyone's hand and gave reassuring smiles to them all.

Stuart saw him to the door, the floor creaking under his solid weight.

Dance too rose. She said to her mother, 'Are you sure the kids won't be too much? I can take them back to Martine's.'

'No, no. I've been looking forward to seeing them.' She pulled on a sweater. 'In fact, I think I'll go outside and visit.'

Dance briefly embraced her, feeling stiffness in her mother's shoulders. For an awkward moment the women held each other's eyes. Then Edie stepped outside.

Dance hugged her father too. 'Why don't you come over for dinner tomorrow?' she asked him.

'We'll see.'

'Really. It'd be good. For Mom. For you, everybody.'

'I'll talk to her about it.'

Dance headed back to the office where she spent the next few hours coordinating stakeouts of the possible victims' houses and of the Brighams' residence, deploying the manpower as best she could. And running the frustratingly hopeless search for the boy, who was proving to be as invisible as the electrons making up the vicious messages that had sent him on his deadly quest.

Comfort.

Pulling up to her house in Pacific Grove at 11:00 p.m., Dance felt a tiny shiver of relief. After this long, long day she was so glad to be home.

The classic Victorian was dark green with gray banisters, shutters and trim – it was in the northwestern part of Pacific Grove; if the time of year, the wind and your attitude about leaning over a shaky railing coincided, you could see the ocean.

Walking into the small entryway, she flicked the light on and locked the door behind her. The dogs charged up to greet her. Dylan, a black-and-tan German shepherd, and Patsy, a dainty flat-coat retriever. They were named respectively for the greatest folk-rock songwriter and for the greatest country-western vocalist in the past hundred years.

Dance reviewed emails but there were no new developments

in the case. In the kitchen, spacious but equipped with appliances from a different decade, she poured a glass of wine and foraged for some leftovers, settling on half a turkey sandwich that hadn't been resident in the fridge for too long.

She fed the dogs and then let them out into the back. But as she was about to return to her computer she jumped at the raucous fuss they made, barking and charging down the stairs. They did this sometimes when a squirrel or cat had had the poor judgment to come for a visit. But that was rare at this time of night. Dance set the wineglass down and, tapping the butt of her Glock, walked out onto the deck.

She gasped.

A cross lay on the ground about forty feet away from the house.

No!

Drawing the gun, she grabbed a flashlight, called the dogs to her and swept the beam into the backyard. It was a narrow space, but extended for fifty feet behind the house and was filled with monkey flowers, scrub oak and maple trees, asters, lupine, potato vines, clover and renegade grass. The only flora that did well here thrived on sandy soil and shade.

She saw no one, though there were places where an intruder could remain hidden from the deck.

Dance hurried down the stairs into the dimness and looked around at the dozen of unsettling shadows cast by branches rocking in the wind.

Pausing, then moving slowly, her eyes on the paths and the dogs, which tracked around the yard, edgy, wary.

Their tense gait and Dylan's raised hackles were unsettling.

She approached the corner of the yard slowly. Looking for movement, listening for footsteps. When she heard and saw no signs of an intruder, she shined the flashlight onto the ground.

It *seemed* to be a cross, but up close Dance couldn't tell if it had been left intentionally or been created by falling branches. It wasn't bound with wire and there were no flowers. But the back gate was a few feet away, which, though locked, could easily have been vaulted by a seventeen-year-old boy.

Travis Brigham, she recalled, knew her name. And could easily find where she lived.

She walked in a slow circle around the cross. Were those footsteps beside it in the trampled grass? She couldn't tell.

The uncertainty was almost more troubling than if the cross had been left as a threat.

Dance returned to the house, stuffing her weapon in the holster.

She locked up and stepped into the living room, filled with furniture as mismatched as that in Travis Brigham's house, but nicer and homier, no leather or chrome. Mostly overstuffed, upholstered in rusts and earth colors. All purchased during shopping trips with her late husband. Dropping onto the sofa, Dance noticed a missed call. She flipped eagerly to the log. It was from Jon Boling, not her mother.

Boling was reporting that the 'associate' had had no luck as yet with cracking the pass code. The supercomputer would be running all night, and he'd let Dance know the progress in the morning. Or, if she wanted, she could call back. He'd be up late.

Dance debated about calling – felt an urge to – but then decided to keep the line free in case her mother called. She then phoned the MCSO, got the senior deputy on duty and requested a Crime Scene run to collect the cross. She told him where it was located. He said he'd get somebody there in the morning.

She then showered; despite the steamy water, she kept shivering, as an unfortunately persistent image lodged in her thoughts: the mask from Kelley Morgan's house, the black eyes, the sewn-shut mouth.

When she climbed into bed, her Glock was three feet away, on the bedside table, unholstered and loaded with a full clip and one 'in the bedroom' – the chamber.

She closed her eyes but, as exhausted as she was, she couldn't sleep.

And it wasn't the pursuit of Travis Brigham that was keeping her awake, nor the scare earlier. Not even the image of that damn mask.

No, the source of her keen restlessness was a simple comment that kept looping over and over in her mind.

Her mother's response to Sheedy's question about witnesses in the ICU the night that Juan Millar was killed.

There were some nurses down on that wing. But that was all. His family was gone. And there were no visitors.

Dance couldn't recall for certain, but she was almost positive that when she'd mentioned the deputy's death to her mother just after it happened, Edie had acted surprised by the news; she'd told her daughter that she'd been so busy on her own wing that she hadn't gone down to the ICU that night.

If Edie hadn't been in intensive care that night, as she'd claimed, then how could she be so certain it was deserted?

WEDNESDAY

17

At 8:00 in the morning, Kathryn Dance walked into her office and smiled to see Jon Boling, in too-large latex gloves, tapping on the keyboard of Travis's computer.

'I know what I'm doing. I watch *NCIS*.' He grinned. 'I like it better than *CSI*.'

'Hey, boss, we need a TV show about us,' TJ said from a table he'd dragged into the corner, his workstation for his search for the origins of the eerie mask from the Kelley Morgan scene.

'I like that.' Boling picked up on the joke. 'A show about kinesics, sure. You could call it *The Body Reader*. Can I be a special guest star?'

Though she was hardly in a humorous mood, Dance laughed.

TJ said, 'I get to be the handsome young sidekick who's always flirting with the gorgeous girl agents. Can we hire some gorgeous girl agents, boss? Not that you aren't. But you know what I mean.'

'How're we doing?'

Boling explained that the supercomputer linked to Travis's hadn't had any luck cracking the boy's pass code.

One hour, or three hundred years.

'Nothing to do but keep waiting.' He pulled off the gloves and returned to tracking down the identities of posters who might be at risk.

'And, Rey?' Dance glanced at quiet Rey Carraneo, who still

was going through the many pages of notes and sketches they'd found in Travis's bedroom.

'Lot of gobbledygook, ma'am,' Carraneo said, the Anglo word very stiff in a Latino mouth. 'Languages I don't recognize, numbers, doodles, spaceships, trees with faces in them, aliens. And pictures of bodies cut open, hearts and organs. Kid's pretty messed up.'

'Any places at all he's mentioned?'

'Sure,' the agent said. 'They just don't seem to be on earth.'

'Here are some more names.' Boling handed her a sheet of paper with another six names and addresses of posters.

Dance looked up the phone numbers in the state database and called to warn them that Travis presented a threat.

It was then that her computer pinged with an incoming email. She read it, surprised to see the sender. Michael O'Neil. He must've been real busy; he rarely sent her messages, preferring to talk to her in person.

K—

Hate to say, but the container situation is heating up big time. TSA and Homeland Sec. are getting worried.

I'll still help you out on the Travis Brigham case – ride herd on forensics and drop in when I can – but this one'll take up most of my time. Sorry.

—M

The case involving the shipping container from Indonesia. Apparently he couldn't put it on hold any longer. Dance was fiercely disappointed. Why *now*? She sighed in frustration. A twinge of loneliness too. She realized that between the Los Angeles homicide case against J. Doe and the roadside crosses situation, she and O'Neil had seen each other almost daily for the past week. That was more, on average, than she'd seen her husband.

She really wanted his expertise in the pursuit of Travis Brigham. And she wasn't ashamed to admit that she simply wanted his company too. Funny how just talking, sharing thoughts and speculations was such an elixir. But his case was clearly important and that was enough for her. She typed a fast reply.

Good luck, miss you.

Backspaced, deleting the final two words and the punctuation. She rewrote: Good luck. Stay in touch.

Then he was gone from her mind.

Dance had a small TV in the office. It was on now and she happened to glance at it. She blinked in shock. On the screen at the moment was a wooden cross.

Did it have to do with the case? Had they found another one?

Then the camera panned on and settled on the Reverend R. Samuel Fisk. It was a report on the euthanasia protest – which now, she realized with a sinking heart, had shifted to focus on her mother. The cross was in the hand of a protester.

She turned up the volume. A reporter was asking Fisk if he'd actually called for the murder of abortion doctors, as *The Chilton Report* had said. With eyes that struck her as icy and calculating, the man of the cloth gazed back at the camera and said that his words had been twisted by the liberal media.

She recalled the Fisk quotation in *The Report*. She couldn't think of a clearer call to murder. She'd be curious to see if Chilton posted a follow-up.

She muted the set. She and the CBI had their own problems with the media. Through leaks, scanners and that magical way the press learns details about cases, the story about the crosses as prelude to murder and that a teenage student was the suspect, had gone public. Calls about the 'Mask Killer', the 'Social Network Killer', the 'Roadside Cross Killer' were now flooding the CBI lines (despite the fact that Travis hadn't managed actually to kill the two intended victims – and that no social networking sites were directly involved).

The calls kept coming in. Even the media-hungry head of the CBI was, as TJ cleverly and carelessly put it, 'Overbywhelmed'.

Kathryn Dance spun around in her chair and gazed out the window at a gnarled trunk that had started as two trees and had grown, through pressure and accommodation, into one, stronger than either alone. An impressive knot was visible just outside the window and she often rested her eyes on it, a form of meditation.

Now she had no time for reflection. She called Peter Bennington, at MCSO forensics, about the scenes at the second cross and Kelley Morgan's house.

The roses left with the second cross were bound with the same type of rubber bands used by the deli near where Travis used to work but they revealed no trace that was helpful. The fiber that Michael O'Neil had gotten from the gray hooded sweatshirt in the Brigham's laundry basket was indeed almost identical to the fiber found near the second cross, and the tiny scrap of brown paper from the woods Ken Pfister had pointed out was most likely from an M&M package – candy that she knew Travis bought. The grain trace from the scene was associated with that used in oat-bran bagels at Bagel Express. At Kelley Morgan's house, the boy had shed no trace or physical evidence except a bit of red rose petal that matched the bouquet with cross number two.

The mask was homemade, but the paste and paper and ink used in its construction were generic and unsourceable.

The gas that had been used in the attempt to murder Kelley Morgan was chlorine – the same that had been used in World War I to such devastating effect. Dance told Bennington, 'There's a report he got it from a neo-Nazi site.' She explained about what she'd learned from Caitlin's friend.

The crime lab boss chuckled. 'Doubt it. It was probably from somebody's kitchen.'

'What?'

'He used household cleaners.' The deputy explained that a few simple substances could make the gas; they were available in any grocery or convenience store. 'But we didn't find any containers or anything that would let us determine the source.'

Nothing at the scene or nearby had given them clues as to where the boy might be hiding out.

'And David stopped by your house a little bit ago.'

Dance hesitated, not sure whom he was speaking of. 'David?'

'Reinhold. He works in the CS Unit.'

Oh, the young, eager deputy.

'He collected the branches left in your backyard. But we still can't tell if they were left intentionally or it was a coincidence. No other trace, he said.'

'He got up early. I left the house at seven.'

Bennington laughed. 'Just two months ago he was writing speeding tickets with the Highway Patrol and now I think he's got his eye on my job.'

Dance thanked the Crime Scene head and disconnected.

Stung with frustration, Dance found herself looking at the photo of the mask. It was just plain awful – cruel and unsettling. She picked up her phone and called the hospital. Identified herself. She asked about Kelley Morgan's condition. It was unchanged, a nurse told her. Still in a coma. She'd probably live, but none of the staff was willing to speculate about whether she'd return to consciousness – or, if so, whether she'd regain a normal life.

Sighing, Kathryn Dance hung up.

And got angry.

She swept the phone up again, found a number in her notebook and, with a heavy finger, punched the keypad hard.

TJ, nearby, watched the stabbing. He tapped Jon Boling on the arm and whispered, 'Uh-oh.'

James Chilton answered on the third ring.

'This is Kathryn Dance, the Bureau of Investigation.'

A brief pause. Chilton would be recalling meeting her . . . and wondering why she was contacting him again. 'Agent Dance. Yes. I heard there was another incident.'

'That's right. Why I'm calling, Mr Chilton. The only way we were able to save the victim – a high school girl – was by tracing her screen name. It took a long time, and a lot of people, to find out who she was and where she lived. We got to her house about a half hour before she died. We saved her but she's in a coma and might not recover.'

'I'm so sorry.'

'And it looks like the attacks are going to continue.' She explained about the stolen bouquets.

'Twelve of them?' His voice registered dismay.

'He's not going to stop until he's killed everybody who's attacked him in your blog. I'm going to ask you again, will you please give us the Internet addresses of the people who've posted?'

'No.'

Goddammit. Dance shivered in rage.

'Because if I did, it would be a breach of trust. I can't betray my readers.'

That again. She muttered, 'Listen to me—'

'Please, Agent Dance, just hear me out. But what I will do . . . write this down. My hosting platform is Central California Internet Services. They're in San Jose.' He gave her the address and phone number, as well as a personal contact. 'I'll call them right now and tell them I won't object to their giving you the addresses of every-body who's posted. If they want a warrant, that's *their* business, but I won't fight it.'

She paused. She wasn't sure of the technical implications but she thought he'd just agreed to what she'd asked for, while saving some journalistic face.

'Well . . . thank you.'

They hung up and Dance called to Boling, 'I think we can get the IP addresses.'

'What?'

'Chilton's had a change of heart.'

'Sweet,' he said, smiling, and seemed like a boy who'd just been told his father'd gotten tickets to a play-off game.

Dance gave it a few minutes and called the hosting company. She was skeptical both that Chilton had called and the service itself would give up the information without a court battle. But to her surprise the representative she spoke with said, 'Oh, Mr Chilton just called. I've got the IP addresses of the posters. I've okayed forwarding them to a dot-gov location.'

She smiled broadly, and gave the hosting employee her email address.

'They're on their way. I'll go back to the blog every few hours or so and get the addresses of the new posters.'

'You're a lifesaver . . . literally.'

The man said grimly, 'This is about that boy who's getting even with people, right? The Satanist? Is it true they found biological weapons in his locker?'

Brother, Dance thought. The rumors were spreading faster than the Mission Hills fire a few years ago.

'We're not sure what's happening at this point.' Always noncommittal.

They disconnected. And a few minutes later her computer dinged with incoming mail.

'Got it,' Dance said to Boling. He rose and walked behind her, put his hand on her chair back, leaning forward. She smelled subtle aftershave. Pleasant.

'Okay. Good. Of course, you know those are the raw computer addresses. We've got to contact all the providers and find out names and physical addresses. I'll get right on it.'

She printed out the list – it contained about thirty individuals' names – and handed it to him. He disappeared back into his corner of the lair and hunkered down in front of his computer.

'May have something, boss.' TJ had been posting pictures of the mask on the Web and in blogs and asking if anybody knew its source. He ran his hand through his curly red hair. 'Pat me on the back.'

'What's the story?'

'The mask is of some character in a computer game.' A glance at the mask. 'Qetzal.'

'What?'

'That's his name. Or *its* name. A demon who kills people with these beams from its eyes. And it can only moan because somebody laced up the lips.'

Dance asked, 'So it's getting even with people who have the ability to communicate.'

'Didn't really run a Dr Phil on him, boss,' TJ said.

'Fair enough.' She smiled.

'The game,' TJ continued, 'is *DimensionQuest*.'

'It's a Morpeg,' Boling announced, without looking up from his own computer.

'What's that?'

'*DimensionQuest* is an M-M-O-R-P-G – massively multiplayer online role-playing game. I call them "Morpegs". And *DQ* is one of the most popular.'

'Helpful to us?'

'I don't know yet. We'll see when we get into Travis's computer.'

Dance liked the professor's confidence. 'When,' not 'if'. She sat back, pulled out her cell phone and called her mother. Still no answer.

Finally she tried her father.

'Hey, Katie.'

'Dad. How's Mom? She never called me.'

'Oh.' A hesitation. 'She's upset, of course. I think she's just not in the mood to talk to anybody.'

Dance wondered how long her mother's conversation had been with Dance's sister, Betsey, last night.

'Has Sheedy said anything else?'

'No. He's doing some research, he said.'

'Dad, Mom didn't say anything, did she? When she was arrested?'

'To the police?'

'Or to Harper, the prosecutor?'

'No.'

'Good.'

She felt an urge to ask him to put her mother on the phone. But she didn't want the rejection if she said no. Dance said brightly, 'You *are* coming over for dinner tonight? Right?'

He assured her they would, though his tone really meant that they'd *try*.

'I love you, Dad. Tell Mom too.'

'Bye, Katie.'

They hung up. Dance stared at the phone for a few minutes.

Then she strode up the hall and into her boss's office, entering without knocking.

Overby was just hanging up. He nodded at the phone. 'Kathryn, any leads in the Morgan girl's attack? Something about biochemicals? News Nine called.'

She closed the door. Overby eyed her uneasily.

'No biological weapons, Charles. It was just rumors.'

Dance ran through the leads: the mask, the state vehicle, Caitlin Gardner's report that Travis liked the seashore, the household chemicals. 'And Chilton's cooperating. He gave the Internet addresses of the posters.'

'That's good.' Overby's phone rang. He glanced at it but let his assistant pick up.

'Charles, did you know my mother was going to be arrested?'

He blinked. 'I . . . no, of course not.'

'What'd Harper tell you?'

'That he was checking the caseloads.' Starch in his words. Defensive. 'What I said yesterday.'

She couldn't tell if he was lying. And she understood why: Dance was breaking the oldest rule in kinesic interrogation. She was being emotional. When that happened, all her skills fell by the wayside. She had no idea if her boss had betrayed her or not.

'He was looking through our files to see if I'd altered anything about the Millar situation.'

'Oh, I doubt that.'

The tension in the room hummed.

Then it vanished, as Overby gave a reassuring smile. 'Ah, you're worrying too much, Kathryn. There'll be an investigation, and the case will all go away. You don't have a thing to worry about.'

Did he know something? Eagerly, she asked, 'Why do you say that, Charles?'

He looked surprised. 'Because she's innocent, of course. Your mother'd never hurt anyone. You know that.'

*   *   *

Dance returned to the Gals' Wing, to the office of her fellow agent Connie Ramirez. The short, voluptuous Latina, with black, black hair always sprayed meticulously in place, was the most decorated agent in the regional office and one of the most recognized in the entire CBI. The forty-year-old agent had been offered executive positions with CBI headquarters in Sacramento – the FBI had sought her out too – but her family had come out of the local lettuce and artichoke fields and nothing was going to displace her from blood. The agent's desk was the antithesis of Dance's – organized and tidy. Framed citations hung on the walls but the biggest photos were of her children, three strapping boys, and Ramirez and her husband.

'Hey, Con.'

'How's your mom doing?'

'You can imagine.'

'This's such nonsense,' she said with a faint trace of a melodious accent.

'Actually, why I'm here. Need a favor. A big one.'

'Whatever I can do, you know that.'

'I've got Sheedy on board.'

'Ah, the cop-buster.'

'But I don't want to wait for discovery to get some of the details. I asked Henry for the hospital's visitor shuts the day Juan died but he's stonewalling.'

'What? Henry? You're his friend.'

'Harper's got him scared.'

Ramirez nodded knowingly. 'You want me to try?'

'If you can.'

'You bet, I'll get over there as soon as I finish interviewing this witness.' She tapped a folder for a big drug case she was running.

'You're the best.'

The Latina agent grew solemn. 'I know how I'd feel if it was my mother. I'd go down there and rip Harper's throat out.'

Dance gave a wan smile at the petite woman's declaration. As she headed for her office, her phone trilled. She glanced at 'Sheriff's Office' on Caller ID, hoping it was O'Neil.

It wasn't.

'Agent Dance.' The deputy identified himself. 'Have to tell you. CHP called in. I've got some bad news.'

18

James Chilton was taking a break from ridding the world of corruption and depravity.

He was helping a friend move.

After the call from the MCSO, Kathryn Dance had rung up Chilton at his home and been directed by Patrizia to this modest, beige California ranch house on the outskirts of Monterey. Dance parked near a large U-Haul truck, plucked the iPod ear buds out and climbed from her car.

In jeans and a T-shirt, sweating, Chilton was wrangling a large armchair up the stairs and into the house. A man with corporate-trimmed hair and wearing shorts and a sweat-limp polo shirt was carting a stack of boxes behind the blogger. A Realtor's sign in the front yard diagonally reported, SOLD.

Chilton came out the front door and walked two steps to the gravel path, bordered by small boulders and potted plants. He joined Dance, wiped his forehead and, being so sweaty and streaked with dust and dirt, nodded in lieu of shaking her hand. 'Pat called. You wanted to see me, Agent Dance? Is this about the Internet addresses?'

'No. We've got them. Thanks. This is something else.'

The other man joined them, fixing Dance with a pleasant, curious gaze.

Chilton introduced them. The man was Donald Hawken.

Familiar. Then Dance recalled: the name appeared in Chilton's blog – in 'On the Home Front', the personal section, she believed. Not one of the controversial posts. Hawken was returning to Monterey from San Diego.

'Moving day, it looks like,' she said.

Chilton explained, 'Agent Dance is investigating that case involving the posts on *The Report*.'

Hawken, tanned and toned, frowned sympathetically. 'And I understand there was another girl attacked. We were listening to the news.'

Dance remained circumspect as always about giving away information, even to concerned citizens.

The blogger explained that the Chiltons and Hawken and his first wife had been close friends a few years ago. The women had hosted dinner parties, the men had golfed regularly – at the anemic Pacific Grove course and, on flush days, at Pebble Beach. About three years ago the Hawkens had moved to San Diego, but he had recently remarried, was selling his company and coming back here.

'Could I talk to you for a minute?' Dance asked Chilton.

As Hawken returned to the U-Haul, the blogger and Dance walked to her Crown Vic. He cocked his head and waited, breathing hard from lugging the furniture into the house.

'I just got a call from the sheriff's office. The Highway Patrol found another cross. With today's date on it.'

His face fell. 'Oh, no. And the boy?'

'No idea of his whereabouts. He's disappeared. And it looks like he's armed.'

'I heard on the news,' Chilton said, grimacing. 'How'd he get a gun?'

'Stole it from his father.'

Chilton's face tightened angrily. 'Those Second Amendment people . . . I took them on last year. I've never had so many death threats in my life.'

Dance got to the crux of her mission. 'Mr Chilton, I want you to suspend your blog.'

'What?'

'Until we catch him.'

Chilton laughed. 'That's absurd.'

'Have you read the postings?'

'It's my blog. Of course I read them.'

'The posters are getting even more vicious. Don't give Travis any more fodder.'

'Absolutely not. I'm not going to be cowed into silence.'

'But Travis is getting the names of victims from the blog. He's reading up on them, finding their deepest fears, their vulnerabilities. He's tracking down where they live.'

'People shouldn't be writing about themselves on public Internet pages. I did a whole blog about that too.'

'Be that as it may, they are posting.' Dance tried to control her frustration. 'Please, work with us.'

'I *have* been working with you. That's as far as I'm willing to go.'

'What can it hurt to take it down for a few days?'

'And if you don't find him by then?'

'Put it up again.'

'Or you come to me and say a few more, then a few more.'

'At least stop taking posts on that thread. He won't get any more names he can target as victims. It'll make our job easier.'

'Repression never leads to anything good,' he muttered, staring right into her eyes. The missionary was back.

Kathryn Dance gave up on the Jon Boling strategy to coddle Chilton's ego. She snapped angrily, 'You're making these bullshit grand pronouncements. "Freedom". "Truth". "Repression". This boy is trying to *kill* people. Jesus Christ, look at it for what it is. Take the damn politics out of it.'

Chilton calmly replied, 'My job is to keep an open forum for public opinion. That's the *First* Amendment . . . I know, you're going to remind me that you were a reporter too and you cooperated if the police wanted some help. But, see, that's the difference. You were beholden to big money, to the advertisers, to whoever's pocket your bosses were in. I'm not beholden to anybody.'

'I'm not asking you to stop reporting on the crimes. Write away to your heart's content. Just don't accept any more posts. Nobody's adding facts, anyway. These people are just venting. And half of what they say is just plain wrong. It's rumors, specu-lation. Rants.'

'And their thoughts aren't valid?' he asked, but not angrily; in fact he seemed to be enjoying the debate. 'Their opinions don't count? Only the articulate and the educated – and the *moderate* – are allowed to comment? Well, welcome to the new world of journalism, Agent Dance. The free exchange of ideas. See, it's not about your big newspapers anymore, your Bill O'Reillys, your Keith Olbermanns. It's about the *people*. No, I'm not suspending the blog and I'm not locking any threads.' He glanced at Hawken, who was wrestling another armchair out of the back of the U-Haul. Chilton said to her, 'Now, if you'll excuse me.'

And he strode to the truck, looking, she decided, just like some martyr on his way to the firing squad, having just deliv-ered a rant about a cause he, though nobody else, fervently believed in.

Like everyone else on the Peninsula – anybody over age six and with any access to the media, that is – Lyndon Strickland was very aware of the Roadside Cross Case.

And, like a lot of people who read *The Chilton Report*, he was angry.

The forty-one-year-old lawyer climbed out of his car and locked the door. He was going for his daily lunchtime run along a path near Seventeen Mile Drive, the beautiful road that leads from Pacific Grove to Carmel, winding past movie stars' and business executives' vacation houses and Pebble Beach golf course.

He heard the sounds of construction for that new highway heading east to Salinas and the farmland. It was progressing fast. Strickland represented several small homeowners whose prop-erty had been taken by eminent domain to make way for the road. He'd been up against the state and against massive Avery Construction itself – and their armada of big legal guns. Not unexpectedly he'd lost the trial, just last week. But the judge had stayed the destruction of his client's houses pending appeal. The lead defense counsel, from San Francisco, had been livid.

Lyndon Strickland, on the other hand, had been ecstatic.

The fog was coming up, the weather chill, and he had the jogging path to himself as he started to run.

Angry.

Strickland had read what people were saying in James Chilton's blog. Travis Brigham was a crazy boy who idolized the shooters at Columbine and Virginia Tech, who stalked girls in the night, who'd half asphyxiated his own brother, Sammy, and left him retarded, who'd intentionally driven a car off the cliff a few weeks ago in some weird suicide/murder ritual, killing two girls.

How the hell had everybody missed the danger signs the boy must've displayed? His parents, his teachers . . . friends.

The image of the mask he'd seen online that morning still gave him the creeps. A chill coursed through his body, only partly from the damp air.

The Mask Killer . . .

And now the kid was out there, hiding in the hills of Monterey County, picking off one by one the people who'd posted negative things about him.

Strickland read *The Chilton Report* frequently. It was on his RSS feed, near the top. He disagreed with Chilton on some issues, but the blogger was always reasonable and always made solid, intellectual arguments in support of his positions. For instance, although Chilton was adamantly opposed to abortion, he'd posted a comment against that wacko Reverend Fisk, who'd called for the murder of abortion doctors. Strickland, who'd often represented Planned Parenthood and other pro-choice organizations, had been impressed with Chilton's balanced stance.

The blogger was also opposed to the desalination plant, as was Strickland, who was meeting with a potential new client – an environmental group interested in hiring him to sue to stop the plant from going forward. He'd just posted a reply supporting the blogger.

Strickland now headed up the small hill that was the hardest part of his jog. The route was downhill from there. Sweating, heart pounding . . . and feeling the exhilaration of the exercise.

As he crested the hill, something caught his eye. A splash of red off the jogging path and a flurry of motion near to the ground. What was it? he wondered. He circled back, paused his stop-watch and walked slowly through the rocks to where he saw a sprinkling of crimson, out of place in the sandy soil, dotted with brown and green plants.

His heart continued to slam in his chest, though now out of fear, not exertion. He thought immediately about Travis Brigham. But the boy was targeting only those who'd attacked him online. Strickland had said nothing about him at all.

Relax.

Still, as he detoured along the trail toward the commotion and spots of red, Strickland pulled his cell phone from his pocket, ready to push 911 if there was any threat.

He squinted, looking down as he approached the clearing. What *was* he looking at?

'Shit,' he muttered, freezing.

On the ground were hunks of flesh sitting amid a scattering of rose petals. Three huge, ugly birds – vultures, he guessed – were ripping the tissue apart, frantic, hungry. A bloody bone sat nearby too. Several crows were hopping close cautiously, grabbing a bit, then retreating.

Strickland squinted, leaning forward, as he noted something else, in the center of the frenzy.

No! . . . A cross had been scraped into the sandy soil.

He understood that Travis Brigham was around here some-where. Heart trilling, the lawyer scanned the bushes and trees and dunes. He could be hiding anywhere. And suddenly it didn't make any difference that Lyndon Strickland had never posted anything about the boy.

As an image of that terrifying mask the boy had left as an

emblem of his attack lodged in his mind, Strickland turned and started to flee back to the path.

He got a mere ten feet before he heard someone push out of the bushes and begin running fast his way.

19

Jon Boling sat in Dance's office, on her sagging couch. The sleeves of his dark blue striped shirt were rolled up and he had two phones going at once, as he stared at printouts of Chilton's blog. He was working to find the physical addresses from the Internet data that the hosting service had provided.

Crooking a Samsung between ear and shoulder, he jotted information and called out, 'Got another one. SexyGurl is Kimberly Rankin, one-two-eight Forest, Pacific Grove.'

Dance took the details down and phoned to warn the girl – and her parents – of the danger and to insist bluntly that she stop posting to the *Report* and to tell her friends to stop too.

How's *that*, Chilton?

Boling was studying the computer screen in front of him. Dance looked over and saw that he was frowning.

'What is it?' she asked.

'The first posts responding in the "Roadside Crosses" thread were mostly local, classmates and people around the Peninsula. Now people from all over the country – hell, from all over the world – are chiming in. They're really going after him – and the Highway Patrol or the police too – for not following up on the accident. And they're dissing the CBI too.'

'Us?'

'Yep. Somebody reported that a CBI agent went to interview Travis at home but didn't detain him.'

'How do they even know Michael and I were there?'

He gestured at the computer. 'The nature of the beast. Information spreads. People in Warsaw, Buenos Aires, New Zealand.'

Dance returned to the crime scene report of the most recent roadside cross on a quiet road in a lightly inhabited part of north Monterey. No witnesses. And little had been found at the scene, aside from the same sort of trace discovered at the earlier scenes, linking Travis to the crime. But there was one discovery that might prove helpful. Soil samples revealed some sand that wasn't generally found in the immediate vicinity of the cross. It couldn't, however, be sourced to a particular location.

And all the while she reviewed these details, she couldn't help but think, who is the next victim?

Is Travis getting close?

And what terrible technique is he going to use this time to frighten and to kill? He seemed to favor lingering deaths, as if in compensation for prolonged suffering he'd been through at the hands of the cyberbullies.

Boling said, 'I've got another name.' He called it out to Dance, who jotted it down.

'Thanks,' she said, smiling.

'You owe me a Junior G-Man badge.'

As Boling cocked his head and bent toward his notes once more, he said something else softly. Perhaps it was her imagination but it almost sounded as if he'd started to say, 'Or maybe dinner,' but swallowed the words before they fully escaped.

Imagination, she decided. And turned back to her phone.

Boling sat back. 'That's all of them for now. The other posters aren't in the area or they have untraceable addresses. But if we can't find them, Travis can't either.'

He stretched and leaned back.

'Not your typical day in the world of academia, is it?' Dance asked.

'Not exactly.' He cast a wry look her way. 'Is this a typical day in the world of law enforcement?'

'Uhm, no, it's not.'

'I guess that's the good news.'

Her phone buzzed. She noted the internal CBI extension. 'TJ.'

'Boss . . .' As had happened on more than one occasion recently, the young agent's typically irreverent attitude was absent. 'Have you heard?'

Dance's heart gave a bit of a flip when she saw Michael O'Neil at the crime scene.

'Hey,' she said. 'Thought I'd lost you.'

He gave a faint startle reaction to that. Then said, 'Juggling both cases. But a crime scene' – he nodded toward a fluttering ribbon of police tape – 'has priority.'

'Thanks.'

Jon Boling joined them. Dance had asked the professor to accompany her. She'd supposed there were several ways in which he could be helpful. Mostly she wanted him here to bounce ideas off of, since Michael O'Neil, she'd believed, wouldn't be present.

'What happened?' she asked the senior deputy.

'Left a little diorama to scare him,' a glance up the trail, 'and then chased him down here. And shot him.' It seemed to Dance that O'Neil was going to give more details but pulled back, probably because of Boling's presence.

'Where?'

The deputy pointed. The body wasn't visible from here.

'I'll show you the initial scene.' He led them along the jogging path. About two hundred yards up a shallow hill, they found a short trail that led to a clearing. They ducked under yellow tape and saw rose petals on the ground and a cross carved in the sandy dirt. There were bits of flesh scattered around and bloodstains too. A bone. Claw marks in the dirt, from vultures and crows, it seemed.

O'Neil said, 'It's animal, the Crime Scene people say. Probably beef, store-bought. My guess is the vic was jogging up the trail back there, saw the fuss and then took a look. He got spooked and ran. Travis got him halfway down the hill.'

'What's his name?'

'Lyndon Strickland. He's a lawyer. Lives nearby.'

Dance squinted. 'Wait. Strickland? I think he posted something on the blog.'

Boling opened his backpack and pulled out a dozen sheets of paper, copies of the blog pages. 'Yep. But not in "Roadside Crosses". He posted a reply about the desalination plant. He's supporting Chilton.'

He handed her the printout:

Reply to Chilton, posted by Lyndon Strickland.

I have to say you've opened my eyes on this issue. Had no idea that somebody's ramrodding this through. I reviewed the filed proposal at the County Planning Office and must say that, though I am an attorney familiar with environmental issues, it was one of the most obfuscatory documents I've ever tried to wade through. I think we need considerably more transparency in order to have meaningful debate on this matter.

Dance asked, 'How did Travis know he'd be here? It's so deserted.'

Boling said, 'These are jogging trails. I'll bet Strickland posted to a bulletin board or blog that he likes running here.'

We give away too much information about ourselves online. Way too much.

O'Neil asked, 'Why would the boy kill *him*?'

Boling seemed to be considering something.

'What, Jon?' Dance asked.

'It's just a thought but remember that Travis is into those computer games?'

Dance explained to O'Neil about the massively multiplayer online role-playing games that Travis played.

The professor continued, 'One aspect of the game is growth.

Your character develops and grows, your conquests expand. You have to do that, otherwise you won't succeed. Following that classic pattern, I think Travis might be expanding his pool of targets. First, it was people who directly attacked him. Now he's included somebody who supports Chilton, even if he has nothing to do with the "Roadside Crosses" thread.'

Boling cocked his head, looking at the bits of meat and the claw marks in the sandy ground. 'That's an exponential increase in the number of possible victims. It'll mean dozens more are at risk now. I'll start checking out the Internet addresses of anyone who's posted anything even faintly supportive of Chilton.'

More discouraging news.

'We're going to examine the body now, Jon,' Dance said. 'You should head back to the car.'

'Sure.' Boling looked relieved that he didn't have to participate in this part of the job.

Dance and O'Neil hiked through the dunes to where the body had been found. 'How's the terrorist thing going? The Container Case?'

The senior deputy gave a wan laugh. 'Moving along. You get Homeland Security involved, FBI, Customs, it's a quagmire. What's that line, you rise to the level of your own unhappiness? Sometimes I'd like to be back in a Police Interceptor handing out tickets.'

'It's "level of incompetence". And, no, you'd hate being back in Patrol.'

'True.' He paused. 'How's your mother holding up?'

That question again. Dance was about to put on a sunny face, but then remembered to whom she was speaking. She lowered her voice. 'Michael, she hasn't called me. When they found Pfister and the second cross, I just left the courthouse. I didn't even say anything to her. She's hurt. I know she is.'

'You found her a lawyer – one of the best on the Peninsula. And he got her released, right?'

'Yes.'

'You've done everything you can. Don't worry about it. She's probably distancing herself from you. For the sake of this case.'

'Maybe.'

Eyeing her, he laughed again. 'But you don't believe that. You're convinced she's mad at you. That she thinks you've let her down.'

Dance was remembering times in her childhood when, at some affront, real or imagined, the staunch woman would turn cold and distant. It was only in partial humor that Dance's father occasionally referred to his wife as 'the staff sergeant'.

'Mothers and daughters,' O'Neil mused out loud, as if he knew exactly what she'd been thinking.

When they reached the body, Dance nodded at the men from the coroner's office, who were setting a green body bag beside the corpse. The photographer had just finished up. Strickland lay on his belly, in jogging attire, now bloody. He'd been shot from behind. Once in the back, once in the head.

'And then there's this.' One of the medics tugged the sweat-shirt up, revealing an image carved into the man's back: a crude approximation of a face, which might've been the mask. Qetzal, the demon from *Dimension-Quest*. This is probably what O'Neil was reluctant to mention in front of Boling.

Dance shook her head. 'Postmortem?'

'Right.'

'Any witnesses?'

'None,' an MCSO deputy said. 'There's that highway construction site about a half mile from here. They heard the shots and called it in. But nobody saw anything.'

One of the Crime Scene officers called, 'Didn't find any significant physical evidence, sir.'

O'Neil nodded and together he and Dance returned to their cars.

Dance noticed Boling was standing beside his Audi, hands clasped in front of him and his shoulders seemed raised slightly. Sure signs of tension. Murder scenes will do that to you.

She said, 'Thanks for coming out here, Jon. This was above and beyond the call of duty. But it was helpful to get your thoughts.'

'Sure.' He sounded as if he was trying to be stoic. She wondered if he'd ever been to a crime scene.

Her phone rang. She noticed Charles Overby's name and number on Caller ID. She'd called earlier and told him about this killing. Now she'd have to tell him that the victim hadn't been guilty of cyberbullying, but was a true innocent bystander. This would throw the area into even more panic.

'Charles.'

'Kathryn, you're at the latest scene?'

'Right. It looks like—'

'Did you catch the boy?'

'No. But—'

'Well, you can give me the details later. Something's come up. Get here as soon as you can.'

20

'So this is the Kathryn Dance.' A big ruddy hand encircled hers, holding it until the bucket of propriety had been filled and then releasing.

Odd, she noted. He hadn't put as much emphasis on the article as you'd expect. Not *the* Kathryn Dance. More like: so this is the *agent*.

Or, this is the *chair*.

But she ignored the curious descriptive since kinesic analysis wasn't a priority at the moment; the man wasn't a suspect, but was, as it turned out, connected to the CBI's boss of bosses. Resembling a college linebacker gone into politics or business, fiftyish Hamilton Royce worked in the attorney general's office in Sacramento. He returned to his chair – they were in Charles Overby's office – and Dance too sat. Royce explained that he was an ombudsman.

Dance glanced at Overby. Itchily squinting toward Royce out of deference or curiosity or probably both, he didn't offer anything else to flesh out the visitor's job description – or mission.

Dance was still angry about her boss's carelessness, if not malfeasance, in suborning Robert Harper's covert operation in the CBI file room.

Because she's innocent, of course. Your mother'd never hurt anyone. You know that . . .

Dance kept her attention on Royce.

'We hear good things about you in Sacramento. I understand your expertise is body language.' The broad-shouldered man, with dark swept-back hair, was wearing a slick suit, its color a blue just the regal side of navy and therefore suggestive of a uniform.

'I'm just an investigator. I tend to use kinesics more than a lot of people.'

'Ah, there she goes, Charles, selling herself short. You said she'd do that.'

Dance offered a cautious smile and wondered what exactly Overby had said and how cautious he'd been in offering or with-holding praise of an employee. Evidence for job and raise reviews, of course. Her boss's face remained neutral. How hard life can be when you're unsure.

Royce continued jovially, 'So you could look me over and tell me what I'm thinking. Just because of how I cross my arms, where I look, whether I blush or not. Tip to my secrets.'

'It's a little more complicated than that,' she said pleasantly.

'Ah.'

In fact she'd already come up with a tentative personality typing. He was a thinking, sensing extravert. And probably had a Machiavellian liar's personality. Accordingly Dance was wary.

'Well, we do hear good things about you. That case earlier in the month, that crazy man on the Peninsula here? That was a tough one. You nailed the fellow, though.'

'We caught some lucky breaks.'

'No, no,' Overby interrupted quickly, 'no breaks, no lucky. She outthought him.'

And Dance realized by saying 'luck', she'd suggested a criticism of herself, the CBI's Monterey office and Overby.

'And what do you do exactly, Hamilton?' She wasn't going for a status-defining 'Mr', not in a situation like this.

'Oh, jack of all trades. A troubleshooter. If there are problems involving state agencies, the governor's office, the assembly, even the courts, I look into it, write a report.' A smile. 'A lot of reports. I hope they get read. You never know.'

This didn't seem to answer her question. She looked at her watch, a gesture that Royce noticed but that Overby did not. As she'd intended.

'Hamilton is here about the Chilton case,' Overby said, then looked at the man from Sacramento to make sure that was all right. Back to Dance: 'Brief us,' he said like a ship captain.

'Sure, Charles,' Dance replied wryly, noting both his tone and the fact Overby had said 'the Chilton case'. *She'd* been thinking of the attacks as the Roadside Cross Case. Or the Travis Brigham Case. Now she had an inkling as to why Royce was here.

She explained about the murder of Lyndon Strickland – the mechanics of the killing and how he figured in the Chilton blog.

Royce frowned. 'So he's expanding his possible targets?'

'We think so, yes.'

'Evidence?'

'Sure, there's some. But nothing specific that leads to where Travis is hiding out. We've got a joint CHP and sheriff's office task force running a manhunt.' She shook her head. 'They're not making much progress. He doesn't drive – he's on a bike – and he's staying underground.' She looked at Royce. 'Our consultant thinks he's using evasion techniques he learned in online games to stay out of sight.'

'Who?'

'Jon Boling, a professor from UC-Santa Cruz. He's very helpful.'

'*And* he's volunteering his time, no charge to us,' Overby slipped in smoothly, as if the words were oiled.

'About this blog,' Royce said slowly. 'How does that figure in, exactly?'

Dance explained, 'Some postings have set the boy off. He was cyberbullied.'

'So, he snapped.'

'We're doing everything we can to find him,' Overby said. 'He can't be far. It's a small peninsula.'

Royce hadn't given much away. But Dance could see from his focused eyes he was not only sizing up the Travis Brigham situation but was neatly folding it into his purpose here.

Which he finally got down to.

'Kathryn, there's a concern in Sacramento about this case, I have to tell you. Everybody's nervous. It's got teenagers, computers, social networking. Now, a weapon's involved. You can't help but think Virginia Tech and Columbine. Apparently those boys from Colorado were his idols.'

'Rumor. I don't know if that's true or not. It was posted on the blog by someone who might or might not have known him.'

And from the flutter of eyebrow and twitch of lip, she realized she might have just played into his hand. With people like Hamilton Royce, you never could be sure if all was straightforward, or if you were fencing.

'This blog . . . I was talking to the AG about it. We're worried that as long as people are posting, it's like gasoline on the flames. You know what I mean? Like an avalanche. Well, mixing my metaphors, but you get the idea. What we were thinking: wouldn't it be better for the blog to shut down?'

'I've actually asked Chilton to do that.'

'Oh, you have?' Overby asked the question.

'And what did he say?'

'Emphatically no. Freedom of the press.'

Royce scoffed. 'It's just a blog. It's not the *Chronicle* or *Wall Street Journal*.'

'He doesn't feel that way.' Dance then asked, 'Has anybody from the AG's office contacted him?'

'No. If the request came from Sacramento, we're worried that he'd post something about *us* bringing the subject up. And that'd spread to the newspapers and TV. Repression. Censorship. And those labels might rub off on the governor and some congressmen. No, we can't do that.'

'Well, he refused,' Dance repeated.

'I was just wondering,' Royce began slowly, his gaze keenly strafing Dance, 'if there was anything you've found about him, something to help persuade him?'

'Stick or carrot?' she asked quickly.

Royce couldn't help but laugh. Savvy people apparently

impressed him. 'He doesn't seem like the carrot sort, from what you've told me.'

Meaning a bribe wouldn't work. Which Dance knew was true, having tried one. But neither did Chilton seem susceptible to threats. In fact, he seemed like the sort who'd relish them. And post something in his blog about any that were made.

Besides, though she didn't like Chilton and thought he was arrogant and self-righteous, using something she'd learned in an investigation to intimidate the man into silence didn't sit well. In any case, Dance could honestly answer, 'I haven't found a thing. James Chilton himself is a small part of the case. He didn't even post anything about the boy – and he deleted Travis's name. The point of the "Roadside Crosses" thread was to criticize the police and highway department. It was the readers who started to attack the boy.'

'So there's nothing incriminating, nothing we can use.'

Use. Odd choice of verb.

'No.'

'Ah, too bad.' Royce *did* seem disappointed. Overby noticed too and looked disappointed himself.

Overby said, 'Keep on it, Kathryn.'

Her voice was a crawl. 'We're working full-out to find the perp, Charles.'

'Of course. Sure. But in the whole scope of the case . . .' His sentence dwindled.

'What?' she asked sharply. The anger about Robert Harper was resurfacing.

Watch it, she warned herself.

Overby smiled in a way that bore only a loose resemblance to a smile. 'In the whole scope of the case it would be helpful to *everybody* if Chilton could be persuaded to stop the blog. Helpful to us and to Sacramento. Not to mention saving the lives of people who've posted comments.'

'Exactly,' Royce said. 'We're worried about more victims.'

Of course the AG and Royce would worry about that. But

they'd also worry about the bad press against the state for not doing everything to stop the killer.

To end the meeting and get back to work, Dance simply agreed. 'If I see anything you can use, Charles, I'll let you know.'

Royce's eyes flickered. Overby missed the irony completely and smiled. 'Good.'

It was then that her phone vibrated with a text message. She read the screen, and gave a faint gasp and looked up at Overby.

Royce asked, 'What is it?'

Dance said, 'James Chilton was just attacked. I have to go.'

21

Dance hurried into Emergency Admitting at Monterey Bay Hospital.

She found TJ looking troubled in the middle of the lobby. 'Boss,' he said, exhaling hard, relieved to see her.

'How is he?'

'He'll be okay.'

'Did you get Travis?'

'It wasn't the boy who did it,' TJ said.

At that moment the double doors to the emergency room swung open and James Chilton, a bandage on his cheek, strode out. 'He attacked me!' Chilton was pointing at a ruddy-faced, solidly built man in a suit. He sat beside the window. A large county deputy stood over him. Without a greeting, Chilton pointed to him and snapped to Dance, 'Arrest him.'

Meanwhile the man leapt to his feet. 'Him. I want him in jail!'

The deputy muttered, 'Mr Brubaker, please sit down.' He spoke forcefully enough so that the man hesitated, delivered a glare to Chilton then dropped back into the fiberglass seat.

The officer then joined Dance and told her what had happened. A half hour before, Arnold Brubaker had been on the grounds of his proposed desalination plant with a survey crew. He'd found Chilton taking pictures of animal habitats there. He tried to grab the blogger's camera and shoved Chilton to the ground. The surveyors called the police.

The injury, Dance assessed, didn't seem serious.

Still, Chilton seemed possessed. 'That man is raping the Peninsula. He's destroying our natural resources. Our flora and fauna. Not to mention destroying an Ohlone burial ground.'

The Ohlone Indians were the first inhabitants of this part of California.

'We aren't building anywhere near the tribal land!' Brubaker yelled. 'That was a rumor. And completely untrue!'

'But the traffic in and out of the area is going to—'

'And we're spending millions to relocate animal populations and—'

'Both of you,' Dance snapped. 'Quiet.'

Chilton, however, had his momentum going. 'He broke my camera too. Just like the Nazis.'

Brubaker replied with a cold smile, 'James, I believe you broke the law first by trespassing on private property. Didn't the Nazis do that too?'

'I have a right to report on the destruction of our resources.'

'And I—'

'Okay,' Dance snapped. 'No more!'

They fell silent as she got the details of the various offenses from the deputy. Finally she approached Chilton. 'You trespassed on private property. That's a crime.'

'I—'

'Shhh. And you, Mr Brubaker, assaulted Mr Chilton, which is illegal unless you're in imminent danger of physical harm from a trespasser. Your remedy was to call the police.'

Brubaker fumed, but he nodded. He seemed upset that all he'd done was bang Chilton's cheek. The bandage was quite small.

'The situation is that you're guilty of minor offenses. And if you want to complain I'll make arrests. But it'll be both of you. One for criminal trespass and one for assault and battery. Well?'

Red-faced, Brubaker began to whine, 'But he—'

'Your answers?' Dance asked with an ominous calm that made him shut up immediately.

Chilton nodded, with a grimace. 'All right.'

Finally, with frustration evident in his face, Brubaker muttered to Dance, 'Okay. Fine. But it's not fair! Seven days a week for the past year, working to help eliminate drought. That's been my life. And *he* sits in that office of his and tears me down, without even looking at the facts. People see what he says in that blog and think it's true. And how can I compete with that? Write a blog of my own? Who has time?' Brubaker delivered a dramatic sigh and headed out the main door.

After he'd gone, Chilton said to Dance, 'He's not building the plant out of the goodness of his heart. There's money to be made and that's his only concern. And I *have* researched the story.'

His voice fell silent as she turned to him and he noticed her somber expression. 'James, you might not have heard the news. Lyndon Strickland was just murdered by Travis Brigham.'

Chilton remained still for a moment. 'Lyndon Strickland, the lawyer? Are you sure?'

'I'm afraid so.'

The blogger's eyes were sweeping the floor of the emergency room, green-and-white tile, mopped clean but scuffed by years of anxious heels and soles. 'But Lyndon posted in the desalination thread, not "Roadside Crosses". No, Travis wouldn't have any complaint with him. It's somebody else. Lyndon'd made a lot of people upset. He was a plaintiff's lawyer and was always taking on controversial causes.'

'The evidence doesn't leave any doubt. It was Travis.'

'But why?'

'We think because his post supported you. Doesn't matter that it was a different blog thread. We think Travis is expanding his pool of targets.'

Chilton greeted this with grim silence, then asked, 'Just because he posted something agreeing with me?'

She nodded. 'And that leads me to something else I've been worried about. That Travis might be after you.'

'But what argument does he have with me? I haven't said a word about him.'

She continued, 'He's targeted somebody who's supporting you. And the extension of that is that he's angry with you too.'

'You really think so?'

'I think we can't afford to dismiss it.'

'But my family's—'

'I've ordered a car stationed outside your house. A deputy from the sheriff's office.'

'Thank you . . . thank you. I'll tell Pat and the boys to be on the lookout for anything odd.'

'You're all right?' She nodded at the bandage.

'It's nothing.'

'You need a ride home?'

'Pat's coming to pick me up.'

Dance started outside. 'Oh, and for God's sake, leave Brubaker alone.'

Chilton's eyes narrowed. 'But do you know the effects that plant is going to have . . .' He fell silent and held up two hands in surrender. 'Okay, okay. I'll stay off his property.'

'Thank you.'

Dance walked outside and turned her phone back on. It rang thirty seconds later. Michael O'Neil. She was comforted to see his number pop up.

'Hey.'

'I just heard a report. Chilton. He was attacked?'

'He's fine.' She explained what had happened.

'Trespassing. Serves him right. I called the office. They're getting the crime scene report back from the Strickland shooting. I pushed 'em to get it done fast. But nothing really helpful jumps out.'

'Thanks.' Dance then lowered her voice – amusing herself because she did so – and told O'Neil about the curious encounter with Hamilton Royce.

'Great. Too many cooks screwing up the broth.'

'I'd like to *put them* in the broth,' Dance muttered. 'And turn up the heat.'

'And this Royce wants to shut down the blog?'

'Yep. Worried about the public relations is my take.'

O'Neil offered, 'I almost feel sorry for Chilton.'

'Spend ten minutes with him; you'll feel different.'

The deputy chuckled.

'I was going to call you anyway, Michael. I've asked Mom and Dad over tonight for dinner. She needs the support. Love it if you could come.' She added, 'You and Anne and the kids.'

A pause. 'I'll try. I'm really swamped on this Container Case. And Anne went up to San Francisco. A gallery's going to be hanging a show of her recent photos.'

'Really? That's impressive.' Dance recalled the one-sided conversation yesterday about Anne O'Neil's impending trip at their attempted breakfast after meeting with Ernie Seybold. Dance had several opinions about the woman, the most unblemished of which had to do with her talent as a photographer.

They disconnected and Dance continued toward her car, unraveling the iPod ear buds. She needed a hit of music. She was scrolling through tunes, trying to decide on Latino or Celtic, when her phone buzzed. Caller ID announced Jonathan Boling.

'Hi,' she said.

'It's all over the CBI here, Chilton was attacked. What happened? Is he all right?'

She gave him the details. He was relieved nobody had been hurt seriously, but she could tell from his voice quality that he had some news for her. She fell silent and he asked, 'Kathryn, you near the office?'

'I wasn't planning on heading back. I've got to pick up the kids and work from home for a while.' She didn't tell him that she wanted to avoid Hamilton Royce and Overby. 'Why?'

'Couple things. I've got names of posters who've supported Chilton. The good news, I suppose, is that there aren't a lot. But that's typical. In blogs more people are contrarians than supporters.'

'Email me the list, and I'll start calling them from home. What else?'

'We'll have Travis's computer cracked in the next hour or so.'

'Really? Oh, that's great.' Tiffany or Bambi was a pretty good hacker, apparently.

'I'm going to mirror his disk on a separate drive. I thought you'd want to see it.'

'You bet.' Dance had a thought. 'You have plans tonight?'

'No, I've put my cat burglary plans on hold while I'm helping you guys.'

'Bring the computer over to my house. I'm having my mother and father and a few friends over for dinner.'

'Well, sure.'

She gave him the address and a time.

They disconnected.

As Dance stood beside her car in the hospital parking lot she noticed several aides and nurses leaving for the day. They were staring at her.

Dance knew several of them and smiled. One or two nodded in greeting but the response was tepid, if not chill. Of course, she realized, they'd be thinking: I'm looking at the daughter of a woman who might have committed murder.

22

'I'll carry the groceries,' Maggie announced as Dance's Pathfinder squealed to a stop in front of their house.

The girl had been feeling independent lately. She grabbed the largest bag. There were four of them; after picking up the children at Martine's, they'd stopped at Safeway for a shopping frenzy. If everyone she'd invited showed up, the dinner party would include nearly a dozen people, among them youngsters with serious appetites.

Listing under the weight of two bags gripped in one hand – an older-brother thing – Wes asked his mother, 'When's Grandma coming over?'

'In a little while, I hope . . . There's a chance she might not come.'

'No, she said she's coming.'

Dance gave a confused smile. 'You talked to her?'

'Yeah, she called me at camp.'

'Me too,' Maggie offered.

So she'd called to reassure the children she was all right. But Dance's face flushed. Why hadn't she called *her*?

'Well, it's great she'll be able to make it.'

They carried the bags inside.

Dance went into her bedroom, accompanied by Patsy.

She glanced at the gun lockbox. Travis was expanding his

targets, and he knew she was one of the officers pursuing him. And she couldn't forget the possible threat – the cross – in her backyard last night. Dance decided to keep the weapon with her. Ever-fastidious about weapons in a household with children, though, she locked the black gun away for a few minutes to take a shower. She stripped off her clothes energetically and stepped into the stream of hot water – trying unsuccessfully to flush away the residue of the day.

She dressed in jeans and an oversize blouse, not tucked in, to obscure the weapon, which sat against the small of her back. Uncomfortable, yet a comfort. Then she hurried into the kitchen.

She fed the dogs and put out a small brushfire between the children, who were sniping over their predinner tasks. Dance stayed patient – she knew they were upset about the incident at the hospital yesterday. Maggie's job was to unpack the groceries, while Wes straightened up for guests. Dance continued to be amazed at how cluttered a house could become, even though only three people lived there.

She thought now, as she often did, about the time when the population was four. And glanced at her wedding picture. Bill Swenson, prematurely gray, lean and with an easy smile, looked out at the camera with his arm around her.

Then she went into the den, booted up her computer and emailed Overby about the assault on Chilton and the confrontation with Brubaker.

She wasn't in the mood to talk to him.

Then Dance retrieved Jon Boling's email with the names of people who'd posted comments favorable to Chilton over the past months. Seventeen.

Could be worse, she supposed.

She spent the next hour finding the numbers of those within a hundred miles and calling to warn them they might be in danger. She weathered their criticism, some of it searing, about the CBI and the police not being able to stop Travis Brigham.

Dance logged on to that day's *Chilton Report*.

She scrolled through all the threads, noting that new posts had appeared in nearly all of them. The latest contributors to the Reverend Fisk and the desalination threads were taking their respective causes seriously – and with intensifying anger. But none of their posts compared to the vicious comments in the 'Roadside Crosses' thread, most of them unleashing undiluted fury at each other, as much as at Travis.

Some of them were curiously worded, some seemed to be probing for information, some seemed to be outright threats. She got the feeling that there were clues as to where Travis was hiding – possibly even tidbits of facts that might suggest whom he was going to attack next. Was Travis actually one of the posters, hiding behind a fake identity or the common pseudonym, 'Anonymous'? She read the exchanges carefully and decided that perhaps there were clues, but the answer eluded her. Kathryn Dance, comfortable with analyzing the spoken word, could come to no solid conclusions as she read the frustratingly silent shouts and mutters.

Finally she logged off.

An email from Michael O'Neil arrived. He gave her the discouraging news that the immunity hearing in the J. Doe case had been pushed back to Friday. The prosecutor, Ernie Seybold, felt that the judge's willingness to go along with the defense's request for the extension was a bad sign. She grimaced at the news and was disappointed that he hadn't called to give her the news over the phone. Neither had he mentioned anything about whether he and the children would come over tonight.

Dance began to organize dinner. She didn't have much skill in the kitchen, as she was the first to admit. But she knew which stores had the most talented prepared-food departments; the meal would be fine.

Listening to the soft braying of a video game from Wes's room, Maggie's keyboard scales, Dance found herself staring into the backyard, recalling the image of her mother's face yesterday afternoon, as her daughter deserted her to see about the second roadside cross.

Your mother will understand.

No, she won't . . .

Hovering over the containers of brisket, green beans, Caesar salad, salmon and twice-baked potatoes, Dance remembered that time three weeks ago – her mother standing in this very kitchen and reporting about Juan Millar in the ICU. With Edie's face feeling his pain, she'd told her daughter what he'd whispered to her.

Kill me . . .

The doorbell now drew her from that disquieting thought.

She deduced who had arrived – most friends and family just climbed the back deck stairs and entered the kitchen without ringing or knocking. She opened the front door to see Jon Boling standing on the porch. He wore that now-familiar, comfortable smile and was juggling a small shopping bag and a large laptop case. He'd changed into black jeans and a dark striped collared shirt.

'Hi.'

He nodded and followed her into the kitchen.

The dogs bounded up. Boling crouched and hugged them as they double-teamed him.

'Okay, guys, outside!' Dance commanded. She flung Milk Bones out the back door and the dogs charged down the steps and into the backyard.

Boling stood, wiped his face from the licks and laughed. He reached into the shopping bag. 'I decided to bring sugar for a hostess gift.'

'Sugar?'

'Two versions: fermented.' He extracted a bottle of Caymus Conundrum white wine.

'Nice.'

'And baked.' A bag of cookies emerged. 'I remembered the way you looked at them in the office when your assistant was trying to fatten me up.'

'Caught that, did you?' Dance laughed. 'You'd be a good kinesic interviewer. We have to be observant.'

His eyes were excited, she could see. 'Got something to show you. Can we sit down somewhere?'

She directed him into the living room, where Boling unpacked yet another laptop, a big one, a brand she didn't recognize. 'Irv did it,' he announced.

'Irv?'

'Irving Wepler, the associate I was telling you about. One of my grad students.'

So, not Bambi or Tiff.

'Everything on Travis's laptop is in here now.'

He began typing. In an instant the screen came to life. Dance didn't know computers could respond so quickly.

From the other room, Maggie hit a sour note on the keyboard.

'Sorry.' Dance winced.

'C sharp,' Boling said without looking up from the screen.

Dance was surprised. 'You a musician?'

'No, no. But I have perfect pitch. Just a fluke. And I don't know what to do with it. No musical talent whatsoever. Not like you.'

'Me?' She hadn't told him her avocation.

A shrug. 'Thought it might not be a bad idea to check you out. I didn't expect you to have more Google hits as a song-catcher than a cop . . . Oh, can I say cop?'

'So far it's not a politically incorrect term.' Dance went on to explain that she was a failed folksinger but had found musical redemption in the project that she and Martine Christensen operated – a website called *American Tunes,* the name echoing Paul Simon's evocative anthem to the country from the 1970s. The site was a lifesaver for Dance, who often had to dwell in some very dark places because of her work. There was nothing like music to pull her safely out of the minds of the criminals she pursued.

Although the common term was 'songcatcher', Dance told him, the job description was technically 'folklorist'. Alan Lomax was the most famous – he'd roam the hinterland of America, collecting traditional music for the Library of Congress in the midtwentieth century. Dance too traveled around the country, when she could, to collect music, though not Lomax's mountain, blues and bluegrass. Today's homegrown American songs were African, Afro-pop, Cajun, Latino, Caribbean, Nova Scotian, East Indian and Asian.

American Tunes helped the musicians copyright their original material, offered the music for sale via download and distributed to them the money listeners paid.

Boling seemed interested. He too, it seemed, trekked into the wilderness once or twice a month. He'd been a serious rock climber at one time, he explained, but had given that up.

'Gravity,' he said, 'is nonnegotiable.'

Then he nodded toward the bedroom that was the source of the music. 'Son or daughter?'

'Daughter. The only strings my son's familiar with come on a tennis racket.'

'She's good.'

'Thank you,' Dance said with some pride; she had worked hard to encourage Maggie. She practiced with the girl and, more time-consuming, chauffeured her to and from piano lessons and recitals.

Boling typed and a colorful page popped up on the laptop's screen. But then his body language changed suddenly. She noticed he was looking over her shoulder, toward the doorway.

Dance should have guessed. She'd heard the keyboard fall silent thirty seconds before.

Then Boling was smiling. 'Hi, I'm Jon. I work with your mom.'

Wearing a backward baseball cap, Maggie was standing in the doorway. 'Hello.'

'Hats in the house,' Dance reminded.

Off it came. Maggie walked right up to Boling. 'I'm Maggie.' Nothing shy about my girl, Dance reflected, as the ten-year-old pumped his hand.

'Good grip,' the professor told her. 'And good touch on the keyboard.'

The girl beamed. 'You play anything?'

'CDs and downloads. That's it.'

Dance looked up and wasn't surprised to see twelve-year-old Wes appear too, looking their way. He was hanging back, in the doorway. And he wasn't smiling.

Her stomach did a flip. After his father's death, Wes could be counted on to take a dislike to the men that his mom saw socially – sensing them, her therapist said, as a threat to their family and to his father's memory. The only man he really liked was Michael O'Neil – in part because, the doctor theorized, the deputy was married and thus no risk.

The boy's attitude was hard for Dance, who'd been a widow for two years, and at times felt a terrible longing for a romantic companion. She wanted to date, she wanted to meet somebody and knew it would be good for the children. But whenever she went out, Wes became sullen and moody. She'd spent hours reassuring him that he and his sister came first. She planned out tactics to ease the boy comfortably into meeting her dates. And sometimes simply laid down the law and told him she wouldn't tolerate any attitude. Nothing had worked very well; and it didn't help that his hostility toward her most recent potential partner had turned out to be far more insightful than her own judgment. She resolved after that to listen to what her children had to say and watch how they reacted.

She motioned him over. He joined them. 'This is Mr Boling.'

'Hi, Wes.'

'Hi.' They shook hands, Wes a bit shy, as always.

Dance was about to add quickly that she knew Boling through work, to reassure Wes and defuse any potential awkwardness. But before she could say anything, Wes's eyes flashed as he gazed at the computer screen. 'Sweet. *DQ!*'

She regarded the splashy graphics of the *DimensionQuest* computer game homepage, which Boling had apparently extracted from Travis's computer.

'Are you guys playing?' The boy seemed astonished.

'No, no. I just wanted to show your mother something. You know Morpegs, Wes?'

'Like, definitely.'

'Wes,' Dance murmured.

'I mean, sure. She doesn't *like* me to say "like".'

Smiling, Boling asked, 'You play *DQ*? I don't know it so well.'

'Naw, it's kind of wizardy, you know. I'm more into *Trinity*.'

'Oh, man,' Boling said with some boyish, and genuine, reverence in his voice. 'The graphics kick butt.' He turned to Dance and said, 'It's S-F.'

But that wasn't much of an explanation. 'What?'

'Mom, science fiction.'

'Sci-fi.'

'No, no, you can't say that. It's S-F.' Eyes rolling broadly ceilingward.

'I stand corrected.'

Wes's face scrunched up. 'But with *Trinity*, you definitely need two gig of RAM and at least two on your video card. Otherwise it's, like . . .' He winced. 'Otherwise it's so slow. I mean, you've got your beams ready to shoot . . . and the screen hangs. It's the worst.'

'RAM on the desktop I hacked together at work?' Boling asked coyly.

'Three?' Wes asked.

'Five. And four on the video card.'

Wes mimicked a brief faint. '*Nooooo*! That is *sooo* sweet. How much storage?'

'Two T.'

'No way! Two *tera*bytes?'

Dance laughed, feeling huge relief that there wasn't any tension between them. But she said, 'Wes, I've never seen you play *Trinity*. We don't have it loaded on our computer here, do we?' She was very restrictive about what the children played on their computers and the websites they visited. But she couldn't oversee them 100 percent of the time.

'No, you don't let me,' he said without any added meaning or resentment. 'I play at Martine's.'

'With the twins?' Dance was shocked. The children of Martine Christensen and Steven Cahill were younger than Wes and Maggie.

Wes laughed. 'Mom!' Exasperated. 'No, with Steve. He's got all the patches and codes.'

That made sense; Steve, who described himself as a green geek, ran the technical side of *American Tunes*.

'Is it violent?' Dance asked Boling, not Wes.

The professor and the boy shared a conspiratorial look.

'Well?' she persisted.

'Not really,' Wes said.

'What does that mean exactly?' asked the law enforcement agent.

'Okay, you can sort of blow up spaceships and planets,' Boling said.

Wes added, 'But not like violent-violent, you know.'

'Right,' the professor assured her. 'Nothing like *Resident Evil* or *Manhunt*.'

'Or *Gears of War*,' Wes added. 'I mean, there you can *chainsaw* people.'

'*What?*' Dance was appalled. 'Have you ever played it?'

'No!' he protested, right on the edge of credibility. 'Billy Sojack at school has it. He told us about it.'

'Make sure you don't.'

'All right. I won't. Anyway,' the boy added, with another glance at Boling, 'you don't *have* to use a chain saw.'

'I never want you to play that game. Or the others that Mr Boling mentioned.' She said this in her best mother voice.

'Okay. Geez, Mom.'

'Promise?'

'Yeah.' The look at Boling said, She just *gets* this way sometimes.

The two males then launched into a discussion of other games and technical issues whose meaning Dance couldn't even guess at. But she was happy to see this. Boling, of course, was no romantic interest, but it was such a relief that she didn't have to worry about conflicts, especially tonight – the evening would be stressful enough. Boling didn't talk down to the boy, nor did he try to impress him. They seemed like peers of different ages, having fun talking.

Feeling neglected, Maggie barged in with, 'Mr Boling, do you have kids?'

'Mags,' Dance interjected, 'don't ask personal questions when you've just met somebody.'

'That's all right. No, I don't, Maggie.'

She nodded, taking in the information. The issue, Dance understood, wasn't about possible playmates. She was really inquiring about his marital status. The girl was ready to marry off her mother faster than Maryellen Kresbach from the office (provided Maggie was 'best woman' – no retro 'maid of honor' for Dance's independent daughter).

It was then that voices sounded from the kitchen. Edie and Stuart had arrived. They walked inside and joined Dance and the children.

'Grams!' Maggie called and charged toward her. 'How are you?'

Edie's face blossomed into a genuine smile – or nearly so, Dance assessed. Wes, his face glowing with relief too, ran to her as well. Though stingy with hugs for Mom lately, the boy wrapped his arms around his grandmother and squeezed tight. Of the two children, he'd taken the arrest incident at the hospital closer to heart.

'Katie,' Stuart said, 'chasing down crazed felons and you still had time to cook.'

'Well, *somebody* had time to cook,' she replied with a smile and a glance at the Safeway shopping bags, hiding near the trash can.

Ecstatic to see her mother, Dance embraced her. 'How are you?'

'Fine, dear.'

Dear . . . Not a good sign. But she was here, at least. That's what counted.

Edie turned back to the children and was enthusiastically

telling them about a TV show she'd just seen on extreme home makeovers. Dance's mother was brilliant at dispensing comfort and rather than talk directly about what happened at the hospital – which would only trouble them more – she reassured the kids by saying nothing about the incident and chatting away about inconsequential things.

Dance introduced her parents to Jon Boling.

'I'm a hired gun,' he said. 'Kathryn made the mistake of asking my advice, and she's stuck with me now.'

They talked about where in Santa Cruz he lived, how long he'd been in the area and the colleges he'd taught at. Boling was interested to learn that Stuart still worked part-time at the famous Monterey Bay aquarium; the professor went often and had just taken his niece and nephew there.

'I did some teaching too,' Stuart Dance offered, when he learned Boling's career. 'I was pretty comfortable in academia; I'd done a lot of research into sharks.'

Boling laughed hard.

Wine was dispensed – Boling's Conundrum white blend first.

But then Boling must've sensed a wind shift and he excused himself to head back to the computer. 'I don't get to eat unless I finish my homework. I'll see you in a bit.'

'Why don't you go out back,' Dance told him, pointing to the deck. 'I'll join you in a minute.'

After he'd collected the computer and wandered outside, Edie said, 'Nice young man.'

'Very helpful. Thanks to him we saved one of the victims.' Dance stepped to the refrigerator to put the wine away. As she did, emotion took the reins and she blurted softly to her mother, 'I'm sorry I had to leave the courtroom so fast, Mom. They found another roadside cross. There was a witness I had to interview.'

Her mother's voice revealed no trace of sarcasm when she said, 'That's all right, Katie. I'm sure it was important. And that poor man today. Lyndon Strickland, the lawyer. He was well known.'

'Yes, he was.' Dance noted the shift of subject.

'Sued the state, I think. Consumer advocate.'

'Mom, what've you heard from Sheedy?'

Edie Dance blinked. 'Not tonight, Katie. We won't talk about it tonight.'

'Sure.' Dance felt like a chastised child. 'Whatever you want.'

'Will Michael be here?'

'He's going to try. Anne's in San Francisco, so he's juggling kids. And working on another big case.'

'Oh. Well, hope he can make it. And how *is* Anne?' Edie asked coolly. She believed that O'Neil's wife's mothering skills left a lot to be desired. And any failures there were a class-A misdemeanor to Edie Dance, bordering on felony.

'Fine, I imagine. Haven't seen her for a while.'

Dance wondered again if in fact Michael would show up.

'You talked to Betsey?' she asked her mother.

'Yes, she's coming up this weekend.'

'She can stay with me.'

'If it's not inconvenient,' Edie offered.

'Why would it be inconvenient?'

Her mother replied, 'You might be busy. With this case of yours. That's your priority. Now, Katie, you go visit with your friend. Maggie and I'll get things started. Mags, come on and help me in the kitchen.'

'Yea, Grandma!'

'And Stu brought a DVD he thinks Wes would like. Sports bloopers. You boys go put that on.'

Her husband took the cue and wandered to the flat-screen TV, calling Wes over.

Dance stood helplessly for a moment, hands at her sides, watching her mother retreat as she chatted happily with her granddaughter. Then Dance stepped outside.

She found Boling at an unsteady table on the deck, near the back door, under an amber light. He was looking around. 'This is pretty nice.'

'I call it the Deck,' she laughed. 'Capital *D*.'

It was here that Kathryn Dance spent much of her time – by

herself and with the children, dogs and those connected to her through blood or through friendship.

The gray, pressure-treated structure, twenty by thirty feet, and eight feet above the backyard, extended along the back of the house. It was filled with unsteady lawn chairs, loungers and tables. Illumination came from tiny Christmas lights, wall lamps, some amber globes. A sink, tables and a large refrigerator sat on the uneven planks. Anemic plants in chipped pots, bird feeders and weathered metal and ceramic hangings from the garden departments of chain stores made up the eclectic decorations.

Dance would often come home to find colleagues from the CBI or MCSO or Highway Patrol sitting on the Deck, enjoying beverages from the battered fridge. It didn't matter if she was home or not, provided the rules were observed: never disrupt the kids' studying or the family's sleep, keep the crudeness down and stay out of the house itself, unless invited.

Dance loved the Deck, which was a site for breakfasts, dinner parties and more formal occasions. She'd been married here.

And she'd hosted the memorial service for her husband on the gray, warped timbers.

Dance now sat on the wicker love seat beside Boling, who was hunched forward over the large laptop. He looked around and said, 'I've got a deck too. But if we were talking constellations, yours'd be Deck Major. Mine'd be Deck Minor.'

She laughed.

Boling nodded at the computer. 'There was very little I found about the local area or Travis's friends. Much less than you'd normally see in a teen's computer. The real world doesn't figure much in Travis's life. He spends most of his time in the synth, on websites and blogs and bulletin boards and, of course, playing his Morpegs.'

Dance was disappointed. All the effort to hack into the computer and it wasn't going to be as helpful as she'd hoped.

'And as for his time in the synth world, most of that is in *DimensionQuest*.' He nodded at the screen. 'I did some research.

It's the biggest online role-playing game in the world. There are about twelve million subscribers to that one.'

'Bigger than the population of New York City.'

Boling described it as a combination of *Lord of the Rings*, *Star Wars* and *Second Life* – the social interaction site where you create imaginary lives for yourself. 'As near as I can tell he was on *DQ* between four and ten hours a day.'

'A *day*?'

'Oh, that's typical for a Morpeg player.' He chuckled. 'Some are even worse. There's a *DimensionQuest* twelve-step program in the real world to help people get over their addiction to the game.'

'Seriously?'

'Oh, yes.' He sat forward. 'Now, there's nothing in his computer about places he'd go or his friends, but I've found something that might be helpful.'

'What's that?'

'Him.'

'Who?'

'Well, Travis himself.'

23

Dance blinked, waiting for a punch line.

But Jon Boling was serious.

'You found him? Where?'

'In Aetheria, the fictional land in *DimensionQuest*.'

'He's online?'

'Not now, but he has been. Recently.'

'Can you find out where he is in real life from that?'

'There's no way of knowing. We can't trace him. I called the gaming company – they're in England – and talked to some executives. *DimensionQuest*'s servers are in India and at any given moment there are a million people online.'

'And since we have his computer, that means he's using a friend's,' Dance said.

'Or he's at a public terminal or he's borrowed or stolen a computer and is logging on through a Wi-Fi spot.'

'But whenever he's online we know he's standing still and we have a chance to find him.'

'In theory, yes,' Boling agreed.

'Why is he still playing? He must know we're looking for him.'

'Like I was saying, he's addicted.'

A nod at the computer: 'Are you sure it's Travis?'

'Has to be. I got into his folders in the game and found a list of avatars he's created to represent himself. Then I had a few of my students go online and look for those names. He's been logging on and off today. The character's name is Stryker – with a *y*. He's in the category of Thunderer, which makes him a warrior. A killer, basically. One of my students – a girl who's played *DimensionQuest* for a few years – found him about an hour ago. He was roaming around the countryside just killing people. She watched him slaughter a whole family. Men, women and children. And then he corpse camped.'

'What's that?'

'In these games, when you kill another character they lose power, points and whatever they're carrying with them. But they're not permanently dead. Avatars come to life again after a few minutes. But they're in a weakened state until they can start to regain power. Corpse camping is when you kill a victim and just wait nearby for them to come back to life. Then you kill them again, when they have no defenses. It's very bad form, and most players don't do it. It's like killing a wounded soldier on the battlefield. But Travis apparently does it regularly.'

Dance stared at the homepage of *DimensionQuest*, an elaborate graphic of foggy glens, towering mountains, fantastical cities, turbulent oceans. And mythical creatures, warriors, heroes, wizards. Villains too, including Qetzal, the spiky demon with the sewn-shut mouth, wide eyes chillingly staring at her.

A bit of that nightmare world had coalesced here on earth, smack within her jurisdiction.

Boling tapped his cell phone, on his belt. 'Irv's monitoring the game. He wrote a bot – an automated computer program – that'll tell him when Stryker's online. He'll call or IM me the instant Travis logs on.'

Dance glanced into the kitchen and saw her mother staring out the window. Her palms were clenched.

'Now, what I was thinking,' Boling continued, 'tracing is out, but if we can find him online and watch him, maybe we can learn something about him. Where he is, who he knows.'

'How?'

'Watching his instant messages. That's how players communicate in *DQ*. But there's nothing we can do until he logs on again.'

He sat back. They sipped wine in silence.

Which was suddenly broken as Wes called, 'Mom!' from the doorway.

Dance jumped and found herself easing away from Boling as she turned toward her son.

'When do we eat?'

'As soon as Martine and Steve get here.'

The boy retreated to the TV. And Dance and Boling walked inside, carting wine and the computer. The professor replaced the unit in his bag and then snagged a bowl of pretzels from the island in the kitchen.

He headed into the living room and offered the bowl to Wes and Stu. 'Emergency rations to keep our strength up.'

'Yeah!' the boy cried, grabbing a handful. Then said, 'Grandpa, go back to that fumble so Mr Boling can see it.'

Dance helped her mother and daughter finish setting out the food, buffet style, on the island in the kitchen.

She and Edie talked about the weather, about the dogs, about the children, about Stuart. Which led to the aquarium, which led to a water referendum, which led to a half dozen other trivial subjects, all of which had one thing in common: they were as far away from the subject of the arrest of Edie Dance as could be.

She watched Wes, Jon Boling and her father sitting together in the living room, with the sports show on the screen. They all laughed hard when a receiver crashed into a Gatorade tank and drenched a cameraman, and were digging into the pretzels and dip as if dinner were an empty promise. Dance had to smile at the homey, comforting scene.

Then she glanced down at her cell phone, disappointed that Michael O'Neil hadn't called.

As she was setting the table on the Deck, the other guests

arrived: Martine Christensen and her husband, Steven Cahill, climbed the stairs, their nine-year-old twin boys in tow. Delighting Wes and Maggie, they also brought with them a long-haired tawny puppy, a briard named Raye.

The couple greeted Edie Dance warmly, avoiding any mention of the cases; either the Roadside Cross attacks or the one involving Edie.

'Hey, girlfriend,' long-haired Martine said to Dance, winking, and passed her a dangerous-looking homemade chocolate cake.

Dance and Martine had been best friends ever since the woman had decided to single-handedly wrest Dance from the addictive lethargy of widowhood and force her back into life.

As if moving from the synth world back to the real, Dance now reflected.

She hugged Steven, who promptly vanished into the den to join the menfolk, his Birkenstocks flapping in time to his long ponytail.

The adults had wine while the children held an impromptu dog show in the backyard. Raye had apparently been doing his homework and was, literally, running circles around Patsy and Dylan, doing tricks and leaping over benches. Martine said he was a star in his obedience and agility classes.

Maggie appeared and said she wanted to take their dogs to school too.

'We'll see,' Dance told her.

Soon candles were lit, sweaters distributed and everybody was sitting around the table, food steaming in the false autumn of a Monterey evening. Conversation was whirling as fast as the wine flowed. Wes was whispering jokes to the twins, who giggled not because of the punch lines but because an older boy was spending time whispering jokes to them.

Edie was laughing at something Martine said.

And for the first time in two days, Kathryn Dance felt the gloom fade.

Travis Brigham, Hamilton Royce, James Chilton . . . and the Dark Knight – Robert Harper – slipped from the forefront of her thoughts and she began to think that life might eventually right itself.

Jon Boling turned out to be quite social and fit right in, though he hadn't known a single soul there before today. He and Steven, the computer programmer, had much to talk about, though Wes kept injecting himself into the conversation.

Everyone studiously avoided talking about Edie's problem, which meant that current affairs and politics took center stage. Dance was amused to note that the first subjects to come up were ones Chilton had written about: the desalination plant and the new highway to Salinas.

Steve, Martine and Edie were adamantly opposed to the plant.

'I suppose,' Dance said. 'But we've all lived here for a long time.' A glance at her parents. 'Aren't you tired of the droughts?'

Martine said she doubted the water produced by the desalination plant would benefit them. 'It'll be sold to rich cities in Arizona and Nevada. Somebody'll make billions and we won't see a drop.'

After that they debated the highway. The group was divided on this, as well. Dance said, 'It'd come in handy for the CBI and sheriff's office if we're running cases in the fields north of Salinas. But that cost-overrun issue is a problem.'

'What overrun?' Stuart asked.

Dance was surprised to see everyone looking at her blankly. She explained what she'd learned by reading *The Chilton Report*: that the blogger had uncovered some possible malfeasance.

'I hadn't heard about that,' Martine said. 'I was so busy reading about the roadside crosses that I didn't pay much attention . . . But I'm sure going to look into it now, I'll tell you.' She was the most political of Dance's friends. 'I'll check out the blog.'

After dinner Dance asked Maggie to bring out her keyboard for a brief concert.

The group retired to the living room, more wine was passed around. Boling lounged back in a deep armchair, joined by Raye the briard. Martine laughed – Raye was a bit bigger than a lapdog – but the professor insisted the puppy stay.

Maggie plugged in and, with the gravity of a recital pianist, sat down and played four songs from her Suzuki *Book Three*, simple arrangements of pieces by Mozart, Beethoven and Clementi. She hardly missed a note.

Everyone applauded and then went for cake, coffee and more wine.

Finally around 9:30, Steve and Martine said they wanted to get the twins to bed, and they headed out the door with the children. Maggie was already making plans to enter Dylan and Patsy in Raye's dog classes.

Edie gave a distant smile. 'We should go too. It's been a long day.'

'Mom, stay for a while. Have another glass of wine.'

'No, no, I'm exhausted, Katie. Come on, Stu. I want to go home.'

Dance received a distracted embrace from her mother, and her comfort from earlier diminished. 'Call me later.' Disappointed at their quick retreat, she watched the taillights disappear up the road. Then she told the children to say good night to Boling. The professor smiled and shook their hands, and Dance sent them off to wash up.

Wes appeared a few minutes later with a DVD. *Ghost in the Shell,* a Japanese anime science fiction tale involving computers.

'Here, Mr Boling. This is pretty sweet. You can borrow it if you want.'

Dance was astonished that her son was behaving so well with a man. Probably he recognized Boling as a business associate of his mother's, not a love interest; still, he'd been known to grow defensive even around her coworkers.

'Well, thanks, Wes. I've written about anime. But I've never seen this one.'

'Really?'

'Nope. I'll bring it back in good shape.'

'Whenever. 'Night.'

The boy hurried back to his room, leaving the two of them together.

But only for a moment. A second later Maggie appeared with a gift of her own. 'This is my recital.' She handed him a CD in a jewel box.

'The one you were talking about at dinner?' Boling asked. 'Where Mr Stone burped during the Mozart?'

'Yeah!'

'Can I borrow it?'

'You can have it. I have about a million of them. Mom made them.'

'Well, thanks, Maggie. I'll burn it on my iPod.'

The girl actually blushed. Unusual for her. She charged off.

'You don't have to,' Dance whispered.

'Oh, no. I will. She's a great girl.'

He slipped the disk into his computer bag and looked over the anime that Wes had lent him.

Dance lowered her voice again, 'How many times have you seen it?'

He chuckled. '*Ghost in the Shell?* Twenty, thirty times . . . along with the two sequels. Damn, you can even spot the white lies.'

'Appreciate your doing that. It means a lot to him.'

'I could tell he was excited.'

'I'm surprised you don't have children. You seem to understand them.'

'No, that never worked out. But if you want children, it definitely helps to have a woman in your life. I'm one of those men you have to be careful of. Don't you say that, all you girls?

'Careful of? Why's that?'

'Never date a man over forty who's never been married.'

'I think nowadays whatever works, works.'

'I just never met anybody I wanted to settle down with.'

Dance noted the flicker of an eyebrow and a faint fluctuation of pitch. She let those observations float away.

Boling began, 'You're . . . ?' His eyes dipped to her left hand, where a gray pearl ring encircled the heart finger.

'I'm a widow,' Dance said.

'Oh, gosh. I'm sorry.'

'Car crash,' she said, feeling only a hint of the familiar sorrow. 'Terrible.'

And Kathryn Dance said nothing more about her husband and the accident for no reason other than she preferred not to talk about them any longer. 'So, you're a real bachelor, hmm?'

'I guess I am. Now there's a word you haven't heard for . . . about a century.'

She went to the kitchen to retrieve more wine, instinctively grabbing a red – since that was Michael O'Neil's favorite – then remembered that Boling liked white. She filled their glasses halfway up.

They chatted about life on the Peninsula – his mountain-biking trips and hikes. His professional life was far too sedentary for him so Boling would often jump into his old pickup truck and head out to the mountains or a state park.

'I'll do some biking this weekend. It'll be some sanity in an island of madness.' He then told her more about the family get-together he'd mentioned earlier.

'Napa?'

'Right.' His brow wrinkled in a cute and charming way. 'My family is . . . how do I put this?'

'A family.'

'Hit the nail on the head,' he said, laughing. 'Two parents healthy. Two siblings I get along with a majority of the time, though I like their children better. Assorted uncles and aunts. It'll be fine. Lot of wine, lot of food. Sunsets – but not a lot of those, thank goodness. Two, tops. That's sort of the way weekends work.'

Again, a silence fell between them. Comfortable. Dance felt no rush to fill it.

But the peace was broken just then as Boling's cell phone hiccuped. He looked at the screen. Immediately his body language had shifted to high alert.

'Travis is online. Let's go.'

24

Under Boling's keystrokes, the *DimensionQuest* homepage loaded almost instantly.

The screen dissolved and a welcome box appeared. Below it was apparently the rating of the game by an organization referred to as ERSB.

Teen
Blood
Suggestive Themes
Alcohol
Violence

Then, with his self-assured typing, Jon Boling took them to Aetheria.

It was an odd experience. Avatars – some fantastical creatures, some human – wandered around a clearing in a forest of massive trees. Their names were in balloons above the characters. Most of them were fighting, but some just walked, ran or rode horses or other creatures. Some flew on their own. Dance was surprised to see that everyone moved nimbly and that the facial expressions were true to life. The graphics were astonishing, nearly movie quality.

Which made the combat and its vicious, excessive bloodletting all the more harrowing.

Dance found herself sitting forward, knee bobbing – a classic indication of stress. She gasped when one warrior beheaded another right in front of them.

'There are real people guiding them?'

'One or two are NPC – those're "nonplayer characters" that the game itself creates. But nearly all of the others are avatars of people who could be anywhere. Cape Town, Mexico, New York, Russia. The majority of the players are men, but there're a lot of women too. And the average age isn't as young as you'd think. Teenage to late twenties mostly but plenty of older players. They could be boys or girls or middle-aged men, black, white, disabled, athletes, lawyers, dishwashers . . . In the synth world, you can be whoever you want to be.'

In front of them another warrior easily killed his opponent. Blood spurted in a geyser. Boling grunted. 'They're not all *equal*, though. Survival depends on who practices the most and who has the most power – power you earn by fighting and killing. It's a vicious cycle, literally.'

Dance tapped the screen and pointed to the back of a woman avatar in the foreground. 'That's you?'

'One of my student's avatars. I'm logging in through her account.'

The name above her was 'Greenleaf'.

'There he is!' Boling said, his shoulder brushing hers as he leaned forward. He was pointing at Travis's avatar, Stryker, who was about a hundred feet away from Greenleaf.

Stryker was a tough, muscular man. Dance couldn't help but notice that while many other characters had beards or ruddy, leathery skin, Travis's avatar was unblemished and his skin as smooth as a baby's. She thought of the boy's concerns about acne.

You can be whoever you want to be . . .

Stryker – a 'Thunderer,' she recalled – was clearly the domin-ant warrior here. People would look his way and turn and leave. Several people engaged him – once two at the same time. He easily killed them both. One time he stunned a huge avatar, a troll or similar beast, with a ray. Then, as it lay shaking on the ground, Travis directed his avatar to plunge a knife into its chest.

Dance gasped.

Stryker bent down and seemed to reach inside the body.

'What's he doing?'

'Looting the corpse.' Boling noted Dance's furrowed brow and added, 'Everyone does it. You have to. The bodies might have something valuable. And if you've defeated them, you've earned the right.'

If these were the values that Travis had learned in the synth world, it was a wonder he hadn't snapped sooner.

She couldn't help but wonder: and where was the boy now in the real world? At a Starbucks Wi-Fi location, with the hood over his head and sunglasses on, so he wouldn't be recognized? Ten miles from here? One mile?

He wasn't at the Game Shed. She knew that. After learning that he spent time there, Dance had ordered surveillance on the place.

As she watched Travis's avatar engage and easily kill dozens of creatures – women and men and animals – she found herself instinctively drawing on her skills as a kinesics expert.

She knew, of course, that computer software was controlling the boy's movement and posture. Yet she was already seeing that his avatar moved with more grace and fluidity than most. In combat he didn't flail away randomly, as some of the characters did. He took his time, he withdrew a bit and then struck when his opponents were disoriented. Several fast blows or stabs later – and the character was dead. He stayed alert, always looking around him.

This was a clue, perhaps, to the boy's strategy of life. Planning the attacks out carefully, learning all he could about his victims, attacking fast.

Analyzing the body language of a computer avatar, she reflected. What an odd case this was.

'I want to talk to him.'

'To Travis? I mean, to Stryker?'

'Right. Get closer.'

Boling hesitated. 'I don't know the navigation commands very well. But I think I can walk all right.'

'Go ahead.'

Using the keypad, Boling maneuvered Greenleaf closer to where Stryker was hunched over the body of the creature he'd just killed, looting it.

As soon as she was within attack distance Stryker sensed Dance's avatar's approach and leapt up, his sword in one hand, an elaborate shield in the other. Stryker's eyes gazed out of the screen.

Eyes dark as the demon Qetzal's.

'How do I send a message?'

Boling clicked on a button at the bottom of the screen and a box opened. 'Just like any instant message now. Type your message and hit "Return". Remember, use abbreviations and leetspeak if you can. The easiest thing to do is just substitute the number three for *e* and four for *a*.'

Dance took a deep breath. Her hands were shaking as she stared at the animated face of the killer.

'*Stryker, U R g00d.*' The words appeared in a balloon over Greenleaf's head as the avatar approached.

'*who r u?*' Stryker stood back, gripping a sword.

'*I'm just some lus3r.*'

Boling told her, 'Not bad, but forget grammar and punctuation. No caps, no periods. Question marks are okay.'

Dance continued, '*saw u fight u r el33t.*' Her breath was coming fast; tension rose within her.

'Excellent,' Boling whispered.

'*what is your realm?*'

'What's he mean?' Dance asked, feeling a sprinkle of panic.

'I think he's asking for your country or the guild you're in. There'd be hundreds of them. I don't know any in this game. Tell him you're a newbie.' He spelled it. 'That's somebody new to a game, but who wants to learn.'

'*just newbie, play for fun, thought u could t33ch*'

There was a pause.

'u mean u r sum n00b'

'What's that?' Dance asked.

'Newbie's just a beginner. A n00b is a loser, somebody who's egotistical and incompetent. It's an insult. Travis has been called a n00b a lot online. LOL him but say you're not. Your really want to learn from him.'

'lol, but no d00d, i w4nt to learn'

'R U hot?'

Dance asked Boling, 'Is he coming on to me?'

'I don't know. It's an odd question under the circumstances.'

'sorta people tell me'

'u board funny'

'Shit, he's catching on that there's a delay in your keyboarding. He's suspicious. Change the subject back to him.'

'like really w4nt to learn, what can u t33ch me?'

A pause. Then: *'1 thing'*

Dance typed, *'whats that?'*

Another hesitation.

Then words appeared in the balloon Travis's avatar. *'2 die'*

And though Dance felt an instinct to slam an arrow key or slide the touchpad to lift an arm and protect herself, there was no time.

Travis's avatar moved in fast. He swung his sword again and again, striking her. In the upper left-hand corner of the screen a box popped up showing two figures, solid white: the headings 'Stryker' was above the one on the left, and 'Greenleaf' on the right.

'No!' she whispered, as Travis slashed away.

The white filling the Greenleaf outline began to empty. Boling said, 'That's your life force bleeding out. Fight back. You have a sword. There!' He tapped the screen. 'Put the cursor on it and left click with the mouse.'

Filled with unreasonable but feverish panic, she began clicking. Stryker easily deflected her avatar's wild blows.

As Greenleaf's power slipped away on the gauge, the avatar

dropped to her knees. Soon the sword fell to the ground. She was on her back, arms and legs splayed. Helpless.

Dance felt as vulnerable as she ever had in real life.

'You don't have much power left,' Boling said. 'There's nothing you can do.' The gauge was nearly drained.

Stryker stopped hacking at Greenleaf's body. He moved closer and looked into the computer monitor.

'who r u?' came the words popping up in the instant message. *'i am greenleaf. Y did U kill me?'*

'WHO R U?'

Boling said, 'All caps. He's shouting. He's mad.'

'pleez?' Dance's hands were shaking and her chest was constricted. It was as if these weren't bits of electronic data but real people; she'd plunged wholly into the synth world.

Travis then directed Stryker to step forward and drive his sword into Greenleaf's abdomen. Blood spurted, and the gauge in the upper left-hand corner was replaced with a message: *'YOU ARE DEAD.'*

'Oh,' Dance cried. Her sweaty hands quivered and her breath stuttered in and out, over her dry lips. Travis's avatar stared at the screen chillingly, then turned and began to run into the forest. Without a pause, he swiped his sword across the neck of an avatar whose back was turned and lopped off the creature's head.

He then vanished.

'He didn't wait to loot the corpse. He's escaping. He wants to get away fast. He thinks something's up.' Boling moved closer to Dance – now it was their legs that brushed. 'I want to see something.' He began to type. Another box appeared. It said, *'Stryker is not online.'*

Dance felt a painful chill rattling through her, ice along her spine.

Sitting back, her shoulder against Jon Boling's, she was thinking: if Travis had logged off, maybe he'd left the location where he'd been online.

And where was he going?

Into hiding?

Or was he intent on continuing his hunt in the real world?

Lying in bed, the hour closing in on midnight.

Two sounds confused: the wind stroking the trees outside her bedroom window and surf on rocks a mile away at Asilomar and along the road to Lovers Point.

Beside her, she felt warmth against her leg, and exhaled breath, soft in sleep, tickled her neck.

She was unable to join in the bliss of unconsciousness, however. Kathryn Dance was as awake as if it were noon.

In her mind a series of thoughts spun past. One would rise to the top for a time, then roll on, like on *Wheel of Fortune*. The subject the clicker settled on most frequently was Travis Brigham of course. In her years of being a crime reporter and a jury consultant and a law enforcement agent, Dance had come to believe that the tendency toward evil could be found in the genes – like Daniel Pell, the cult leader and killer she'd pursued recently – or could be acquired: J. Doe in Los Angeles, for instance, whose murderous inclinations had come later in life.

Dance wondered where Travis fell on the spectrum.

He was a troubled, dangerous young man, but he was also someone else, a teenager yearning to be normal – to have clear skin, to have a popular girl like him. Was it inevitable from birth that he'd slip into this life of rage? Or had he begun like any other boy yet been so battered by circumstance – his abusive father, troubled brother, gawky physique, solitary nature, bad complexion – that his anger couldn't burn away as it did in most of us, like midmorning fog?

For a long, thick moment, pity and loathing were balanced within her.

Then she saw Travis's avatar staring her down and lifting his sword.

like really w4nt to learn, what can u t33ch me?

2 die . . .

Next to her the warm body shifted slightly, and she wondered if she was giving off minuscule tensions that disturbed sleep. She was trying to remain motionless, but that, as a kinesics expert, she knew was impossible. Asleep or waking, if our brain functioned, our bodies moved.

The wheel spun on.

Her mother, and the euthanasia case, now paused at the top. Though she'd asked Edie to call when they got back to the inn, she hadn't. This hurt, but didn't surprise, Dance.

Then the wheel spun again and the J. Doe case in Los Angeles paused at the apogee. What would come of the immunity hearing? Would it be delayed again? And the ultimate outcome? Ernie Seybold was good. But was he good enough?

Dance honestly didn't know.

This musing in turn led to thoughts of Michael O'Neil. She understood there were reasons that he hadn't been able to be here tonight. But his not calling? That was unusual.

The Other Case . . .

Dance laughed at the jealousy.

She occasionally tried to picture herself and O'Neil together, had he not been married to svelte and exotic Anne. On the one hand, it was too easy. They'd spent days together on cases, and the hours moved by seamlessly. The conversation flowed, the humor. Yet they also disagreed, sometimes to the point of anger. But she believed their passionate disagreements only added to what they had together.

Whatever that was.

Her thoughts wheeled on, unstoppable.

Click, click, click . . .

At least until they stopped at Professor Jonathan Boling.

And beside her the soft breathing became a soft rattle.

'Okay, that's it,' Dance said, rolling onto her other side. 'Patsy!'

The flat-coat retriever stopped snoring as she awoke and lifted her head off the pillow.

'On the floor,' Dance commanded.

The dog stood, assessed that no food or ball playing figured in the deal and leapt off the bed to join her companion, Dylan, on the shabby rug they used as a futon, leaving Dance once more alone in bed.

Jon Boling, she reflected. Then decided perhaps it was better not to spend much time on him.

Not just yet.

In any case, at that moment, her musings vanished as the mobile phone by the bed, sitting next to her weapon, trilled.

Instantly, she flipped the light on, shoved her glasses on her nose and laughed, seeing the Caller ID.

'Jon,' she said.

'Kathryn,' Boling said. 'I'm sorry to call so late.'

'It's okay. I wasn't asleep. What's up? Stryker?'

'No. But there's something you have to see. The blog – *The Chilton Report*. You better go online now.'

In her sweats, the dogs nearby, Dance was sitting in the living room, all the lights off, though moonlight and a shaft of street-light painted iridescent swatches of blue-white on the pine floor. Her Glock pressed against her spine, the heavy gun tugging down the limp elastic waistband of her sweats.

The computer finished its interminable loading of the software.

'Okay.'

He said, 'Look over the latest posting of the blog.' He gave her the URL.

http://www.thechiltonreport.com/html/june27update.html

She blinked in surprise. 'What . . . ?'

Bolling told her, 'Travis hacked the *Report*.'

'How?'

The professor gave a cold laugh. 'He's a teenager, that's how.'

Dance shivered as she read. Travis had posted a message over the beginning of the June 27 blog. To the left was a crude drawing of the creature Qetzal from *DimensionQuest*. Around the eerie face, its lips sewn shut and bloody, were cryptic numbers and words. Beside it was a text posting in large, bold letters. It was even more troubling than the picture. Half English, half leetspeak.

> I will OWN u all!
> i = win, u = fail!!
> u r d3ad
> 3v3ry 1 of u
> – post3d by TravisDQ

She didn't need a translator for this one.

Below this was another picture. The awkward color rendering showed a teenage girl or woman lying on her back, mouth open in a scream, as a hand plunged a sword into her chest. Blood spurted skyward.

'That picture . . . it's disgusting, Jon.'

After a pause: 'Kathryn,' he said in a soft voice. 'Do you notice anything about it?'

As she studied the awkward drawing, Dance gave a gasp. The victim had brownish hair, pulled back in a ponytail, and was wearing a white blouse and black skirt. On her belt was a darkened area on the hip, which could have been a weapon holster. The outfit was similar to what Dance had been wearing when she'd met Travis yesterday.

'It's me?' she whispered to Boling.

The professor said nothing.

Was the picture old, maybe a fantasy about the death of a girl or woman who'd slighted Travis somehow in the past?

Or had he drawn it today, despite the fact he was on the run from the police?

Dance had a chilling image of the boy, hovering over the paper with pencil and crayon, creating this crude depiction of a synth world death he hoped to make real.

The wind is a persistent aspect of the Monterey Peninsula. Usually bracing, sometimes weak or tentative but never absent. Day and night, it churns the blue-gray ocean, which false to its name is never calm.

One of the windiest places for miles around is China Cove, at the south end of Point Lobos State Park. The chill, steady breath from the ocean numbs the skin of hikers, and picnics are a dicey proposition if paper plates and cups figure as the dishware. Seabirds here labor even to stay in place if they aim into the breeze.

Now, nearly midnight, the wind is fickle, surging and vanishing, and at its strongest, it kicks up towering gray spumes of seawater.

It rustles the scrub oak.

It bends the pine.

It flattens the grasses.

But one thing that's immune to the wind tonight is a small artifact on the seaside shoulder of Highway 1.

It's a cross, about two feet high and made of black branches. In the middle is a torn cardboard disk with tomorrow's date penned in blue. Sitting at the base, weighted down by stones, is a bouquet of red roses. At times petals fly off and skitter across the highway. But the cross itself doesn't flutter or bend. Clearly it was driven deep into the sandy dirt by the roadside with powerful blows, its creator adamant that it remain upright and visible for all to see.

THURSDAY

25

Kathryn Dance, TJ Scanlon and Jon Boling were in her office. The time was 9:00 a.m. and they'd been there for close to two hours.

Chilton had removed Travis's threat and the two pictures from the thread.

But Boling had downloaded them and made copies.

u r d3ad.

3v3ry 1 of u.

And the pictures, too.

Jon Boling said, 'It might be possible to trace the posting.' A grimace. 'But only if Chilton cooperates.'

'Is there anything in the picture of Qetzal – those numbers and codes and words? Anything that might help?'

Boling said that they were mostly about the game and had probably been made a long time ago. In any case, even the puzzle-master could find no clues in the weird notations.

The others in the room scrupulously avoided commenting that the second picture, of the stabbing, bore a resemblance to Dance herself.

She was about to phone the blogger, when she got a call. Barking a laugh as she looked at Caller ID, she picked up. 'Yes, Mr Chilton?'

Boling looked at her with an ironic gaze.

'I don't know if you saw . . . ?'

'We did. Your blog got hacked.'

'The server had good security. The boy's got to be smart.'
A pause. Then the blogger continued, 'I wanted to let you
know, we tried to trace the hack. He's using a proxy site somewhere in Scandinavia. I've called some friends over there, and
they're pretty certain they know what the company is. I have
the name and their address. Phone number too. It's outside
of Stockholm.'

'Will they cooperate?'

Chilton said, 'Proxy services rarely do unless there's a warrant.
That's why people use them, of course.'

An international warrant would be a nightmare procedurally
and Dance had never known one to be served earlier than two
or three weeks after it was issued. Sometimes the foreign authorities ignored them altogether. But it was something. 'Give me
the information. I'll try.'

Chilton did.

'I appreciate your doing this.'

'And there's something else.'

'What's that?'

'Are you in the blog now?'

'I can be.'

'Read what I just posted a few minutes ago.'

She logged on.

http://www.thechiltonreport.com/html/june28.html

First was an apology to the readers, surprising Dance with its
humility. Then came:

AN OPEN LETTER TO TRAVIS BRIGHAM

This is a personal plea, Travis. Now that your name is public, I hope you won't
mind my using it.

My job is to report the news, to ask questions, not to get involved in the stories
I report on. But I have to get involved now.

Please, Travis, there's been enough trouble. Don't make it worse for yourself. It's not too late to put an end to this terrible situation. Think of your family, think of your future. Please . . . call the police, give yourself up. There are people who want to help you.

Dance said, 'That's brilliant, James. Travis might even contact you about surrendering.'

'And I've frozen the thread. Nobody else can post to it.' He was silent for a moment. 'That picture . . . it was terrible.'

Welcome to the real world, Chilton.

She thanked him and they hung up. She scrolled to the end of the 'Roadside Crosses' thread and read the most recent – and apparently last – posts. Although some seemed to have been posted from overseas, she once again couldn't help wondering if they contained clues that might help her find Travis or anticipate his next moves. But she could draw no conclusions from the cryptic postings.

Dance logged off and told TJ and Boling about what Chilton had written.

Boling wasn't sure it would have much effect – the boy, in his assessment, was past reasoning with. 'But we'll hope.'

Dance doled out assignments; TJ retreated to his chair at the coffee table to contact the Scandinavian proxy, and Boling to his corner to check out the names of possible victims from a new batch of Internet addresses – including those who'd posted to threads other than 'Roadside Crosses.' He'd identified thirteen more.

Charles Overby, in a politician's blue suit and white shirt, stepped into Dance's office. His greeting: 'Kathryn . . . say, Kathryn, what's this about the kid posting threats?'

'Right, Charles. We're trying to find out where he hacked in from.'

'Six reporters have already called me. And a couple of them got my home phone number. I've put them off but I can't wait anymore. I'm holding a press conference in twenty minutes. What can I tell them?'

'That the investigation is continuing. We're getting some manpower help from San Benito for the search. There've been sightings but nothing's panned out.'

'Hamilton called me too. He's pretty upset.'

Sacramento's Hamilton Royce, of the too-blue suit, the quick eyes and the ruddy complexion.

Agent in Charge Overby had had a rather eventful morning, it seemed.

'Anything more?'

'Chilton's stopped the posts on the thread and asked Travis to surrender.'

'Anything tech, I mean?'

'Well, he's helping us trace the boy's uploads.'

'Good. So we're doing *something*.'

He meant: something the viewers of prime-time TV would appreciate. As opposed to the sweaty, unstylish police work they'd been engaged in the last forty-eight hours. Dance caught Boling's eye, which said he too was taken aback by the comment. They looked away from each other immediately before a shared look of shock bloomed.

Overby glanced at his watch. 'All right. My turn in the barrel.' He wandered off to the press conference.

'Does he know what that expression means?' Boling asked her.

'About the barrel? I don't know, myself.'

TJ gave a chortling laugh but said nothing. He smiled at Boling, who said, 'It's a joke I won't repeat. It involves horny sailors out to sea for a long time.'

'Thanks for not sharing.' Dance dropped into her desk chair, sipped the coffee that had materialized and, what the hell, went for half of the doughnut that also had appeared as a gift from the gods.

'Has Travis – well, Stryker – been back online?' she called to Jon Boling.

'Nope. Haven't heard from Irv. But he'll be sure to let us know. I don't think he's ever slept. He's got Red Bull in his veins.'

Dance picked up the phone and called Peter Bennington at

MCSO forensics for the latest information on the evidence. The gist was that while there was by now plenty of evidence to get a murder conviction against Travis, there were no leads as to where he might be hiding out, except those traces of soil they'd found earlier – a location different from that where the cross had been left. David Reinhold, that eager young deputy from the sheriff's office, had taken it on himself to collect samples from around Travis's house; the dirt didn't match.

Sandy soil . . . *So* helpful, Dance reflected cynically, in an area that boasted more than fifteen miles of the most beautiful beaches and dunes in the state.

Despite his ability to report that the CBI was 'doing something techie', Charles Overby got T-boned at the press conference.

The TV in Dance's office was on and they were able to watch the crash live.

Dance's briefing to Overby had been accurate, except for one small detail, albeit one she hadn't known.

'Agent Overby,' a reporter asked, 'what are you doing to protect the community in light of the new cross?'

Deer in the headlights.

'Uh-oh,' TJ whispered.

Shocked, Dance looked from him to Boling. Then back to the screen.

The reporter continued that she'd heard a report a half hour earlier on a radio scanner. Carmel police had found another cross with today's date, June 28, near China Cove on Highway 1.

Overby sputtered in response, 'I was briefed just before coming here by the agent in charge of the case, and she apparently wasn't aware of it.'

There were two senior women agents in the Monterey office of the CBI. It would be easy to find out who the 'she' in question was.

Oh, you son of a bitch, Charles.

She heard another reporter ask, 'Agent Overby, what do you say to the fact that the town, the whole Peninsula's in a panic?

There've been reports of homeowners shooting at innocent people who happen to walk into their yards.'

A pause. 'Well, that's not good.'

Oh, brother . . .

Dance shut the TV off. She called the MCSO and learned that, yes, another cross, with today's date, had been found near China Cove. A bouquet of red roses too. Crime Scene was collecting the evidence and searching the area.

'There were no witnesses, Agent Dance,' the deputy added.

After she hung up, Dance turned to TJ. 'What do the Swedes tell us?'

TJ had phoned the proxy service company and left two urgent messages. They had not returned his call yet, despite it being a business day in Stockholm and only past lunchtime.

Five minutes later Overby stormed into the office. 'Another cross? Another cross? What the hell happened?'

'I just found out about it myself, Charles.'

'How the hell did *they* hear?'

'The press? Scanners, contacts. The way they always find out what we're doing.'

Overby rubbed his tanned forehead. Skin flakes drifted. 'Well, where are we with it?'

'Michael's people are running the scene. If there's evidence they'll let us know.'

'*If* there's evidence.'

'He's a teenager, Charles, not a pro. He's going to leave *some* clues that'll lead us to where he's hiding. Sooner or later.'

'But if he left a cross that means he's also going to try to kill somebody today.'

'We're contacting as many people as we can find who might be at risk.'

'And the computer tracing? What's going on there?'

TJ said, 'The company's not calling us back. We've got Legal putting together a foreign warrant request.'

The head of the office grimaced. 'That's just great. Where's the proxy?'

'Sweden.'

'They're better than the Bulgarians,' Overby said, 'but it'll be a month before they even get around to responding. Send the request, to cover our asses, but don't waste time on it.'

'Yes, sir.'

Overby stormed off, fishing his mobile out of his pocket.

Dance snagged her own phone and called Rey Carraneo and Albert Stemple into her office. When they arrived she announced, 'I'm tired of being on the defensive here. I want to pick the top five or six potential victims – the ones who've posted the most vicious attacks on Travis, and the posters who're the most supportive of Chilton. We're going to get them out of the area and then set up surveillance at their houses or apartments. He's got a new victim in mind and when he shows up, I want him to get one big goddamn surprise. Let's get on it.'

26

'How's he holding up?' Lily Hawken asked her husband, Donald.

'James? He's not saying much but it's got to be tough on him. Patrizia too, I'm sure.'

They were in the den of their new house in Monterey.

Unpacking, unpacking, unpacking . . .

The petite blonde stood in the middle of the room, feet apart slightly, looking down at two plastic bags of drapes. 'What do you think?'

Hawken was a bit overwhelmed at the moment and couldn't care less about window treatments, but his wife of nine months and three days had taken on much of the burden of the move from San Diego and so he set down the tools he was using to assemble the coffee table and looked from the red to the rust and back again.

'The ones on the left.' Remaining ready to retreat at a moment's notice if that was the wrong answer.

But it was apparently correct. 'That's where I was leaning,' she said. 'And the police have a guard at his house? They think the boy is going to attack him?'

Hawken resumed assembling the table. Ikea. Damn, they have some pretty clever designers. '*He* doesn't think so. But you know Jim. Even if he did, he's not the sort to head for the hills.'

Then he reflected that Lily didn't really know James Chilton at all; she hadn't even met him yet. It was only through what he'd told her that she had an understanding of his friend.

Just as he knew about many aspects of her life from conversation and hint and deduction. Such was life under these circumstances – second marriages for both of them; he, coming out of mourning, Lily, recovering from a tough divorce. They'd met through friends and had started dating. Wary at first, they'd realized almost simultaneously how starved for intimacy and affection they were. Hawken, a man who hadn't believed that he would ever get married again, proposed after six months – on the gritty rooftop beach bar of the W hotel in downtown San Diego, because he couldn't wait to plot out a more suitable setting.

Lily, though, had described the event as the most romantic thing she could think of. The large diamond ring on a white ribbon slipped over the neck of her Anchor Steam bottle helped.

And here they were starting a new life back in Monterey.

Donald Hawken assessed his situation and decided that he was happy. Boyishly happy. Friends had told him that a second marriage after losing a spouse was different. As a widower he would have changed fundamentally. He wouldn't be capable of that adolescent feeling permeating every cell of his being. There'd be companionship, there'd be moments of passion. But the relationship would essentially be a friendship.

Wrong.

It was adolescent and more.

He'd had an intense, consuming marriage to Sarah, who was sultry and beautiful and a woman one could be intensely in love with, as Hawken had been.

But his love for Lily was just as strong.

And, okay, he'd finally gotten to the point where he could admit that the sex was better with Lily – in the sense that it was far more comfortable. In bed Sarah had been, well, formidable, to put it mildly. (Hawken now nearly smiled at some memories.)

He wondered how Lily would feel about Jim and Pat Chilton. Hawken had told her how they'd been such close friends, the couples getting together frequently. Attending their kids' school and sports events, parties, barbecues . . . He'd noticed Lily's smile shift slightly when he'd told her about this past. But he'd reassured her that, in a way, Jim Chilton was a stranger to him too. Hawken had been so depressed after Sarah's death that he'd lost contact with nearly all his friends.

But now he was returning to life. He and Lily would finish getting the house ready and then collect the children, who were staying with their grandparents in Encinitas. And his life would settle back into the pleasant routine on the Peninsula he remembered from years before. He'd reconnect with his best friend, Jim Chilton, rejoin the country club, see all his friends again.

Yes, this was the right move. But a cloud had appeared. Small, temporary, he was sure, but a blemish nonetheless.

By coming to the place that had been his and Sarah's home, it was as if he'd resurrected a part of her. The memories popped like fireworks.

Here in Monterey, Sarah being the thoughtful hostess, the passionate art collector, the shrewd businesswoman.

Here, Sarah being the sultry, energetic and consuming lover.

Here, Sarah intrepidly donning a wetsuit and swimming in the harsh ocean, climbing out, chilled and exhilarated – unlike her last swim, near La Jolla, not climbing out of the water at all, but wafting into the shore, limp, eyes open and unseeing, her skin matching the water temperature degree for degree.

At this thought, Hawken's heart now added an extra beat or two.

Then he took several deep breaths and slipped the memories away. 'Want a hand?' He glanced at Lily and the drapes.

His wife paused, then set down her work. She approached, took his hand and put it on the V of skin below her throat. She kissed him hard.

They smiled at each other, and his wife returned to the windows.

Hawken finished the glass-and-chrome table and dragged it in front of the couch.

'Honey?' The tape measure was drooping in Lily's hand and she was looking out the back window.

'What?'

'I think somebody's out there.'

'Where, in the backyard?'

'I don't know if it's our property. It's on the other side of the hedge.'

'Then it's definitely somebody else's yard.'

Your dollar doesn't buy you much dirt here on the Central Coast of California.

'He's just standing there, looking at the house.'

'Probably wondering if a rock-and-roll band or druggies are moving in.'

She climbed down a step. 'Just standing there,' she repeated. 'I don't know, honey, it's a little spooky.'

Hawken walked to the window and looked out. From this perspective he couldn't see much, but it was clear that a figure was peering through the bushes. He wore a gray sweatshirt with the hood pulled up.

'Maybe the neighbor's kid. They're always curious about people moving in. Wondering if we have kids their age. I was.'

Lily wasn't saying anything. He could sense her discomfort, as she stood with her narrow hips cocked, frowning eyes framed by blond hair flecked with moving-carton-cardboard dust.

Time for the chivalry part.

Hawken walked into the kitchen and pulled open the back door. The visitor was gone.

He stepped out farther, then heard his wife call, 'Honey!'

Alarmed, Hawken turned and sped back inside.

Lily, still on the ladder, was pointing out another window. The visitor had moved into the side yard – definitely on their property now, though still obscured by plantings.

'Damnit. Who the hell is he?'

He glanced at the phone but decided not to call 911. What if it was the neighbor or the neighbor's son? That would pretty much ruin any chance for a friendship forever.

When he looked back the figure was gone.

Lily climbed off the ladder. 'Where is he? He just vanished. Fast.'

'No idea.'

They gazed out the windows, scanning.

No sign of him.

This was far spookier, *not* being able to see him.

'I think we should—'

Hawken's voice stopped with a gasp as Lily cried, 'A gun – he's got a gun, Don!' She was staring out a front window.

Her husband grabbed his phone, calling to his wife, 'The door! Lock it.'

Lily lunged.

But she was too late.

The door was already swinging wide.

Lily screamed and Don Hawken pulled her to the floor beneath him, in a noble but, he understood, useless gesture to save the life of his bride.

27

Ours of opera . . .

Sitting in Kathryn Dance's office, alone now, Jonathan Boling was cruising through Travis Brigham's computer, in a frantic pursuit of the meaning of the code.

ours of opera . . .

He was sitting forward, typing fast, thinking that if Dance had been here, the kinesics expert within her could have drawn some fast conclusions from his posture and the focus of his eyes: he was a dog scenting prey.

Jon Boling was on to something.

Dance and the others were out at the moment, setting up surveillance. Boling had remained in her office to prowl through the boy's computer. He'd found a clue and was now trying to locate more data that would let him crack the code.

ours of opera . . .

What did it mean?

A curious aspect of computers is that these crazy plastic and metal boxes contain ghosts. A computer hard drive is like a network of secret passages and corridors, leading farther and farther into the architecture of computer memory. It's possible – with considerable difficulty – to exorcise these hallways and rid them of the ghosts of data past, but usually most bits of information we've created or acquired remain forever, invisible and fragmented.

Boling was now wandering these hallways, using a program one of his students had hacked together, reading the scraps of data lodged in obscure places, like the wisps of souls inhabiting a haunted house.

Thinking of ghosts put him in mind of the DVD Kathryn Dance's son had lent him last night. *Ghost in the Shell*. He reflected on the nice time he'd had at her house, how much he'd enjoyed meeting her friends and family. The children especially. Maggie was adorable and funny and would, he knew without a doubt, become a woman every bit as formidable as her mother. Wes was more laid-back. He was easy to talk to and brilliant. Boling often speculated about what his own children would have been like if he'd settled down with Cassie.

He thought of her now, hoped she was enjoying her life in China.

Recalled the weeks prior to her leaving.

And withdrew his generous wishes about contentment in Asia.

Then Boling put thoughts of Cassandra aside, and concentrated on his ghost hunt in the computer. He was getting close to something important in that shred of binary code that translated into the English letters *ours of opera*.

Boling's puzzle-loving mind, which could often be counted on to come up with curious leaps of logic and insight, automatically concluded that those words were fragments of 'hours of operation'. Travis had looked at that phrase online just before he'd vanished. The implication of this was that perhaps, just perhaps, these words referred to a location the boy was interested in.

But computers don't store related data in the same place. The code for 'ours of opera' might be found in a spooky closet in the basement, while the name of whatever they referred to could be in a hallway in the attic. Part of the physical address in one place, the rest in another. The brain of a computer is constantly making decisions about breaking up the data and storing bits and pieces in places that make sense to it but are incomprehensible to a layperson.

And so Boling was following the trail, strolling through the dark corridors filled with spooks.

He didn't think he'd been this engaged in a project for months, maybe years. Jonathan Boling enjoyed university work. He was curious by nature and he liked the challenge of research and writing, the stimulating conversations with fellow faculty members and with his students, getting young people excited about learning. Seeing the eyes of a student intensify suddenly when random facts coalesced into understanding was pure pleasure to him.

But at the moment, those satisfactions and victories seemed minor. Now, he was on a mission to save lives. And nothing else mattered to him but unlocking the code.

ours of opera . . .

He looked at another storeroom in the haunted house. Nothing but jumbled bits and bytes. Another false lead.

More typing.

Nothing.

Boling stretched and a joint popped loudly. Come on, Travis, why were you interested in this place? What appealed to you about it?

And do you still go there? Does a friend work there? Do you buy something from its shelves, display cases, aisles?

Ten more minutes.

Give up?

No way.

Then he strolled into a new part of the haunted house. He blinked and gave a laugh. Like joining pieces of a jigsaw puzzle, the answer to the code 'ours of opera' materialized.

As he gazed at the name of the place, its relationship to Travis Brigham was ridiculously obvious. The professor was angry at himself for not deducing it even without the digital clue. Looking up the address, he pulled his phone off his belt and called Kathryn Dance. It rang four times and went to voice mail.

He was about to leave a message, but then he looked at his notes. The place wasn't far from where he was right now. No more than fifteen minutes.

He flipped the phone shut with a soft snap and stood, pulled on his jacket.

With an involuntary glance at the picture of Dance and her children, dogs front and center, he stepped out of her office and headed for the front door of the CBI.

Aware that what he was about to do was possibly a very bad idea, Jon Boling left the synth world to continue his quest in the real.

'It's clear,' Rey Carraneo told Kathryn Dance as he returned to the living room where she stood over Donald and Lily Hawken. Dance's pistol was in her hand as she was looking vigilantly out the windows and into the rooms of the small house.

The couple, shaken and unsmiling, sat on a new couch, the factory plastic wrap still covering it.

Dance replaced her Glock. She hadn't expected the boy to be inside – he'd been hiding in the side yard and had appeared to flee when the police arrived – but Travis's expertise at the game of *DimensionQuest,* his skill at combat, made her wonder if the teenager had somehow *seemed* to escape but had actually slipped inside.

The door opened and massive Albert Stemple stuck his head in. 'Nup. He's gone.' The man was wheezing – both from the pursuit and from the residual effects of the gas at Kelley Morgan's house. 'Got the deputy lookin' up and down the streets. And we got a half dozen more cars on the way. Somebody saw somebody in a hooded sweatshirt on a bicycle heading through the alleys, making for downtown. I called it in. But . . .' He shrugged. Then the bulky agent vanished and his boots clomped down the steps as he went to join in the manhunt.

Dance, Carraneo, Stemple and the MCSO deputy had arrived ten minutes ago. As they'd been meeting with likely targets, an idea had occurred to Dance. She thought about Jon Boling's theory: that, expanding his targets, Travis might include people merely mentioned favorably in the blog, even if they hadn't posted.

Dance had gone to the site once again and read through the blog's homepage.

http://www.thechiltonreport.com

One name that stood out was Donald Hawken, an old friend of James Chilton's, who was mentioned in the 'On the Home Front' section. Hawken might be the victim for whom Travis had left the cross on the windswept stretch of Highway 1.

So they'd driven to the man's house, their purpose to get Hawken and his wife out of danger and set up surveillance at the house.

But upon arriving, Dance had seen a figure in a hood, possibly holding a gun, lurking in the bushes to the side of the ranch. She'd sent Albert Stemple and the MCSO deputy after the intruder, and Rey Carraneo, with Dance behind him, barged into the house, guns drawn, to protect Hawken and his wife.

They were still badly shaken; they'd assumed Carraneo was the killer when the plainclothes agent had burst through the door, his weapon high.

Dance's Motorola crackled and she answered. It was Stemple again. 'I'm in the backyard. Got a cross carved into this patch of dirt and rose petals scattered around it.'

'Roger that, Al.'

Lily closed her eyes, lowered her head to her husband's shoulder.

Four or five minutes, Dance was thinking. If we'd gotten here just that much later, the couple would be dead.

'Why us?' Hawken asked. 'We didn't do anything to him. We didn't post. We don't even know him.'

Dance explained about the boy's expanding his targets.

'You mean, anybody even mentioned in the blog's at risk?'

'Seems that way.'

Dozens of police had descended on the area within minutes, but the calls coming in made clear that Travis was nowhere to be found.

How the hell does a kid on a bicycle get away? Dance thought, frustrated. He just vanishes. Where? Somebody's basement? An abandoned construction site?

Outside, the first of the press cars were beginning to arrive, the vans with the dishes atop, the cameramen prodding their equipment to life.

About to stoke the panic in town that much hotter.

More police showed up too, including several bicycle patrol officers.

Dance now asked Hawken, 'You still have your house in the San Diego area?'

Lily replied, 'It's on the market. Hasn't sold yet.'

'I'd like you to go back there.'

'Well,' he said, 'there's no furniture. It's in storage.'

'You have people you can stay with?'

'My parents. Donald's children are staying with them now.'

'Then go back there until we find Travis.'

'I guess we could,' Lily said.

'You go,' Hawken said to her. 'I'm not leaving Jim.'

'There's nothing you can do to help him,' Dance said.

'There sure is. I can give him moral support. This is a terrible time. He needs friends.'

Dance continued, 'I'm sure he appreciates your loyalty, but look at what just happened. That boy knows where you live and he obviously wants to hurt you.'

'You might catch him in a half hour.'

'We might not. I really have to insist, Mr Hawken.'

The man showed a bit of businessman's steel. 'I won't leave him.' Then the edge left his voice as he added, 'I have to explain something.' The smallest of glances at his wife. A pause, then: 'My first wife, Sarah, died a couple of years ago.'

'I'm sorry.'

The dismissive shrug that Dance knew oh so well.

'Jim dropped everything; he was at my door within the hour. He stayed by me and the children for a week. Helped us and Sarah's family with everything. Food, the funeral arrangements.

He even took turns with the housework and laundry. I was paralyzed. I just couldn't do anything. I think he might've saved my life back then. He certainly saved my sanity.'

Again Dance couldn't suppress the memories of the months after her own spouse's death – when Martine Christensen, much like Chilton, had been there for her. Dance would never have hurt herself, not with the children, but there were plenty of times when, yes, she thought she might go mad.

She understood Donald Hawken's loyalty.

'I'm not leaving,' the man repeated firmly. 'There's no point in asking.' Then he hugged his wife. 'But you go back. I want you to leave.'

Without a moment's hesitation, Lily said, 'No, I'm staying with you.'

Dance noted the look. Adoration, contentment, resolve . . . Her own heart flipped as she thought, *He* lost his first spouse, recovered and found love again.

It can happen, Dance thought. See?

Then she closed the door on her own life.

'All right,' she agreed reluctantly. 'But you're leaving here right now. Find a hotel and stay there, stay out of sight. And we're going to put a guard on you.'

'That's fine.'

It was then that a car screeched to a stop in front of the house, a voice shouting in alarm. She and Carraneo stepped out onto the porch.

'S'okay,' Albert Stemple said, his voice a lazy drawl, minus the Southern accent. 'Only Chilton.'

The blogger had apparently heard the news and hurried over. He raced up the steps. 'What happened?' Dance was surprised to hear panic in his voice. She'd detected anger, pettiness, arrogance earlier, but never this sound. 'Are they all right?'

'Fine,' she said. 'Travis was here, but Donald's fine. His wife too.'

'What happened?' The collar of the blogger's jacket was askew. Hawken and Lily stepped outside. 'Jim!'

Chilton ran forward and embraced his friend. 'Are you all right?'

'Yes, yes. The police got here in time.'

'Did you catch him?' Chilton asked.

'No,' Dance said, expecting Chilton to launch into criticism for their not capturing the boy. But he took her hand firmly and gripped it. 'Thank you, thank you. You saved them. Thank you.'

She nodded awkwardly and released his hand. Then Chilton turned to Lily with a smile of curiosity.

Dance deduced that they'd never met before, not in person. Hawken introduced them now and Chilton gave Lily a warm embrace. 'I'm so sorry about this. I never, not in a million years, thought it would affect you.'

'Who would have?' Hawken asked.

With a rueful smile, Chilton said to his friend, 'With an introduction to the Monterey Peninsula like this, she's not going to want to stay. She's going to move back tomorrow.'

Lily finally cracked a fragile smile. 'I would. Except we've already bought the drapes.' A nod at the house.

Chilton laughed. 'She's funny, Don. Why doesn't she stay and *you* go back to San Diego?'

'Afraid you're stuck with both of us.'

Chilton then grew serious. 'You have to leave until this is over.'

Dance said, 'I've been trying to talk them into that.'

'We're not leaving.'

'Don—' Chilton began.

But Hawken laughed, nodding at Dance. 'I have police permission. She agreed. We're going to hide out in a hotel. Like Bonnie and Clyde.'

'But—'

'No buts, buddy. We're here. You can't get rid of us now.'

Chilton opened his mouth to object, but then noted Lily's wry grin. She said, 'You don't want to be telling this girl what to do, Jim.'

The blogger gave another laugh and said, 'Fair enough. Thank you. Get to a hotel. Stay there. In a day or two this'll all be over with. Things'll get back to normal.'

Hawken said, 'I haven't seen Pat and the boys since I left. Over three years.'

Dance eyed the blogger. Something else about him was different. Her impression was that she was seeing for the first time his human side, as if this near-tragedy had pulled him yet further from the synth world into the real.

The crusader was, at least temporarily, absent.

She left them to their reminiscences and walked around back. A voice from the bushes startled her. 'Hello.'

She looked behind her to see the young deputy who'd been helping them out, David Reinhold.

'Deputy.'

He grinned. 'Call me David. I heard he was here. You almost nailed him.'

'Close. Not close enough.'

He was carrying several battered metal suitcases, stenciled with *MCSO – CSU* on the side. 'Sorry I couldn't tell anything for certain about those branches in your backyard – that cross.'

'I couldn't tell either. Probably it was just a fluke. If I trimmed the trees like I should, it never would've happened.'

His bright eyes glanced her way. 'You have a nice house.'

'Thanks. Despite the messy backyard.'

'No. It's real comfortable-looking.'

She asked the deputy, 'And how 'bout you, David? You live in Monterey?'

'I did. Had a roommate, but he left, so I had to move to Marina.'

'Well, appreciate your efforts. I'll put in a good word with Michael O'Neil.'

'Really, Kathryn? That'd be great.' He glowed.

Reinhold turned away and began cordoning off the backyard. Dance stared at what was in the center of the yellow tape trapezoid: the cross etched into the dirt and the sprinkling of petals. From there, her eyes rose and took in the sweeping decline from the heights of Monterey down to the bay, where a sliver of water could be seen.

It was a panoramic view, beautiful.

But today it seemed as disturbing as the terrible mask of Qetzal, the demon in *DimensionQuest*.

You're out there somewhere, Travis.

Where, where?

28

Playing cop.

Tracking down Travis the way Jack Bauer chased terrorists.

Jon Boling had a lead: the possible location from which Travis had sent the blog posting of the mask drawing and the horrific stabbing of the woman who looked a bit like Kathryn Dance. The place where the boy would be playing his precious *DimensionQuest*.

The 'hours of operation' he'd found in the ghostly corridors of Travis's computer referred to Lighthouse Arcade, a video and computer gaming center in New Monterey.

The boy would be taking a risk going out in public, of course, considering the manhunt. But if he picked his routes carefully, wore sunglasses and a cap and something other than the hoodie the TV reports were depicting him in, well, he could probably move around with some freedom.

Besides, when it came to online gaming and Morpegs, an addict had no choice but to risk detection.

Boling piloted his Audi off the highway and onto Del Monte then Lighthouse and headed into the neighborhood where the arcade was located.

He was enjoying a certain exhilaration. Here he was, a forty-one-year-old professor, who lived largely by his brain. He'd never thought of himself as suffering from an absence of bravery. He'd done some rock climbing, scuba diving, downhill skiing. Then too, the world of ideas carried risk of harm – to careers and reputations and contentment. He'd battled it out with fellow professors. He also had been a victim of vicious online attacks, much like those against Travis, though with better spelling, grammar and punctuation. Most recently he'd been attacked for taking a stand against file sharing of copyrighted material.

He hadn't expected the viciousness of the attacks. He was trounced . . . called a 'fucking capitalist', a 'bitch whore of big business'. Boling particularly liked 'professor of mass destruction'.

Some colleagues actually stopped talking to him.

But the harm he'd experienced, of course, was nothing compared with what Kathryn Dance and her fellow officers risked day after day.

And which he himself was now risking, he reflected.

Playing cop . . .

Boling realized that he'd been helpful to Kathryn and the others. He was pleased about that and pleased at their recognition of his contribution. But being so close to the action, hearing the phone calls, watching Kathryn's face as she took down information about the crimes, seeing her hand absently stroke the black gun on her hip . . . he felt a longing to participate.

And anything else, Jon? he wryly asked himself.

Well, okay, maybe he was trying to impress her.

Absurd, but he'd felt a bit of jealousy seeing her and Michael O'Neil connect.

You're acting like a goddamn teenager.

Still, something about her lit the fuse. Boling had never been able to explain it – who could, really? – when that connection occurred. And it happened fast or never. Dance was single, he was too. He'd gotten over Cassie (okay, pretty much over); was Kathryn getting close to dating again? He believed he'd gotten a few signals from her. But what did he know? He had none of her skill – body language.

More to the point, he was a man, a species genetically fitted with persistent oblivion.

Boling now parked his gray A4 near Lighthouse Arcade, on a side street in that netherworld north of Pacific Grove. He remembered when this strip of small businesses and smaller apartments, dubbed New Monterey, had been a mini–Haight Ashbury, tucked between a brawling army town and a religious retreat. (Pacific Grove's Lovers Point was named for lovers of *Jesus,* not one another.) Now the area was as bland as a strip mall in Omaha or Seattle.

The Lighthouse Arcade was dim and shabby and smelled, well, gamy – a pun he couldn't wait to share with her.

He surveyed the surreal place. The players – most of them boys – sat at terminals, staring at the screens, teasing joysticks and pounding on keyboards. The playing stations had high, curving walls covered with black sound-dampening material, and the chairs were comfortable, high-backed leather models.

Everything a young man would need for a digital experience was here. In addition to the computers and keyboards there were noise-cancelling headsets, microphones, touch pads, input devices like car steering wheels and airplane yokes, three-D glasses, and banks of sockets for power, USB, Firewire, audiovisual and more obscure connections. Some had Wii devices.

Boling had written about the latest trend in gaming: total immersion pods, which had originated in Japan, where kids would sit for hours and hours in a dark, private space, completely sealed off from the real world, to play computer games. This was a logical development in a country known for *hikikomori,* or 'withdrawal', an increasingly common lifestyle in which young people, boys and men mostly, became recluses, never leaving their rooms for months or years at a time, living exclusively through their computers.

The noise was disorienting: a cacophony of digitally generated sounds – explosions, gunshots, animal cries, eerie shrieks and laughs – and an ocean of indistinguishable human voices speaking into microphones to fellow gamers somewhere in the world. Responses rattled from speakers. Occasionally cries and expletives would issue hoarsely from the throats of desperate players as they died or realized a tactical mistake.

The Lighthouse Arcade, typical of thousands around the globe, represented the last outpost of the real world before you plunged into the synth.

Boling felt a vibration on his hip. He looked down at his mobile. The message from Irv, his grad student, read: *Stryker logged on five minutes ago in DQ!!*

As if he'd been slapped, Boling looked around. Was Travis *here*? Because of the enclosures, it was impossible to see more than one or two stations at a time.

At the counter a long-haired clerk sat oblivious to the noise; he was reading a science fiction novel. Boling approached. 'I'm looking for a kid, a teenager.'

The clerk lifted an ironic eyebrow.

I'm looking for a tree in a forest.

'Yeah?'

'He's playing *DimensionQuest*. Did you sign somebody in about five minutes ago?'

'There's no sign-in. You use with tokens. You can buy 'em here or from a machine.' The clerk was looking Boling over carefully. 'You his father?'

'No. Just want to find him.'

'I can look over the servers. Find out if anybody's logged onto *DQ* now.'

'You could?'

'Yeah.'

'Great.'

But the kid wasn't making any moves to check the servers; he was just staring at Boling through a frame of unclean hair.

Ah. Got it. We're negotiating. Sweet. Very private-eye-ish, Boling thought. A moment later two twenties vanished into the pocket of the kid's unwashed jeans.

'His avatar's name is Stryker, if that helps,' Boling told him.

A grunt. 'Be back in a minute.' He vanished onto the floor.

Boling saw him emerge on the far side of the room and walk toward the back office.

Five minutes later he returned.

'Somebody named Stryker, yeah, he's playing *DQ*. Just logged on. Station forty-three. It's over there.'

'Thanks.'

'Uh.' The clerk went back to his S-F novel.

Boling, thinking frantically: what should he do? Have the clerk evacuate the arcade? No, then Travis would catch on. He should just call 911. But he better see if the boy was alone. Would he have his gun with him?

He had a fantasy of walking past casually, ripping the gun from the boy's belt and covering him till the police arrived.

No. Don't do that. Under any circumstances.

Palms sweating, Boling slowly walked toward station 43. He took a fast look around the corner. The computer had the Aetherian landscape on the screen, but the chair was empty.

Nobody was in the aisles, though. Station 44 was empty but at 42 a girl with short green hair was playing a martial arts game.

Boling walked up to her. 'Excuse me.'

The girl was delivering crippling blows to an opponent. Finally the creature fell over dead and her avatar climbed on top of the body and pulled its head off. 'Like, yeah?' She didn't glance up.

'The boy who was just here, playing *DQ*. Where is he?'

'Like, I don't know. Jimmy walked past and said something and he left. A minute ago.'

'Who's Jimmy?'

'You know, the clerk.'

Goddamn! I just paid forty dollars to that shit to tip off Travis. Some cop I am.

Boling glared at the clerk, who remained conspicuously lost in his novel.

The professor slammed through the exit door and sprinted outside. His eyes, accustomed to the darkness, stung. He paused in the alleyway, squinting left and right. Then caught a glimpse of a young man, walking quickly away, head down.

Don't do anything stupid, he told himself. He pulled his BlackBerry from its holster.

Ahead of him, the boy broke into a run.

After exactly one second of debate, Jon Boling did too.

29

Hamilton Royce, the ombudsman from the attorney general's office in Sacramento, disconnected the phone. It drooped in his hand as he reflected on the conversation he'd just had – a conversation conducted in the language known as Political and Corporate Euphemism.

He lingered in the halls of the CBI, considering options.

Finally he returned to Charles Overby's office.

The agent-in-charge was sitting back in his chair watching a press report about the case streaming on his computer. How the police had come close to catching the killer at the house of a friend of the blogger's but had missed him and he'd escaped possibly to terrorize more people on the Monterey Peninsula.

Royce reflected that simply reporting that the police had saved the friend didn't have quite the stay-tuned-or-else veneer of the approach the network had chosen to take.

Overby typed and a different station came up. The special report anchor apparently preferred Travis to be the 'Video Game Killer', rather than defining him by masks or roadside crosses. He went on to describe how the boy tormented his victims before he killed them.

Never mind that only one person had died or that the bastard got shot in the back of the head, fleeing. Which would tend to minimize the torment.

Finally he said, 'Well, Charles, they're getting more concerned. The AG.' He lifted his phone like he was showing a shield during a bust.

'We're *all* pretty concerned,' Overby echoed. 'The whole Peninsula's concerned. It's really our priority now. Like I was saying.' His face was cloudy. 'But is Sacramento having a problem with how we're handling the case?'

'Not per se.' Royce let this nonresponse buzz around Overby's head like a strident hornet.

'We're doing everything we can.'

'I like that agent of yours. Dance.'

'Oh, she's top-notch. Nothing gets by her.'

A leisurely nod, a thoughtful nod. 'The AG feels bad about those victims. I feel bad about them.' Royce poured sympathy into his voice, and tried to recall the last time he really felt bad. Probably when he missed his daughter's emergency appendectomy because he was in bed with his mistress.

'A tragedy.'

'I know I'm sounding like a broken record. But I really do feel that that blog is the problem.'

'It is,' Overby agreed. 'It's the eye of the hurricane.'

Which is calm and frames a beautiful blue sky, Royce corrected silently.

The CBI chief offered, 'Well, Kathryn *did* get Chilton to post a plea for the boy to come in. And he gave us some details about the server – a proxy in Scandinavia.'

'I understand. It's just . . . as long as that blog's up, it's a reminder that the job isn't getting done.' Meaning: by *you*. 'I keep coming back to that question about something helpful to us, something about Chilton.'

'Kathryn said she'd keep an eye peeled.'

'She's busy. I wonder if there's something in what she's *already* found. I don't really want to deflect Agent Dance from the case. I wonder if I should take a gander.'

'You?'

'You wouldn't mind, would you, Charles? If I just took a peek at the files. I could bring perspective. My impression, actually, is that Kathryn's maybe too kind.'

'Too kind?'

'You were sharp, Charles, to hire her.' The agent in charge accepted this compliment, though, Royce knew, Kathryn Dance had predated Overby's presence in the CBI here by four years. He continued, 'Clever. You saw she was an antidote to the cynicism of old roosters like you and me. But the price of that is a certain . . . naivete.'

'You think she's got something on Chilton and doesn't know it?'

'Could be.'

Overby was looking tense. 'Well, I'll apologize for her. Put it down to distraction, why don't we? Her mother's case. Not focusing up to par. She's doing the best she can.'

Hamilton Royce was known for his ruthlessness. But he would never have sold out a loyal member of his team with a comment like that. He reflected that it was almost impressive to see the top three darker qualities of human nature displayed so boldly: cowardice, pettiness and betrayal. 'Is she in?'

'Let me find out.' Overby made a call and spoke to someone who Royce deduced was Dance's assistant. He hung up.

'She's still at the crime scene at the Hawken house.'

'So, then, I'll just have a look-see.' But then Royce seemed to have a thought. 'Of course, probably better if I weren't disturbed.'

'Here's an idea. I'll call her assistant back, ask her to do something. Run an errand. There are always reports needing to get copied. Or, I know: get her input about workload and hours. It would make sense for me to take her pulse. I'm that kind of boss. She'd never suspect anything's out of the ordinary.'

Royce left Overby's office, walked down corridors whose routes he'd memorized, and paused near Dance's. He waited in the hallway until he saw that the assistant – an efficient-looking woman named Maryellen – took a call. Then, with a perplexed frown, she stood and headed up the corridor, leaving Hamilton Royce free to plunder.

*   *   *

When he got to the end of the alley, Jon Boling paused and looked to the right, down a side street, in the direction that Travis had disappeared. From here the ground descended toward Monterey Bay and was filled with small single-family bungalows, beige and tan apartment buildings and abundant groundcover. Though Lighthouse Avenue, behind him, was ripe with traffic the side road was empty. Thick fog had come up and the scenery was gray.

Well, now that the kid had gotten away, he thought, Kathryn Dance wasn't likely to be very impressed with his detection work.

He called 911 and reported that he'd seen Travis Brigham and gave his location. The dispatcher reported that a police car would be at the arcade in five minutes.

Okay, that was enough of the adolescent behavior, he told himself. His skill was academia, teaching, intellectual analysis.

The world of ideas, not action.

He turned around to head back to the arcade to meet the police car. But then a thought occurred to him: that this quest of his maybe wasn't so out of character, after all. Maybe it was less a case of silly masculine preening than an acknowledgment of a legitimate aspect of his nature: answering questions, unraveling mysteries, solving puzzles. Exactly what Jonathan Boling had always done: understanding society, the human heart and mind.

One more block. What could it hurt? The police were on their way. Maybe he'd find somebody on the street who'd noticed the boy get into a car or climb through a window of a nearby house.

The professor turned back and started down the gray, gritty alley toward the water. He wondered when he'd see Kathryn again. Soon, he hoped.

It was in fact the image of her green eyes that was prominently in his mind when the boy leapt out from behind the Dumpster three feet away and got Boling in a neck lock. Smelling unwashed clothing and adolescent sweat, he choked as the silver blade of the knife began its leisurely transit to his throat.

30

Speaking on her phone, Kathryn Dance sped up to the front of James Chilton's house in Carmel. Parking, she said, 'Thanks again,' to the caller and hung up. She parked and walked up to the Monterey County Sheriff's Office car, in which a deputy sat on guard detail.

She approached him. 'Hey, Miguel.'

'Agent Dance, how you doing? Everything's quiet here.'

'Good. Mr Chilton's back, isn't he?'

'Yes.'

'Do me a favor?'

'You bet.'

'Get out of the car and just stand here, maybe lean against the door, so people can get a good look at you.'

'Something going down?'

'I'm not sure. Just stay there for a bit. Whatever happens, don't move.'

He seemed uncertain but climbed out of the car.

Dance now walked up to the front door and pushed the buzzer. The musician within her detected the slightly flat tone of the final chime.

Chilton opened the door and blinked to see Dance. 'Is everything okay?'

Then, after a glance over her shoulder, Dance pulled her handcuffs out of their holster.

Chilton glanced down. 'What—?' he gasped.

'Turn around and put your hands behind your back.'

'What is this?'

'Now! Just do it.'

'This is—'

She took him by the shoulder and turned him around. He started to speak, but she simply said, 'Shh.' And ratcheted on the cuffs. 'You're under arrest for criminal trespass on private property.'

'What? Whose?'

'Arnold Brubaker's land – the site of the desalination plant.'

'Wait, you mean yesterday?'

'Right.'

'You let me go!'

'You weren't arrested then. Now, you are.' She recited the Miranda warning.

A dark sedan sped up the street, turned and ground along the gravel drive up to the house. Dance recognized it as a unit of the Highway Patrol. The two officers in the front – bulky men – glanced at Dance curiously and climbed out. They looked over at the county sheriff's office car and Deputy Miguel Herrera, who touched his radio on his hip as if wanting to call somebody to see what this was all about.

Together the new arrivals walked toward Dance and her prisoner. They noted the handcuffs.

In a perplexed voice, Dance said, 'Who're you?'

'Well,' the older of the troopers said, 'CHP. Who are you, ma'am?'

She fished for her wallet in her purse and showed her ID to the troopers. 'I'm Kathryn Dance, CBI. What do you want here?'

'We're here to take James Chilton into custody.'

'My prisoner?'

'Yours?'

'That's right. We just arrested him.' She shot a glance to Herrera.

'Wait a minute here,' Chilton barked.

'Quiet,' Dance ordered.

The senior trooper said, 'We have an arrest warrant for James Chilton. And a warrant to take possession of his computers, files, business records. Anything related to *The Chilton Report*.'

They displayed the paperwork.

'That's ridiculous,' Chilton said. 'What the fuck is going on here?'

Dance repeated bluntly, 'Quiet.' Then to the troopers: 'What's the charge?'

'Criminal trespass.'

'At Arnold Brubaker's property?'

'That's right.'

She laughed. 'That's what I just arrested him for.'

Both of the troopers stared at her then at Chilton, buying time, and then, independently, they nodded. Apparently there was, in their experience, no precedent for anything like this.

'Well,' one of the officers contributed, 'we have a warrant.'

'I understand. But he's already been arrested and the CBI already has jurisdiction over his files and computers. We're collecting them in a few minutes.'

'This is fucking bullshit,' Chilton blurted.

'Sir, I'd watch your language,' the younger, and bigger, of the troopers snapped.

The silence roared.

Then Kathryn Dance squinted a smile into her face. 'Wait. Who's the one requested the warrant? Was it Hamilton Royce?'

'That's right. The AG's office in Sacramento.'

'Oh, sure.' Dance was relaxing. 'I'm sorry, this's a misunderstanding. *I* was the senior officer on the trespass on call but we had an affidavit issue and I had to delay taking him into custody. I mentioned it to Hamilton. He probably thought I was so busy on the Roadside Cross Case—'

'That Mask Killer. That thing. You're running that?'

'Sure am.'

'Freaky.'

'It is, yep,' Dance agreed. Then continued, 'Hamilton probably figured I was so busy on that one that he'd take over on the trespass.' A disparaging nod of the head. 'But frankly, Mr Chilton pissed me off so much I wanted to finish up the collar myself.'

She gave a conspiratorial smile that the troopers joined in briefly. Then she continued, 'This's my fault. I should've told him. Let me make a call.' She pulled her phone off her belt and dialed. Then cocked her head. 'This's Agent Dance,' she said and explained about her arrest of James Chilton. Silence for a moment. 'I've already collared him . . . We've got the paperwork back at HQ . . . Sure.' She nodded. 'Good,' Dance said in a conclusory tone, and disconnected on the woman's voice explaining that the temperature was fifty-six degrees and rain was forecast on the Monterey Peninsula tomorrow.

'It's all set, we'll process him.' A smile. 'Unless you really want to cool your heels at the Salinas lockup for four hours.'

'Nup, that's okay, Agent Dance. You need any help getting him in the car?' The big trooper was looking over James Chilton as if the blogger weighed a hundred pounds more and was capable of breaking through the cuff chain with a flex of his muscles.

'No, that's okay. We'll handle it.'

With a nod, the men walked off, climbed in their car and left.

'Listen to me,' Chilton growled, his face red. 'This is bullshit and you know it.'

'Just relax, okay?' Dance turned him around and undid the cuffs.

'What's this all about?' He was rubbing his wrists. 'I thought you were arresting me.'

'I did. I've decided to let you go, though.'

'Are you fucking with me?'

'No, I'm saving you.' Dance slipped the cuffs back into her holster. Smiling, she waved to a very perplexed Herrera. He nodded back.

'You were being set up, James.'

Not long before, Dance had gotten a call from her assistant. Maryellen had grown suspicious when Charles Overby called once to see if Dance was in the office and then again to ask her to come to his office to discuss her job satisfaction, something he'd never done.

En route to Overby's office, the woman had stalled and remained in the Gals' Wing, hiding in a side corridor. Hamilton Royce slipped into her boss's office. After five minutes or so he'd then stepped outside and made a cell phone call. Maryellen had gotten close enough to overhear part of it – Royce was calling a magistrate in Sacramento, who was apparently a friend, and asking for an arrest warrant against Chilton. Something to do with trespass.

Maryellen didn't understand the implications of what had happened, but she called Dance immediately with the news, then continued to Overby's office.

Dance gave Chilton an abbreviated version of the story, omitting Royce's name.

'Who was behind it?' he fumed.

She knew the blogger would, in a posting, go after whoever was behind his arrest and she couldn't afford the kind of publicity nightmare that would create. 'I'm not divulging that. All I'll say is that some people want your blog suspended until we catch Travis.'

'Why?'

She said sternly, 'For the same reasons *I* wanted it shut down. To keep people from posting and giving Travis more targets.' A faint smile. 'And because it looks bad for the state if we're not doing everything we can to protect the public – which means shutting you down.'

'And stopping the blog is *good* for the public? I expose corruption and problems; I don't encourage them.' Then he climbed off the soapbox. 'And you arrested me so they couldn't serve the warrant?'

'Yep.'

'What's going to happen?'

'One of two things. The troopers'll go back home and report to their supervisor that they can't serve the warrant because you're already under arrest. And it'll go away.'

'What's the second thing?'

A collision between excrement and fan, Dance reflected. She said nothing, merely shrugged.

But Chilton got it. 'You put yourself on the line for me? Why?'

'I owe you. You've been cooperating with us. And if you want to know another reason: I don't agree with all of your politics but I *do* agree you have the right to say what you want. If you're wrong, you can get sued and the courts'll decide. But I'm not going to be part of some vigilante movement to shut you up because people don't like your approach.'

'Thank you,' he said and the gratitude was obvious in his eyes.

They shook hands. Chilton said, 'Better get back online.'

Dance returned to the street and thanked Miguel Herrera, the perplexed deputy, and returned to her car. She called TJ and left a message to run a full backgrounder on Hamilton Royce. She wanted to know what kind of enemy she'd just made.

Part of which question was apparently about to be answered; her phone buzzed and Caller ID showed Overby's number.

Oh, well, she'd guessed all along it would be door number two.

Shit and fan . . .

'Charles.'

'Kathryn, I think we have a bit of a problem. Hamilton Royce is here with me on speaker.'

She was tempted to hold the phone away from her ear.

'Agent Dance, what's this about Chilton getting arrested by you? And the CHP not being able to serve their warrant?'

'I didn't have any options.'

'No options? What do you mean?'

Struggling to keep her voice calm, she said, 'I've decided I don't want to shut the blog down. We know Travis reads it. Chilton's asked him to come in. The boy may see that and try to contact the blog. Maybe negotiate a surrender.'

'Well, Kathryn.' Overby sounded desperate. 'On the whole, Sacramento's thinking it's still better to close down the thing. Don't you agree?'

'Not really, Charles. Now, Hamilton, you went through my files, didn't you?'

A land mine of a pause. 'I didn't review anything that wasn't public knowledge.'

'Doesn't matter. It was a breach of professional responsibility. It might even be a crime.'

'Kathryn, really,' Overby protested.

'Agent Dance.' Royce was sounding calm now, ignoring Overby as efficiently as she was. She recalled a common observation during her interrogations: a man in control is a dangerous man. 'People are dying, and Chilton doesn't care. And, yes, it's making us all look bad, from you to Charles to the CBI to Sacramento. All of us. And I don't mind admitting it.'

Dance had no interest in the substance of his argument. 'Hamilton, you try something like this again, with or without a warrant, and the matter'll end up with the attorney general and the governor. And the press.'

Overby was saying, 'Hamilton, what she means is—'

'I think he's pretty clear on what I mean, Charles.'

Her phone then beeped with a text message from Michael O'Neil.

'I've got to take this.' She disconnected the call, cutting off both her boss and Royce.

She lifted her phone and read the stark words on the screen.

K—
Travis spotted in New Monterey. Police lost him. But have report of another victim. He's dead. In Carmel, near end of Cypress Hills Road, west. I'm en route. Meet you there?
—M

She texted, *Yes*. And ran for the car.

Flicking on the flashing lights, which she tended to forget the car even had – investigators like her rarely had to play Hot Pursuit – Dance sped into the afternoon gloom.

Another victim . . .

This attack would have happened not long after they'd foiled the attempt on Donald Hawken and his wife. She'd been right. The boy, probably frustrated that he hadn't been successful, had gone on immediately to find another victim.

She found the turnoff, braked hard and eased the long car down the winding country road. The vegetation was lush but the overcast leached the color from the plants and gave Dance the impression that she was in some otherworldly place.

Like Aetheria, the land in *DimensionQuest*.

She pictured the image of Stryker in front of her, holding his sword comfortably.

like really w4nt to learn, what can u t33ch me?
2 die . . .

Pictured too the boy's crude drawing of the blade piercing her chest.

Then a flash caught her eyes: white lights and colored ones.

She drove up and parked beside the other cars – Monterey County Sheriff's Office – and a Crime Scene van. Dance climbed out, headed into the chaos. 'Hey.' She nodded to Michael O'Neil, greatly relieved to see him, even if this was only a temporary respite from the Other Case.

'You check out the scene?' she asked.

'Just got here myself,' he explained.

They walked toward where the body lay, covered with a dark green tarp. Yellow police tape starkly marked the spot.

'Somebody spotted him?' she asked an MCSO deputy.

'That's right, Agent Dance. Nine-one-one call in New Monterey. But by the time our people got there he was gone. So was the good citizen.'

'Who's the vic?' O'Neil asked.

He replied, 'I don't know yet. It was pretty bad, apparently. Travis used the knife this time. Not the gun. And looks like he took his time.'

The deputy pointed into a grass-filled area about fifty feet away from the road.

She and O'Neil walked over the sandy ground. In a minute or two they arrived at the taped-off area, where a half dozen uniformed and plainclothes officers were standing, and a Crime Scene officer crouched beside the corpse covered by a green tarp.

They nodded a greeting to an MCSO deputy, a round Latino man Dance had worked with for years.

'What's the word on the vic's ID?' she asked.

'A deputy's got his wallet.' The deputy indicated the body. 'They're checking it out now. All we know so far is male, forties.'

Dance looked around. 'Wasn't killed here, I assume?' There were no residences or other buildings nearby. Nor would the victim have been hiking or jogging here – there were no trails.

'Right.' The officer continued, 'There wasn't much blood. Looks like the perp drove the body here and dumped it. Found some tire tracks in the sand. We're guessing Travis boosted the guy's own car, threw him in the trunk. Like that first girl. Tammy. Only this time, he didn't wait for the tide. Stabbed him to death. As soon as we've got the deceased's ID, we can put out a call on the wheels.'

'You're sure Travis did it?' Dance asked.

The deputy offered, 'You'll see.'

'And he was tortured?'

'Looks that way.'

They paused at the Crime Scene tape about ten feet from the corpse. The CS officer, in a jumpsuit like a spaceman, was taking measurements. He glanced up and saw the two officers. He nodded a greeting and through his protective goggles lifted an eyebrow. 'You want to see?' he called.

'Yes,' Dance replied, wondering if he asked thinking a woman might not be comfortable seeing the carnage. Yes, in this day and age, it still happened.

Though, in fact, she was steeling herself for the sight. The nature of her work involved the living, mostly. She'd never grown fully immune to the images of death.

He began to lift the cover when a voice called from behind her, 'Agent Dance?'

She glanced back to see another officer in uniform walking up to her. He was holding something in his hand.

'Yes?'

'Do you know a Jonathan Boling?'

'Jon? Yes.' She was staring at a business card in his hand. And recalled that somebody had taken the victim's wallet to verify ID.

A horrifying thought: was the victim Jon?

Her mind did one of its leaps – *A to B to X*. Had the professor learned something from Travis's computer or in his search for victims and, with Dance away, decided to investigate by himself?

Please, no!

She glanced briefly at O'Neil, horror in her eyes, and lunged for the body.

'Hey!' the CS tech shouted. 'You'll contaminate the scene!'

She ignored him and flung back the tarp.

And gasped.

With mixed relief and horror, she stared down.

It wasn't Boling.

The lean bearded man in slacks and a white shirt had been repeatedly stabbed. One glazed eye was half open. A cross was carved into his forehead. Rose petals, red ones, were scattered over his body.

'But where did that come from?' she asked the other deputy, nodding at Boling's business card, her voice shaking.

'I was trying to tell you – he's at the road block, over there. Just drove up. He wants to see you. It's urgent.'

'I'll talk to him in a minute.' Dance inhaled deeply, shaken.

Another deputy came up with the dead man's wallet in a plastic bag. 'Got the ID. His name's Mark Watson. He's a retired engineer. Went out to the store a few hours ago. Never got home.'

'Who is he?' O'Neil asked. 'Why was he picked?'

Dance dug into her jacket pocket and retrieved the list of everyone mentioned in the blog who might be a potential target.

'He posted in the blog – a reply to the "Power to the People" thread. About the nuclear plant. It doesn't agree or disagree with Chilton about the location of the plant. It's neutral.'

'So *anybody* connected to the blog at all could be at risk now.'

'I'd think so.'

O'Neil looked her over. He touched her arm. 'You okay?'

'Just . . . kind of a scare.'

She found herself thumbing Jon Boling's card. She told O'Neil she was going to see what he wanted and began down the path, her heart only now returning to a normal beat from the fright.

At the roadside she found the professor standing beside his car, the door open. She frowned. In the passenger seat was a teenager with spiky hair. He was wearing an Aerosmith T-shirt under a dark brown jacket.

Boling waved to her. She was struck by the look of urgency on his face, unusual for him.

And by the intensity of the relief she felt that he was all right.

Which gave way to curiosity when she saw what was stuck in the waistband of his slacks; she couldn't tell for certain but it seemed to be the hilt of a large knife.

31

Dance, Boling and the teenager were in her office at the CBI. Jason Kepler was a seventeen-year-old student in Carmel South High, and he, not Travis, was Stryker.

Travis had created the avatar years ago, but he'd sold it online to Jason, along with 'like, a shitload of Reputation, Life Points and Resources'.

Whatever those were.

Dance recalled that Boling had told her that players could sell their avatars and other accoutrements of the game.

The professor explained about his finding a reference in Travis's data to the Lighthouse Arcade's hours of operation.

Dance was grateful for the man's brilliant detective work. (Though she was absolutely going to dress him down later for not calling 911 immediately upon learning that the boy was at the arcade and for going after him alone.) On her desk behind them, in an evidence envelope, was the kitchen knife that Jason had used to threaten Boling. It was a deadly weapon and he was technically guilty of assault and battery. Still, since Boling hadn't actually been injured and the boy had voluntarily handed over the blade to the professor, she was probably going to be satisfied with giving the kid a stern warning.

Boling now explained what had happened: he himself had

been the victim of a sting, orchestrated by the young teen who sat before them now. 'Tell her what you told me.'

'What it is, I was worried about Travis,' Jason told them wide-eyed. 'You don't know what it's like seeing somebody who's in your family getting attacked like he was, in the blog.'

'Your family?'

'Yeah. In the game, in *DQ*, we're brothers. I mean, we've never met or anything, but I know him real good.'

'Never met?'

'Well, sure, but not in the real world, only in Aetheria. I wanted to help him. But I had to find him first. I tried calling and IM'ing and I couldn't get through. All I could think of was hanging out at the arcade. Maybe I could talk him into turning himself in.'

'With a knife?' Dance asked.

His shoulders lifted, then sagged. 'I figured it couldn't hurt.'

The boy was skinny and unhealthily pale. Here it was summer vacation and, ironically, he probably got outside now far less often than in the fall and winter, when he'd have to go to school.

Boling took over the narrative. 'Jason was in the Lighthouse Arcade when I got there. The manager was a friend of his and when I asked about Stryker he pretended to go check out something but instead he told Jason about me.'

'Hey, I'm sorry, man. I wasn't going to stab you or anything. I just wanted to find out who you were and if you had any idea where Travis was. I didn't know you were with this Bureau of Investigation thing.'

Boling gave a sheepish smile at the impersonation-of-an-officer part. He added that he knew she'd want to talk to Jason but he thought it best to take him directly to her, rather than wait for the city police to show up.

'We just jumped in the car and called TJ. He told us where you were.'

It was a good decision, and only marginally illegal.

Dance now said, 'Jason, we don't want Travis to get hurt either. And we don't want him to hurt anybody else. What can you tell us about where he might go?'

'He could be *anywhere*. He's really smart, you know. He knows how to live outside in the woods. He's an expert.' The boy noted their confusion and said, 'See, *DQ*'s a game, but it's also real. I mean, you're in the Southern Mountains, it gets like fifty below zero, and you *have* to learn how to stay warm and if you don't you'll freeze to death. And you have to get food and water and everything. You learn what plants're safe and what animals you can eat. And how to cook and store food. I mean, they have real recipes. You *have* to cook them right in the game or they don't work.' He laughed. 'There've been newbies who've tried to play and they're like, "All we want to do is fight trolls and demons," and they end up starving to death because they couldn't take care of themselves.'

'You play with other people, don't you? Could any of them know where Travis might be?'

'Like, I asked everybody in the family and nobody knows where he is.'

'How many are in your family?'

'About twelve of us. But him and me are the only ones in California.'

Dance was fascinated. 'And you all live together? In Aetheria?'

'Yeah. I know them better than I know my real brothers.' He gave a grim laugh. 'And in Aetheria, they don't beat me up and steal money from me.'

Dance was curious. 'You have parents?'

'In the real world?' He shrugged, a gesture Dance interpreted as meaning 'Sort of.'

She said, 'No, in the game.'

'Some families do. We don't.' He gave a wistful look. 'We're happier that way.'

She was smiling. 'You know, you and I've met, Jason.'

The boy looked down. 'Yeah, I know. Mr Boling told me. I kinda killed you. Sorry. I thought you were just some newb who was dissing us because of Trav. I mean our family – well, our whole guild order – has been totally dissed because of him and all the posts on that blog. It's happening a lot. A raiding party from the north traveled all the way from Crystal Island to wipe us out. We made this allegiance and stopped them. But Morina was killed. She was our sister. She's come back but she lost all her Resources.'

The skinny boy shrugged. 'I get pushed around a lot, you know. At school. That's why I picked an avatar that's a Thunderer, a warrior. Kind of makes me feel better. Nobody fucks with me there.'

'Jason, one thing that might be helpful: if you could give us the strategies Travis would use to attack people. How he'd stalk them. Weapons. Anything that might help us figure out how to outthink him.'

But the boy seemed to be troubled. 'You really don't know very much about Travis, do you?'

Dance was about to say they knew all too much. But interviewers know when to let the subject take over. With a glance at Boling, she said, 'No, I guess we don't.'

'I want to show you something,' Jason said, standing up.

'Where?'

'In Aetheria.'

Kathryn Dance once again assumed the identity of the avatar Greenleaf, who was fully resurrected.

As Jason typed, the character appeared on the screen in a forest clearing. As before, the scenery was beautiful, the graphics astonishingly clear. Dozens of people were wandering around, some armed, some carrying bags or packs, some leading animals.

'This is Otovius, where Travis and me hang out a lot. It's a nice place . . . You mind?'

He bent forward toward the keys.

'No,' Dance told him. 'Go ahead.'

He typed, then received a message: *Kiaruya is not logged on.*

'Bummer.'

'Who's that?' Boling asked.

'My wife.'

'Your what?' Dance asked the seventeen-year-old.

He blushed. 'We got married a couple months ago.'

She laughed in astonishment.

'Last year I met this girl in the game. She's totally cool. She's been all the way through the Southern Mountains. By herself! She didn't die once. And me and her hit it off. We went on some quests. I proposed. Well, sort of *she* did. But I wanted to too. And we got married.'

'Who is she really?'

'Some girl in Korea. But she got a bad grade in a couple of her classes—'

'In the real world?' Boling asked.

'Yeah. So her parents took away her account.'

'You're divorced?'

'Naw, just on hold for a while. Till she gets her math scores up to a B again.' Jason added, 'Funny. Most people who get married in *DQ* stay married. In the real world a lot of our parents're divorced. I hope she gets back online soon. I miss her.' He jabbed a finger at the screen. 'Anyway, let's go to the house.'

Under Jason's direction, Dance's avatar maneuvered around the landscape, past dozens of people and creatures.

Jason led them to a cliff. 'We could walk there, but that'd, you know, take a while. You can't pay for a Pegasus ride because you haven't earned any gold yet. But I can give you transport points.' He began to type. 'It's like my dad's frequent flier thing.'

He keyboarded some more codes and then had the avatar climb on the winged horse and off they flew. The flight was breathtaking. They soared over the landscape, around thick clouds. Two suns burned in the azure sky and occasionally other flying creatures would cruise past, as did dirigibles and bizarre flying machines. Below, Dance saw cities and villages. And, in a few places, fires.

'Those're battles,' Jason said. 'Look pretty epic.' He sounded as if he regretted missing the chance to lop off some heads.

A minute later they arrived at a seashore – the ocean was bright green – and slowly eased in for a landing on a rolling hill-side overlooking the turbulent water.

Dance remembered Caitlin saying that Travis liked the shoreline because it reminded him of some place in a game he played.

Jason showed her how to dismount the horse. And, under her own controls, she navigated Greenleaf toward where Jason pointed, a cottage.

'That's the house. We all built it together.'

Like a barn raising in the 1800s, Dance reflected.

'But Travis earned all the money and the supplies. He paid for it. We hired trolls to do the heavy work,' he added without a bit of irony.

When her avatar was at the door, Jason gave her a verbal password. She spoke it into the computer's microphone and the door opened. They walked inside.

Dance was shocked. It was a beautiful, spacious house, filled with bizarre but cozy furniture, out of a Dr Seuss book. There were walkways and stairs that led to various rooms, windows of odd shapes, a huge, burning fireplace, a fountain and a large pool.

A couple of pets – some goofy hybrid of a goat and salamander – walked around croaking.

'It's nice, Jason. Very nice.'

'Yeah, well, we make cool homes in Aetheria 'cause where we live, I mean, in the real world, our places aren't so nice, you know. Okay, like, here's what I wanted to show you. Go there.' He directed her past a small pond populated with shimmery green fish. Her avatar stopped at a large metal door. It was barred with several locks. Jason gave her another pass code and the door slowly opened – accompanied by creaking sound effects. She sent Greenleaf through the doorway, down a flight of stairs and into what looked like a drugstore combined with an emergency room.

Jason looked at Dance and noticed she was frowning.

He said, 'Understand?'

'Not exactly.'

'That's what I meant about knowing Travis. He's not about weapons and battle strategy or any of that. He's about this. It's his healing room.'

'Healing room?' Dance asked.

The boy explained, 'Travis hated fighting. He created Stryker as a warrior when he first started playing, but he didn't like that. That's why he sold him to me. He's a healer, not a fighter. And I mean a healer at the forty-ninth level. You know how good that makes him? He's the best. He's awesome.'

'A healer?'

'That's his avatar's name. Medicus – it's some foreign language for "doctor".'

'Latin,' Boling said.

'Ancient Rome?' Jason asked.

'Right.'

'Sweet. Anyway, Travis's other professions are herb growing and potion making. This is where people come to be treated. It's like a doctor's office.'

'Doctor?' Dance mused. She rose from her desk, found the stack of papers they'd taken from Travis's room and flipped through them. Rey Carraneo had been right – the pictures were of cut-up bodies. But they weren't the victims of crimes; they were of patients during surgery. They were very well done, technically accurate.

Jason continued, 'Characters from all over Aetheria would come to see him. Even the game designers know about him. They asked him for advice in creating NPCs. He's a total legend. He's made thousands of dollars by making these healing potions, buffers, life regenerators and power spells.'

'In real money?'

'Oh, yeah. He sells them on eBay. Like how I bought Stryker.'

Dance recalled the strongbox they'd found under the boy's bed. So this was how he'd made the cash.

Jason tapped the screen. 'Oh, and there?' He was indicating a glass case in which rested a crystal ball on the end of a gold stick. 'That's the scepter of healing. It took him, like, fifty quests to earn it. Nobody ever got one before, in the whole history of *DQ*.' Jason winced. 'He almost lost it once . . .' An awestruck expression washed over his face. 'That was one messed-up night.'

The boy sounded as if the event were a tragedy in real life. 'What do you mean?'

'Well, Medicus and me and some of us in the family were on this quest in the Southern Mountains, which're like three miles high and really dangerous places. We were looking for this magical tree. The Tree of Seeing, it's called. And, this was sweet, we found the home of Ianna, the Elvish queen, who everybody's heard of but never seen. She's way famous.'

'She's an NPC, right?' Boling asked.

'Yeah.'

He reminded Dance, 'A nonplayer character. One that's created by the game itself.'

Jason seemed offended at the characterization. 'But the algorithm is awesome! She's beyond any bot you've ever seen.'

The professor nodded an apologetic concession.

'So we're there and just hanging and talking and she's telling us about the Tree of Seeing and how we can find it, and all of a sudden we're attacked by this raiding party from the Northern Forces. And everybody's fighting, and this asshole shoots the queen with a special arrow. She's going to die. Trav tries to save her but his healing isn't working. So he decides to Shift. We're like, no, man, don't do it! But he did anyway.'

The boy was speaking with such reverence that Dance found herself leaning forward, her leg bobbing with tension. Boling too was staring at him.

'What's that, Jason? Go on.'

'Okay, what it is, sometimes, if somebody's dying, you can submit your life to the Entities in the High Realm. It's called Shifting. And the Entities start taking *your* life force and giving it to the person who's dying. Maybe the person will come back before your life force is gone. But it might take all your life force and you'll die, and they'll die too. Only when you die because you've Shifted, you lose everything. I mean *everything* you've done and earned, all your points, all your Resources, all your Reputation, for as long as you've been playing the game. They all, like, just go away. If Travis'd died, he would've lost the scepter, his house, his gold, his flying horses . . . He would have to start over like a newbie.'

'He did that?'

Jason nodded. 'It was, like, way close. He was almost out of life force, but the queen revived. She kissed him. That was, like, epic! And then the elves and us got together and kicked some Northern Force ass. Man, that night rocked. It was epic win. Everybody who plays the game still talks about it.'

Dance was nodding. 'Okay, Jason, thanks. You can log off.'

'Like, you don't want to play anymore? You were kind of getting a feel for how to move.'

'Maybe later.'

The boy tapped the keys and the game closed.

Dance glanced at her watch. 'Jon, could you take Jason back home? There's somebody I need to talk to.'

A to B to X . . .

32

'I'd like to see Caitlin, please.'

'You're . . . ?' asked Virginia Gardner, the mother of the girl who'd survived the June 9 car crash.

Dance identified herself. 'I spoke to your daughter the other day at summer school.'

'Oh, you're the policewoman. You arranged for the guard for Cait at the hospital the other day, and out in front of our house.'

'That's right.'

'Have you found Travis?'

'No, I—'

'Is he nearby?' the woman asked breathlessly, looking around.

'No, he's not. I'd just like to ask your daughter a few more questions.'

The woman invited Dance into the entryway of the huge contemporary house in Carmel. Dance recalled that Caitlin was headed for some nice undergrad and medical schools. Whatever Dad or Mom did, it seemed they could afford the tuition.

Dance surveyed the massive living room. There were stark abstracts on the walls – two huge, spiky black-and-yellow paintings and one with bloody red splotches. She found them troubling to look at. She thought how different this was from the cozy feel of Travis's and Jason's house in the *DimensionQuest* game.

Yeah, well, we make cool homes in Aetheria 'cause where we live, I mean, in the real world, our places aren't so nice, you know . . .

The girl's mother disappeared and a moment later returned with Caitlin, in jeans and a lime green shell under a tight-fitting white sweater.

'Hi,' the teenager said uneasily.

'Hello, Caitlin. How you feeling?'

'Okay.'

'Hoping you'll have a minute or two. I have a few follow-up questions.'

'Sure, I guess.'

'Can we sit down somewhere?'

'We can go in the sunroom,' Mrs Gardner said.

They passed an office and Dance saw a University of California diploma on the wall. Medical school. Caitlin's father.

The mother and daughter on the couch, Dance in a straight-backed chair. She scooted it closer and said, 'I wanted to give you an update. There was another killing today. Have you heard?'

'Oh, no,' Caitlin's mother whispered.

The girl said nothing. She closed her eyes. Her face, framed by limp blond hair, seemed to grow paler.

'Really,' the mother whispered angrily, 'I'll never see how you could go out with somebody like that.'

'Mom,' Caitlin whined, 'what do you mean, "go out"? Christ, I never went out with Travis. I never *would*. Somebody like him?'

'I just mean he's obviously dangerous.'

'Caitlin,' Dance interrupted. 'We're really desperate to find him. We're just not having any luck. I'm learning more about him from friends, but—'

Her mother again: 'Those Columbine kids.'

'Please, Mrs Gardner.'

An affronted look, but she fell silent.

'I told you everything I could think of the other day.'

'Just a few more questions. I won't be long.' She scooted the chair closer yet and pulled out a notebook. She opened it and flipped through the pages carefully, pausing once or twice.

Caitlin was immobile as she stared at the notebook.

Dance smiled, looking into the girl's eyes. 'Now, Caitlin, think back to the night of the party.'

'Uh-huh.'

'Something interesting's come up. I interviewed Travis before he ran off. I took some notes.' A nod at the notebook resting on her lap.

'You did? You talked to him?'

'That's right. I didn't pay much attention until I'd spoken to you and some other people. But now I'm hoping to piece together some clues as to where he's hiding.'

'How hard could it be to find—' Caitlin's mother began, as if she couldn't stop herself. But she fell silent under Dance's stern glance.

The agent continued, 'Now, you and Travis talked some, right? That night.'

'Not really.'

Dance was frowning slightly and flipping through her notes.

The girl added, 'Well, except when it was time to leave. I meant during the party he was hanging by himself mostly.'

Dance said, 'On the ride home you did, though.' Tapping the notebook.

'Yeah, talked some. I don't remember too much. It was all a blur, with the crash and all.'

'I'm sure it was. But I'm going to read you a couple of statements and I'd like you to fill in the details. Tell me if anything jogs your memory about what Travis said on the drive home, before the accident.'

'I guess.'

Dance consulted her notebook. 'Okay, here's the first one: "The house was pretty sweet but the driveway freaked me out."' She looked up. 'I was thinking maybe that meant Travis had a fear of heights.'

'Yeah, that's what he was talking about. The driveway was on this hillside, and we were talking about it. Travis said he'd always had this fear of falling. He looked at the driveway and he said why didn't they have a guardrail on it.'

'Good. That's helpful.' Another smile. Caitlin reciprocated. Dance returned to the notes. 'And this one? "I think boats rule. I've always wanted one."'

'Oh, that? Yeah. We were talking about Fisherman's Wharf. Travis really thought it'd be cool to sail to Santa Cruz.' She looked away. 'I think he wanted to ask me to go with him, but he was too shy.'

Dance smiled. 'So he might be hiding out on a boat somewhere.'

'Yeah, that could be it. I think he said something about how neat it would be to stow away on a boat.'

'Good . . . Here's another one. "She has more friends than me. I only have one or two I could hang out with."'

'Yeah, I remember him saying that. I felt sorry for him, that he didn't have many friends. He talked about it for a while.'

'Did he mention names? Anybody he might be staying with? Think. It's important.'

The teenager squinted and her hand rubbed her knee. Then sighed. 'Nope.'

'That's okay, Caitlin.'

'I'm sorry.' A faint pout.

Dance kept the smile on her face. She was steeling herself for what was coming next. It would be difficult – for the girl, for her mother, for Dance herself. But there was no choice.

She leaned forward. 'Caitlin, you're not being honest with me.'

The girl blinked. 'What?'

Virginia Gardner muttered, 'You can't say that to my daughter.'

'Travis didn't tell me any of those things,' Dance said, her voice neutral. 'I made them up.'

'You lied!' the mother snapped.

No, she hadn't, not technically. She'd crafted her words carefully and never said they were actual statements from Travis Brigham.

The girl had gone pale.

The mother grumbled, 'What is this, some kind of trap?'

Yes, that was exactly what it was. Dance had a theory and she needed to prove it true or false. Lives were at stake.

Dance ignored the mother and said to Caitlin, 'But you were playing along as if Travis *had* said all of those things to you in the car.'

'I . . . I was just trying to be helpful. I felt bad I didn't know more.'

'No, Caitlin. You thought you might very well have talked with him about them in the car. But you couldn't remember because you were intoxicated.'

'No!'

'I'm going to ask you to leave now,' the girl's mother blurted.

'I'm not through,' Dance growled, shutting up Virginia Gardner.

The agent assessed: with her science background – and her survival skills in this household – Caitlin had a thinking and sensing personality type, according to the Myers-Briggs index. She struck Dance as probably more introverted than extraverted. And, though her liar's personality would fluctuate, she was at the moment an adaptor.

Lying for self-preservation.

If Dance had had more time she might have drawn the truth out slowly and in more depth. But with the Myers-Briggs typing and Caitlin's personality of adaptor, Dance assessed she could push and not have to coddle, the way she had with Tammy Foster.

'You were drinking at the party.'

'I—'

'Caitlin, people saw you.'

'I had a few drinks, sure.'

'Before coming here I talked to several students who were there. They said that you, Vanessa and Trish drank almost a fifth of tequila after you saw Mike with Brianna.'

'Well . . . okay, so what?'

'You're seventeen,' her mother raged, 'that's what!'

Dance said evenly, 'I've called an accident reconstruction service, Caitlin. They're going to look over your car at the police impound lot. They measure things like seat and rearview mirror adjustment. They can tell the height of the driver.'

The girl was completely still, though her jaw trembled.

'Caitlin, it's time to tell the truth. A lot depends on it. Other people's lives are at stake.'

'What truth?' her mother whispered.

Dance kept her eyes on the girl. 'Caitlin was driving the car that night. Not Travis.'

'No!' Virginia Gardner wailed.

'Weren't you, Caitlin?'

The teenager said nothing for a minute. Then her head dropped, her chest collapsed. Dance read pain and defeat through her body. Her kinesic message was: yes.

Her voice breaking, Caitlin said, 'Mike left with that little slut hanging on him and her hand down the back of his jeans! I knew they went back to his place to fuck. I was going to drive there . . . I was going to . . .'

'All right,' her mother ordered, 'that's enough.'

'Be quiet!' the girl yelled to her mother and started to sob. She turned to Dance. 'Yes, I was driving!' The guilt had finally detonated within her.

Dance continued, 'After the accident Travis pulled you into the passenger seat and he got in the driver's. He pretended he was driving. He did that to save you.'

She thought back to the initial interview with Travis.

I didn't do anything wrong!

The boy's assertion had registered as deceptive to Dance. But she believed that he meant he was lying about the attack on Tammy; in fact what he'd done wrong was to lie about who was driving the car that night.

The idea had occurred to Dance when she was looking over the house of Travis – Medicus – and his family in Aetheria. The fact that the boy spent virtually every moment he could in the *DimensionQuest* game as a doctor and healer, not a killer like Stryker, made her begin to doubt the boy's tendency toward violence. And when she'd learned that his avatar had been willing to sacrifice his life for the Elvish queen, she realized that it was possible Travis had done the same in the real world – taking the blame for the car crash so that the girl he admired from afar wouldn't go to jail.

Caitlin, tears flowing from her closed eyes, pressed back into the couch, her body a knot of tension. 'I just lost it. We got drunk and I wanted to go find Mike and tell him what a shit he was. Trish and Vanessa were more wasted than me so I was going to drive, but Travis followed me outside and kept trying to stop me. He tried to take the keys. But I wouldn't let him. I was so mad. Trish and Vanessa were in the backseat and Travis just jumped in the passenger seat and he was like, "Pull over, Caitlin, come on, you can't drive." But I was acting like an asshole.

'I just kept going, ignoring him. And then, I don't know what happened, we went off the road.' Her voice faded and her expression was one of the most sorrowful and forlorn Kathryn Dance had ever seen, as she whispered, 'And I killed my friends.'

Caitlin's mother, her face white and bewildered, eased forward tentatively. She put her arm around her daughter's shoulders. The girl stiffened momentarily and then surrendered, sobbing and pressing her head against her mother's chest.

After a few minutes, the woman, crying herself, looked at Dance. 'What's going to happen?'

'You and your husband should find a lawyer for Caitlin. Then call the police right away. She should surrender voluntarily. The sooner the better.'

Caitlin wiped her face. 'It's hurt so bad, lying. I was going to say something. I really, really was. But then people started to attack Travis – all those things they said – and I knew if I told the truth they'd attack me.' She lowered her head. 'I couldn't do it. All those things people'd say about me . . . they'd be up on their site forever.'

More worried about her image than the deaths of her friends.

But Dance wasn't here to expiate the teenager's guilt. All she'd needed was confirmation of her theory that Travis had taken the fall for Caitlin. She rose and left the mother and daughter, offering the briefest of farewells.

Outside, jogging toward her car, she hit speed-dial button three – Michael O'Neil.

He answered on the second ring. Thank God the Other Case wasn't keeping him completely incommunicado.

'Hey.' He sounded tired.

'Michael.'

'What's wrong?' He'd grown alert; apparently her tone told stories too.

'I know you're swamped, but any chance I could come by? I need to brainstorm. I've found something.'

'Sure. What?'

'Travis Brigham isn't the Roadside Cross Killer.'

Dance and O'Neil were in his office in the Monterey County Sheriff's Office in Salinas.

The windows looked out on the courthouse, in front of which were two dozen of the Life First protesters, along with the wattle-necked Reverend Fisk. Apparently bored with protesting in front of Stuart and Edie Dance's empty house, they'd moved to where they stood a chance of getting some publicity. Fisk was talking to the associate she'd seen earlier: the brawny redheaded bodyguard.

Dance turned away from the window and joined O'Neil at his unsteady conference table. The place was filled with ordered stacks of files. She wondered which were related to the Indonesian container case. O'Neil rocked back on two legs of a wooden chair. 'So, let's hear it.'

She explained quickly about how the investigation had led to Jason and then into the *DimensionQuest* game and ultimately to Caitlin Gardner and the confession that Travis had taken the fall for her.

'Infatuation?' he asked.

But Dance said, 'Sure, that's part of it. But there's something else going on. She wants to go to medical school. That's important to Travis.'

'Medical school?'

'Medicine, healing. In that game he plays, *DimensionQuest,* Travis is a famous healer. I'm thinking one of the reasons he protected her was because of that. His avatar is Medicus. A doctor. He feels a connection to her.'

'That's a little farfetched, don't you think? After all, it's just a game.'

'No, Michael, it's more than a game. The real world and the synth world are getting closer and closer, and people like Travis are living in both. If he's a respected healer in *DimensionQuest* he's not going to be a vindictive killer in the real world.'

'So he takes the fall for Caitlin's crash, and whatever people say about him in the blog, the last thing in the world he wants is to draw attention to himself by attacking anybody.'

'Exactly.'

'But Kelley . . . before she passed out she told the medic that it was Travis who attacked her.'

Dance shook her head. 'I'm not sure she actually saw him. She *assumed* it was him, maybe because she knew she'd posted about him and the mask at her window was from the *DimensionQuest* game. And the rumors were he was behind the attacks. But I think the real killer was wearing a mask or got her from behind.'

'How do you deal with the physical evidence? Planted?'

'Right. It'd be easy to read up online about Travis, to follow him, learn about his job at the bagel place, his bicycle, the fact that he plays *DQ* all the time. The killer could have made one of those masks, stolen the gun from Bob Brigham's truck, planted the trace evidence at the bagel shop and stolen the knife when the employees weren't looking. Oh, and something else: the M&M's? The flecks of wrapper at the crime scene?'

'Right.'

'Had to be planted. Travis wouldn't eat chocolate. He bought packets for his brother. He was worried about his acne. He had books in his room about what foods to avoid. The real killer didn't know that. He must've seen Travis buy M&M's at some point and assumed they were a favorite candy, so he left some trace of the wrapper at the scene.'

'And the sweatshirt fibers?'

'There was a posting in the *Report* about the Brigham family being so poor that they couldn't afford a washer and dryer. And it mentioned which laundromat they went to. I'm sure the real perp read that and staked the place out.'

O'Neil nodded. 'And stole a hooded sweatshirt when the mother was out or wasn't looking.'

'Yep. And there were some pictures posted in the blog under Travis's name.' O'Neil hadn't seen the drawings and she described them briefly, omitting the fact that the last one bore a resemblance to her. Dance continued, 'They were crude, what an adult would think of a teenager's drawing. But I saw some pictures that Travis had done – of surgery. He's a great artist. Somebody else drew them.'

'It would explain why nobody's been able to find the real killer, despite the manhunt. He pulls on a hoodie for the attack, then throws it and the bicycle in his trunk and drives off down the street like anybody else. Hell, he could be fifty years old. Or he could be a she, now that I think about it.'

'Exactly.'

The deputy fell silent for a moment. His thoughts had apparently arrived at the exact spot where Dance's awaited. 'He's dead, isn't he?' the deputy asked. 'Travis?'

Dance sighed at this harsh corollary of her theory. 'It's possible. But I'm hoping not. I like to think he's just being held somewhere.'

'The poor kid was in the wrong place at the wrong time.' Rocking back and forth. 'So, to find where the real perp is, we've got to figure out who's the intended victim. It's not somebody who posted an attack on Travis; they were just set up to mislead us.'

'My theory?' Dance offered.

O'Neil looked at her with a coy smile. 'Whoever the perp is, he's really after Chilton?'

'Yep. The perp was setting the stage, first going after people who'd criticized Travis, then those friendly with Chilton and finally the blogger himself.'

'Somebody who doesn't want to be investigated.'

Dance replied, 'Or who wants revenge for something he'd posted in the past.'

'Okay, all we need to find out is who wants to kill James Chilton,' Michael O'Neil said.

Dance gave a sour laugh. 'The easier question is: who doesn't?'

33

'James?'

There was a pause on the other end of the line. The blogger said, 'Agent Dance.' His voice sounded weary. 'More bad news?'

'I've found some evidence that suggests Travis isn't leaving the crosses.'

'What?'

'I'm not positive, but the way things are looking, the boy could be a scapegoat and somebody's making it look like he's the killer.'

Chilton whispered, 'And he was innocent all along?'

'I'm afraid so.' Dance explained what she'd learned – about who was really behind the wheel of the car on June 9 – and about the likelihood of the evidence being planted.

'And I think *you're* the ultimate target,' she added.

'Me?'

'You've posted some pretty inflammatory stories throughout your career. And you're writing now about controversial topics. I think some people'd be happy to see you stop. You've been threatened before, I assume.'

'Plenty of times.'

'Go back through your blog, find the names of everybody who's threatened you, who might want to get even for something you've said, or who's concerned that you're investigating something now they might not want published. Pick the most credible suspects. And go back a few years.'

'Sure. I'll come up with a list. But you think I'm really at risk?'

'I do, yes.'

He fell silent. 'I'm worried about Pat and the boys. Do you think we should leave the area? Maybe go to our vacation house? It's in Hollister. Or get a hotel room?'

'Probably the hotel's safer. You'd be on record as owning the other house. I can arrange for you to check into one of the motels we use for witnesses. It'll be under a pseudonym.'

'Thanks. Give us a few hours. Pat'll get things packed up, and we'll leave right after a meeting I have scheduled.'

'Good.'

She was about to hang up when Chilton said, 'Wait. Agent Dance, one thing?'

'What?'

'I've got an idea – of who might be number one on the list.'

'I'm ready to write.'

'You won't need a pen and paper,' Chilton replied.

Dance and Rey Carraneo slowly approached the luxurious house of Arnold Brubaker, the man behind the desalination plant that would, according to James Chilton, destroy the Monterey Peninsula.

It was Brubaker whom Chilton fingered as the number-one choice of suspect. Either the desalination tsar himself, or a person hired by him. And Dance thought this was likely. She was online on the car's computer, reading the 'Desalinate . . . and Devastate' thread on the June 28 posting.

http://www.thechiltonreport.com/html/june28.html

From Chilton's reporting and the posts, Dance deduced that the blogger had found out about Brubaker's Las Vegas connections, which suggested organized crime, and the man's private real estate dealings, which hinted at secrets he might not want exposed.

'Ready?' Dance asked Carraneo as she logged off.

The young agent nodded, and they climbed from the car.

She knocked on the door.

Finally the red-faced entrepreneur – flushed from the sun, not booze, Dance deduced – answered the knock. He was surprised to see visitors. He blinked and said nothing for a moment. 'From the hospital. You're . . . ?'

'Agent Dance. This is Agent Carraneo.'

His eyes zipped behind her.

Looking for backup? she wondered.

And if so, for *her* backup? Or Brubaker's own?

She felt a trickle of fear. People who kill for money were the most ruthless, in her estimation.

'We're following up on that incident with Mr Chilton. You mind if I ask you a few questions?'

'What? That prick filed charges after all? I thought we—'

'No, no charges. Can we come in?'

The man remained suspicious. His eyes avoiding Dance's, he nodded them inside and blurted, 'He's crazy, you know. I mean, I think he's certifiable.'

Dance gave a noncommittal smile.

With another glance outside, Brubaker closed the door. He locked it.

They walked through the house, impersonal, many rooms empty of furniture. Dance believed she heard a creak from nearby. Then another from a different room.

Was the house settling, or did Brubaker have assistants here? Assistants, or muscle?

They walked into an office filled with papers, blueprints, pictures, photographs, legal documents. A carefully constructed scale model of the desalination plant took up one of the tables.

Brubaker lifted several huge bound reports off chairs and gestured them to sit. He did too, behind a large desk.

Dance noticed certificates on the wall. There were also pictures of Brubaker with powerful-looking men in suits – politicians or other businesspeople. Interrogators love office walls; they reveal much about people. From these particular pictures she deduced that Brubaker was smart (degrees and professional course completions) and savvy politically (honors and keys from cities and counties). And tough; his company apparently had built desalination plants in Mexico and Colombia. Photos showed him surrounded by sunglassed, vigilant men – security guards. The men were the same in all of the pictures, which meant they were Brubaker's personal minders, not provided by the local government. One held a machine gun.

Were they the source of the creaks nearby – which she'd heard again, closer, it seemed?

Dance asked about the desalination project, and he launched into a lengthy sales pitch about the latest technology the plant would use. She caught words like 'filtration', 'membranes', 'freshwater holding tanks'. Brubaker gave them a short lecture on the reduced costs of new systems that was making desalination economically feasible.

She took in little information, but instead feigned interest and soaked up his baseline behavior.

Her first impression was that Brubaker didn't seem troubled at their presence, though High Machs were rarely moved by any human connections – whether romantic, social or professional. They even approached confrontation with equanimity. It was one aspect that made them so efficient. And potentially dangerous.

Dance would have liked more time to gather baseline information, but she felt a sense of urgency so she stopped his spiel and asked, 'Mr Brubaker, where were you at one p.m. yesterday and eleven a.m. today?'

The times of Lyndon Strickland's and Mark Watson's deaths.

'Well, why?' A smile. But Dance had no idea what was behind it.

'We're looking into certain threats against Mr Chilton.'

True, though not, of course, the whole story.

'Oh, he libels me, and now *I'm* accused?'

'We're not accusing you, Mr Brubaker. But could you answer my question, please?'

'I don't have to. I can ask you to leave right now.'

This was true. 'You can refuse to cooperate. But we're hoping you won't.'

'You can hope all you want,' he snapped. The smile now grew triumphant. 'I see what's going on here. Could it be that you got it all wrong, Agent Dance? That maybe it isn't some psychotic teenager who's been gutting people like in some bad horror film. But somebody who's been using the kid, setting him up to take the fall for killing James Chilton?'

That was pretty good, Dance thought. But did it mean that he was threatening them? If he was the 'somebody' he referred to, then, yes, he was.

Carraneo stole a brief glance at her.

'Which means you've pretty much had the wool pulled over your eyes.'

There were too many important rules in interviewing and interrogation for any of them to be number one, but high at the top was: never let the personal insults affect you.

Dance said reasonably, 'There's been a series of very serious crimes, Mr Brubaker. We're looking into all possibilities. You have a grudge against James Chilton, and you've assaulted him once already.'

'And, really,' he said in a dismissive tone, 'do you think it'd be the smartest thing in the world to get into a public brawl with a man I'm secretly trying to kill?'

Either very stupid or very smart, Dance responded silently. She then asked, 'Where were you at the times I mentioned? You can tell us, or you can refuse and we'll keep investigating.'

'You're as much of a prick as Chilton is. Actually, Agent Dance, you're worse. You hide behind your shield.'

Carraneo stirred but said nothing.

She too was silent. Either he was going to tell them or he was going to throw them out.

Wrong, Dance realized. There was a third option, one that had been percolating since she'd been listening to the eerie creaks in the seemingly deserted house.

Brubaker was going for a weapon.

'I've had enough of this,' he whispered, and, eyes wide in anger, yanked open the top desk drawer. His hand shot inside.

Dance flashed on her children's faces, then her husband's and then Michael O'Neil's.

Please, she thought, praying for speed . . .

'Rey, behind us! Cover!'

And when Brubaker looked up he was staring into the muzzle of her Glock pistol, while Carraneo was facing the opposite way, aiming at the door to the office.

Both agents were crouching.

'Jesus, take it easy!' he cried.

'Clear so far,' Carraneo said.

'Check it out,' she ordered.

The young man eased to the door and, standing to the side, pushed it open with his foot. 'Clear.'

He spun around to cover Brubaker.

'Lift your hands slowly,' Dance said, her Glock steady enough. 'If you have a weapon in your hand, drop it immediately. Don't lift it or lower it. Just drop it. If you don't – now – we will shoot. Understand?'

Arnold Brubaker gasped. 'I don't have a gun.'

She didn't hear a weapon hit the expensive floor, but he was lifting his hands very slowly.

Unlike Dance's, they weren't shaking at all.

In the developer's ruddy fingers was a business card, which he flicked toward her contemptuously. The agents holstered their weapons. They sat.

Dance looked at the card, reflecting that a situation that couldn't get any more awkward just had. On the card was the gold-embossed seal of the Department of Justice – the eagle and the fine print. She knew FBI agent's cards very well. She still had a large box of them at home: her husband's.

'At the time you mentioned, yesterday, I was meeting with Amy Grabe.' Special agent in charge of the San Francisco office of the Bureau. 'We were meeting here and at the site. From about eleven a.m. to three p.m.'

Oh.

Brubaker said, 'Desalination and water-based infrastructure projects are terrorist targets. I've been working with Homeland Security and the FBI to make sure that if the project gets under way, there'll be adequate security.' He looked at her calmly and with contempt. The tip of his tongue touched a lip. 'I'm hoping it will be *federal* officers involved. I'm losing confidence in the local constabulary.'

Kathryn Dance wasn't about to apologize. She'd check with SAC Amy Grabe, whom she knew and, despite differences of opinion, respected. And even though an alibi wouldn't absolve him from hiring a thug to commit the actual crimes, it was hard for Dance to believe that a man working closely with the FBI and DHS would risk murder. Besides, everything about Brubaker's demeanor suggested he was telling the truth.

'All right, Mr Brubaker. We'll check out what you're telling us.'

'I hope you do.'

'I appreciate your time.'

'You can find your own way out,' he snapped.

Carraneo cast a sheepish glance her way. Dance rolled her eyes.

When they were at the door, Brubaker said, 'Wait. Hold on.' The agents turned. 'Well, was I right?'

'Right?'

'That you think somebody killed the boy and set him up to be the fall guy in some plot to kill Chilton?'

A pause. Then she thought: why not? She answered, 'We think it's possible, yes.'

'Here.' Brubaker jotted something on a slip of paper and offered it. 'He's somebody you ought to be looking at. He'd love for the blog – and the blogger – to disappear.'

Dance glanced at the note.

Wondering why she hadn't thought of the suspect herself.

34

Parked on a dusty street near the small town of Marina, five miles north of Monterey, Dance was alone in her Crown Vic, on the phone with TJ.

'Brubaker?' she asked.

'No criminal record,' he told her. And his work – and the alibi – with the FBI was confirmed.

He still might've hired somebody for the job, but this information did ease him out of the hot seat.

Attention was now on the man whose name Brubaker had given her. The name on the slip of paper was Clint Avery and she was presently gazing at him from about one hundred yards away, through a chain-link fence – topped with razor wire – that surrounded his massive construction company.

The name Avery had never come up as someone involved in the case. For very good reason: the builder had never posted on the blog and Chilton had never written about him in the *Report*.

Not by name, that is. The 'Yellow Brick Road' thread didn't mention Avery specifically. But questioned the government's decision to build the highway and the bidding process, by implication also criticizing the contractor – which Dance should have known was Avery Construction, since she'd been flagged down by a company team at the site of the highway work when she'd been on her way to Caitlin Gardner's summer school two days ago. She hadn't put the two pieces together.

TJ Scanlon now told her, 'Seems that Clint Avery was connected with a company investigated for using substandard materials about five years ago. Investigation got dropped real fast. Maybe Chilton's reporting might get the case reopened.'

A good motive to kill the blogger, Dance agreed. 'Thanks, TJ. That's good . . . And Chilton's got you the list of other suspects?'

'Yep.'

'Any others stand out?'

'Not yet, boss. But I'm glad I don't have as many enemies as he does.'

She gave a brief laugh and they disconnected.

From the distance, Dance continued to study Clint Avery. She'd seen pictures of him a dozen times – on the news and in the papers. He was hard to miss. Though he would certainly have been a millionaire many times over, he was dressed the same as any other worker: a blue shirt sprouting pens in the breast pocket, tan work slacks, boots. The sleeves were rolled up and she spotted a tattoo on his leathery forearm. In his hand was a yellow hard hat. A big walkie-talkie sat on his hip. She wouldn't have been surprised to see a six-shooter; his broad, mustachioed face looked like a gunslinger's.

She started the engine and drove through the gates. Avery noticed her car. He squinted slightly and seemed to recognize hers immediately as a government car. He concluded his discussion with a leather-jacketed man, who walked away. Quickly.

She parked. Avery Construction was a no-nonsense company, devoted to one purpose: building things. Huge stores of construction materials, bulldozers, Cats, backhoes, trucks and jeeps. There was a concrete plant on the premises and what appeared to be metal- and wood-working shops, large diesel tanks for feeding the vehicles, Quonset huts and storage sheds. The main office was made up of a number of large, functional buildings, all low. No graphic designer or landscaper had been involved in the creation of Avery Construction.

Dance identified herself. The head of the company was cordial and shook hands, his eyes crinkling lines into the tanned face as he glanced at her ID.

'Mr Avery, we're hoping you can help us. You're familiar with the crimes that have been occurring around the Peninsula?'

'The Mask Killer, that boy, sure. I heard someone else was killed today. Terrible. How can I help you?'

'The killer's leaving roadside memorials as a warning that he's going to commit more crimes.'

He nodded. 'I've seen that on the news.'

'Well, we've noticed something curious. Several of the crosses have been left near sites of your construction projects.'

'They have?' Now a frown, his brow creasing significantly. Was it out of proportion to the news? Dance couldn't tell. Avery started to turn his head, then stopped. Had he instinctively been looking toward his leather-jacketed associate?

'How can I help?'

'We want to talk to some of your employees to see if they've noticed anything out of the ordinary.'

'Such as?'

'Passersby behaving suspiciously, unusual objects, maybe footprints or bicycle tire tread marks in areas that were roped off for construction. Here's a list of locations.' She'd written down several earlier in the car.

Concern on his face, he looked over the list then slipped the sheet into his shirt pocket and crossed his arms. This in itself meant little kinesically, since she hadn't had time to get a baseline reading. But arm and leg crossing are defensive gestures and can signify discomfort. 'You want me to give you a list of employees who've worked around there? Since the killings began, I assume.'

'Exactly. It would be a big help.'

'I assume you'd like this sooner rather than later.'

'As soon as possible.'

'I'll do what I can.'

She thanked him and walked back to the car, then drove out of the parking lot and up the road. Dance pulled up beside a dark blue Honda Accord nearby. She was pointed the opposite way, so her open window was two feet from Rey Carraneo's. He sat in the driver's seat of the Honda in shirtsleeves, without a tie. She'd seen him dressed this casually only twice before: at a Bureau picnic and one very bizarre barbecue at Charles Overby's house.

'He's got the bait,' Dance said. 'I have no idea if he'll bite.'

'How did he react?'

'Hard to call. I didn't have time to take a baseline. But my sense was that he was struggling to seem calm and cooperative. He was more nervous than he let on. I'm also not so sure about one of his helpers.' She described the man in the leather jacket. 'Either one of them leaves, stay close.'

'Yes, ma'am.'

Patrizia Chilton opened the door and said hello to Greg Ashton, the man her husband called an Über Blogger – in that cute but slightly obnoxious way of Jim's.

'Hi, Pat,' Ashton said. They shook hands. The slim man, in expensive tan slacks and a nice sports coat, nodded toward the squad car sitting in the road. 'That deputy? He wouldn't give anything away. But he's here because of those killings, right?'

'They're just taking precautions.'

'I've been following the story. You must be pretty upset.'

She gave a stoic smile. 'That's putting it mildly. It's been a nightmare.' She liked being able to admit to how she felt. She couldn't always do that with Jim. She believed she had to be supportive. In fact, she was sometimes furious at his role as a relentless investigative journalist. It was important, she understood, but sometimes she just plain hated the blog.

And now . . . endangering the family and forcing them to move to a hotel? This morning she'd had to ask her brother, a big man who'd been a bouncer in college, to escort the boys to their day camp, stay there and bring them back.

She bolted the door behind them. 'Can I get you anything?' Patrizia asked Ashton.

'No, no, I'm fine, thanks.'

Patrizia walked him to the door of her husband's office, her eyes taking in the backyard through a large window in the hallway.

A tap of concern in her chest.

Had she seen something in the bushes behind the house? Was it a person?

She paused.

'Something wrong?' Ashton asked.

Her heart was pounding hard. 'I . . . Nothing. Probably just a deer. I have to say this whole case has got my nerves shaken.'

'I don't see anything.'

'It's gone,' she said. But was it? She couldn't tell. Yet she didn't want to alarm their guest. Besides, all the windows and doors were locked.

They arrived at her husband's office and stepped inside. 'Honey,' she said. 'It's Greg.'

'Ah, right on time.'

The men shook hands.

Patrizia said, 'Greg said he doesn't care for anything. How 'bout you, honey?'

'No, I'm fine. Any more tea and I'll be in the bathroom for the whole meeting.'

'Well, I'll leave you two boys to do your work and get back to packing.' Her heart sank again at the thought of moving into a hotel. She hated being driven from her home. At least the boys would consider it an adventure.

'Actually,' Ashton said, 'hold on a minute, Pat. I'm going to do a video of Jim's operation to post on my site. I want to include you too.' He set his briefcase on the table and opened it up.

'*Me?*' Patrizia gasped. 'Oh, no. I haven't done my hair. And my makeup.'

Ashton said, 'First of all, you look fantastic. But most important, blogging isn't about hair and makeup. It's about authenticity. I've shot dozens of these and I've never let anybody so much as put on lipstick.'

'Well, I guess.' Patrizia was distracted, thinking about the motion she'd seen behind the house. She should tell the deputy out front about it.

Ashton laughed. 'It's only a webcam anyway, medium resolution.' He held up the small video camera.

'You're not going to ask me questions, are you?' She was growing panicky at the thought. Jim's blog alone had hundreds of thousands of viewers. Greg Ashton's probably had many more. 'I wouldn't know what to say.'

'It'll be sound bites. Just talk about what it's like to be married to a blogger.'

Her husband laughed. 'I'll bet she has plenty to say.'

'We can do as many takes as you want.' Ashton set a tripod up in the corner of the room and mounted the camera.

Jim straightened his desktop, organizing the dozens of stacks of journals and papers. Ashton laughed and shook a finger. 'We want it authentic, Jim.'

Another laugh. 'Okay. Fair enough.' Jim replaced the papers and magazines.

Patrizia looked at herself in a small decorative mirror up on the wall, and ran her fingers through her hair. No, she decided defiantly. She was going to get fixed up, no matter what he said. She turned to tell Ashton this.

She had only a moment to blink, and no time to protect herself, when Ashton's fist swung directly into her cheek and collided hard with bone, breaking skin and knocking her to the floor.

Eyes wide in horror and bewilderment, Jim leapt toward him.

And froze as Ashton thrust a gun into his face.

'No!' Patrizia cried, scrabbling to her feet. 'Don't hurt him!'

Ashton tossed Patrizia a roll of duct tape and ordered her to bind her husband's hands behind him.

She hesitated.

'Do it!'

Hands shaking, tears streaming, confused, she did as she'd been told.

'Honey,' she whispered as she wrapped his hand behind the chair. 'I'm scared.'

'Do what he says,' her husband told her. Then he glared at Ashton. 'What the hell is this?'

Ashton ignored him and dragged Patrizia by the hair to the corner. She squealed, tears falling. 'No . . . no. It hurts. No!'

Ashton taped her hands as well.

'Who are you?' Jim whispered.

But Patrizia Chilton could answer that one herself. Greg Ashton was the Roadside Cross Killer.

Ashton noticed Jim looking outside. He muttered, 'The deputy? He's dead. There's nobody to help you.'

Ashton pointed the video camera at Jim's pale, horrified face, tears welling in his eyes. 'You want more hits on your precious *Report*, Chilton? Well, you're going to get 'em. I'll bet it'll be a record. I don't think we've ever seen a blogger killed on webcam before.'

35

Kathryn Dance was back at CBI headquarters. She was disappointed to learn that Jonathan Boling had returned to Santa Cruz. But since he'd come up with the platinum find – Stryker, well, Jason – there wasn't much else for him to do at the moment.

Rey Carraneo called in with some interesting news. He explained that Clint Avery had left his company ten minutes ago. The agent had followed him along the winding roads in the Pastures of Heaven, the name that literary legend John Steinbeck had given to the lush, agriculturally fertile area. There he'd stopped twice, on the shoulder. Both times he'd met with someone. First, two somber men – dressed like cowboys – in a fancy pickup truck. The second time, a white-haired man in a nice suit, behind the wheel of a Cadillac. The meetings seemed suspicious; Avery was clearly nervous. Carraneo had gotten the plates and was running profiles.

Avery was now headed toward Carmel, Carraneo right behind him.

Dance was discouraged. She'd hoped that her meeting with Avery would flush the construction boss – force him to speed to a safe house, where he'd stashed evidence – and perhaps Travis himself.

But apparently not.

Still, the men Avery'd met with might've been hired guns who were behind the killings. The DMV report would give her some clues, if not answers.

TJ stuck his head in her doorway. 'Hey, boss, you still interested in Hamilton Royce?'

The man who was probably at that very moment considering how to bring her career down in flames. 'Give me a one-minute précis.'

'A what?' TJ asked.

'Synopsis. Summary. Digest.'

'"Précis" is a word? Learn something new every day . . . Okay. Royce's a former lawyer. Left practice mysteriously and quickly. He's a tough guy. Works mostly with six or seven different departments in the state. Ombudsman's his official title. Unofficially he's a fixer. You see that movie *Michael Clayton*?'

'With George Clooney, sure. Twice.'

'Twice?'

'George Clooney.'

'Ah. Well, that's what Royce does. Lately he's been doing a lot of work for senior people in the lieutenant governor's office, the state energy commission, the EPA, and the Finance Committee of the Assembly. If there's a problem, he's there.'

'What sort of problem?'

'Committee disagreements, scandals, public relations, pilfering, contract disputes. I'm still waiting to hear back on more details.'

'Let me know if there's anything I can use.' Picking one of the man's favorite verbs.

'Use? To do what?'

'We had a falling-out, Royce and me.'

'So you want to blackmail him?'

'That's a strong word. Let's just say I'd like to keep my job.'

'I want you to keep your job too, boss. You let me get away with murder. Hey, what's with Avery?'

'Rey's tailing him.'

'Love that word. Almost as good as "shadow".'

'What's the progress on Chilton's list of suspects?'

TJ explained that tracking them down was going slowly. People had moved or were unlisted, they were out, names had changed.

'Give me half,' she said. 'I'll get going on it too.'

The young agent handed her a sheet of paper. 'I'll give you the small list,' he said, 'because you're my favorite boss.'

Dance looked over the names, considering how best to proceed. She heard in her mind Jon Boling's words. *We give away too much information about ourselves online. Way too much.*

Kathryn Dance decided she'd get to the official databases in a while – National Criminal Information Center, Violent Criminal Apprehension Program, California Open Warrants and consolidated DMV.

For now, she'd stick to Google.

Greg Schaeffer studied James Chilton, who sat bloodied and frightened before him.

Schaeffer had been using the pseudonym Greg Ashton to get close to Chilton without arousing suspicions.

Because the name 'Schaeffer' might raise alarms in the blogger.

But then again it might not have; it wouldn't surprise Schaeffer one bit if Chilton regularly forgot about the victims who suffered because of his blog.

This thought infuriated Schaeffer all the more and when Chilton started to sputter, 'Why—?' he slugged him once more.

The blogger's head snapped back against the upper part of his desk chair and he grunted. Which was all fine, but the son of a bitch wasn't looking terrified enough to satisfy Schaeffer.

'Ashton! Why're you doing this?'

Schaeffer leaned forward, gripped Chilton by the collar. He whispered, 'You're going to read a statement. If you don't sound sincere, if you don't sound remorseful, your wife will die. Your children too. I know they'll be home from camp soon. I've been following them. I know the schedule.' He turned to Chilton's wife. 'And I know your brother's with them. He's a big guy, but he's not bulletproof.'

'Oh, God, no!' Patrizia gasped, dissolving into tears. 'Please!'

And now, at last, there was real fear in Chilton's face. 'No, don't hurt my family! Please, please . . . I'll do whatever you want. Just don't hurt them.'

'Read the statement and sound like you mean it,' Schaeffer warned, 'then I'll leave them alone. I'll tell you, Chilton, I've got nothing but sympathy for them. They deserve a better life than being with a piece of shit like you.'

'I'll read it,' the blogger said. 'But who are you? Why are you doing this? You owe me an answer.'

Schaeffer was seized by a wave of fury. '*Owe* you?' he growled. 'Owe you? You arrogant asshole!' He slammed his fist into Chilton's cheek once more, leaving the man stunned. 'I owe you nothing.' He leaned forwards and snapped, 'Who am I, who am I? Do you know anybody whose lives you destroy? No, of course not. Because you sit in that fucking chair, a million miles away from real life, and you say whatever you want to say. You type some shit on your keyboard, send it out into the world and then you're on to something else. Does the concept of *consequences* mean anything to you? Accountability?'

'I try to be accurate. If I got something wrong—'

Schaeffer burned. 'You are so fucking blind. You don't understand you can be factually right and still be wrong. Do you *have* to tell every secret in the world? Do you *have* to destroy lives for no reason – except your ratings?'

'Please!'

'Does the name Anthony Schaeffer mean anything to you?'

Chilton's eyes closed momentarily. 'Oh.' When he opened them again they were filled with understanding, and perhaps remorse. But that didn't move Schaeffer one bit.

At least Chilton remembered the man he'd destroyed.

Patrizia asked, 'Who's that? Who does he mean, Jim?'

'Tell her, Chilton.'

The blogger sighed. 'He was a gay man who killed himself after I outed him a few years ago. And he was . . . ?'

'My brother.' His voice cracked.

'I'm sorry.'

'Sorry,' Schaeffer scoffed.

'I apologized for what happened. I never wanted him to die! You must know that. I felt terrible.'

Schaeffer turned to Patrizia, 'Your husband, the voice of the moral and just universe, didn't like it that a deacon in a church could also be gay.'

Chilton snapped back, 'That wasn't the reason. He headed a big anti–gay marriage campaign in California. I was attacking his hypocrisy, not his sexual orientation. And his immorality. He was married, he had children . . . but when he was on business trips he'd call up gay prostitutes. He was cheating on his wife, sometimes with three men a night!'

The blogger's defiance was back and Schaeffer wanted to hit him once more, so he did, hard and fast.

'Tony was struggling to find God's path. He slipped a few times. And you made it sound like he was a monster! You never even gave him a chance to explain. God was helping him find the way.'

'Well, God wasn't doing a very good job. Not if—'

The fist struck again.

'Jim, don't argue with him. Please!'

Chilton lowered his head. Finally he looked desperate and filled with sorrow and fear.

Schaeffer enjoyed the delicious sense of the man's despair. 'Read the statement.'

'All right. I'll do whatever you want. I'll read it. But my family . . . please.' The agony in Chilton's face was like fine wine to Schaeffer.

'You have my word on it.' He said this sincerely, though he was reflecting that Patrizia would outlive her husband by no more than two seconds – a humane act, in the end. She wouldn't want to go on without him. Besides, she was a witness.

As for the children, no, he wouldn't kill them. For one thing they weren't due home for nearly an hour and he'd be long gone by then. Also, he wanted the sympathy of the world. Killing the blogger and his wife was one thing. The children were something else.

Beneath the camera Schaeffer taped a piece of the paper containing the statement he'd written that morning. It was a moving piece – and had been drafted in a way to make sure that nobody would associate the crime with him.

Chilton cleared his throat and looked down. He began to read. 'This is a statement—' His voice broke.

Beautiful! Schaeffer kept the camera running.

Chilton started over. 'This is a statement to those who've been reading my blog, *The Chilton Report*, over the years. There is nothing more precious in the world than a man's reputation and I have devoted my life to needlessly and randomly destroying the reputations of many fine, upstanding citizens.'

He was doing a good job.

'It's easy to buy a cheap computer and a website and some blog software and in five minutes you've got a venue for your personal opinions – a venue that will be seen by millions of people around the world. This leads to an intoxicating sense of power. But it's a power that isn't earned. It's a power that's stolen.

'I've written many things about people that were merely rumors. Those rumors spread and they became accepted as the truth, even though they were total lies. Because of my blog the life of a young man, Travis Brigham, has been destroyed. He has nothing more to live for. And neither do I. He has sought justice against the people who attacked him, people who were my friends. And now he's rendering justice against me. I'm ultimately respon-sible for destroying his life.'

Glorious tears were streaking down his face. Schaeffer was in purest heaven.

'I now accept responsibility for destroying Travis's reputation and those of the others I've carelessly written about. The sentence that Travis now serves on me will stand as a warning to others: the truth is sacred. Rumors are not the truth . . . Now, good-bye.'

He inhaled deeply and looked at his wife.

Schaeffer was satisfied. The man had done a good job. He paused the webcam and checked the screen. Only Chilton was in the image. The wife wasn't. He didn't want an image of her death, just the blogger's. He pulled back a bit so the man's entire torso was visible. He'd shoot him once, in the heart, and let him die on camera, then upload the post to a number of social networking sites and to other blogs. Schaeffer estimated it would take two minutes for the video to appear on YouTube and would be viewed by several million people before the company took it down. By then, though, the pirate software that allowed the downloading of streaming videos would have captured it and the footage would spread throughout the world like cancer cells.

'They'll find you,' Chilton muttered. 'The police.'

'But they won't be looking for *me*. They'll be looking for Travis Brigham. And, frankly, I don't think anybody's going to be looking very hard. You've got a lot of enemies, Chilton.'

He cocked the gun.

'No!' Patrizia Chilton wailed desperately, frantic. Schaeffer resisted a tempting impulse to shoot her first.

He kept the gun steady on his target and noted a resigned and, it seemed, ironic smile crossing James Chilton's face.

Schaeffer hit the 'Record' button on the camera again and began to pull the trigger.

When he heard, 'Freeze!'

The voice was coming from the open office doorway. 'Drop the weapon. Now!'

Jolted, Schaeffer glanced back, at a slim young Latino man in a white shirt, sleeves rolled up. Pointing a weapon his way. A badge on his hip.

No! How had they found him?

Schaeffer kept the gun steadily on the blogger's chest and snapped to the cop, '*You* drop it!'

'Lower the weapon,' was the officer's measured reply. 'This is your only warning.'

Schaeffer growled, 'If you shoot me, I'll—'

He saw a yellow flash, sensed a tap to his head and then the universe went black.

36

The dead rolled, the living walked.

The body of Greg Ashton – it was really Greg *Schaeffer,* Dance had learned – was wheeled down the stairs and over the lawn on the rickety gurney to the coroner's bus, while James and Patrizia Chilton walked slowly to an ambulance.

Another casualty, everyone was horrified to learn, was the MCSO deputy who'd been guarding the Chiltons, Miguel Herrera.

Schaeffer, as Ashton, had stopped at Herrera's car. The guard had called Patrizia and been told that the man was expected. Then Schaeffer had apparently shoved the gun against Herrera's jacket and fired twice, the proximity to the body muting the sound.

The deputy's supervisor from the MCSO was present, along with a dozen other deputies, shaken, furious at the murder.

As for the walking wounded, the Chiltons didn't seem too badly hurt.

Dance was, however, keeping an eye on Rey Carraneo – who'd been the first on the scene, spotted the dead deputy, and raced into the house after calling for backup. He'd seen Schaeffer about to shoot Chilton. Carraneo gave the killer a by-the-book warning, but when the man had tried to negotiate, the agent had simply fired two very efficient rounds into his head. Discussions with gun-toting suspects only occur in movies and TV shows – and bad ones, at that. Police never lower or set down their weapons. And they never hesitate to take out a target if one presents itself.

Rules number one, two and three are: shoot.

And he had. Superficially the young agent seemed fine, his body language unchanged from the professional, upright posture he wore like a rented tux. But his eyes told a different story, revealing the words looping through his mind at the moment: *I just killed a man. I just killed a man.*

She'd make sure he took some time off with pay.

A car pulled up and Michael O'Neil climbed out. He spotted Dance and joined her. The quiet deputy wasn't smiling.

'I'm sorry, Michael.' She gripped his arm. O'Neil had known Miguel Herrera for several years.

'Just shot him down?'

'That's right.'

His eyes closed briefly. 'Jesus.'

'Wife?'

'No. Divorced. But he's got a grown son. He's already been notified.' O'Neil, otherwise so calm, with a facade that revealed so little, looked with chilling hatred at the green bag containing Greg Schaeffer's body.

Another voice intruded, weak, unsteady. 'Thank you.'

They turned to face the man who'd spoken: James Chilton. Wearing dark slacks, a white T-shirt and a navy blue V-neck sweater, the blogger seemed like a chaplain humbled by battle-front carnage. His wife was at his side.

'Are you all right?' Dance asked them.

'I'm fine, yes. Thank you. Just beat up a bit. Cuts and bruises.' Patrizia Chilton said she too wasn't seriously injured.

O'Neil nodded to them and asked Chilton, 'Who was he?'

Dance answered, 'Anthony Schaeffer's brother.'

Chilton gave a blink of surprise. 'You figured it out?'

She explained to O'Neil about Ashton's real name. 'That's the interesting thing about the Internet – those role-playing games and sites. Like *Second Life*. You can create whole new identities for yourself. Schaeffer's been spending the past few months seeding the name "Greg Ashton" around online as this blogging and RSS maven. He did that to seduce his way into Chilton's life.'

'I outed his brother Anthony in a blog several years ago,' Chilton explained. 'He was the one I told Agent Dance about when I first met her – one of the things I regretted about the blog – that he killed himself.'

O'Neil asked Dance, 'How did you find out about him?'

'TJ and I were checking out the suspects. It wasn't likely that Arnold Brubaker was the killer. I was still suspicious of Clint Avery – the guy behind the highway project – but we didn't have anything specific yet. So I was working on the list of people who'd sent James threats.'

The small list . . .

Chilton said, 'Anthony Schaeffer's wife was on the list. Sure. She'd threatened me a few years ago.'

Dance continued, 'I went online to find out as many details about her as I could. I found her wedding pictures. The best man at their wedding was Greg, Anthony's brother. I recognized him from when I came to your house the other day. I checked him out. He traveled here on an open ticket about two weeks ago.' As soon as she'd learned this she'd called Miguel Herrera but couldn't get through, so she sent Rey Carraneo here. The agent, following Clint Avery, was not far from Chilton's house.

O'Neil asked, 'Did Schaeffer say anything about Travis?'

Dance showed him the plastic envelope containing the hand-written note, with the references to Travis, making it seem that the boy was the one about to shoot Chilton.

'He's dead, you think?'

O'Neil's and Dance's eyes met. She said, 'I'm not going on that assumption. Ultimately, sure, Schaeffer'd have to kill the boy. But he might not have done it yet. He might want to make it look like Travis killed himself after he'd finished with Chilton. Make the case tidier. That means he could still be alive.'

The senior deputy took a phone call. He stepped away, eyes

straying to the MCSO car where Herrera had been so ruthlessly killed. He disconnected after a moment. 'Got to head off. Have to interview a witness.'

'You? Interviewing?' she chided. Michael O'Neil's technique at interviewing involved gazing unsmilingly at the subject and asking him over and over again to tell O'Neil what he knew. It could be effective, but it wasn't efficient. And O'Neil didn't really enjoy it.

He consulted his watch. 'Any chance you could do me a favor?'

'Name it.'

'Anne's flight from San Francisco was delayed. I can't miss this interview. Can you pick up the kids at day care?'

'Sure. I'm going to get Wes and Maggie after camp anyway.'

'Meet me at Fisherman's Wharf at five?'

'Sure.'

O'Neil headed off, with yet another dark glance at Herrera's car.

Chilton gripped his wife's hand. Dance recognized postures that bespoke a graze with mortality. She thought back to the arrogant, self-righteous crusader Chilton had been when she first met him. Very different now. She recalled that something about him seemed to have softened earlier – when he'd learned that his friend Don Hawken and his wife had nearly been killed. Now, there'd been another shift, away from the stony visage of a missionary.

The man gave a bitter smile. 'Oh, did he sucker me in . . . He played right to my fucking ego.'

'Jim—'

'No, honey. He did. You know, this's all my fault. Schaeffer picked Travis. He read through the blog, found somebody who'd be a good candidate to be a fall guy and set up a seventeen-year-old boy as my killer. If I hadn't started the "Roadside Crosses" thread and mentioned the accident, Schaeffer wouldn't have any incentive to go after him.'

He was right. But Kathryn Dance tended to avoid the what-if game. The playing field was far too soupy. 'He would've picked somebody else,' she pointed out. 'He was determined to get revenge against you.'

But Chilton didn't seem to hear. 'I should just shut the fucking blog down altogether.'

Dance saw resolve in his eyes, frustration, anger. Fear, too, she believed. Speaking to both of them, he said firmly, 'I'm going to.'

'To what?' his wife asked.

'Shut it down. The *Report*'s finished. I'm not destroying anybody else's life.'

'Jim,' Patrizia said softly. She brushed some dirt off her sleeve. 'When our son had pneumonia, you sat beside his bed for two days and didn't get a bit of sleep. When Don's wife died, you walked right out of that meeting at Microsoft headquarters to be there for him – you gave up a hundred-thousand-dollar contract. When my dad was dying, you were with him more than the hospice people. You do good things, Jim. That's what you're about. And your blog does good things too.'

'I—'

'Shhh. Let me finish. Donald Hawken needed you and you were there. Our children needed you and you were there. Well, the world needs you too, honey. You can't turn your back on that.'

'Patty, people died.'

'Just promise me you won't make any decisions too fast. This has been a terrible couple of days. Nobody's thinking clearly.'

A lengthy pause. 'I'll see. I'll see.' Then he hugged his wife. 'But one thing I *do* know is that I can go on hiatus for a few days. And we're going to get away from here.' Chilton said to his wife, 'Let's go up to Hollister tomorrow. We'll spend a long weekend with Donald and Lily. You still haven't met her. We'll bring the boys, cook out . . . do some hiking.'

Patrizia's face blossomed into a smile. She rested her head against his shoulders. 'I'd like that.'

He'd turned his attention to Dance. 'There's something I've been thinking about.'

She cocked an eyebrow.

'A lot of people would've thrown me to the wolves. And I probably deserved to be thrown. But you didn't. You didn't like me, you didn't approve, but you stood up for me. That's intellectual honesty. You don't see that much. Thank you.'

Dance gave a faint, embarrassed laugh, acknowledging the compliment – even as she thought of the times when she *had* wanted to throw him to the wolves.

The Chiltons returned to the house to finish packing and arrange for a motel that night – Patrizia didn't want to stay in the house until the office had been scrubbed clean of every trace of Schaeffer's blood. Dance could hardly blame her.

The agent now joined the MCSO Crime Scene chief, an easygoing middle-aged officer she'd worked with for several years. She explained that there was a possibility that Travis might still be alive, stashed in a hideout somewhere. Which meant he'd have a dwindling supply of food and water. She had to locate him. And soon.

'You find a room key on the body?'

'Yep. Cyprus Grove Inn.'

'I want the room, and Schaeffer's clothes and his car gone over with a microscope. Look for anything that might give us a clue where he might've put the boy.'

'You bet, Kathryn.'

She returned to her car, phoning TJ. 'You got him, boss. I heard.'

'Yep. But now I want to find the boy. If he's alive, we may only have a day or two until he starves to death or dies of thirst. All-out on this one. MCSO's running the scenes at Chilton's house and at the Cyprus Grove – where Schaeffer was staying. Call Peter Bennington and ride herd on the reports. Call Michael if you need to. Oh, and find me witnesses in nearby rooms at the Cyprus Grove.'

'Sure, boss.'

'And contact CHP, county and city police. I want to find the last roadside cross – the one Schaeffer left to announce Chilton's death. Peter should go over it with every bit of equipment they've got.' Another thought occurred to her. 'Did you ever hear back about that state vehicle?'

'Oh, that Pfister saw, right?'

'Yeah.'

'Nobody's called. I don't think we're prioritized.'

'Try again. And make it a priority.'

'You coming in, boss? Overbearing wants to see you.'

'TJ.'

'Sorry.'

'I'll be in later. I've got to follow up on one thing.'

'You need help?'

She said she didn't, though the truth was she sure as hell didn't want to do this one solo.

37

Sitting in her car, parked in the driveway, Dance gazed at the Brigham's small house: the sad lean of the gutters and curl of the shingles, the dismembered toys and tools in the front and side yards. The garage so filled with discards that you couldn't get more than half a car hood under its roof.

Dance was sitting in the driver's seat of her Crown Vic, the door shut. Listening to a CD she and Martine had been sent from a group in Los Angeles. The musicians were Costa Rican. She found the music both cheerful and mysterious, and wanted to know more about them. She'd hoped that when she and Michael were in L.A. on the J. Doe murder case she'd have a chance to meet with them and do some more recordings.

But she couldn't think about that now.

She heard the rumble of rubber on gravel and looked into the rearview mirror to see Sonia Brigham's car pause as it turned past the hedge of boxwood.

The woman was alone in the front seat. Sammy sat in the back.

The car didn't move for a long moment and Dance could see the woman staring desperately at the police cruiser. Finally Sonia teased her battered car forward again and drove past Dance to the front of the house, braked and shut the engine off.

With a fast look Dance's way, the woman climbed out and

strode to the back of the car and lifted out the laundry baskets, and a large bottle of Tide.

His families so poor that they can't even afford a washer and drier . . . Who goes to laundromats? Lusers that's who. . . .

The blog post that told Schaeffer where to find a sweatshirt to steal to help him frame Travis.

Dance climbed out of her own vehicle.

Sammy looked at her with a probing expression. The curiosity of their first meeting was gone; now he was uneasy. His eyes were eerily adult.

'You know something about Travis?' he asked, and didn't sound as odd as he had earlier.

But before Dance could say anything, his mother shooed him off to play in the backyard.

He hesitated, still staring at Dance, then wandered off, uncomfortable, fishing in his pockets.

'Don't go far, Sammy.'

Dance took the bottle of detergent from under Sonia's pale arm and followed her toward the house. Sonia's jaw was firm, eyes straight forward.

'Mrs—'

'I have to put this away,' Sonia Brigham said in a clipped tone.

Dance opened the unlocked door for her. She followed Sonia inside. The woman moved straight into the kitchen and separated the baskets. 'If you let them sit . . . the wrinkles, you know what it's like.' She smoothed a T-shirt.

Woman to woman.

'I washed it thinking I could give it to him.'

'Mrs Brigham, there are some things you should know. Travis wasn't driving the car on June 9. He took the blame.'

'*What?*' She stopped fussing with her laundry.

'He had a crush on the girl who was driving. She'd been drinking. He tried to get her to pull over and let him drive. She crashed before that happened.'

'Oh, heavens!' Sonia lifted the shirt to her face, as if it could ward off the impending tears.

'And he wasn't the killer, leaving the crosses. Someone set it up to make it seem like he'd left them and caused those deaths. A man with a grudge against James Chilton. We stopped him.'

'And Travis?' Sonia asked desperately, fingers white as they gripped the shirt.

'We don't know where he is. We're looking everywhere, but we haven't found any leads yet.' Dance explained briefly about Greg Schaeffer and his plan for revenge.

Sonia wiped her round cheeks. There was prettiness still in her face, though obscured. The remnants of the prettiness evident in the picture of her in the state fair stall taken years earlier. Sonia whispered, 'I knew Travis wouldn't hurt those people. I told you that.'

Yes, you did, Dance thought. And your body language told me that you were telling the truth. I didn't listen to you. I listened to logic when I should have listened to intuition. Long ago Dance had done a Myers-Briggs analysis of herself. She got into trouble when she strayed too far from her nature.

She replaced the shirt, smoothed the cotton again. 'He's dead, isn't he?'

'We have no evidence he is. Absolutely none.'

'But you think so.'

'It'd be logical for Schaeffer to keep him alive. I'm doing everything we can to save him. That's one of the reasons I'm here.' She displayed a picture of Greg Schaeffer, a copy from his DMV picture. 'Have you ever seen him? Maybe following you? Talking to neighbors?'

Sonia pulled on battered glasses and looked at the face for a long time. 'No. I can't say I have. So he's him. The one done it, took my boy?'

'Yes.'

'I told you no good would come of that blog.'

Her eyes slipped toward the side yard, where Sammy was disappearing into the ramshackle shed. She sighed. 'If Travis *is* gone, telling Sammy . . . oh, that'll destroy him. I'll be losing two sons at once. Now, I've got to put the laundry away. Please go now.'

Dance and O'Neil stood next to each other on the pier, leaning against the railing. The fog was gone, but the wind was steady. Around Monterey Bay you always had one or the other.

'Travis's mother,' O'Neil said, speaking loudly. 'That was tough, I'll bet.'

'Hardest part of it all,' she said, her hair flying. Then asked him, 'How was the interview?' Thinking of the Indonesian investigation.

The Other Case.

'Good.'

She was glad O'Neil was running the case, regretted her jealousy. Terrorism kept all law enforcers up nights. 'If you need anything from me let me know.'

His eyes on the bay, he said, 'I think we'll wrap it in the next twenty-four hours.'

Below them were their children, the four of them, on the sand at water's edge. Maggie and Wes led the expedition; being grandchildren of a marine biologist, they had some authority.

Pelicans flew solemnly nearby, gulls were everywhere, and not far offshore, a brown curl of sea otter floated easily on its back, inverted elegance. It happily smashed open mollusks against a rock balanced on its chest. Dinner. O'Neil's daughter, Amanda, and Maggie stared at it gleefully, as if trying to figure out how to get it home as a pet.

Dance touched O'Neil's arm and pointed at ten-year-old Tyler, who was crouching beside a long whip of kelp and poking it cautiously, ready to flee if the alien creature came to life. Wes stood protectively near in case it did.

O'Neil smiled but she sensed from his stance and the tension in his arm that something was bothering him.

Only a moment later he explained, calling over the blast of wind, 'I heard from Los Angeles. The defense is trying to move the immunity hearing back again. Two weeks.'

'Oh, no,' Dance muttered. 'Two weeks? The grand jury's scheduled for then.'

'Seybold's going all-out to fight it. He didn't sound optimistic.'

'Hell.' Dance grimaced. 'War of attrition? Keep stalling and hope it all goes away?'

'Probably.'

'We won't,' she said firmly. 'You and me, we won't go away. But will Seybold and the others?'

O'Neil considered this. 'If it takes much more time, maybe. It's an important case. But they have a lot of important cases.'

Dance sighed. She shivered.

'You cold?'

Her forearm was docked against his.

She shook her head. The involuntary ripple had come from thinking of Travis. As she'd been looking over the water, she'd wondered if she was also gazing at his grave.

A gull hovered directly in front of them. The angle of attack of his wings adjusted perfectly for the velocity of the wind. He was immobile, twenty feet above the beach.

Dance said, 'All along, you know, even when we thought he was the killer, I felt sorry for Travis. His home life, the fact he's a misfit. Getting cyberbullied like that. And Jon was telling me the blog was just the tip of the iceberg. People were attacking him in instant messages, emails, on other bulletin boards. It's just so sad it's turned out this way. He was innocent. Completely innocent.'

O'Neil said nothing for a moment. Then: 'He seems sharp. Boling, I mean.'

'He is. Getting the names of the victims. And tracking down Travis's avatar.'

O'Neil laughed. 'Sorry, but I keep picturing you going to Overby about a warrant for a character in a computer game.'

'Oh, he'd do the paperwork in a minute if he thought there was a press conference and a good photo op involved. I could've beaned Jon, though, for going to that arcade alone.'

'Playing hero?'

'Yep. Save us from amateurs.'

'He married, have a family?'

'Jon? No.' She laughed. 'He's a bachelor.'

Now there's a word you haven't heard for . . . about a century.

They fell silent, watching the children, who were totally lost in their seaside exploration. Maggie was holding her hand out and pointing to something, probably explaining to O'Neil's children the name of a shell she'd found.

Wes, Dance noted, was by himself, standing on a damp flat, the water easing up close to his feet in foamy lines.

And as she often did, Dance wondered if her children would be better off if she had a husband, and they had a home with a father. Well, of course they would.

Depending on the man, of course.

There was always that.

A woman's voice behind them. 'Excuse me. Are those your children?'

They turned to see a tourist, to judge by the bag she held from a nearby souvenir shop.

'That's right,' Dance said.

'I just wanted to say that it's so nice to see a happily married couple with such lovely children. How long have you been married?'

A millisecond pause. Dance answered, 'Oh, for some time.'

'Well, bless you. Stay happy.' The woman joined an elderly man leaving a gift shop. She took his arm and they headed toward a large tour bus, parked nearby.

Dance and O'Neil laughed. Then she noticed a silver Lexus pull up in a nearby parking lot. As the door opened, she was aware that O'Neil had eased away from her slightly, so that their arms no longer touched.

The deputy smiled and waved to his wife as she climbed from the Lexus.

Tall, blond Anne O'Neil, wearing a leather jacket, peasant blouse, long skirt and belt of dangly metal, smiled as she approached. 'Hello, honey,' she said to O'Neil and hugged him, kissed his cheek. Her eyes lit on Dance. 'Kathryn.'

'Hi, Anne. Welcome home.'

'The flight was awful. I got tied up at the gallery and didn't make it in time to check my bag. I was right on the borderline.'

'I was in an interview,' O'Neil told her. 'Kathryn picked up Tyler and Ammie.'

'Oh, thanks. Mike said you've closed the case. That one about the roadside crosses.'

'A few hours ago. Lot of paperwork, but, yeah, it's done.' Not wanting to talk about it any longer, Dance said, 'How's the photo exhibition going?'

'Getting ready,' said Anne O'Neil, whose hair brought to mind the word 'lioness'. 'Curating's more work than taking the pictures.'

'Which gallery?'

'Oh, just Gerry Mitchell's. South of Market.' The tone was dismissive, but Dance guessed the gallery was well known. Whatever else, Anne never flaunted ego.

'Congratulations.'

'We'll see what happens at the opening. Then there are the reviews afterward.' Her sleek face grew solemn. In a low voice: 'I'm sorry about your mother, Kathryn. It's all crazy. How's she holding up?'

'Pretty upset.'

'It's like a circus. The newspaper stories. It made the news up there.'

A hundred and thirty miles away? Well, Dance shouldn't've been surprised. Not with the prosecutor Robert Harper playing the media game.

'We've got a good attorney.'

'If there's anything I can do . . .' The ends of Anne's metal belt tinkled like a wind chime in the breeze.

O'Neil called down to the beach, 'Hey, guys, your mother's here. Come on!'

'Can't we stay, Dad?' Tyler pleaded.

'Nope. Time to get home. Come on.'

Reluctantly the children trudged toward the adults. Maggie was dispensing shells. Dance was sure she'd be giving the good ones to the O'Neil children and her brother.

Wes and Maggie piled into Dance's Pathfinder for the short ride to the inn where her parents were staying. Once again, they'd spend the night with Edie and Stuart. The perp was dead, so the threat to her personally was gone, but Dance was adamant about finding Travis alive. She'd possibly be working late into the night.

They were halfway to the inn when Dance noticed that Wes had grown quiet.

'Hey, young man, what's up?'

'Just wondering.'

Dance knew how to reel in details from reluctant children. The trick was patience. 'About what?'

She was sure it had to do with his grandmother.

But it didn't.

'Is Mr Boling coming over again?'

'Jon? Why?'

'Just, *The Matrix*'s on TNT tomorrow. Maybe he hasn't seen it.'

'I'll bet he has.' Dance was always amused by the way children assumed that they're the first to experience something and that prior generations lived in sorrowful ignorance and deprivation. Mostly, though, she was surprised that the boy had even asked the question. 'You like Mr Boling?' she ventured.

'No . . . I mean, he's okay.'

Maggie contradicted, 'You said you liked him! You said he was neat. As neat as Michael.'

'I did not.'

'Yes, you did!'

'Maggie, you are so wrong!'

'All right,' Dance commanded. But her tone was amused. In fact, there was something about the sibling bickering that she found comforting, a bit of normalcy in this turbulent time.

They arrived at the inn, and Dance was relieved to see that the protestors still had not found the location where her parents were hiding out. She walked Wes and Maggie to the front door. Her father greeted her. She hugged him hard and looked inside.

Her mother was on the phone, focusing on what was apparently a serious conversation.

Dance wondered if she was talking to her sister, Betsey.

'Any word from Sheedy, Dad?'

'Nothing more, no. The arraignment's tomorrow afternoon.' He brushed absently at his thick hair. 'I heard you got the fellow, that killer. And the boy was innocent?'

'We're looking for him right now.' Her voice lowered so the children couldn't hear. 'Frankly, the odds are he's dead, but I'm hoping for the best.' She hugged the man. 'I've got to get back to the search now.'

'Good luck, honey.'

As she turned to leave she waved once more to her mother. Edie reciprocated with a distant smile and nod, then, still on the phone, gestured her grandchildren to her and gave them big hugs.

Ten minutes later Dance walked into her office, where a message awaited her.

A curt note from Charles Overby:

Could you send me the report on disposition of the Chilton blog case. All the details, sufficient for a meaningful announcement to the press. Will need within the hour. Thank you.

And you're welcome for a case solved, a perp dead and no more victims.

Overby was pissy, she supposed, because she'd refused to kowtow to Hamilton Royce, the fixer.

Who was about as far from George Clooney as one could be.

Meaningful announcement . . .

Dance composed a lengthy memo, giving the details of Greg Schaeffer's plan, how they'd learned of his identity and his death. She included information about the murder of Miguel Herrera, the deputy with the MCSO guarding the Chilton house, and the update on the all-out search for Travis.

She sent the memo off via email, hitting the mouse harder than usual.

TJ stuck his head in the door of her office. 'You hear, boss?'

'About what in particular?'

'Kelley Morgan's regained consciousness. She'll live.'

'Oh, that's so good to hear.'

'Be a week or so in therapy, the deputy over there said. That stuff screwed up her lungs pretty bad, but she'll be okay, eventually. Looks like there won't be any brain damage.'

'And what'd she say about ID'ing Travis?'

'He got her from behind, half strangled her. He whispered something about why'd she posted things about him? And then she passed out, woke up in the basement. Assumed it was Travis.'

'So Schaeffer didn't want her to die. He set it up to make her think it was Travis but never let her see him.'

'Makes sense, boss.'

'And Crime Scene – at Schaeffer's and Chilton's? Any leads to where the boy might be?'

'Nothing yet. And no witnesses around the Cyprus Grove.'

She sighed. 'Keep at it.'

The time was now after 6:00 p.m. She realized she hadn't eaten since breakfast. She rose and made for the lunchroom. She needed coffee and wanted something indulgent: homemade cookies or doughnuts. Maryellen's well in the Gals' Wing had run dry. At the least she could enter a negotiation with the temperamental vending machine: a rumpled dollar in exchange for a packet of toasted peanut butter crackers or Oreos.

As she stepped into the cafeteria she blinked. Ah, luck.

On a paper plate full of crumbs sat two oatmeal raisin cookies. More of a miracle, the coffee was relatively fresh.

She poured a cup, added 2 percent milk and snagged a cookie. Exhausted, she plunked herself down at a table. She stretched and fished her iPod out of her pocket, mounting the ear buds and scrolling through the screen to find solace in more of Badi Assad's arresting Brazilian guitar.

She hit 'Play', took a bite of cookie and was reaching for the coffee when a shadow hovered.

Hamilton Royce was looking down at her. His temporary ID was pinned to his shirt. The big man's arms hung at his sides.

Just what I need. If thoughts could sigh, hers would have been clearly audible.

'Agent Dance. Can I join you?'

She gestured to an empty chair, trying not to look too invitational. But she did pull out the ear buds.

He sat, the chair squeaking, plastic and metal in tension under his frame, and leaned forward, elbows on the table, hands clasped in front of him. This position generally signifies directness. She noted his suit again. The blue didn't work. Not dark enough. Or, alternatively, she thought unkindly, he should be wearing a sailor's hat with a shiny brim.

'I heard. The case is over, correct?'

'We've got the perp. We're still searching for the boy.'

'For Travis?' Royce asked, surprised.

'That's right.'

'But he's dead, don't you think?'

'No.'

'Oh.' A pause. 'That's the one thing I regret,' Royce said. 'That's the worst of it all. That innocent boy.'

Dance noted that this reaction, at least, was honest.

She said nothing more.

Royce offered, 'I'll be headed back to Sacramento in a day or two. Look, I know we had some problems earlier . . . Well, disagreements. I wanted to apologize.'

Decent of him, though she remained skeptical. She said, 'We saw things differently. I didn't take any offense. Not personally.'

But, professionally, she thought, I was totally pissed you tried to flank me.

'There was a lot of pressure from Sacramento. I mean, a *lot*. I got carried away in the heat of the moment.' He looked away, partly embarrassed. And partly deceptive too; he *didn't* feel that bad, Dance noticed. But she gave him credit for trying to make nice. He continued, 'Not often that you're in a situation like this, is it? Where you have to protect somebody as unpopular as

Chilton.' He didn't seem to expect an answer. He gave a hollow laugh. 'You know something? In a funny way I've come to admire him.'

'Chilton?'

A nod. 'I don't agree with much of what he says. But he's got moral character. And not a lot of people do nowadays. Even in the face of a murder threat, he stayed the course. And he'll probably keep right on going. Don't you think?'

'I assume so.' She said nothing about the possible termination of *The Chilton Report*.

That wasn't her business, or Royce's.

'You know what I'd like to do? Apologize to *him* too.'

'Would you?'

'I tried his house. Nobody was answering. Do you know where he is?'

'He and his family're going to their vacation home in Hollister tomorrow. Tonight, they're staying at a hotel. I don't know where. Their house is a crime scene.'

'Well, I suppose I could email him at his blog.'

She was wondering if this would ever happen.

Then, silence. Time for my exit, Dance thought. She snagged the last cookie, wrapped it in a napkin and headed for the lunchroom door. 'Have a safe drive, Mr Royce.'

'Again, I'm truly sorry, Agent Dance. I look forward to working with you in the future.'

Her kinesic skills easily fired off a message that his comment had contained two lies.

38

Jonathan Boling, looking pleased, was walking up to Dance in the lobby of the CBI. She handed him a temporary pass.

'Thanks for coming in.'

'I was beginning to miss the place. I thought I'd been fired.'

She smiled. When she'd called him in Santa Cruz she'd interrupted a paper-grading session for one of his summer school courses (she'd wondered if she would catch him prepping for a date) and Boling had been delighted to abandon the job and drive back to Monterey.

In her office, she handed him his last assignment: Greg Schaeffer's laptop. 'I'm really desperate to find Travis, or his body. Can you go through it, look for any references to local locations, driving directions, maps . . . anything like that?'

'Sure.' He indicated the Toshiba. 'Passworded?'

'Not this time.'

'Good.'

He opened the lid and began to type. 'I'll search for everything with a file access or creation date in the past two weeks. Does that sound good?'

'Sure.'

Dance tried not to smile once more, watching him lean forward enthusiastically. His fingers played over the keys like a concert pianist's. After a few moments he sat back. 'Well, it doesn't look like he used it for much of his mission here, other than to research for blogs and RSS feeds, and emails to friends and business associates – and none of them have anything to do with his plot to kill Chilton. But those are just the undeleted records. He's been deleting files and websites regularly for the past week. Those, I'd guess, might be more what you're interested in.'

'Yep. Can you reconstruct them?'

'I'll go online and download one of Irv's bots. That'll roam the free space on his C: drive and put back together anything he's deleted recently. Some of it will be only partial and some will be distorted. But most of the files should be ninety percent readable.'

'That'd be great, Jon.'

Five minutes later Irv's bot was silently roaming through Schaeffer's computer, looking for fragments of deleted files, reassembling them and storing them in a new folder that Boling had created.

'How long?' she asked.

'A couple of hours, I'd guess.' Boling looked at his watch and suggested they get a bite of dinner. They climbed into his Audi and headed to a restaurant not far from CBI headquarters, on a rise overlooking the airport and, beyond that, the city of Monterey and the bay. They got a table on the deck, warmed with overhead propane heaters, and sipped a Viognier white wine. The sun was now melting into the Pacific, spreading out and growing violently orange. They watched it in silence as tourists nearby snapped pictures that would have to be Photoshopped to even approximate the grandeur of the real event.

They talked about her children, about their own childhoods. Where they were from originally. Boling commented that he believed only twenty percent of the Central Coast population comprised native Californians.

Silence flowed between them again. Dance sensed his shoulders rising and was expecting what came next.

'Can I ask you something?'

'Sure.' She meant it, no reservations.

'When did your husband die?'

'About two years ago.'

Two years, two months, three weeks. She could give him the days and hours too.

'I've never lost anybody. Not like that.' Though there was a wistfulness in his voice, and his eyelids flickered like venetian blinds troubled by the wind. 'What happened, you mind if I ask?'

'Not at all. Bill was an FBI agent, assigned to the local resident agency. But it wasn't work-related. An accident on Highway One. A truck. The driver fell asleep.' A wisp of a laugh. 'You know, I never thought about it until just now. But his fellow agents and friends put flowers by the roadside for about a year after it happened.'

'A cross?'

'No, just flowers.' She shook her head. 'God, I hated that. The reminder. I'd drive miles out of my way to avoid the place.'

'Must've been terrible.'

Dance tried not to practice her skills as a kinesics expert when she was out socially. Sometimes she'd read the kids, sometimes she'd read a date. But she remembered when she'd caught Wes in some minor lie and he grumbled, 'It's like you're Superman, Mom. You've got X-ray word vision.' Now she was aware that, although Boling's face kept its sympathetic smile, his body language had subtly changed. The grip on his wineglass stem tightened. On his free hand, fingers rubbed compulsively. Behaviors she knew he wasn't even aware of.

Dance just needed to prime the pump. 'Come on, Jon. Your turn to spill. What's your story? You've been pretty vague on the bachelor topic.'

'Oh, nothing like your situation.'

He was minimizing something that hurt, she could see that. She wasn't even a therapist, let alone his. But they'd spent some time under fire and she wanted to know what was troubling him. She touched his arm briefly. 'Come on. Remember, I interrogate people for a living. I'll get it out of you sooner or later.'

'I never go out with somebody who wants to waterboard me on the first date. Well, depending.'

Jon Boling, Dance had come to realize, was a man who used clever quips as armor.

He continued, 'This is the worst soap opera you'll ever hear . . . The girl I met after leaving Silicon Valley? She ran a bookstore in Santa Cruz. Bay Beach Books?'

'I think I've been there.'

'We hit it off real well, Cassie and I. Did a lot of outdoor things together. Had some great times traveling. She even survived some visits to my family — well, actually it's only me who has trouble surviving those.' He thought for a minute. 'I think the thing is that we laughed a lot. That's a clue. What kind of movies do you like best? We watched comedies mostly. Okay, she was separated, not divorced. Legal separation. Cassie was completely honest about it. I knew it all up front. She was getting the paperwork together.'

'Children?'

'She had two, yes. Boy and girl like you. Great kids. Split the time between her and her ex.'

You mean, her not-quite-ex, Dance corrected silently, and, of course, knew the arc of the story.

He sipped some more of the cold, crisp wine. A breeze had come up and as the sun melted, the temperature fell. 'Her ex was abusive. Not physically; he never hurt her or the kids, but he'd insult her, put her down.' He gave an astonished laugh. '*This* wasn't right, *that* wasn't right. She was smart, kind, thoughtful. But he just kept dumping on her. I was thinking about this last night.' His voice faded at that comment, having just given away a bit of data he wished he hadn't. 'He was an emotional serial killer.'

'That's a good way to put it.'

'And naturally she went back to him.' His face was still for a moment as he relived a specific incident, she supposed. Our hearts rarely respond to the abstract; it's the tiny slivers of sharp memory that sting so. Then the facade returned in the form of a tight-lipped smile. 'He got transferred to China, and they went with him, Cassie and the kids. She said she was sorry, she'd always love me, but she *had* to go back to him . . . Never quite got the obligatory part in relationships. Like, you *have* to breathe, you *have* to eat . . . but staying with a jerk? I don't get the *neces-sary*. But here I am going on about . . . oh, shall we say an "epic" bad call on my part, and *you* had a real tragedy.'

Dance shrugged. 'In my line of work, whether it's murder or manslaughter or criminally negligent homicide, a death's still a death. Just like love; when it goes away, for whatever reason, it hurts all the same.'

'I guess. But all I'll say is it's a real bad idea to fall in love with somebody who's married.'

Amen, thought Kathryn Dance again, and nearly laughed out loud. She tipped a touch more wine into her glass.

'How 'bout that,' he said.

'What?'

'We've managed to bring up two extremely personal *and* depressing topics in a very short period of time. Good thing we're not on a date,' he added with a grin.

Dance opened the menu. 'Let's get some food. They have—'

' – the best calamari burgers in town here,' Boling said. She laughed. She'd been about to say exactly the same.

The computer search was a bust.

She and the professor returned from their squid and salads to her office, both eager to see what Irv's bot had found. Boling sat down, scrolled through the file and announced with a sigh, 'Zip.'

'Nothing?'

'He just deleted those emails and files and research to save space. Nothing secretive, and nothing local at all.'

The frustration was keen, but there was nothing more to do. 'Thanks, Jon. At least I got a nice dinner out of it.'

'Sorry.' He looked truly disappointed that he couldn't be of more help. 'I guess I better finish up grading those papers. And pack.'

'That's right, your family reunion's this weekend.'

He nodded. A tight smile and he said, 'Woooo-hoooo,' with forced enthusiasm.

Dance laughed.

He hovered near her. 'I'll call you when I get back. I want to know how things work out. And good luck with Travis. I hope he's okay.'

'Thanks, Jon. For everything.' She took his hand and gripped it firmly. 'And I especially appreciate your not getting stabbed to death.'

A smile. He squeezed her hand and turned away.

As she watched him walk down the corridor a woman's voice interrupted her thoughts. 'Hey, K.'

Dance turned to see Connie Ramirez, walking down the hallway toward her.

'Con.'

The other senior agent looked around and nodded toward Dance's office. Then stepped inside, closing the door. 'Found a few things I thought you might be interested in. From the hospital.'

'Oh, thanks, Con. How'd you do it?'

Ramirez considered this. 'I was deceptively honest.'

'I like that.'

'I flashed my shield and gave them some details of another case I'm running. That medical fraud case.'

The CBI investigated financial crimes too. And the case Ramirez was referring to was a major insurance scam – the perps used identification numbers of doctors who were deceased to file bogus claims in their names.

It was the sort of thing, Dance reflected, that Chilton himself might write about in his blog. And it was a brilliant choice for Connie; staffers at the hospital were among the victims, and would have an interest in helping investigators.

'I asked them to show me the log-in sheets. The whole month's worth, so Henry didn't get suspicious. They were more than happy to comply. And here's what I found: the day Juan Millar died there was one visiting physician – the hospital has a continuing-ed lecture series and he was probably there for that. There were also six job applicants – two for maintenance spots, one for the cafeteria and three nurses. I've got copies of their résumés. None of them look suspicious to me.

'Now, what's interesting is this: there were sixty-four visitors at the hospital that day. I correlated the names and the people they were there to see, and every one of them checks out. Except one.'

'Who?'

'It's hard to read the name, either the printed version or the signature. But I think it's Jose Lopez.'

'Who was he seeing?'

'He only wrote "patient".'

'That was a safe bet, in a hospital,' Dance said wryly. 'Why is it suspicious?'

'Well, I figured that if somebody was there to kill Juan Millar, he or she would have to have been there before – either as visitors or to check out security and so on. So I looked at everybody who'd signed in to see him earlier.'

'Brilliant. And you checked their handwriting.'

'Exactly. I'm no document examiner but I found a visitor who'd been to see him a number of times, and I'd almost guarantee the handwriting's the same as this Jose Lopez's.'

Dance was sitting forward. 'Who?'

'Julio Millar.'

'His brother!'

'I'm ninety percent sure. I made copies of everything.' Ramirez handed Dance sheets of paper.

'Oh, Connie, this is brilliant.'

'Good luck. If you need anything else, just ask.'

Dance sat alone in her office, considering this new information. Could Julio actually have killed his brother?

At first, it seemed impossible, given the loyalty and love that Julio displayed for his young sibling. Yet there was no doubt that the killing had been an act of mercy, and Dance could imagine a conversation between the two brothers – Julio leaning forward as Juan whispered a plea to put him out of his misery.

Kill me . . .

Besides, why else would Julio have faked a name on the sign-in sheet?

Why had Harper and the state investigators missed this connection? She was furious, and had a suspicion that they knew about it, but were downplaying the possibility because it would be better publicity against the death-with-dignity act for Robert Harper to go after the mother of a state law enforcement agent. Thoughts of prosecutorial malfeasance buzzed around her head.

Dance called George Sheedy and left a message about what Connie Ramirez had found. She then called her mother to tell her directly about it. There was no answer.

Damnit. Was she screening calls?

She disconnected then sat back, thinking about Travis. If he was alive, how much longer would he have? A few days, without water. And what a terrible death it would be.

Another shadow in her doorway. TJ Scanlon appeared, 'Hey, boss.'

She sensed something was urgent.

'Crime scene results?'

'Not yet, but I'm riding 'em hard. *Rawhide,* remember? This's something else. Heard from MCSO. They got a call – anonymous – about the Crosses Case.'

Dance sat up slightly. 'What was it?'

'The caller said he'd spotted, quote, "something near Harrison Road and Pine Grove Way". Just south of Carmel.'

'Nothing more than that?'

'Nope. Just "something". I checked the intersection. It's near that abandoned construction site. And the call was from a pay phone.'

Dance debated for a moment. Her eyes dipped to a sheet of paper, a copy of the postings on *The Chilton Report*. She rose and pulled on her jacket.

'You going to go over there to check it out?' TJ asked uncertainly.

'Yep. Really want to find him, if there's any way.'

'Kind of a weird area, boss. Want backup?'

She smiled. 'I don't think I'm going to be in much danger.'

Not with the perp presently residing in the Monterey County morgue.

The ceiling of the basement was painted black. It contained eighteen rafters, also black. The walls were a dingy white, cheap paint, and were made up of 892 cinder blocks. Against the wall were two cabinets, one gray metal, one uneven white wood. Inside were large stocks of canned goods, boxes of pasta, soda and wine, tools, nails, personal items like toothpaste and deodorant.

Four metal poles rose to the dim ceiling, supporting the first floor. Three were close to each other, one farther away. They were painted dark brown but they were also rusty and it was hard to tell where the paint ended and the oxidation began.

The floor was concrete and the cracks made shapes that became familiar if you stared at them long enough: a sitting panda, the state of Texas, a truck.

An old furnace, dusty and battered, sat in the corner. It ran on natural gas and switched on only rarely. Even then, though, it didn't heat this area much at all.

The size of the basement was thirty-seven feet by twenty-eight, which could be calculated easily from the cinder blocks, which were exactly twelve inches wide by nine high, though you had to add an eighth of an inch to each one for the mortar that glued them together.

A number of creatures lived down here too. Spiders, mostly. You could count seven families, if that was what spiders lived in, and they seemed to stake out territories so as not to offend – or get eaten by – the others. Beetles and centipedes too. Occasional mosquitoes and flies.

Something larger had shown an interest in the stacks of food and beverages in the far corner of the basement, a mouse or a rat. But it'd grown timid and left, never to return.

Or been poisoned and died.

One window, high in the wall, admitted opaque light but no view; it was painted over, off-white. The hour was now probably 8:00 or 9:00 p.m. – since the window was nearly dark.

The thick silence was suddenly shattered as footsteps pounded across the first floor, above. A pause. Then the front door opened, and slammed shut.

At last.

Finally, now that his kidnapper had left, Travis Brigham could relax. The way the schedule of the past few days had turned out, once his captor left at night he wouldn't be back till morning. Travis now curled up in the bed, pulling the gamy blanket around him. This was the high point of his day: sleep.

At least in sleep, Travis had learned, he could find some respite from despair.

39

The fog was thick and briskly streamed overhead as Dance turned off the highway and began to meander down winding Harrison Road. This area was south of Carmel proper – on the way to Point Lobos and Big Sur beyond – and was deserted, mostly hilly woods; a little farmland remained.

Coincidentally it was close to the ancient Ohlone Indian land near which Arnold Brubaker hoped to build his desalination plant.

Smelling pine and eucalyptus, Dance slowly followed her headlights – low beams because of the fog – along the road. Occasional driveways led into darkness broken by dots of light. She passed several cars, also driving slowly, coming from the opposite direction, and she wondered if it had been a driver who'd called in the anonymous report that had sent her here, or one of the residents.

Something . . .

That was certainly a possibility but Harrison Road was also a shortcut from Highway 1 to Carmel Valley Road. The call could have come from anybody.

She soon arrived at Pine Grove Way and pulled over.

The construction site that the anonymous caller had mentioned was a half-completed hotel complex – now never to be finished, since the main building had burned under suspicious circumstances. Insurance fraud was initially suspected but the perps turned out to be environmentalists who didn't want the land scarred by the development. (Ironically, the green terrorists miscalculated; the fire spread and destroyed hundreds of acres of pristine woods.)

Most of the wilderness had grown back, but for various reasons the hotel project never got under way again and the complex remained as it now was: several acres of derelict buildings and foundations dug deep in the loamy ground. The area was surrounded by leaning chain-link fences marked with *Danger* and *No Trespassing* signs, but a couple of times a year or so teens would have to be rescued after falling into a pit or getting trapped in the ruins while smoking pot or drinking or, in one case, having sex in the least comfortable and unromantic location imaginable.

It was also spooky as hell.

Dance grabbed her flashlight from the glove compartment and climbed out of her Crown Vic.

The damp breeze wafted over her, and she shivered with a jolt of fear.

Relax.

She gave a wry laugh, clicked on the flashlight and started forward, sweeping the Magna-Lite beam over the ground tangled with brush.

A car swept past on the highway, tires sticky on the damp asphalt. It eased around a corner and the sound stopped instantly as if the vehicle had beamed into a different dimension.

As she looked around her, Dance was supposing that the 'something' the anonymous caller had reported was the last roadside cross, the one intended to announce James Chilton's death.

There was, however, none to be seen in the immediate vicinity.

What else could the person have meant?

Could they have seen or heard Travis himself?

This would be a perfect place to stash him.

She paused and listened for any calls for help.

Nothing but the breeze through the oaks and pines.

Oaks . . . Dance pictured one of the improvised roadside crosses. Pictured the one in her backyard too.

Should she call in and order a search? Not just yet. Keep looking.

She wished she had the anonymous caller here. Even the most reluctant witness could be the source of all the information she needed; look at Tammy Foster, whose lack of cooperation hadn't slowed down the investigation at all.

Tammy's computer. It's got the answer. Well, maybe not the answer. But an answer . . .

But she didn't have the caller; she had her flashlight and a spooky, deserted construction site.

Looking for 'something'.

Dance now slipped through one of the several gates in the chain link, the metal bent by years of trespassers, and eased through the grounds, moving slowly. The main building had collapsed completely under the flames. And the others – service sheds, garages and complexes of hotel rooms – were boarded up. There were a half dozen open foundation pits. They were marked with orange warning signs, but the fog was thick and reflected back much light into Dance's eyes; she moved carefully for fear of tumbling down into one.

Easing through the compound, one step at a time, pausing, looking for footprints.

What the hell had the caller seen?

Then, Dance heard a noise in the distance, but not that distant. A loud snap. Another.

She froze.

Deer, she guessed. They were plentiful in the area. But other animals lived here too. Last year a mountain lion had killed a tourist jogging not far from here. The animal had sliced the poor woman apart then vanished. Dance unbuttoned her jacket and tapped the butt of her Glock for reassurance.

Another snap then a creak.

Like a hinge of an old door opening.

Dance shivered in fear, reflecting that just because the Roadside Cross Killer was no longer a threat, that didn't mean meth cookers or gangbangers weren't hanging around here.

But heading back never entered her mind. Travis could be here. Keep going.

Another forty feet or so into the compound, Dance was looking for the structures that might house a kidnap victim, looking for buildings with padlocks, looking for footprints.

She thought she heard another sound – almost a moan. Dance came close to calling out the boy's name. But instinct told her not to.

And then she stopped fast.

A human figure was silhouetted in the fog no more than ten yards awayt. Crouching, she thought.

She gasped, clicked the light out and drew her gun.

Another look. Whoever – whatever – it might have been was gone.

But the image wasn't imagination. She was certain she'd seen somebody, male, she believed from the kinesics.

Now, footsteps were sounding clearly. Branches snapping, leaves rustling. He was flanking her, to her right. Moving, then pausing.

Dance fondled the cell phone in her pocket. But if she made a call, her voice would give away her position. And she had to assume that whoever was here in the dark on a damp, foggy night wasn't present for innocent purposes.

Retrace your steps, she told herself. Back to the car. Now. Thinking of the shotgun in her trunk, a weapon she'd fired once. In training.

Dance turned around and moved quickly, every step making a loud crinkle through the leaves. Every step shouting, Here I am, here I am.

She stopped. The intruder didn't. His steps telegraphed his transit over the leaves and underbrush as he continued on, somewhere in the dark fog to her right.

Then they stopped.

Had he stopped too? Or was he on leafless ground, moving in for an attack?

Just get back to the car, get under cover, rack the 12-gauge and call in backup.

It was fifty, sixty feet back to the chain-link fence. In the dim ambient light – moon diffused by fog – she surveyed the ground. Some places seemed less leaf-strewn than others, but there was no way to proceed quietly. She told herself she couldn't wait any longer.

But still the stalker was silent.

Was he hiding?

Had he left?

Or was he coming up close under cover of the dense foliage?

Near panicking, Dance whirled but saw nothing other than the ghosts of buildings, trees, some large tanks, half buried and rusting.

Dance crouched, wincing from the pain in her joints – from the chase, and the tumble, the other day at Travis's house. Then she moved toward the fence as quickly as she could. Resisting the nearly overwhelming urge to break into a run over ground strewn with construction-site booby traps.

Twenty-five feet to the chain link.

A snap nearby.

She stopped fast, dropped to her knees and lifted her weapon, searching for a target. She was holding her flashlight in her left hand and nearly clicked it on. But instinct once again told her not to. In the fog the beam would half blind her and give the intruder a perfect target.

Not far away a raccoon slipped from a hiding place and moved stiffly away, its kinesic message irritation at the disturbance.

Dance rose, turned back toward the fence and moved quickly over the leaves, looking behind her often. Nobody was in pursuit that she could see. Finally she pushed through the gate and began jogging toward her car, cell phone in her left hand, open, as she scrolled through previously dialed listings.

It was then that a voice from very close behind her echoed through the night. 'Don't move,' the man said. 'I have a gun.'

Heart slamming, Dance froze. He'd flanked her completely, gotten through another gate or silently scaled the fence.

She debated: if he *was* armed and wanted to kill her she'd be dead by now. And, with the mist and dimness, maybe he hadn't seen her weapon in her hand.

'I want you down on the ground. Now.'

Dance began to turn.

'No! On the ground!'

But she kept turning until she was facing the intruder and his outstretched arm.

Shit. He *was* armed, the gun aimed directly at her.

But then she looked at the man's face and blinked. He wore a Monterey County Sheriff's Office uniform. She recognized him. It was the young, blue-eyed deputy who'd helped her out several times earlier. David Reinhold.

'Kathryn?'

'What are you doing here?'

Reinhold shook his head, a faint smile on his face. He didn't answer, just looked around. He lowered his weapon, but didn't slip it back into the holster. 'Was it you? In there?' he finally asked, glancing back to the construction site.

She nodded.

Reinhold continued to look around, tense, his kinesics giving off signals that he was still ready for combat.

Then a tinny voice said from her side, 'Boss, that you? You calling?'

Reinhold blinked at the sound.

Dance lifted her mobile and said, 'TJ, you there?' When she'd heard the intruder come up behind her she'd hit 'Dial.'

'Yeah, boss. What's up?'

'I'm at that construction site off Harrison. I'm here with Deputy Reinhold from the sheriff's office.'

'Did you find anything?' the young agent asked.

Dance felt her legs going weak, her heart pounding, now that the initial fright was over. 'Not yet. I'll call you back.'

'Got it, boss.'

They disconnected.

Reinhold finally holstered his weapon. He inhaled slowly and puffed air out of his smooth cheeks. 'That just about scared the you-know-what out of me.'

Dance asked him, 'What are you doing here?'

He explained that the MCSO had gotten a call an hour ago about 'something' having to do with the case near the intersection of Pine Grove and Harrison.

The call that had spurred Dance to come here.

Since Reinhold had worked on the case, he explained, he'd volunteered to check it out. He'd been searching the construction site when he'd seen the beam of a flashlight and come closer to investigate. He hadn't recognized Dance in the fog and was worried that she might be a meth cooker or drug dealer.

'Did you find anything that suggests Travis is here?'

'Travis?' he asked slowly. 'No. Why, Kathryn?'

'Just seems that this'd be a pretty good place to hide a kidnap victim.'

'Well, I searched pretty carefully,' the young deputy told her. 'Didn't see a thing.'

'Still,' she said. 'I want to be sure.'

And called TJ back to arrange for a search party.

In the end they did learn what the anonymous caller had seen.

The discovery was made not by Dance or Reinhold, but by Rey Carraneo, who'd come here along with a half dozen other officers from the CHP, the MCSO and the CBI.

The 'something' *was* a roadside cross. It had been planted on Pine Grove, not Harrison Road, about a hundred feet from the intersection.

But the memorial had nothing to do with Greg Schaeffer or Travis Brigham or the blog entries.

Dance sighed angrily.

This cross was fancier than the others, carefully made, and the flowers below it were daisies and tulips, not roses.

Another difference was that this one had a name on it. Two, in fact.

JUAN MILLAR, R.I.P.
MURDERED BY EDITH DANCE

Left by somebody from Life First – the anonymous caller, of course.

Angrily, she plucked it from the ground and flung it into the compound.

With nothing to search, and no evidence to examine, no witnesses to interview, Kathryn Dance trudged back to her car and returned home, wondering just how fitful her sleep would be.

If indeed she could sleep at all.

FRIDAY

40

At 8:20 a.m., Dance steered the Ford Crown Vic into the parking lot of the Monterey County Courthouse.

She was eagerly anticipating the crime scene reports on Schaeffer and any other information TJ and the MCSO had found about where the killer was keeping Travis. But in fact her thoughts were largely elsewhere: she was wondering about the curious call she'd received early that morning – from Robert Harper, asking if she would stop by his office.

Apparently at his desk by 7:00, the special prosecutor had sounded uncharacteristically pleasant and Dance decided it was possible that he'd heard from Sheedy about the Julio Millar situation. Her thoughts actually extended to a dismissal of her mother's case, and lodging charges against Juan's brother. She had a feeling that Harper wanted to discuss some type of a face-saving arrangement. Maybe he'd drop the charges against Edie completely, and immediately, if Dance agreed not to go public with any criticism of his prosecution of the case.

She parked in the back of the courthouse, looking over the construction work around the parking lot; it had been here that the woman partner of the cult leader Daniel Pell had engineered the man's escape by starting the fire that had caused Juan Millar's terrible burns.

She nodded hello to several people she knew from the court

and from the sheriff's office. Speaking to a guard, she learned where Robert Harper's office was. The second floor, near the law library.

A few minutes later she arrived – and was surprised to find the quarters quite austere. There was no secretary's anteroom; the special prosecutor's door opened directly onto the corridor across from a men's room. Harper was alone, sitting at a large desk, the room bare of decoration. There were two computers, rows of law books and dozens of neat stacks of papers on both a gray metal desk and a round table near the single window. The blinds were down, though he would have a striking view of lettuce fields and the mountains east.

Harper was in a pressed white shirt and narrow red tie. His slacks were dark and his suit jacket hung neatly on a hanger on a coatrack in the corner of the office.

'Agent Dance. Thanks for coming in.' He subtly inverted the sheet of paper he'd been reading, and closed the lid of his attaché case. Inside, she'd caught a glimpse of an old law book.

Or maybe a Bible.

He rose briefly and shook her hand, again keeping his distance.

As she sat, his closely set eyes examined the table beside her to see if there was anything that she ought not to observe. He seemed satisfied that all secrets were safe. He took in, very briefly, her navy blue suit – tailored jacket and pleated skirt – and white blouse. She'd worn her interrogation clothes today. Her glasses were the black ones.

Predator specs.

She'd be happy to reach an accommodation if it got her mother off, but she wasn't going to be intimidated.

'You've spoken to Julio Millar?' she asked.

'Who?'

'Juan's brother.'

'Oh. Well, I have, a while ago. Why are you asking?'

Dance felt her heart begin pounding faster. She noted a stress reaction – her leg moved slightly. Harper, on the other hand, was motionless. 'I think Juan begged his brother to kill him. Julio faked a name on the hospital sign-in sheet, and did what his brother wanted. I thought that's what you wanted to talk to me about.'

'Oh,' Harper said, nodding. 'George Sheedy called about that. Just a bit ago. I guess he didn't get a chance to call you and tell you.'

'Tell me what?'

With a hand tipped in perfectly filed nails, Harper lifted a folder from the corner of his desk and opened it up. 'On the night his brother died, Julio Millar *was* in the hospital. But I confirmed that he was meeting with two members of the MBH security staff in connection with a suit against the California Bureau of Investigation for negligence in sending his brother to guard a patient that you knew, or should have known, was too dangerous for a man of Juan's experience to handle. He was also considering suing you personally on a discrimination charge for singling out a minority officer for a dangerous assignment. And for exacerbating his brother's condition by interrogating him. At the exact time of Juan's death, Julio was in the presence of those guards. He put a fake name in the check-in log because he was afraid you'd find out about the suit and try to intimidate him and his family.'

Dance's heart clenched to hear these words, delivered so evenly. Her breathing was rapid. Harper was as calm as if he were reading from a book of poetry.

'Julio Millar has been cleared, Agent Dance.' The smallest of frowns. 'He was one of my first suspects. Do you think I wouldn't have considered him?'

She fell silent and sat back. In an instant, all hope had been destroyed.

Then, to Harper, the matter was concluded. 'No, why I asked you here . . .' He found another document. 'Will you stipulate that this is an email you wrote? The addresses match, but there are no names on it. I can trace it back to you but it'll take some time. As a courtesy, could you tell me if it's yours?'

She glanced at the sheet. It was a photocopy of an email she'd written to her husband when he was away on a business trip at an FBI seminar in Los Angeles several years ago.

How's everything going down there? You get to Chinatown, like you were thinking?

Wes got a perfect on the English test. He wore the gold star on his forehead until it fell off and had to buy some more. Mags decided to donate all her Hello Kitty stuff to charity – yes, all of it (yea!!!!)

Sad news from Mom. Willy, their cat, finally had to be put down. Kidney failure. Mom wouldn't hear of the vet doing it. She did it herself, an injection. She seemed happier afterward. She hates suffering, would rather lose an animal than see it suffer. She told me how hard it was to see Uncle Joe at the end, with the cancer. Nobody should have to go through that, she said. A shame there was no assisted suicide law.

Well, on a happier note: got the website back online and Martine and I uploaded a dozen songs from that Native American group down in Ynez. Go online if you can. They're great!

Oh and went shopping at Victoria's Secret. Think you'll like what I got. I'll do some modeling!! Come home soon!

Her face burned – in shock and rage. 'Where did you get this?' she snapped.

'A computer at your mother's house. Under a warrant.'

Dance recalled. 'It was *my* old computer. I gave it to her.'

'It was in her possession. Within the scope of the warrant.'

'You can't introduce that.' She waved at the email printout.

'Why not?' He frowned.

'It's irrelevant.' Her mind jumped around. 'And it's a privileged communication between husband and wife.'

'Of course it's relevant. It goes to your mother's state of mind in committing mercy killing. And as for the privilege: since neither you nor your husband are subjects of the prosecution, any communications should be fully admissible. In any case, the judge will decide.' He seemed surprised she hadn't realized this. '*Is* it yours?'

'You'll have to depose me before I respond to anything you ask.'

'All right.' He seemed only faintly disappointed at her failure to cooperate. 'Now, I should tell you that I consider it a conflict of interest for you to be involved in this investigation, and using Special Agent Consuela Ramirez to do legwork for you doesn't vitiate that conflict.'

How had he found that out?

'This case emphatically does not fall within the jurisdiction of the CBI and if you continue to pursue it, I'll lodge an ethics complaint against you with the attorney general's office.'

'She's my mother.'

'I'm sure you're emotional about the situation. But it's an active investigation and soon to be an active prosecution. Any interference from you is unacceptable.'

Shaking with rage, Dance rose and started for the door.

Harper seemed to have an afterthought. 'One thing, Agent Dance. Before I move to admit that email of yours into evidence, I want you to know that I'll redact the information about buying that lingerie, or whatever it was, at Victoria's Secret. *That* I do consider irrelevant.'

Then the prosecutor slid toward him the document he'd been reviewing when she arrived, turned it over and began reading once again.

In her office Kathryn Dance was staring at the entwined tree trunks outside her window, still angry with Harper. She was thinking again about what would happen if she was forced to testify against her mother. If she didn't, she'd be held in contempt. A crime. It could mean jail and the end of her career as a law enforcer.

She was drawn from this thought by TJ's appearance.

He looked exhausted. He explained he'd spent much of the night working with Crime Scene to examine Greg Schaeffer's room at the Cyprus Grove Inn, his car and Chilton's house. He had the MCSO report.

'Excellent, TJ.' She regarded his bleary, red eyes. 'You get any sleep?'

'What's that again, boss? "Sleep"?'

'Ha.'

He handed her the crime scene report. 'And I finally got more four-one-one on our friend.'

'Which one?'

'Hamilton Royce.'

Didn't matter now, she supposed, with the case closed, and apologies – such as they were – delivered. But she was curious. 'Go on.'

'His latest assignment was for the Nuclear Facilities Planning Committee. Until he got here he'd been billing the nukers sixty hours a week. And by the way, he's expensive. I think I need a raise, boss. Am I a six-figure kind of agent?'

Dance smiled. She was glad that his humor seemed to be returning. 'You're worth seven figures in my book, TJ.'

'I love you too, boss.'

The implication of the information then struck her. She riffled through copies of *The Chilton Report*.

'That son of a bitch.'

'What's that?'

'Royce was trying to get the blog shut down – for his *client's* sake. Look.' She tapped the printout.

POWER TO THE PEOPLE

Posted by Chilton.

Rep. Brandon Klevinger . . . Ever heard of his name? Probably not.

And the state representative looking after some fine folks in Northern California would rather keep a low profile.

No such luck.

Representative Klevinger is the head of the state's Nuclear Facilities Planning

Committee, which means the bomb – oops, excuse me, the buck – stops with him on the issue of those little gadgets called reactors.

And you want to know something interesting about them?

No – go away, Greenies. Go whine elsewhere! I have no problem with nuclear energy; we need it to achieve energy independence (from certain *interests* overseas whom I've written about at great length). But what I do object to is this: nuclear power loses its advantage if the price for the plants and the energy expended in the construction outweigh the advantages.

I've learned that Rep. Klevinger just happens to have been on a couple of posh golfing trips to Hawaii and Mexico with his newfound 'friend', Stephen Ralston. Well, guess what, boys and girls? Ralston happens to have put in bids for a proposed nuclear facility north of Mendocino.

Mendocino . . . Lovely place. And very pricey to build in. Not to mention that it seems the cost of delivering the power to where it's needed will be huge. (Another developer has proposed a far cheaper and more efficient location about fifty miles south of Sacramento.) But a source has snuck me the Nuclear Committee's preliminary report and it reveals that Ralston's probably going to get the go-ahead to build in Mendocino.

Has Klevinger done anything illegal or wrong?

I'm not saying yes or no. I just ask the question.

'He was lying all along,' TJ said.

'Sure was.'

Still, she couldn't concentrate on Royce's duplicity just now. There was, after all, no need to blackmail him at this point, considering he was headed home in a day or two.

'Good work.'

'Just dotting my *j*'s.'

As he left she hunched over the MCSO report. She was a little surprised that David Reinhold, the eager kid – the one she'd played cat-and-mouse with last night – hadn't brought it in person.

From: Dep. Peter Bennington, MCSO Crime Scene Unit

To: Kathryn Dance, Special Agent, California Bureau of Investigation — Western Division.

Re: June 28 homicide at house of James Chilton, 2939 Pacific Heights Court, Carmel, California.

Kathryn, here's the inventory.

Greg Schaeffer's body

One Cross brand wallet, containing Calif. driver's license, credit cards, AAA membership card, all in name of Gregory Samuel Schaeffer

$329.52 cash

Two keys to Ford Taurus, California registration ZHG128

One motel key to Room 146, Cyprus Grove Inn

One key to BMW 530, California registration DHY783, registered to Gregory S. Schaeffer, 20943 Hopkins Drive, Glendale, CA

One claim ticket for car at LAX long-term parking, dated June 10

Miscellaneous restaurant and store receipts

One cell phone. Only calls to local phone numbers: James Chilton, restaurants

Trace on shoes, consistent with sandy dirt found at prior scenes of roadside crosses

Fingernail trace inconclusive

Room 146, Cypress Grove Inn, registered in name of Greg Schaeffer

Miscellaneous clothing and toiletries

One 1-liter bottle, Diet Coke

Two bottles Robert Mondavi Central Coast Chardonnay wine

Leftover Chinese food, three orders

Miscellaneous groceries

One Toshiba laptop computer and power pack (transferred to California Bureau of Investigation; see chain-of-custody record)

One Hewlett-Packard DeskJet printer

One box of 25-count Winchester .38 Special ammunition, containing 13 rounds

Miscellaneous office supplies

Printouts of The Chilton Report *from March of this year to present*

Approximately 500 pages of documents relating to the Internet, blogs, RSS feeds

Items in Gregory Schaeffer's possession found at James Chilton's house

One Sony digital camcorder

One SteadyShot camera tripod

Three USB cables

One roll, Home Depot brand duct tape

One Smith & Wesson revolver, loaded with 6 rounds of .38 Special ammunition

One Baggie containing 6 extra rounds of ammunition

Hertz Ford Taurus, California registration HG128, parked 1/2 block away from James Chilton's house

One bottle orange-flavored Vitamin Water, half full

One rental agreement, Hertz, naming Gregory Schaeffer as lessee

One McDonald's Big Mac wrapper

One map of Monterey County, provided by Hertz, no marked locations (infrared analysis negative)

Five empty coffee cups, 7-Eleven. Only Schaeffer's fingerprints

Dance read the list twice. She couldn't be upset at the job

Crime Scene had done. It was perfectly acceptable. Yet it offered no clues whatsoever as to where Travis Brigham was being held. Or where his body was buried.

Her eyes slipped out the window, and settled on the thick, barky knot, the point where two independent trees became one, then continued their separate journey toward the sky.

Oh, Travis, Kathryn Dance thought.

Unable to resist the thought that she'd let him down.

Unable, finally, to resist the tears.

41

Travis Brigham woke up, peed in the bucket beside the bed and washed his hands with bottled water. He adjusted the chain connecting the shackle around his ankle to a heavy bolt in the wall.

Thought once again of that stupid movie, *Saw*, where two men had been chained to a wall, just like this, and could escape only by sawing their legs off.

He drank some Vitamin Water, ate some granola bars and returned to his mental investigation. Trying to piece together what had happened to him, why he'd ended up here.

And who was the man who'd done this terrible thing?

He recalled the other day, those police or agents at the house. His father being a dick, his mother being all weepy-eyed and weak. Travis had grabbed his uniform and his bike and headed for his sucky job. He'd wheeled the bike a short way into the woods behind his house and then just lost it. He'd dropped his bike and sat down beside the huge oak tree and started crying his head off.

Hopeless! Everybody hated him.

Then, wiping his nose as he sat beneath the oak, a favorite spot – it reminded him of a place in Aetheria – he'd heard footsteps behind him, moving fast.

Before he could turn toward the sound, his vision went all

yellow and every muscle in his body contracted at once, from neck to toe. His breath went away and he passed out. And then he woke up here in the basement, with a headache that wouldn't stop. Somebody'd hit him with a Taser, he knew. He'd seen how they work on YouTube.

The Big Fear turned out to be a false alarm. Feeling carefully – down his pants, behind – he realized nobody'd done anything to him – not *that* way. Though it made him all the more uneasy. Rape would've made some sense. But this . . . just being kidnapped, held here like in some kind of Stephen King story? What the hell was going on?

Travis now sat up on the cheap folding bed that shook every time he moved. He looked around his prison once more, the filthy basement. The place stank of mold and oil. He surveyed the food and drink left for him: mostly chips and packaged crackers and Oscar Mayer snack boxes – ham or turkey. Red Bull and Vitamin Water and Coke to drink.

A nightmare. Everything about his life this month was an unbearable nightmare.

Starting with the graduation party at that house in the hills off Highway 1. He'd only gone because some of the girls said Caitlin was hoping he'd be there. No, she really, really is! So he'd hitched all the way down the highway, past Garrapata State Park.

Then he walked inside, and to his horror he'd seen only the kewl people, none of the slackers or gamers. The Miley Cyrus crowd.

And worse, Caitlin looked at him like she didn't even recognize him. The girls who'd told him to come were giggling, along with their jock boyfriends. And everybody else was staring at him, wondering what the hell a geek like Travis Brigham was doing there.

It was all a setup, just to make fun of him.

Pure fucking hell.

But he wouldn't turn around and run. No way. He'd hung around, looked over the million CDs the family had, flipped through some channels, ate kick-ass food. Finally, sad and embarrassed, he'd decided, it was time to head back, wondering if he'd get a ride that time of night, near midnight. He'd seen Caitlin, wasted on tequila, pissed about Mike D'Angelo and Bri leaving together. She was fumbling for her keys and muttering about following the two of them and . . . well, she didn't know what.

Travis had thought: be a hero. Take the keys, get her home safe. She won't care you're not a jock. She won't care if your face is all red and bumpy.

She'll know who you are on the inside . . . she'll love you.

But Caitlin had jumped into the driver's seat, her friends in the back. Being all, 'Girlfriend, girlfriend . . .' Travis hadn't let it go. He'd climbed right into the car beside her and tried to talk her out of driving.

Hero . . .

But Caitlin had sped off, plummeting down the driveway and onto Highway 1, ignoring his pleas to let him drive.

'Like, please, Caitlin, pull over!'

But she hadn't even heard him.

'Caitlin, come on! Please!'

And then . . .

The car flying off the road. The sound of metal on stone, the screams — Sounds louder than anything Travis had ever heard.

And still I had to be the goddamn hero.

'Caitlin, listen to me. Can you hear me? Tell them I was driving the car. I haven't had anything to drink. I'll tell them I lost control. It won't be a big deal. If they think you were driving, you'll go to jail.'

'Trish, Van? . . . Why aren't they saying anything?'

'Do you hear me, Cait? Get into the passenger seat. Now! The cops'll be here any minute. I was driving! You hear me?'

'Oh, shit, shit, shit.'

'Caitlin!'

'Yes, yes. You were driving . . . Oh, Travis. Thank you!'

As she threw her arms around him, he felt a sensation like none other he'd ever experienced.

She loves me, we'll be together!

But it didn't last.

Afterward, they'd talked some, they'd gone for coffee at Starbucks, lunch at Subway. But soon the times together grew awkward. Caitlin would fall silent and start looking away from him.

Eventually she stopped returning his calls.

Caitlin became even more distant than she'd been before his good deed.

And then look what happened. Everybody on the Peninsula – no, everybody in the *world* – started hating him.

H8 to break it to you but [the driver] is a total fr33k and a luser . . .

But even then Travis couldn't give up hope. The night Tammy Foster got attacked, Monday, he'd been thinking about Caitlin and couldn't sleep, so he went to her house. To see if she was all right, though mostly thinking, in his fantasy, maybe she'd be hanging out in the backyard or on her front porch. She'd see him and say, 'Oh, Travis, I'm sorry I've been so distant. I'm just getting over Trish and Van. But I do love you!'

But the house had been dark. He'd bicycled back home at 2:00 a.m.

The next day the police had shown up and asked him where he'd been that night. He'd instinctively lied and said he was at the Game Shed. Which of course they'd found out he hadn't been. And now they'd definitely think he was the one behind the attack on Tammy.

Everybody hating me . . .

Travis now recalled waking up here after he'd been Tasered. The big man standing over him. Who was he? One of the fathers of the girls killed in the accident?

Travis had asked. But the man had only pointed out the bucket to use for a toilet, the food and water. And had warned, 'My associates and I are going to be checking on you, Travis. You stay quiet at all times. If you don't . . .' He showed the boy a soldering iron. 'Okay?'

Crying, Travis had blurted, 'Who *are* you? What did I do?'

The man plugged the soldering iron into the wall socket.

'No! I'm sorry. I'll be quiet! I promise!'

The man unplugged the iron. And then clomped up the stairs. The basement door had closed. More footsteps and the front door had slammed. A car started. And Travis was left alone.

He remembered the following days as a blur, filled with increasing hallucinations or dreams. To stave off boredom – and madness – he played *DimensionQuest* in his mind.

Now, Travis gasped, hearing the front door opening upstairs. Thumps of footsteps.

His captor was back.

Travis hugged himself and tried not to cry. Be quiet. You know the rules. Thinking of the Taser. Thinking of the soldering iron.

He stared at the ceiling – his ceiling, his kidnapper's floor – as the man roamed through the house. Five minutes later, the steps moved in a certain pattern. Travis tensed; he knew what that sound meant. He was coming down here. And, yeah, a few seconds later the lock on the basement door snapped. Footsteps on the squeaky stairs, descending.

Travis now shrank back on the bed as he saw his captor come closer. The man normally would have with him an empty bucket and would take the full one upstairs. But today he carried only a paper bag.

This terrified Travis. What was inside?

The soldering iron?

Something worse?

Standing over him, he studied Travis closely. 'How do you feel?'

Like shit, you asshole, what do you think?

But he said, 'Okay.'

'You're weak?'

'I guess.'

'But you've been eating.'

A nod. Don't ask him why he's doing this. You want to, but

don't. It's like the biggest mosquito bite in the world. You have to scratch it; but don't. He's got the soldering iron.

'You can walk?'

'I guess.'

'Good. Because I'm giving you a chance to leave.'

'Leave? Yes, please! I want to go home.' Tears popped into Travis's eyes.

'But you have to earn your freedom.'

'Earn it? I'll do anything . . . What?'

'Don't answer too quickly,' the man said ominously. 'You might choose not to.'

'No, I'll—'

'Shh. You can choose not to do what I'm going to ask. But if you don't, you'll stay here until you starve to death. And there'll be other consequences. Your parents and brother will die too. There's somebody outside their house right now.'

'Is my brother okay?' Travis asked in a frantic whisper.

'He's fine. For now.'

'Don't hurt them! You can't hurt them!'

'I can hurt them and I will. Oh, believe me, Travis. I will.'

'What do you want me to do?'

The man looked him over carefully. 'I want you to kill somebody.'

A joke?

But the kidnapper wasn't smiling.

'What do you mean?' Travis whispered.

'Kill somebody, just like in that game you play. *DimensionQuest*.'

'Why?'

'That doesn't matter, not to you. All you need to know is if you don't do what I'm asking, you'll starve to death here, and my associate will kill your family. Simple as that. Now's your chance. Yes or no?'

'But I don't know how to kill anybody.'

The man reached into the paper bag and took out a pistol wrapped in a Baggie. He dropped it on the bed.

'Wait! That's my father's! Where did you get it?'

'From his truck.'

'You said my family's fine.'

'They are, Travis. I didn't hurt him. I stole it a couple of days ago, when they were asleep. Can you shoot it?'

He nodded. In fact, he'd never fired a real gun. But he'd played shooting games in arcades. And he watched TV. Anybody who watched *The Wire* or *The Sopranos* knew enough about guns to use one. He muttered, 'But if I do what you want, you'll just kill me. And then my family.'

'No, I won't. It's better for me if you're alive. You kill who I tell you to, drop the gun and run. Go wherever you want. Then I'll call my friend and tell him to leave your family alone.'

There was a lot about this that didn't make sense. But Travis's mind was numb. He was afraid to say yes, he was afraid to say no.

Travis thought of his brother. Then his mother. An image of his father smiling even came to mind. Smiling when he looked at Sammy, never at Travis. But it was a smile nonetheless and seemed to make Sammy happy. That was the important thing.

Travis, did you bring me M's?

Sammy . . .

Travis Brigham blinked tears from his eyes and whispered, 'Okay. I'll do it.'

42

Even without the benefit of excessive lunchtime Chardonnay, Donald Hawken was feeling maudlin.

But he didn't care.

He rose from the couch where he'd been sitting with Lily and embraced James Chilton, who was entering the living room of his vacation house in Hollister, carrying several more bottles of white wine.

Chilton gripped him back, only mildly embarrassed. Lily chided her husband, 'Donald.'

'Sorry, sorry, sorry.' Hawken laughed. 'But I can't help it. The nightmare's over. God, what you've been through.'

'What we've *all* been through,' Chilton said.

The story of the psycho was all over the news. How the Mask Killer wasn't the boy but was really some crazy man who'd been trying to avenge a posting that Chilton had put on his report several years ago.

'And he was actually going to shoot you on camera?'

Chilton lifted an eyebrow.

'Jesus our Lord,' said Lily, looking pale – and surprising Hawken, since she was a professed agnostic. But Lily, like her husband, was a bit tipsy too.

'I'm sorry about that boy,' Hawken said. 'He was an innocent victim. Maybe the saddest victim of all.'

'Do you think he's still alive?' Lily wondered.

'I doubt it,' Chilton said grimly. 'Schaeffer would have to kill him. Leave no traces. I'm heartsick about it.'

Hawken was pleased he'd rejected the request – well, from that Agent Dance it had almost been an *order* – to go back to San Diego. No way. He thought back to those dismal days when Sarah had died and James Chilton had sped to his side.

This is what friends did.

Breaking the pall that had descended, Lily said, 'I've got an idea. Let's plan a picnic for tomorrow. Pat and I can cook.'

'Love it,' Chilton said. 'We know this beautiful park nearby.'

But Hawken wasn't through being maudlin. He lifted his glass of Sonoma-Cutrer. 'Here's to friends.'

'To friends.'

They sipped. Lily, her pretty face crowned with curly golden hair, asked, 'When're they coming up? Pat and the kids?'

Chilton glanced at his watch. 'She left about fifteen minutes ago. She'll pick the boys up from camp. Then head up here. Shouldn't be too long.'

Hawken was amused. The Chiltons lived close to one of the most beautiful waterfronts in the world. And yet for their vacation house they'd chosen a rustic old place in the hills forty-five minutes inland, hills that were decidedly dusty and brown. Yet the place was quiet and peaceful.

Y ningunos turistas. A relief after summertime Carmel, filled to the gills with out-of-towners.

'Okay,' Hawken announced. 'I can't wait any longer.'

'Can't wait?' Chilton asked, a perplexed smile on his face.

'What I told you I was bringing.'

'Oh, the painting? Really, Don. You don't need to do that.'

'It's not "need". It's something I want to do.'

Hawken went into the guest bedroom where he and Lily were staying and returned with a small canvas, an impressionistic painting of a blue swan on a darker blue background. His late wife, Sarah, had bought it in San Diego or La Jolla. One day, while Jim Chilton was in Southern California to help after her death, Hawken had found the man staring at the painting admiringly.

Hawken had decided at that moment that someday he'd give the artwork to his friend, in gratitude for all he'd done during those terrible times.

Now, the three of them gazed at the bird taking off from the water.

'It's beautiful,' Chilton said. He propped the painting up on the mantel. 'Thank you.'

Hawken, now a half glass of wine more maudlin yet, was lifting his glass to make a toast when a door squeaked in the kitchen.

'Oh,' he said, smiling. 'Is that Pat?'

But Chilton was frowning. 'She couldn't be here that fast.'

'But I heard something. Didn't you?'

The blogger nodded. 'I did, yes.'

Then, looking toward the doorway, Lily said, 'There's some-body there. I'm sure.' She was frowning. 'I hear footsteps.'

'Maybe—' Chilton began.

But his words were cut off as Lily screamed. Hawken spun around, dropping his wineglass, which shattered loudly.

A boy in his late teens, hair askew, face dotted with acne, stood in the doorway. He seemed stoned. He was blinking and looking around, disoriented. In his hand was a pistol. Shit, Hawken thought, they hadn't locked the back door when they'd arrived. This kid had wandered inside to rob them.

Gangs. Had to be gangs.

'What do you want?' Hawken whispered. 'Money? We'll give you money!'

The boy continued to squint. His eyes settled on Jim Chilton and narrowed.

Then Donald Hawken gasped. 'It's the boy from the blog! Travis Brigham!' Skinnier and paler than in the pictures on TV. But there was no doubt. He *wasn't* dead. What was this all about? But one thing he understood: the boy was here to shoot his friend Jim Chilton.

Lily grabbed her husband's arm.

'No! Don't hurt him, Travis,' Hawken cried and felt an urge to step in front of Chilton, to protect him. Only his wife's grip kept him from doing so.

The boy took a step closer to Chilton. He blinked, then looked away – toward Hawken and Lily. He asked in a weak voice, 'They're the ones you want me to kill?'

What did he mean?

And James Chilton whispered, 'That's right, Travis. Go ahead and do what you agreed. Shoot.'

Squinting against the raw light that stung his eyes like salt, Travis Brigham stared at the couple – the people his captor had told him, in the basement a half hour ago, he had to kill: Donald and Lily. His kidnapper had explained that they'd be arriving soon and would be upstairs – in this house, the very one whose basement he'd spent the past three or four days in.

Travis couldn't understand why his kidnapper wanted them dead. But that didn't matter. All that mattered was keeping his family alive.

Travis, did you bring me M's?

He lifted the gun, aimed at them.

As the couple blurted words he hardly heard, he tried to hold the weapon steady. This took all his effort. After days of being chained to a bed, he was weak as a bird. Even the climb up the stairs had been a chore. The gun was weaving.

'No, please no!' someone cried, the man or the woman. He couldn't tell. He was confused, disoriented by the glaring light. It stung his eyes. Travis aimed at the man and woman, but still, he kept wondering: who are they, Donald and Lily? In the basement the man had said, 'Look at them like characters in that game you play. *DimensionQuest*. Donald and Lily're only avatars, nothing more than that.'

But these people sobbing in front of him *weren't* avatars. They were real.

And they seemed to be his captor's friends – at least in their minds. 'What's going on? Please, don't hurt us.' From Lily. 'James, please!'

But the man – James, it seemed – just kept his eyes, cool eyes, on Travis. 'Go ahead. Shoot!'

'James, no! What are you saying?'

Travis steadied the gun, pointing it at Donald. He pulled back the hammer.

Lily screamed.

And then something in Travis's mind clicked.

James?

The boy from the blog.

Roadside Crosses.

Travis blinked. 'James Chilton?' Was this the blogger?

'Travis,' the captor said firmly, stepping behind him, pulling another gun from his back pocket. He touched it to Travis's head. 'Go ahead and do it. I told you not to say anything, don't ask questions. Just shoot!'

Travis asked Donald, 'He's James Chilton?'

'Yes,' the man whispered.

What, Travis wondered, was going on here?

Chilton shoved the gun harder into Travis's skull. It hurt. 'Do it. Do it, or you'll die. And your family will die.'

The boy lowered the gun. He shook his head. 'You don't have any friends at my house. You were lying to me. You're doing this alone.'

'If you don't do it, I'll kill you and then go to their house and kill them. I swear I will.'

Hawken cried, 'Jim! Is this . . . for God's sake, what *is* this?'

Lily cried uncontrollably.

Travis Brigham understood now. Shoot them or not, he was dead. His family would be all right; Chilton had no interest in them. But he was dead. A faint laugh eased from his throat and he felt tears sting eyes already stinging from the sunlight.

He thought of Caitlin, her beautiful eyes and smile.

Thought of his mother.

Thought of Sammy.

And of all the terrible things that people had said about him in the blog.

Yet he'd done nothing wrong. His life was about nothing more than trying to get through school as best he could, to play a game that made him happy, to spend some time with his brother and look after the boy, to meet a girl who wouldn't mind that he was a *geek* with troubled skin. Travis had never in his life hurt anybody intentionally, never dissed anyone, never posted a bad word about them.

And the whole world had attacked him.

Who'd care if he killed himself?

Nobody.

So Travis did the only thing he could. He lifted the gun to his own chin.

Look at the luser, his life is epic FAIL!!!

Travis's finger slipped around the trigger of the gun. He began to squeeze.

The explosion was fiercely loud. Windows shook, acrid smoke filled the room, and a delicate porcelain cat tumbled from the mantelpiece and shattered on the hearth into dozens of pieces.

43

Kathryn Dance's car turned onto the long dirt driveway that led to James Chilton's vacation house in Hollister.

She was reflecting on how wrong she'd been.

Greg Schaeffer wasn't the Roadside Cross killer.

Everyone else had been misled too but Dance took no solace from that. She'd been content to assume that Schaeffer was the guilty party and that he'd killed Travis Brigham. With the man dead, there'd be no more attacks.

Wrong . . .

Her phone rang. She wondered who was calling, but decided it was best not to look at Caller ID as she wove up the serpentine drive, with drop-offs on either side.

Another fifty yards.

She saw the home ahead of her, a rambling old farmhouse that would have looked in place in Kansas if not for the substantial hills surrounding it. The yard was scruffy, filled with untended patches of grass, gray broken branches, overgrown gardens. She would have thought that James Chilton would have a nicer vacation home, considering the inheritance from his father-in-law and his beautiful house in Carmel.

Even in the sun, the place exuded a sense of eeriness.

But that was, of course, because Dance knew what had happened inside.

How could I have read everything so wrong?

The road straightened and she continued on. She fished the phone off the seat and looked at the screen. Jonathan Boling had called. But the message flag wasn't up. She debated hitting 'Last Received Call'. But instead picked Michael O'Neil's speed-dial button. After four rings it went to voice mail.

Maybe he was on the Other Case.

Or maybe he was talking to his wife, Anne.

Dance tossed the phone onto the passenger seat.

As she pulled close to the house, Dance counted a half dozen police cars. Two ambulances as well.

The San Benito County sheriff, whom she'd worked with regularly, saw her and motioned her forward. Several officers stepped aside, and she drove over the uneven grass to where the sheriff was standing.

She saw where Travis Brigham lay on a gurney, his face covered.

Dance slammed the gearshift into park and climbed out, then walked quickly toward the boy. She noted his bare feet, the welts on his ankle, his pale skin.

'Travis,' she whispered.

The boy jerked, as if she'd awakened him from a deep sleep.

He lifted the damp cloth and ice pack off his bruised face. He blinked and focused his eyes on her. 'Oh, uh, Officer . . . I, like, can't remember your name.'

'Dance.'

'Sorry.' He sounded genuinely contrite at the social slip.

'Not a problem at all.' Kathryn Dance hugged the boy hard.

The boy would be fine, the medic explained.

His worst injury from the ordeal – in fact, the only serious one – was from hitting his forehead on the mantel in the living room of Chilton's house when the San Benito County SWAT team stormed the place.

They had been conducting furtive surveillance – as they awaited Dance's arrival – when the commander had seen through the window that the boy had entered the living room with a gun.

James Chilton too had pulled a weapon. For some reason, it then appeared that Travis was going to take his own life.

The commander had ordered his officers in. They'd launched flash-bang grenades into the room, which detonated with stunning explosions, knocking Chilton to the floor and the boy into the mantelpiece. The officers raced inside and relieved them of their weapons. They'd cuffed Chilton and dragged him outside, then escorted Donald Hawken and his wife to safety and gotten Travis to the paramedics.

'Where's Chilton?' Dance asked.

'He's over there,' the sheriff said, nodding to one of the county deputy's cars, in which the blogger sat, handcuffed, his head down.

She'd get to him later.

Dance glanced at Chilton's Nissan Quest. The doors and tailgate were open and Crime Scene had removed the contents: most notable were the last roadside cross and bouquet of red roses – now tinged with brown. Chilton would have been planning to leave them nearby, after he'd killed the Hawkens. Travis's bike also rested near the tailgate, and in a clear evidence bag was the gray hoodie that Chilton had stolen and worn to impersonate the boy and that he'd picked fibers off to leave at the scenes.

Dance asked the paramedic, 'And the Hawkens? How're they?'

'Shaken up, as you can imagine, a bit bruised, hitting the deck when we moved in. But they'll be fine. They're on the porch.'

'You doing okay?' Dance asked Travis.

'I guess,' he answered.

She realized what a foolish question it was. Of course he wasn't okay. He'd been kidnapped by James Chilton and been ordered to murder Donald Hawken and his wife.

Apparently rather than going through with that task he'd chosen to die.

'Your parents will be here soon,' she told him.

'Yeah?' The boy seemed cautious at this news.

'They were real worried about you.'

He nodded, but she read skepticism in his face.

'Your mother was crying, she was so happy when I told her.'

That was true. Dance had no idea what the father's reaction had been.

A deputy brought the boy a soft drink.

'Thank you.' He drank the Coke thirstily. For his days in captivity, he wasn't doing too badly. A medic had looked over the raw chafing on his leg; it wouldn't need treatment other than a bandage and antibiotic cream. The injury was from the shackles, she realized, and a wave of fury coursed through her. She glared at Chilton, who was being transferred from the San Benito to a Monterey County car, but the blogger's eyes remained downcast.

'What's your sport?' the Coke-toting cop asked the boy, trying to make conversation and put Travis at ease.

'Like, I game, mostly.'

'That's what I mean,' the young crew-cut officer said, taking the skewed response to be a result of the boy's temporary hearing loss from the flash-bangs. More loudly he asked, 'What's your fave? Soccer, football, basketball?'

The boy blinked at the young man in the blue outfit. 'Yeah, I play all those some.'

'Way to go.'

The trooper didn't realize that the sports equipment involved only a Wii or game controller and that the playing field was eighteen inches diagonally.

'But start out slow. Bet your muscles've atrophied. Find a trainer.'

'Okay.'

A rattling old Nissan, the red finish baked matte, pulled up, rocking along the dirt driveway. It parked and the Brighams climbed out. Sonia, tearful, lumbered over the grass and hugged her son hard.

'Mom.'

His father too approached. He stopped beside them, unsmiling, looking the boy up and down. 'You're thin, pale, you know what I mean? You hurtin' anywhere?'

'He'll be okay,' the paramedic said.

'How's Sammy?' Travis asked.

'He's at Gram's,' Sonia said. 'He's in a state, but all right.'

'You found him, you saved him.' The father, still unsmiling, was speaking to Dance.

'We all did, yes.'

'He kept you down there, in that basement?' he said to his son.

The boy nodded, not looking at either of them. 'Wasn't so bad. Got cold a lot.'

His mother said, 'Caitlin told everybody what happened.'

'She did?'

As if he were unable to control himself the father muttered, 'You shouldn'ta took the blame for—'

'Shhh,' the mother hissed sharply. His brow furrowed but the man fell silent.

'What's going to happen to her?' Travis asked. 'Caitlin?'

His mother said, 'That's not our concern. We don't need to worry about that now.' She looked at Dance. 'Can we go home? Is it all right if we just go home?'

'We'll get a statement later. No need right now.'

'Thank you,' Travis said to Dance.

His father said the same and shook her hand.

'Oh, Travis. Here.' Dance handed him a piece of paper.

'What's that?'

'It's somebody who wants you to call him.'

'Who?'

'Jason Kepler.'

'Who's that? . . . Oh, Stryker?' Travis blinked. 'You *know* him?'

'He went looking for you, when you were missing. He helped us find you.'

'He did?'

'He sure did. He said you'd never met him.'

'Like, not in person, no.'

'You only live five miles from each other.'

'Yeah?' He gave a surprised smile.

'He wants to get together with you sometime.'

He nodded with a curious expression on his face, as if the idea of meeting a synth world friend in the real was very strange indeed.

'Come on home, baby,' his mother said. 'I'll make a special dinner. Your brother can't wait to see you.'

Sonia and Bob Brigham and their son walked back to the car. The father's arm rose and slipped around his son's shoulders. Briefly. Then it fell away. Kathryn Dance noted the tentative contact. She believed not in divine salvation but in the proposition that we poor mortals are fully capable of saving ourselves, if conditions and inclinations are right, and the evidence of this potential is found in the smallest of gestures, like the uncertain resting of a large hand on a bony shoulder.

Gestures, more honest than words.

'Travis?' she called.

He turned.

'Maybe I'll see you sometime . . . in Aetheria.'

He held his arm over his chest, palm outward, which she supposed was a salute among the inhabitants of his guild. Kathryn Dance resisted the temptation to reciprocate.

44

Dance walked across the yard to Donald and Lily Hawken, her Aldo shoes gathering dust and plant flecks. Crisp grasshoppers fled from her transit.

The couple sat on the front porch steps of Chilton's vacation house. Hawken's face was harrowing to see. The betrayal had clearly affected him to his core.

'Jim did this?' he whispered.

'I'm afraid so.'

Another thought shook him. 'My God, what if the children had been here? Would he have . . . ?' He couldn't complete the sentence.

His wife stared at the dusty yard, wiping sweat off her brow. Hollister's a long way from the ocean, and summer air, trapped by the knobby hills, heated up fiercely by midday.

Dance said, 'Actually, it was his second attempt to kill you.'

'Second?' Lily whispered. 'You mean at the house? When we were unpacking the other day?'

'That's right. That was Chilton too, wearing one of Travis's hoodies.'

'But . . . is he insane?' Hawken asked, mystified. 'Why would he want to kill us?'

Dance had learned that in her line of work nothing is gained by soft-pedaling. 'I can't say for absolute certain, but I think James Chilton murdered your first wife.'

A heartbreaking gasp. Eyes wide with disbelief. 'What?'

Lily now lifted her head and turned to Dance. 'But she died in an accident. Swimming near La Jolla.'

'I'm getting some details from San Diego and the Coast Guard to be sure. But it's pretty likely that I'm right.'

'He couldn't have. Sarah and Jim were very . . .' Hawken's words dissolved.

'Close?' Dance asked.

He was shaking his head. 'No. It's not possible.' But then he blurted angrily, 'Are you saying they were having an affair?'

A pause, then she said, 'I think so, yes. I'll be getting some evidence in the next few days. Travel records. Phone calls.'

Lily put her arm around her husband's shoulders. 'Honey,' she whispered.

Hawken said, 'I remember that they'd always enjoy each other's company when we'd go out. And, with me, Sarah was a challenge. I was always traveling. Maybe two, three days a week. Not a lot. But she sometimes said I was neglecting her. Kind of joking – I didn't take it all that seriously. But maybe she meant it, and Jim stepped in to fill the gap. Sarah was always pretty demanding.'

The tone of delivery suggested to Dance that the sentence could have ended with 'in bed'.

She added, 'I'm guessing that Sarah wanted Chilton to leave Patrizia and marry her.'

A bitter laugh. 'And he said no?'

Dance shrugged. 'That's what occurred to me.'

Hawken considered this. He added in hollow tones, 'It wasn't a good thing to say no to Sarah.'

'I thought about the timing. You moved to San Diego about three years ago. It was around then that Patrizia's father died, and she inherited a lot of money. Which meant that Chilton could keep writing his blog – he started working on it full-time then. I think he was beginning to get a sense he was on a mission to save the world and Patrizia's money could let him do that. So he broke it off with your wife.'

Hawken asked, 'And Sarah threatened to expose him if he didn't leave Pat?'

'I think she was going to broadcast that James Chilton, the moral voice of the country, had been having an affair with his best friend's wife.'

Dance believed that Chilton lied to Sarah, agreeing to get the divorce, and met her in San Diego. She could imagine his suggestion of a romantic picnic, at a deserted cove near La Jolla. A swim at the beautiful seashore preserve there. Then an accident – a blow to the head. Or maybe he just held her underwater.

'But why was he going to kill us?' Lily asked, with a troubled look back at the house.

Dance said to Donald Hawken, 'You'd been out of touch for a while?'

'After Sarah died, I was so depressed I gave up on everything, stopped seeing all my old friends. Most of my time went to the children. I was a recluse . . . until I met Lily. Then I started to resurface.'

'And you decided to move back.'

'Right. Sell the company and come back.' Hawken was understanding. 'Sure, sure, Lily and I would get together with Jim and Patrizia, some of our old friends around here. At some point we'd have to reminisce. Jim used to come to Southern California a bit before Sarah died. He would've lied to Pat about it; it'd only be a matter of time before he'd get caught.' Hawken's head swiveled to the house, his eyes wide. '*The Blue Swan* . . . Yes!'

Dance lifted an eyebrow.

'I told Jim I wanted to give him one of my late wife's favorite paintings. I remembered him staring at it when he stayed with me after Sarah died.' A scoffing laugh. 'I'll bet it was Jim's. He probably bought it years ago and one day when Sarah was over at his place she told him she wanted it. Maybe he told Patrizia he sold it to somebody. If she saw the painting now she'd wonder how Sarah had gotten it.'

This would explain Chilton's desperation – why he'd take the risk of murdering. The righteous blogger lecturing the world on morality about to be exposed for having an affair – with a woman who'd died. Questions would be raised, an investigation started. And the most important thing in his life – his blog – would have been destroyed. He had to eliminate that threat.

The Report *is too important to jeopardize* . . .

Lily asked, 'But that man at the house, Schaeffer? The statement that James was going to read – it mentioned Travis.'

'I'm sure Schaeffer's plans didn't originally involve Travis. He'd wanted to kill Chilton for some time – probably since his brother's death. But when he heard about the Roadside Crosses attacks, he rewrote the statement to include Travis's name – so no one would suspect Schaeffer himself.'

Hawken asked, 'How did you figure out Jim was the one, not Schaeffer?'

Mostly, she explained, because of what *wasn't* in the crime scene reports TJ had just delivered to her.

'What *wasn't* there?' Hawken asked.

'First,' she explained, 'there wasn't any cross to announce the murder of Chilton. The killer had left crosses in public places before the other attacks. But nobody could find the last cross. Second, the perp had used Travis's bicycle, or his own, to leave tread marks to implicate the boy. But Schaeffer didn't have a bike anywhere. And then the gun he threatened Chilton with? It wasn't the Colt stolen from Travis's father. It was a Smith and Wesson. Finally, there were no flowers or florist's wire in his car or hotel room.

'So, I considered the possibility that Greg Schaeffer wasn't the Roadside Cross Killer. He just lucked into the case and decided to use it. But, if he wasn't leaving the crosses, who could it be?'

Dance had gone back through the list of suspects. She'd thought of the minister, Reverend Fisk, and his bodyguard, possibly *CrimsoninChrist*. They were certainly fanatics and had threatened Chilton directly in their postings on the blog. But TJ had gone to see Fisk, the minder and several other key members of the group. They all had alibis for the times of the attacks.

She'd also considered Hamilton Royce – the troubleshooter from Sacramento, being paid to shut down the blog because of what Chilton was posting about the Nuclear Facilities Planning Committee. It was a good theory, but the more she'd thought about it, the less likely it seemed. Royce was too obvious a suspect, since he'd already tried to get the blog closed down – and very publicly – by using the state police.

Clint Avery, the construction boss, was a possibility too. But she'd learned that Avery's mysterious meetings after Dance had left his company were with a lawyer specializing in equal employment law and two men who ran a day-labor service. In an area where most employers worried about hiring too many undocumented aliens, Avery was worried about getting sued for hiring too few minorities. He was uneasy with Dance, it seemed, because he was afraid she was really there investigating a civil rights complaint that he was discriminating against Latinos.

Dance had also fleetingly considered Travis's father as the perp, actually wondering if there was some psychological connection between the branches and roses and Bob Brigham's job as a landscaper. She'd even considered that the perp might be Sammy – troubled, but maybe a savant, cunning, and possibly filled with resentment against his older brother.

But even though the family had its problems, those were pretty much the same problems all families had. And both father and son were accounted for during some of the attacks.

With a shrug Dance said to the Hawkens, 'Finally I ran out of suspects. And came to James Chilton himself.'

'Why?' he asked.

A to B to X . . .

'I was thinking about something a consultant of ours told me about blogs – about how dangerous they were. And I asked myself: what if Chilton wanted to kill someone? What a great weapon the *Report* was. Start a rumor, then let the cybermob take over. Nobody would be surprised when the bullied victim snapped. There's your perpetrator.'

Hawken pointed out, 'But Jim didn't say anything about Travis in the blog.'

'And that's what was so brilliant; it made Chilton seem completely innocent. But he didn't *need* to mention Travis. He knew how the Internet works. The merest hint he'd done something wrong and the Vengeful Angels would take over.

'If Chilton was the perp, I wondered then who was the intended victim. There was nothing about the two girls, Tammy or Kelley, to suggest he wanted to kill them. Or Lyndon Strickland or Mark Watson. You were the other potential victims, of course. I thought back to everything I'd learned about the case. I remembered something odd. You told me that Chilton had hurried to your house in San Diego to be with you and the children the day your wife died. He was there within the hour.'

'Right. He'd been in L.A. at a meeting. He got the next commuter flight down.'

Dance said, 'But he'd told his wife he was in *Seattle* when he heard that Sarah had died.'

'Seattle?' Hawken appeared confused.

'In a meeting at Microsoft headquarters. But, no, he was actually in San Diego. He'd been there all along. He never left town after drowning Sarah. He was waiting to hear from you and to get to your house. He needed to.'

'Needed to? Why?'

'You said he stayed with you, even helped you with the cleaning?'

'That's right.'

'I think he wanted to go through the house and destroy anything among Sarah's possessions that suggested they were having an affair.'

'Jesus,' Hawken muttered.

She explained a few of the other connections between Chilton and the crimes: he was a triathlon competitor, which meant he biked. Dance recalled seeing all the sports equipment in Chilton's garage, among them several bicycles.

'Then, the soil.' She explained about finding the mismatched dirt near one of the roadside crosses. 'Crime Scene found identical trace on Greg Schaeffer's shoes. But the ultimate source was the gardens in Chilton's front yard. That's where Schaeffer picked it up.'

Dance reflected that she'd actually gazed right at the source of the dirt when she'd first been to the blogger's house, as she examined the landscaping.

'And then there was his van, the Nissan Quest.' She told them about the witness Ken Pfister seeing the state vehicle near one of the crosses. Then she gave a wry smile. 'But it was actually Chilton himself who was driving – after planting the second cross.'

She pointed to the blogger's van, parked nearby. It bore the bumper sticker she remembered from the first day she'd been to his house: *If you DESALINATE, you DEVASTATE.*

It was the last syllable on that sticker that Ken Pfister had seen as the van drove past: *STATE.*

'I went to the magistrate with what I'd found and got a warrant. I sent officers to search Chilton's house in Carmel. He'd discarded most of the evidence, but they found a few red rose petals and a bit of cardboard similar to what was used on the crosses. I remembered that he said he was coming here with you. So I called San Benito County and told them to send a tactical team here. The only thing I didn't guess was that Chilton was going to force Travis himself to shoot you.'

She interrupted the man's effusive thanks – he seemed about to cry – with a glance at her watch. 'I have to leave now. You go home, get some rest.'

Lily hugged Dance. Hawken shook her hand in both of his. 'I don't know what to say.'

Disengaging, she walked to the Monterey County Sheriff's Office squad car, where James Chilton sat. His thinning hair was plastered to the side of his head. He watched her approach with a hurt gaze on his face. Almost a pout.

She opened the back door, leaned down.

He hissed, 'I don't need shackles on my feet. Look at this. It's degrading.'

Dance noted the chains. Noted them with satisfaction.

He continued, 'They put them on, some deputies did, and they were smiling! Because they claimed I kept the boy shackled. This's all bullshit. This is all a mistake. I've been framed.'

Dance nearly laughed. Apart from all the other evidence, there were three eyewitnesses – Hawken, his wife and Travis – to his crimes.

She recited his Miranda rights.

'Somebody did that already.'

'Just making sure you really understand them. Do you?'

'My rights? Yes. Listen, back there, yes, I had a gun. But people had been out to kill me. Of course I'm going to protect myself. Somebody's setting me up. Like you said, somebody I'd posted about in my blog. I saw Travis come into the living room and I pulled out my gun – I started carrying one when *you* said I was in danger.'

Ignoring the rambling, she said, 'We're going to take you to Monterey County and book you, James. You can call your wife or your attorney then.'

'Do you hear what I'm saying? I've been framed. Whatever that boy's claiming, he's unstable. I was playing along with him, with his delusions. I was going to shoot him if he'd tried to hurt Don and Lily. Of course I was.'

She leaned forward, controlling her emotions as best she could. Which wasn't easy. 'Why'd you target Tammy and Kelley, James? Two teenage girls who never did anything to you.'

'I'm innocent,' he muttered.

She continued, as if he hadn't spoken. 'Why them? Because you didn't like adolescent attitude? You didn't like them tainting your precious blog with their obscenities? You didn't like bad grammar?'

He said nothing, but Dance believed there was a flicker of acknowledgment in his eyes. She pushed ahead. 'And why Lyndon Strickland? And Mark Watson? You killed them just because they posted under their real names and they were easy to find, right?'

Chilton was looking away now, as if he knew he was telegraphing the truth with his eyes.

'James, those pictures you uploaded to the blog, pretending to be Travis? You drew them yourself, didn't you? I remembered from your bio in the *Report* that you were a graphic designer and art director in college.'

He said nothing.

The anger flared hotter. 'Did you *enjoy* drawing the one of me getting stabbed?'

Again, silence.

She stood. 'I'll be by at some point to interview you. You can have your attorney present if you like.'

Then he turned to her, his face imploring. 'One thing, Agent Dance? Please?'

She lifted an eyebrow.

'There's something I need. It's important.'

'What's that, James?'

'A computer.'

'What?'

'I need access to a computer. Soon. Today.'

'You get phone calls from the lockup. No computer.'

'But the *Report* . . . I've got to upload my stories.'

Now she couldn't contain the laugh. He was not at all concerned about his wife or children, only about the precious blog. 'No, James, that's not going to happen.'

'But I have to. I *have* to!'

Hearing those words and seeing his frantic gaze, Kathryn Dance finally understood James Chilton. The readers were nothing to him. He'd easily murdered two of them and was fully prepared to kill more.

The truth was nothing to him. He'd lied over and over again.

No, the answer was simple: like the players in *DimensionQuest*, like so many people lost in the synth world, James Chilton was an addict. Addicted to his messianic mission. Addicted to the seductive power of spreading the word – his word – to the minds and hearts of people throughout the world. The more who read his musings, his rants, his praise, the more exquisite the high.

She leaned down, close to his face. 'James. I will do everything possible to make sure that whatever prison you go to, you will never be able to get online ever again. Never in your life.'

His face turned livid and he began screaming, 'You can't do that! You can't take my blog away. My readers need me. The country needs me! You can't!'

Dance closed the door and nodded to the deputy behind the wheel.

45

The flashing lights – on personal business – were against regulations, but Dance didn't care. The emergency accessories were a wise idea, given that she was speeding at twice the limit down Highway 68 back to Salinas from Hollister. Edie Dance was being arraigned in twenty minutes, and she was going to be there, front and center.

She was wondering when her mother's trial would happen. Who would testify? What exactly would the evidence show?

Again she thought, dismayed: will I be called to the stand?

And what would happen if Edie was convicted? Dance knew California prisons. The population was largely illiterate, violent, their minds ruined by drugs or alcohol or simply damaged from birth. Her mother's heart would wither in a place like that. The punishment *would* be the death penalty, after all – capital punishment for the soul.

And she was furious with herself for writing that email to Bill, the one commenting on her mother's decision to put down one of her ailing pets. Years ago, an offhand comment. Out of proportion to the devastating effect it could have on her mother's fate.

Which put her in mind of *The Chilton Report*. All of those postings about Travis Brigham. All wrong, completely wrong . . . yet they would be in existence, on servers and in the hearts of individual computers, forever. People might see them five or ten or twenty years from now. Or a hundred. And never know the truth.

Dance was shaken out of her troubling meditation by the buzz of her phone.

It was a text message from her father.

I'm at the hospital with your mother. Get here as soon as you can.

Dance gasped. What was this about? The arraignment was supposed to be starting in fifteen minutes. If Edie Dance was in the hospital it was only for one reason. She was ill or injured.

Dance immediately punched her father's mobile number, but it went right to voice mail. Of course, he'd shut it off in the hospital.

Had she been attacked?

Or had she tried to kill herself?

Dance shoved the accelerator down and drove faster. Her mind tumbling, out of control now. Thinking that if her mother *had* tried to kill herself, it was because she knew Robert Harper had a solid case against her, and that it would be futile to fight it.

So her mother *had* committed murder. Dance recalled the damning comment, revealing Edie's knowledge of the ICU corridors at the time Juan Millar died.

There were some nurses down on that wing. But that was all. His family was gone. And there were no visitors . . .

She sped past Salinas, Laguna Seca and the airport. Twenty minutes later she was pulling into the circular drive of the hospital. The car skidded to a violent stop, breaching the handicapped space. Dance leapt out and sprinted to the main entrance door and wedged through before the automatic panels had fully opened.

At the admissions station, an alarmed receptionist looked up and said, 'Kathryn, are you—?'

'Where's my mother?' the agent gasped.

'She's downstairs and—'

Dance was already pushing through the doorway and downward. Downstairs meant only one thing: the intensive care unit.

Ironically the very place where Juan Millar had died. If Edie was there, at least she was alive.

On the bottom floor she shoved through the door, hurrying toward ICU, when she happened to glance into the cafeteria.

Breathing hard, Dance pulled up fast, a stitch in her side. She looked through the open doorway and saw four people sitting at a table, coffee in front of them. They were the director of the hospital, the security chief Henry Bascomb, Dance's father and . . . Edie Dance. They were engaged in a discussion and were looking over documents on the table before them.

Stuart glanced up and smiled, gesturing with an index figure, meaning, Dance guessed, they'd only be a moment or two. Her mother glanced her way and then, expression neutral, returned her attention to the hospital director.

'Hi,' a man's voice said from behind her.

She turned, blinking in surprise to see Michael O'Neil.

'Michael, what's going on?' Dance asked breathlessly.

With furrowed brows, he asked, 'Didn't you get the message?'

'Just the text from Dad that they were here.'

'I didn't want to bother you in the middle of an operation. I spoke to Overby and gave him the details. He was supposed to call when you were finished.'

Oh. Well, this was one glitch she couldn't lay at the feet of her thoughtless boss; she'd been in such a hurry to get to the arraignment, she'd never told him they'd wrapped the Chilton take-down.

'I heard Hollister went okay.'

'Yeah, everybody's fine. Chilton's in custody. Travis's got a banged head. That's it.' But the Roadside Cross Case was far from her mind. She stared into the cafeteria. 'What's going on, Michael?'

'The charges against your mother've been dropped,' he said.

'What?'

O'Neil hesitated, looking almost sheepish, and then said, 'I didn't tell you, Kathryn. I couldn't.'

'Tell me what?'

'The case I've been working on?'

The Other Case . . .

'It had nothing to do with the container situation. That's still on hold. I took on your mother's case as an independent investigation. I told the sheriff I was going to do it. Pretty much insisted. He agreed. Stopping Harper *now* was our only chance. If he'd gotten a conviction . . . well, you know the odds of getting a verdict overturned on appeal.'

'You never said anything.'

'That was the plan. I could run it but I couldn't mention anything to you. I had to be able to testify that you knew nothing about what I was doing. Conflict of interest, otherwise. Even your parents didn't know. I talked to them about the case, but only informally. They never suspected.'

'Michael.' Dance again felt rare tears sting. She gripped his arm and their eyes met, brown on green.

He said, frowning, 'I knew she wasn't guilty. Edie taking somebody's life? Crazy.' He grinned. 'You notice I've been talking to you in text messages a lot lately, emails?'

'Right.'

'Because I couldn't lie to you in person. I knew you'd spot it in a minute.'

She laughed, recalling how vague he'd been about the Container Case.

'But who killed Juan?'

'Daniel Pell.'

'Pell?' she whispered in astonishment.

O'Neil explained, though, that it wasn't Pell himself who'd killed Juan Millar, but one of the women connected with him – the partner that Dance had been thinking of yesterday as she'd driven her children to see their grandparents.

'She knew the threat you presented, Kathryn. She wanted desperately to stop you.'

'Why did you think of her?'

'Process of elimination,' O'Neil explained. 'I knew your mother couldn't've done it. I knew Julio Millar hadn't – he was accounted for the whole time. His parents weren't there, and there were no other fellow officers present. So I asked who'd have a motive to blame your mother for the death? Pell came to mind. You were running the manhunt to find him and getting closer. Your mother's arrest would distract you, if not force you off the case altogether. He couldn't do it himself, so he used his partner.'

He explained that the woman had slipped into the hospital by pretending to be applying for a job as a nurse.

'The job applications,' Dance said, nodding, recalling what Connie's investigation had found. 'There wasn't any connection between them and Millar, though, so we didn't pay any attention.'

'Witnesses said that she was wearing a nurse's uniform. As if she'd just gotten off a shift at another hospital and had come over to MBH to apply for a job.' The deputy continued, 'I had her computer examined and found that she'd searched for drug interactions on Google.'

'The evidence in the garage?'

'She planted it. I had Pete Bennington take the garage apart. A CS team found some hairs – that Harper's people had missed, by the way. They were hers. DNA match. I'm sure she'll take a plea.'

'I feel so bad, Michael. I almost believed she'd . . .' Dance couldn't even bring herself to say the words. 'I mean, Mom looked so upset when she told me that Juan asked her to kill him. And then she claimed she wasn't on the ICU floor when Juan was killed, but she let slip that she *knew* the place was deserted except for some nurses.'

'Oh, she'd talked to one of the ICU doctors and *he* commented to your mother that all the visitors had left. Edie was never on the wing at all.'

A miscommunication and an assumption. Not much excuse for *that* in her line of work, she thought wryly. 'And Harper? He's going forward with the case?'

'Nope. He's packing up and going home to Sacramento. He's handed off to Sandy.'

'What?' Dance was shocked.

O'Neil laughed, noting her expression. 'Yep. Not much interested in justice. Only interested in a high-profile conviction, the mother of a government agent.'

'Oh, Michael.' She squeezed his arm again. And he put his hand on hers, then was looking away. She was struck by his countenance. What was she seeing? A vulnerability, a hollowness?

O'Neil started to say something and then didn't.

Maybe to apologize for lying to her and withholding the truth about his investigation. He looked at his watch. 'Got a few things to take care of.'

'Hey, you okay?'

'Just tired.'

Alarm bells sounded within Dance. Men are never 'just tired'. What they mean is, no, they're not okay at all but they don't want to talk.

He said, 'Oh, almost forgot. I heard from Ernie, the L.A. case? The judge refused to push off the immunity hearing. It's starting in about a half hour.'

Dance displayed crossed fingers. 'Let's hope.' She then hugged him, hard.

O'Neil fished his car keys out of his pocket and headed up the stairs, apparently in too much of a hurry to wait for the elevator.

Dance glanced into the cafeteria. She noted that her mother was no longer at the table. Her shoulders slumped. Damnit. She's gone.

But then she heard a woman's voice behind her. 'Katie.'

Edie Dance had come out the side door and presumably waited to join her daughter until O'Neil left.

'Michael told me, Mom.'

'After the charges were dismissed, I came by here to see the people who supported me, to thank them.'

The people who supported me . . .

There was silence for a moment. The PA system gave an incomprehensible announcement. Somewhere a baby cried. The sounds faded.

And from Edie's expression and words, Kathryn Dance knew the complete weave of what had happened between mother and daughter in the past few days. The difficulty had nothing to do with her leaving the courthouse early the other day. The issue was more fundamental. She blurted, 'I didn't think you'd done it, Mom. Really.'

Edie Dance smiled. 'Ah, and coming from you, from a kinesics expert, Katie? Tell me what to look for to see if you're telling a fib.'

'Mom—'

'Katie, you thought it was *possible* I'd killed that young man.'

Dance sighed, wondered how big the vacuum in her soul was at the moment. The denial died in her mouth and she said in a shaky voice, 'Maybe, Mom. Okay, maybe. I didn't think less of you. I still loved you. But, okay, I thought you might have.'

'Your face, in the courtroom at the bail hearing. Just looking at your face, I knew you were considering it. I knew you were.'

'I'm so sorry,' Dance whispered.

Then Edie Dance did something completely uncharacteristic. She took her daughter by the shoulders, firmly, more firmly than Dance believed she'd ever been held by the woman, even as a child. 'Don't you dare say that.' Her words were harsh.

Dance blinked and began to speak.

'Shhhhh, Katie. Listen. I was up all night after the bail hearing. Thinking about what I'd seen in your eyes, what you suspected about me, let me finish. I was up all night, hurt, furious. But then, finally I understood something. And I felt so proud.'

A warm smile softened the round contours of the woman's face. 'So proud.'

Dance was confused.

Her mother continued, 'You know, Katie, a parent never knows if they get it right. I'm sure you've wrestled with that.'

'Oh, only about ten times a day.'

'You always hope, you pray, that you give your children the resources they need, the attitude, the courage. That's what it's all about, after all. Not fighting their battles, but getting them prepared to fight on their own. Teaching them to make judgments, to think for themselves.'

The tears were streaming down Dance's cheeks.

'And when I saw you questioning what I might've done, looking at what had happened, I knew that I'd got it one hundred percent right. I raised you not to be blind. You know, prejudice blinds people, hate blinds people. But loyalty and love blind people too. You looked past everything, for the truth.' Her mother laughed. 'Of course, you got it wrong. But I can't fault you for that.'

The women embraced and Edie Dance said, 'Now, you're still on duty. Go on back to the office. I'm still mad at you. But I'll get over it in a day or two. We'll go shopping and then have dinner at Casanova. Oh, and Katie, you're picking up the check.'

46

Kathryn Dance returned to her office at CBI and wrote up the final disposition on the case.

She sipped the coffee that Maryellen Kresbach had brought her and looked over the pink phone message slips that the assistant had stacked beside a plate containing a very thick cookie.

She considered the messages at length and returned none of the calls but ate 100 percent of the cookie.

Her phone beeped. A text from Michael O'Neil:

K – judge has ruled in L.A. Will release decision in next few hours. Keep your fingers crossed. Lot going on today, but will talk to you soon. – M.

Please, please, please . . .

A final sip of coffee and Dance printed out the report for Overby and took it down to his office. 'Here's the disposition, Charles.'

'Ah. Good.' The man added, 'That was a surprise, the direction the case took.' He read the report fast. She noticed a gym bag, tennis racket and small suitcase behind his desk. It was late afternoon on a summer Friday, and he was probably leaving directly from the office for his weekend place.

She detected a certain chilliness in his posture, attributable undoubtedly to her flying off the handle with Hamilton Royce.

And so she was looking forward to what was coming next. Sitting opposite her boss, she said, 'There's one final thing, Charles. It's about Royce.'

'What's that?' He looked up, began smoothing her memo, as if wiping off dust.

She explained what TJ had uncovered about Royce's mission – to stop the blog not to save victims, but to derail Chilton's exposé about the state representative's being wined and dined by the nuclear plant developer. 'He used us, Charles.'

'Ah.' Overby continued to fiddle with some papers.

'He bills his time to the Nuclear Facilities Planning Committee – which is headed by the representative Chilton was writing about in the "Power to the People" thread of the blog.'

'I see. Royce, hmm.'

'I want to send a memo to the AG. It's probably not a crime, what Royce did, but it's definitely unethical – using me, using us. It'll cost him his job.'

More fiddling. Overby was considering this.

'Are you okay with my doing that?' She asked this because it was clear he wasn't.

'I'm not sure.'

She laughed. 'Why not? He went through my desk. Maryellen saw him. He used state police for his own agenda.'

Overby's eyes dipped to the papers on his desk. They were as ordered as could be. 'Well, it'll take up our time and resources. And it could be . . . awkward for us.'

'Awkward?'

'Bring us into that interagency crap. I hate that.'

This was hardly an argument. Life in state government is all about interagency crap.

At the end of a chewy silence, Overby seemed to come up with a thought. His eyebrow lifted a bit. 'Besides, I think you might not have time to pursue it.'

'I'll fit it in, Charles.'

'Well, the thing is, there's this . . .' He found a file on his credenza and extracted a stapled document several pages long.

'What's that?'

'Matter of fact' – the second eyebrow joined in – 'it's *from* the AG's office.' He pushed the papers forward across the desk. 'It seems there was a complaint made against you.'

'Me?'

'Apparently you made racist remarks to a county employee.'

'Charles, that's crazy.'

'Ah, well, it went all the way to Sacramento.'

'Who complained?'

'Sharanda Evans. County Social Services.'

'I've never met her. It's a mistake.'

'She was at Monterey Bay Hospital when your mother was arrested. She was looking after your children.'

Oh, the woman who'd collected Wes and Maggie from the hospital play area.

'Charles, she wasn't "looking after" them. She was taking them into custody. She didn't even try to call me.'

'She claims you uttered racist comments.'

'Jesus Christ, Charles, I said she was incompetent. That's all.'

'She didn't interpret it that way. Now, since you generally have a good reputation and no history of problems in the past, the AG's not inclined to open a formal complaint. Still, it's got to be looked into.'

He seemed torn about this dilemma.

But not that torn.

'He wanted some input from people on the ground about how to proceed.'

From Overby himself, he meant. And she understood too exactly what was going on here: Dance had embarrassed Overby in front of Royce. Maybe the ombudsman had gotten the impression that the man couldn't control his employees. A CBI-instigated complaint against Royce would call Overby's leadership into question.

'Of *course* you're not racist. But the woman's pretty hot under the collar about it, this Ms. Evans.' He stared at the inverted letter in front of Dance the way one would gaze at autopsy photos.

How long've you had this job? . . . Either not long enough, or way too long.

Kathryn Dance realized that her boss was negotiating: if she didn't go any further with the complaint about Royce's impropriety, Overby would tell the AG that the social worker's claim had been fully investigated and that there was no merit to it.

If Dance did pursue the Royce matter, she might lose her job.

This sat between them for a moment. Dance was surprised that Overby was showing no kinesic evidence that he was feeling stress. She, on the other hand, observed her foot bobbing like a piston.

I think I have the big picture, Dance thought cynically. She came close to saying it, but didn't.

Well, she had a decision to make.

Debating.

He tapped the complaint report with his fingers. 'A shame when things like this happen. We have our core work, then other stuff intrudes.'

After the Roadside Cross Case, after the roller-coaster with the J. Doe case in Los Angeles, after the harrowing days worrying about her mother, Dance decided she didn't have the heart for a fight, not over this.

'If you think a complaint against Royce would be too distracting, Charles, I'll respect that, of course.'

'It's best probably. Let's get back to work – that's what we need to do. And this we'll just put away too.' He took the complaint and slipped it into the file.

How blatant can we be, Charles?

He smiled. 'No more distractions.'

'Back to work,' Dance echoed.

'Okay, I see it's late. Have a good weekend. And thanks for wrapping the case, Kathryn.'

'Good night, Charles.' Dance rose and left the office. She wondered if he felt as unclean as she did.

She doubted it very, very much.

Dance returned to the Gals' Wing and was just at her office door when a voice behind her called, 'Kathryn?'

She turned to see somebody she didn't recognize at first. Then it struck her – it was David Reinhold, the young deputy from the sheriff's office. He wasn't in uniform, but was wearing jeans, a polo shirt and jacket. He smiled and glanced down. 'Off duty.' He approached her and stopped a few feet away. 'Hey, I heard about the Roadside Cross Case.'

'Kind of a surprise,' she said.

His hands were jammed in his pockets. He seemed nervous. 'I'll say. That boy'll be okay, though?'

'He'll be fine.'

'And Chilton? Did he confess?'

'I bet he doesn't need to. We've got him on witnesses and PE. Cold.' She nodded toward her office, lifting an eyebrow, inviting him inside.

'I have some things to take care of . . . I stopped by earlier and you were out.'

A curious thing to say. And she noted that he seemed even more nervous now. His body language was giving off high amperage of stress.

'I just wanted to say, I've really enjoyed working with you.'

'Appreciate your help.'

'You're a very special person,' Reinhold stammered.

Uh-oh. Where was this going?

Reinhold was avoiding her eyes. He cleared his throat. 'I know you don't really know me very well.'

He's at least a decade younger than I am, she thought. He's a kid. Dance was struggling to keep from smiling or looking too maternal. She wondered where he was going to invite her on a date.

'Anyway, what I'm trying to say is . . .'

But he said nothing, just pulled an envelope from his pocket and handed it to her.

'What I'm trying to say is that I hope you'll consider my application to join the CBI.' Reinhold added, 'Most older people in police work aren't very good mentors. I know you'd be different. I'd appreciate the chance to learn from you.'

Struggling not to laugh, Dance said, 'Well, David, thanks. I don't think we're hiring right at the moment. But I promise you, when we do, I'll make sure to get this to the top of the list.'

'Really?' He beamed.

'You bet. You have a good night now, David. And thanks again for your help.'

'Thanks, Kathryn. You're the best.'

For an older person . . .

Smiling, she walked into her office and dropped heavily into her chair. She sat, staring at the entwined tree trunks outside her window. Her cell phone chimed. Not much in the mood to talk to anybody, she looked down at the Caller ID window.

After three rings of debate she hit 'Answer'.

47

A butterfly eased along the fence and vanished into the neighbor's yard. It wasn't the time of year for Monarchs, the migratory lepidoptera that gave Pacific Grove its subtitle of 'Butterfly Town, U.S.A.', and Kathryn Dance wondered what kind it was.

She was sitting on the Deck, which was slick from the late-afternoon fog. It was quiet now, she was alone. The children and the dogs were at her parents'. She wore faded jeans, a green sweatshirt, stylish Wish shoes, from the Brown company's Fergie line – a treat she'd allowed herself after the conclusion of the case. She sipped white wine.

Her laptop was open in front of her. Dance had logged on as a temporary administrator to *The Chilton Report* after she'd found the access pass codes in one of James Chilton's files. She consulted the book she'd been reading from, finished typing the text and uploaded it.

http://www.thechiltonreport.com/html/final.html

Dance read the results. Gave a faint smile.
Then logged off.
She heard heavy footsteps on the stairs leading up from the side of the house and turned to see Michael O'Neil.
'Hey.' He smiled.

She had been expecting a phone call about the magistrate's ruling in Los Angeles as to whether the J. Doe case would proceed; he'd seemed so preoccupied at the hospital, she hadn't expected him to show up here in person. No matter, Michael O'Neil was always welcome. She tried to read his expression. She was usually good at this – she knew him so well – but he still had on a poker face.

'Wine?'

'Sure.'

She retrieved a second glass from the kitchen and poured him his favorite red.

'I can't stay long.'

'Okay.' Dance could barely control herself. 'Well?'

The smile escaped. 'We won. Got the word twenty minutes ago. The judge blew the defense out of the water.'

'For real?' Dance asked, slipping into adolescent-speak.

'Yep.'

She rose and hugged him hard. His arms slid around her back and pressed her to his solid chest.

They stepped apart and clinked glasses.

'Ernie presents to the grand jury in two weeks. There's no doubt they'll return a bill. They want us down there on Tuesday, nine a.m., to plan out the testimony. You up for a trip?'

'Oh, you bet I am.'

O'Neil moved to the railing. He was gazing out into the backyard, staring at a wind chime that Dance had been meaning to pick up from the spot, where she'd dumped it on a windy – and sleepless – night some time ago. He fell silent.

Something was coming, Dance could tell.

She grew alarmed. What was the story? Illness?

Was he moving?

He continued, 'I was wondering . . .'

She waited. Her breath was fast. The wine in her glass rocked like the turbulent Pacific.

'The meeting's on Tuesday and I was wondering if you wanted to stay down in L.A. a few extra days. We could see the sights.

Get those eggs Benedict we were hoping for. Or maybe we could go out for sushi in West Hollywood and watch people trying to be cool. I could even buy a black shirt.' He was rambling.

Which Michael O'Neil never did. Ever.

Dance blinked. Her heart thudded as fast as the wings of the hummingbird hovering over the crimson feeder nearby. 'I . . .'

He laughed and his shoulders slumped. She couldn't imagine what her expression looked like. 'Okay. There's something else I guess I ought to say.'

'Sure.'

'Anne's leaving.'

'What?' She gasped.

Michael O'Neil's face was an amalgam of emotion: hope, uncertainty, pain. Perhaps the most obvious was bewilderment.

'She's moving to San Francisco.'

A hundred questions filled her mind. She asked the first, 'The children?'

'They'll be with me.'

This news wasn't surprising. There was no better father than Michael O'Neil. And Dance had always had her doubts about Anne's skills at mothering, and about her desire to handle the job.

Of course, she realized. The split-up was the source of O'Neil's troubled look at the hospital. She remembered his eyes, how hollow they seemed.

He continued, speaking with the clipped tone of somebody who'd been doing a lot of rapid-fire – and not wholly realistic – planning. Men were guilty of this more often than women. He was telling her about the children's visiting their mother, about the reactions of his family and Anne's, about lawyers, about what Anne would be doing in San Francisco. Dance nodded, concentrating on his words, encouraging, mostly just letting him talk.

She picked up immediately on the references to 'this gallery owner' and a 'friend of Anne's in San Francisco' and 'he'. The deduction she made didn't truly surprise her, though she was furious with the woman for hurting O'Neil.

And hurt he was, devastated, though he didn't know it yet.

And me? Dance thought. How do *I* feel about this?

Then she promptly tucked that consideration away, refusing to examine it right now.

O'Neil stood like a schoolboy who'd asked a girl to the eighth-grade dance. She wouldn't have been surprised if he'd jammed his hands into his pockets and stared down at his shoe tips. 'So I was just wondering, about next week. A few extra days?'

Where do we go from here? Dance thought. If she could hover over herself, looking down as a kinesic analyst, what was her body language saying? She was, on the one hand, deeply moved by the news. On the other, she was as cautious as a war-zone soldier approaching a roadside package.

The appeal of a trip with Michael O'Neil was almost overwhelming.

Yet the answer, of course, could not be yes. For one thing, O'Neil needed to be there for his children, completely there, one hundred percent there. They might not – *should* not – have been told about their parents' problems at this point. Yet they would know something. Children's intuition is a primary force of nature.

But there was another reason for Dance and O'Neil not to share personal time in Los Angeles.

And, coincidentally, it appeared just now.

'Hello?' called a man's voice from the side yard.

Dance held Michael O'Neil's eye, gave a tight smile and called, 'Up here. In the back.'

More footsteps on the stairs and Jonathan Boling joined them. He gave a smile to O'Neil and the two men shook hands. Like Dance, he was in jeans. His knit shirt was black, under a Lands' End windbreaker. He wore hiking boots.

'I'm a little early.'

'Not a problem.'

O'Neil was smart, and more, he was savvy. Dance could see that he understood instantly. His first reaction was dismay that he'd put her in a difficult position.

His eyes offered a sincere apology.

And hers insisted that none was necessary.

O'Neil was amused too and gave Dance a smile not unlike the one they'd shared when last year they'd heard on the car radio the Sondheim song 'Send in the Clowns', about potential lovers who just can't seem to get together.

Timing, they both knew, was everything.

Dance said evenly, 'Jonathan and I are going to Napa for the weekend.'

'Just a little get-together at my parents' place. I always like to bring along somebody to run interference.' Boling was downplaying the getaway. The professor was smart too – he'd seen Dance and O'Neil together – and understood that he'd walked into the middle of something now.

'It's beautiful up there,' O'Neil said.

Dance remembered that he and Anne had spent their honeymoon at an inn near the Cakebread Vineyard up in wine country.

Could we just shoot these ironies dead, please? Dance thought. And she realized that her face was burning with a girlish blush.

O'Neil asked, 'Wes is at your mom and dad's?'

'Yep.'

'I'll call him. I want to cast off at eight tomorrow.'

She loved him for keeping the fishing date with the boy, even though Dance would be out of town and O'Neil had plenty to cope with. 'Thanks. He's really looking forward to it.'

'I'm getting a copy of the decision from L.A. I'll email it to you.'

She said, 'I want to talk, Michael. Call me.'

'Sure.'

O'Neil would understand that she meant talking about him and Anne and the impending separation, not the J. Doe case.

And Dance understood that he *wouldn't* call, not while she was away with Boling. He was that kind of person.

Dance felt a fast urge – a hungry urge – to hug the deputy again, put her arms around him, and she was about to. But for a man who remained unskilled at kinesic analysis, O'Neil instantly picked up on her intention. He turned and walked to the stairs. 'Got to collect the kids. Pizza night. Bye, Jon. And, hey, thanks for all your help. We couldn't've done it without you.'

'You owe me a tin badge,' Boling said with a grin and asked Dance if he could carry anything out to the car. She pointed out the shopping bag full of soda, water, snacks and CDs for the drive north.

Dance found herself clutching her wineglass to her chest as she watched O'Neil start down the deck stairs. She wondered if he'd turn back.

He did, briefly. They shared yet another smile, and then he was gone.

Acknowledgments

With thanks to Katherine Buse, whose excellent research gave me the lowdown on blogs and life in the synth world and who taught me how to survive (at least for a while) in massively multiplayer online role-playing games. Thanks too for the savvy editorial skills of Jane Davis, Jenna Dolan, Donna Marton, Hazel Orme and Phil Metcalf. My appreciation to James Chilton's webmaster, my sister, Julie Reece Deaver, and thanks, as always, to Madelyn and to the puppies – all of them.

About the Author

A former journalist, folksinger and attorney, Jeffery Deaver is an international number-one bestselling author. His novels have appeared on a number of bestseller lists around the world, including *The New-York Times*, *The Times* of London and *The Los Angeles Times*. His books are sold in 150 countries and translated into 25 languages. The author of twenty novels and two collections of short stories, he's been awarded the Steel Dagger and the Short Story Dagger from the British Crime Writers' Association, is a three-time recipient of the Ellery Queen Reader's Award for Best Short Story of the year and is a winner of the British Thumping Good Read Award. His standalone thriller *The Bodies Left Behind* won the Novel of the Year in the International Thriller Awards 2009, and the Lincoln Rhyme thriller *The Cold Moon* won a Grand prix from the Japanese Adventure Fiction Association and was named Book of the Year by the Mystery Writers Association of Japan.

He's been nominated for six Edgar Awards from the Mystery Writers of America, an Anthony Award and a Gumshoe Award. His book *A Maiden's Grave* was made into an HBO movie starring James Garner and Marlee Matlin, and his novel *The Bone Collector* was a feature release from Universal Pictures, starring Denzel Washington and Angelina Jolie. His most recent books are *The Broken Window*, *The Sleeping Doll* and *The Bodies Left*

Behind. And, yes, the rumors are true, he did appear as a corrupt reporter on his favorite soap opera, *As the World Turns*.

The next Lincoln Rhyme novel publishes in 2010.

Readers can visit his website at www.jefferydeaver.com.

Read on for an excerpt from the electrifying
new Lincoln Rhyme thriller . . .

THE BURNING WIRE

Jeffery Deaver

Coming out in July 2010

HODDER &
STOUGHTON

The driver eased the M70 bus through traffic toward the stop on 57th Street near where Tenth Avenue blended into Amsterdam. He was in a pretty good mood. The new bus was a kneeling model, which lowered to the sidewalk to make stepping aboard easier, and featured a handicapped ramp, great steering and, most important, a rump-friendly driver's seat.

Lord knew he needed that, spending eight hours a day in it.

Today was beautiful, clear and cool. April. One of his favorite months. It was about 11:30 a.m. and the bus was crowded as people were heading east for lunch dates or errands on their hour off. Traffic was moving slowly as he nosed the huge vehicle closer to the stop, where four or five people waited beside a lamppost covered with flyers.

He was approaching the bus stop and he happened to look past the people waiting to get on board, his eyes taking in the old, brown building behind the stop. An early twentieth-century building, it had several gridded windows but was always dark inside; he'd never seen anybody going in or out. A spooky place, like a prison. On the front was a flaking sign in white paint on a blue background.

ALGONQUIN CONSOLIDATED POWER COMPANY
SUBSTATION MH-10

PRIVATE PROPERTY

DANGER. HIGH VOLTAGE. TRESPASS PROHIBITED.

He rarely paid attention to the place but today something had caught his eye, something, he believed, out of the ordinary. Dangling from the window, about ten feet off the ground, was a wire, about a half-inch in diameter. It was covered with dark insulation up to the end. There, the plastic or rubber was stripped away, revealing silverish metal strands; it was bolted to a fitting of some kind, a flat piece of brass. Damn big hunk of wire, the driver thought.

And just hanging out the window. Was that *safe*?

He now braked the bus to a complete stop and hit the door release. The kneeling mechanism engaged and the big vehicle dipped. The metal lower step was now just inches from the sidewalk. The driver turned his broad, ruddy face toward the door, which eased open with a satisfying hydraulic hiss. The folks began to climb on board. 'Morning,' the driver said cheerfully.

A woman in her eighties, clutching an old shabby Henri Bendel shopping bag, nodded back and, using a cane, staggered to the rear, ignoring the empty seats in the front reserved for the elderly and disabled.

How could you not just *love* New Yorkers?

Then sudden motion in the rearview mirror. Flashing yellow lights. A truck was speeding up behind him. Algonquin Consolidated. Three workers stepped outside and stood in a close group, talking among themselves. They held boxes of tools and thick gloves and jackets. They didn't seem happy as they walked slowly toward the substation, staring at it, heads close together as they debated something. One of those heads was shaking ominously.

Then the driver turned to the last passenger about to board, a young Latino, clutching his MetroCard and pausing outside the bus. He too was gazing at the substation. Frowning. The driver noticed his head was raised, as if he was sniffing the air.

An acrid scent. Yes, something was burning. The smell reminded him of the time that an electric motor in the wife's washing machine had shorted out and the insulation burned. Nauseating. A wisp of smoke was coming from the doorway of the substation.

So that's what the Algonquin people were doing here.

That'd be a mess. The driver wondered if it would mean a power outage and the stoplights would go out. That'd be it for him. The cross-town trip, normally twenty minutes, would be hours. Well, in any event, he'd better clear the area for the Fire Department. He gestured the passenger on board. 'Hey, mister, I gotta go. Come on. Get on—'

As the passenger, still frowning at the smell, turned around and stepped onto the bus, the driver heard what sounded like pops coming from inside the substation. Sharp, almost like gunshots. Then a flash of light, light like a dozen suns, filled the entire sidewalk between the bus and the cable dangling from the window.

The Latino passenger disappeared into a cloud of flame.

The driver's vision collapsed to gray afterimages. The sound was like a ripping crackle and shotgun blast at the same time, stunning his ears. Though belted into his seat, his upper body was slammed backward against the side window.

Through numb ears, he heard the echoes of his passengers' screams.

Through half-blinded eyes, he saw fire.

As he began to pass out, the driver wondered if he himself might very well be the source of the fire.

'He was spotted a few hours ago. In Mexico City.'

'Not Tijuana?' Lincoln Rhyme asked.

'No. Landing there was a diversion, it looks like.' The woman's voice blossomed crisply from the speakerphone. 'He snuck onto a truck at Tijuana Airport and somebody drove him to the capital.'

Amelia Sachs, sitting beside Lincoln Rhyme's candy-apple-red Storm Arrow wheelchair, leaned forward and spoke into the black box of the speakerphone. 'They're sure it's him?' Sachs tugged at her long red hair and twined it into a severe ponytail.

'They have prints confirming it. And a visual too, both at the airport and in Mexico City. I'm having TJ upload a security tape. It'll be just a minute.' Her voice faded as she turned to her protégé and gave him instructions about the tape.

A little past noon, Rhyme and Sachs were in the ground-floor parlor turned forensic laboratory of his townhouse on Central Park West, what had been a gothic Victorian structure in which had possibly resided – Rhyme liked to think – some very un-quaint Victorians. Tough businessmen, dodgy politicians, high-class crooks. Maybe an incorruptible police commissioner who liked to bang heads. Rhyme had written a classic book on old-time crime in New York and had used his sources to try to track the genealogy of his building. But he could find no pedigree.

The woman they were speaking with was in a more modern

structure, Rhyme had to assume, 3000 miles away: the Monterey office of the California Bureau of Investigation. CBI Agent Kathryn Dance had worked with Rhyme and Sachs several years ago, on a case involving the very man they were now closing in on. Richard Logan was, they believed, his real name. Though Lincoln Rhyme thought of him mostly by his nickname: the Watchmaker.

He was a professional criminal, one who planned his crimes with the precision he devoted to his hobby and passion – constructing timepieces. Rhyme and the killer had clashed several times; Rhyme had foiled one of his plans but failed to stop another. Still, Lincoln Rhyme considered the overall score a loss for himself since the Watchmaker wasn't in custody.

Rhyme leaned his head back in his wheelchair, picturing Logan. He'd seen the man in person, up close. Body lean, hair a dark boyish mop, eyes gently amused at being questioned by the police, never revealing the mass murder he was planning. His serenity seemed to be innate, and it was what Rhyme found to be perhaps the most disturbing quality of the man. Emotion breeds mistake and carelessness, and no one could ever accuse Richard Logan of being emotional.

He could be hired for larceny or illegal arms or any other scheme that needed elaborate planning and ruthless execution, but was generally hired for murder – killing witnesses or whistle-blowers or political or corporate figures. Recent intelligence revealed he'd taken a murder assignment in Tijuana, but by the time they'd gotten details of his transit, four or five days had passed. And he'd disappeared.

Rhyme had called Kathryn Dance, who had many contacts south of the border – and who had herself nearly been killed by the Watchmaker's associate a few years earlier. Given the proximity of California to Tijuana, Dance was representing the Americans in the operation to arrest and extradite him, working with a senior investigator with the Ministerial Federal Police, a young, hardworking officer named Arturo Diaz.

'You ready for the video?' Dance asked.

'Go ahead.' Rhyme shifted one of his few working fingers – the index finger of his right hand – and moved the electric wheelchair closer to the screen. He was a C4 quadriplegic, paralyzed from the neck down.

On one of the several flat-screen monitors in the lab came a grainy night-vision image of an airport. Trash and discarded cartons, cans and drums littered the ground on both sides of the fence in the foreground. A private cargo jet taxied into view, a rear hatch opened and a man dropped out. He stretched and then oriented himself. He was Anglo and seemed to have the build of the Watchmaker and Rhyme was positive it was the killer. He had no baggage. Crouching, the man ran toward and hid behind a work shed. A few minutes later a worker came by, carrying a package. Logan swapped it for a letter-sized envelope. The worker left and a maintenance truck pulled up. Logan climbed into the back and hid under some tarps. The truck disappeared from view.

Dance said, 'They found the truck in Mexico City this morning.'

'What's the ID confirmation?' Rhyme asked.

'Our DEA people at the airport found the worker. The envelope was empty but it had Logan's prints. And the truck too. Some locals were dismantling it for parts, outside Mexico City, but Diaz's men managed to find prints on some water bottles and a coffee cup.'

'What was in the package?'

'The DEA people're interrogating the worker. I wanted to try to tease some information out of him myself but it'll take too long for me to get the okay.'

Rhyme and Sachs shared a smile at this. The teasing reference was a bit of modesty on Dance's part. She was a kinesics – body language – expert and one of the top interrogators in the country. But the testy relationship between the sovereign states in question was such that a California cop would have plenty of paperwork to negotiate before she could slip into Mexico for a formal interrogation, whereas the U.S. Drug Enforcement Agency already had a sanctioned presence there.

'Where was Logan spotted in the capital?'

A business district. He was trailed to a hotel, but Diaz's men couldn't narrow it down beyond that.' Dance added that Diaz's boss, a very senior police official, would be taking over the investigation. 'It's encouraging that they're taking it all pretty seriously.'

Yes, encouraging, Rhyme thought. But frustrating too. To be on the verge of finding the prey and yet to have so little control over the case . . . He found himself breathing more quickly. He was considering the last time he and the Watchmaker had been up against each other; Logan had outthought everybody. And easily killed the man he'd been hired to murder. Rhyme had had all the facts at hand to figure out what Logan was up to. Yet he'd misread the strategy completely.

After disconnecting the call, Sachs wiped some sweat from Rhyme's forehead – he hadn't been aware of the moisture – and they sat silent for a moment, looking out the window at the blur of a peregrine falcon sweeping into view. It veered up to its nest on Rhyme's second floor.

A male voice intruded, 'Well, did you get him?'

'Who?' Rhyme snapped. 'And how artful a verb is "get"?'

Thom Reston, Lincoln Rhyme's caregiver, said, 'The Watchmaker.'

'No,' grumbled Rhyme.

'But you're close, aren't you?' asked the trim man, wearing dark slacks, a businessman's starched yellow shirt and a floral tie.

'Oh, close,' Rhyme muttered. '*Close*. That's very helpful. Next time you're being attacked by a mountain lion, Thom, how would you feel if the park ranger shot really *close* to it? As opposed to, oh, say, actually *hitting* it?'

'Aren't mountain lions endangered?' Thom asked, not even bothering with an ironic inflection. He was impervious to Rhyme's edge. He'd worked for the forensic detective for years, longer than many married couples. And the aide was as seasoned as the toughest spouse.

'Ha. Very funny. Endangered.'

Sachs walked around behind Rhyme's wheelchair and gripped his shoulders, massaged. Sachs was tall and in better shape than most NYPD detectives her age and, though arthritis often plagued her knees and lower extremities, her arms and hands were strong and largely pain-free.

They wore their working clothes: Rhyme was in sweat slacks, black, and a knit shirt of dark green. Sachs had shed her navy blue jacket but was wearing matching slacks and a white cotton blouse, one button open at the collar, pearls present. Her Glock was high on her hip in a fast-draw polymer holster, and two magazines sat side by side in holsters of their own, along with a Taser.

He enjoyed the fingers digging into his flesh. It was as if the small percentage of remaining sensation in his body was enhanced. He glanced down at the useless legs. He closed his eyes.

Thom now looked him over carefully, 'You all right, Lincoln?'

'All right? Aside from the fact that the perp I've been searching for for years slipped out of our grasp and is now hiding out in the second largest metropolitan area in this hemisphere, I'm just peachy.'

'That's not what I'm talking about. You look tired.'

'You're right. Actually I need some medicine.'

'Medicine?'

'Whisky. I'd feel better with some whisky.'

'No, you wouldn't.'

'Well, why don't we try an experiment. Science. Cartesian. Rational. Who can argue with that? I know how I feel now. Then I'll have some whisky and I'll tell you how I feel after. I'll report back to you.'

'No. It's too early.'

'It's afternoon.'

'By a few minutes.'

'Goddamn it.' Rhyme sounded gruff, as often, but in fact he was losing himself in Sachs's massage. A few strands of red hair had escaped from her ponytail and hung tickling against his cheek. He didn't move away. Since he'd apparently lost the single malt battle, he was ignoring Thom, but the aide brought his attention around quickly by saying, 'When you were on the phone, Lon called.'

'He did? Why didn't you tell me?'

'You said you didn't want to be disturbed while you were talking with Kathryn.'

'Well, tell me now.'

'He'll call back. Something about a case. A problem.'

'Really?' The Watchmaker receded somewhat at this news. Rhyme understood that there was another source of his bad mood: boredom. He'd just finished analyzing the evidence for a complicated organized crime case and was facing several weeks with nothing to do. So he was buoyed by the thought of another job. Like Amelia Sachs craving speed, Rhyme needed problems, challenges, input. One of the difficulties with a severe disability that few people focus on is the absence of anything new. The same settings, the same people, the same activities . . . and the same platitudes, the same empty reassurances, the same reports from unemotional doctors.

What had saved his life after his injury – literally, since he'd been considering assisted suicide – was his tentative steps back into his prior passion: using science to solve crimes.

You could never be bored when you confronted mystery.

Thom persisted, 'Are you sure you're up for it? You're looking a little pale.'

'Haven't been to the beach lately, you know.'

But then all considerations of Rhyme's health vanished as his phone blared and Detective Lieutenant Lon Sellitto's number showed up on caller ID.

Rhyme used a working finger on his right hand to answer.

'Lon.'

'Linc, listen, here's the thing.' He was harried and, to judge from the surround-sound acoustics piping from the speaker, apparently driving somewhere quickly. 'We may have a terrorist situation going on.'

'Situation? That's not very specific.'

'Okay, how's this? Somebody fucked with the power company, shot a five-thousand-degree spark at a Metro bus and shut down the electric grid for six square blocks south of Lincoln Center. That specific enough for you?'

A Lincoln Rhyme thriller

The
BROKEN WINDOW

Jeffery
DEAVER

He is watching you.

He knows you, better than you know yourself.
And he is using his knowledge to plan your death.

But you are not his only victim.
He is also watching our killer.

He is about to get away with the perfect murder . . .

Out now in paperback

HODDER

The BODIES LEFT BEHIND

Jeffery DEAVER

YOU CAN RUN. YOU CAN HIDE. BUT YOU CAN'T ESCAPE . . .

A distant lake house in Wisconsin.
A call to police emergency is cut short.
A phone glitch, or something more sinister?
Off-duty deputy Brynn McKenzie goes to find out.

And stumbles onto the scene of a murder. Before she can call for backup,
she finds herself the next potential victim. Deprived of her phone,
weapon and car, Brynn flees, along with the only survivor of the crime.

These unlikely allies can survive only by escaping into the dense,
deserted woods, on a desperate trek to safety. And ultimately to a life
or death choice. Flight. Or fight?

Out now in paperback

HODDER